MW01633338

SKIM

MILK, MONEY & MURDER

STEVE BYRNE

ISBN: 978-1-927591-29-1

PHOTOS:
page 8: Ford City, 1920

page 12 - 13: Soldiers Off To War, Windsor Station, Windsor Ontario, 1915

page 206 - 207: Aerial View of Ford City & Walkerville Ontario, 1921

Walter P. Reuther archives

Book & Cover Design:
Walkerville Publishing Inc.
walkerville.com

Printed in Canada

To my family:
Susie, Erin, Sara, and Danny.

To my little brother, Dennis,
who was an accomplished storymaker.

Inspired by my great-grandfather,
Ontario Liquor Control Inspector
Maxime Mousseau.

AUTHOR'S NOTE

This story is a work of fiction.

However, many of the settings — the towns, scene locations, and streets — are real, as are some characters:

THE PURPLE GANG from Detroit was a notorious and much-feared Jewish organized-crime syndicate during Prohibition (1918-1933). They were led for a time by the nefarious Bernstein brothers. The Purples resorted to intimidation and violence to maintain control of their illicit activities on both sides of the border. Their role as middlemen between Canadian whiskey suppliers and the infamous Al Capone's empire in Chicago and points beyond is undisputed. Rumour has it that those who ran afoul of the Purples ended up with "cement shoes," the Detroit River becoming their watery grave.

....

BLAISE DIESBOURG, also known as "King Canada" during this colourful period, was a farmer in Belle River, part of Maidstone Township. His connection to the Al Capone syndicate and his use of his own personal airplane and landing strips to run booze across Lake St. Clair to Michigan is embedded in local lore. His cousin, Paul Poisson, served as a colonel in the medical branch during the Great War and won the Military Cross. In 1921, Poisson became the first mayor of Tecumseh, Ontario. Today, the Tecumseh Legion Hall is still called the Colonel Paul Poisson Branch and has recently been adorned with a mural depicting his image.

....

MAXIME MOUSSEAU, my great-grandfather, was the chief Ontario liquor-control inspector for this region during Prohibition. A God-fearing man who performed his duties admirably, Maxime was, by all accounts, incorruptible, unlike many officials at the time. Also raised in Belle River, he eventually moved to Windsor and went to school at both Windsor Collegiate Institute and Assumption College. Maxime was married at 21 years old and had five children, one of whom was my grandmother, Bernadette Monforton. In 1913, his wife died; he remarried three years later.

During Prohibition, Maxime banished one of his sons, Lawrence, to Chicago because of his illegal involvement with the "devil's liquid." Maxime Mousseau died in June of 1931 at his home on Church Street after a period officially described as a "general breakdown, brought on by his duties as a government official."

PART I

A ship in harbour is safe,
but that is not what ships are for.

John Augustus Shedd

OOSE KNEW IT WAS WRONG; HE KNEW IT COULD BE DANGEROUS. "What the hell," he thought to himself as he began planning the operation. He was tired of being the fool. Of being on the outside, looking in.

Maurice "Moose" Ducharme had been through an entire lifetime in the 36 years he'd been alive. Where had all his hard work, honesty, loyalty, and service gotten him? He lived in a run-down, rented home with his wife and two children, breaking his back early every morning loading and delivering milk, constantly struggling to pay the bills while others had the balls to get in the game. His family deserved more! He was determined to give his family more than his useless father had given him. So the moral struggle raging inside him recently was being won by greed—and by the sheer exhaustion of always trying to get one step ahead.

Moose was only a couple of years removed from doing his bit for the Empire in the Great War. But when he'd come home in 1919 to Ford City, on the eastern edge of the Windsor, Ontario, shoreline, his community and the government that were so eager and proud to see him off didn't seem to care much now about his sacrifice or his lot in life. They weren't going to help him, so it was time for Moose to take matters into his own hands, even if that threatened his good name, his marriage and his freedom.

When Moose enlisted in the fall of 1914, he was 29, a good deal older than the average recruit. Like people in every corner of the Empire, he read about the growing tensions in Europe, the assassination of an unknown archduke in some far-off land, and how it led to Britain's standoff with Germany. The patriotism he felt, combined with the not-so-subtle pressure from the community, convinced him that he could sacrifice the six months or so it would take the British Empire to crush the lowly Huns.

Sara, his beautiful young wife, reluctantly supported his decision, even with two young children at home. Unlike Moose, she accepted her daily struggles and Spartan lifestyle in true Irish-immigrant fashion. Petite and strawberry blonde with sparkling green eyes, Sara O'Hollaren hadn't fallen for Maurice because of money, social position, or promises of a better future. Nor was she smitten with the immense, athletic frame that had helped him become a local football legend. Her attraction was simple—he was a handsome, quiet, sincere, and well-mannered young man.

By the time they wed in a simple service at their local church in 1906, Maurice had been employed at a number of general-labourer jobs around town, where his size and strength were in high demand and where his fellow workers continued calling him by his old football nickname, Moose.

Their first child, a son named Jack, arrived at the end of their first year of marriage. Jackie was their pride and joy, with the soft, fair features of his mother and the calm, quiet demeanour—as well as the bulk—of the Ducharme clan.

By the time their second child was on her way, Moose had landed a well-paying, seemingly secure job at the Walkerville Wagon Works Company when it expanded in 1910. His natural strength and hard work were rewarded at three dollars a day. The company was in the heart of the small town of Walkerville, named after the family of Hiram Walker, the founder of the nearby world-class distillery. The wagon-works company kept expanding to fulfil the growing demand for automobiles built by the Ford Motor Company on both sides of the border.

Any hopes that the young couple had to create a large French-Irish family were dashed with the delivery of their second child. Moose agonized throughout the night, hearing Sara's painful screams and the midwife's growing concerns. By the time the sun rose, a local doctor had joined the fray, and when little Anne-Marie arrived, she was dangerously underweight and blue, while Moose's poor wife nearly bled out. Although Sara recovered quickly, the doctor informed them that the damage done during delivery would make having any more children highly unlikely. Despite their disappointment, Moose and Sara felt blessed to have each other, two children, a steady income, and a bright future.

Months later, baby Annie seemed the picture of health, with little red tufts on her head and a full, round face sporting dimples—but Sara sensed something was not right. The baby's eyes seemed more and more vacant, and she had little reaction to things in front of her. After a costly visit to a specialist, it was discovered that the difficult birth hadn't just damaged the mother; loss of oxygen had also left little Annie blind.

So it was with a good deal of relief when Moose began his steady work at the wagon factory, making carriage parts and wheels for a growing community. Within three years, he was promoted to supervisor and given a much-needed pay raise. The doctors and special school where they hoped to send Annie in the future were going to be expensive.

By the fall of 1914, however, war recruitment was at a fever pitch in Ford City, Walkerville, Windsor, and across the nation. Ads in the Border City Star, posters plastered around town, recruitment drives, public rallies, and even Sunday church homilies encouraged all healthy young males—loyal Empire subjects—to sign up. Mounting pressure made it impossible for those who avoided the call from King and Country to be looked upon as anything less than cowards. This was especially true for Moose and other French Canadians, who might appear to be sympathetic to the French majority in the province of Quebec—a majority who refused to enlist in an "English war" they did not support.

It was under these circumstances that Moose came home from work one afternoon and announced to Sara, "I've signed on."

Sara was quiet for several seconds. "I suppose I knew you had to," she said with calm resignation. She walked over to him, wrapped her arms around his waist, put her head to his barrel chest, and asked, "How much longer do we have you before they ship you out?"

"Physical's on Monday, and we leave the last Saturday of the month," he answered as he blankly stared in the direction of seven year-old Jackie, playing with his wooden truck on the floor of the kitchen, and Annie, sitting and chewing on a cracker in her high chair. "I won't be long, luv. Some say we could even be home by Christmas, and we'll get on like I was never gone."

With concern that was hard to hide, Sara responded, "I pray you are right, Maurice."

Not unexpectedly, Moose passed the physical easily, and on a crisp, cool October morning, the Ducharme family walked the five blocks together to the trolley station on nearby Sandwich Street. The trolley line ran along the shores of the Detroit River and connected the communities to the east with the growing city of Windsor. Moose was carrying a gunny sack over his shoulder with the limited provisions he would need. As the trolley neared the train station at the foot of Goyeau Street a short time later, more and more people filled the streets, and they began to hear faint music. As the family made their way onto the train-station lot, a parade-like atmosphere awaited them. "It's a Long Way to Tipperary" was being played, somewhat poorly, by a four-piece military band. The music accompanied the young family as they greeted some friends, neighbours, and other recruits on the station's cobblestone platform. Sara's mother Clair and Moose's parents were already there. Marie, his mother, was nervously chatting in her thick French accent with a group of women as his father, Henri, hung back with his back against the station's stone wall.

Some time later, when the dignitaries finished a few patriotic messages and the recruits began their long goodbyes, the band started up again. Sara's tears and Jackie's lock on his meaty leg gave Moose considerable pause, but after hugs and one last kiss for his wife, he was away. Boarding the train, he bumped heavily into a much younger and considerably slighter fellow, causing him to tumble to the platform like his daughter's rag doll. Neither of these strangers could have guessed the profound affect they were destined to have on one another.

A loud whistle and release of steam announced the train's departure for Toronto and onward to Valcartier, Quebec, for basic training. Rolling away with steel wheels screeching against the track, Moose joined dozens of the others and hung out the window, waving goodbye to loved ones and a community they prayed they would return to soon.

S ARA HAD HELD BACK HER TEARS, BUT AS THE TRAIN CRAWLED OUT OF THE STATION, she let them flow. She was unable to wave like every-one else as her hands were occupied with An-nie, straddled on her right hip, and Jackie, holding tightly to her left hand. Her mother and mother-in-law were gathered protectively around her, caught up in the moment of sombre patriotism and waving en-thusiastically, while Moose's father stood expression-less. As the train rolled down the track and slowly out of sight, the band stopped abruptly, the music re-placed by the murmurs and quiet sobs of loved ones left on the platform.

The crowd dispersed slowly as if many were reluc-tant to believe where their young men were headed. Sara turned to receive hugs goodbye and begin her walk back home.

"I'm around to help with the little ones, Sara," Clair assured her; "all you have to do is ask."

"Oui, oui, Cherie," Marie Ducharme chimed in as her husband stood back, his head down, his cap pulled low over his forehead.

Sara wiped her eyes, saying, "Thank you. That's appreciated, but I really don't know what we are go-ing to need...prayers for Maurice, mostly, I guess."

Then, looking down at her son, she added, "We are just going to have to figure this all out, aren't we, Jackie?"

Jackie looked somewhat confused by her question as they all began their slow stroll out of the station together. The Ducharmes broke away for a walk towards downtown Windsor, while Clair insisted on joining Sara and the kids for the trolley ride home.

Sara had always been very close to her mother. Growing up the youngest of five children, she had watched the way her mother completely exhausted her time and energy, as well as her limited finances, raising a family on her own. When Sara was too little to remember, her father died tragically from a fall on a construction site. The company showed sympathy towards Clair and provided a meagre death benefit, but after the funeral and all the kind words of condolence, Clair was left to her own devices, a single mother caring for a large brood on her own.

The O'Hollaren family, like so many other Irish immigrant families of the day, struggled to get by and relied heavily on the charity of others—loving neighbours and friends—as well as on their unwavering Catholic faith. As soon as Sara's older siblings were of age, they picked up jobs of any kind to help support the family.

By the time Sara was fifteen years old, two of her siblings were already married and moved away, while the other two were working steady jobs, lightening the financial burden on Clair considerably. This was to be of great benefit to Sara's future. Her academic excellence during this time, a result of a sharp mind and her mother's insistence on focused study, made Sara's dream of becoming a school-teacher an attainable goal.

Two years later, the entire family celebrated Sara's acceptance into Normal School. There were few professional opportunities for young women of the day, and her love of children and education made teaching a natural fit. By the time she graduated a year later, she had already secured a teaching position at a one-room schoolhouse in nearby Sandwich East Township.

A beautiful and smart young woman like Sara drew constant interest from young men in the area. Because of her profession, unblemished reputation, and good standing in the community, she had many suitors, but most were of elevated class or education and came with the arrogance and stuffiness that Sara despised. She was also fully aware that marriage meant having to resign her teaching position. She loved her job and had no intention of giving it up just to marry.

Then she met Maurice Ducharme. The local Catholic parish, Our Lady of the Lake, nestled near the shore of the Detroit River, held a monthly bazaar that raised money to help the poorest of the poor in their community. While Sara was bringing in some canned preserves that her mother donated one cool spring evening, she ran into Moose—literally, bumping into him as he helped unload a wagon.

"Pardon me, miss," he starting saying, as he looked down at her and caught his breath. Her bright, beautiful eyes and pretty face had immediate impact.

"My fault, surely," Sara responded with an innocent grin. "I've been known to be a bit clumsy. Please forgive me."

In response, Moose stumbled to the point of embarrassment. All he could do was smile and look down at his hands nervously working the seam of his wool cap.

After a number of awkward seconds, Sara added, "Well, sorry again," and turned to go.

Moose's speeding heart rate, combined with the thought of a missed opportunity to get to know this striking young woman, caused him to panic. With her back turned and several steps away, he burst out, "I'm Maurice! Maurice Ducharme!"

His deep, booming voice echoed into the cavernous church hall, causing others to take notice. His face flushed.

This outburst caught Sara by surprise, and she turned her head, flashing a coy smile. "Nice to meet you, Maurice Ducharme. I'm Sara. Sara O'Hollaren." She stepped forward, offering her hand, and Moose shook it roughly, causing her body to be pulled off balance. Sara giggled at the awkwardness of this gentle giant, which helped to ease his obvious discomfort.

While Moose stood mesmerized by her exquisite features, they chatted briefly about the bazaar and mutual church acquaintances. For her part, Sara was impressed by Moose's shyness and humility despite his size and handsome features. His dark, wavy hair matched his eyes, and his square jaw framed an honest-looking face. His clothing indicated he was not from the wealthy class nor trying to pretend he was, which made him even more appealing.

After several minutes of small talk, an awkward pause signalled an end to their encounter. "Well, Maurice. It was a pleasure meeting you. I do hope we meet again," Sara said, once again extending her hand.

"So do I," Moose replied as he took her hand more gently and his eyes searched the floor. "When might that be?"

"I'm guessing you're a member of the parish, so I suspect I will see you at mass on Sunday."

"I look forward to it" was his reply, even though he was already considering the fact that, despite his mother's best attempts, he did not attend mass regularly. "Goodbye, Sara O'Hollaren."

"And goodbye to you, Maurice Ducharme," she said with a smile that made Moose weak at the knees.

They went their separate ways, both excited and hoping that they would see each other again soon.

While Sara shared every detail of the meeting with her mother, Moose kept the encounter to himself. He had few close friends to share the news with, and he certainly didn't want to get his mother's hopes stirred. He found her continued inquiries about potential marriage prospects annoying. He knew his father would have little interest in the matter.

As Sunday neared, Moose realized he had two problems. One was the reaction he would receive when he suddenly presented himself in his Sunday best and showed interest in attending mass.

That might be explained easily enough. The other problem was more of a concern. Lady of the Lake was a large, vibrant parish at the foot of Ford City, across Sandwich Street from the river, and it held three masses every Sunday. Unfortunately, he did not know which one Sara would be attending, so he simply took a chance and accompanied his parents to their usual mass.

Moose appeared in the kitchen on Sunday morning, thirty minutes before the 10 a.m. service. His hair was neatly combed back and he was wearing his only suit, which clung to his oversized frame far too snugly. His pant legs fell far short of his well-worn leather shoes. His mother was pleasantly surprised by the unexpected sight, but did not want to question him and risk a change of heart. She just smiled and looked at her husband, whose eyes moved slowly from his son to his wife and then back into his coffee mug.

Minutes later, as they walked the several blocks to the church, Moose was becoming increasingly nervous. Rounding the corner of Sandwich Street to the church's front sidewalk, Marie and Moose greeted friends and neighbours as her husband stood back uncomfortably. While hands were being shaken and pleasantries passed, Moose was preoccupied and using his considerable height to search anxiously over the heads of other parishioners.

Sara had little concern about being at the right mass to see her gentle giant again. Her mother attended church regularly and was a parish committee member, so she not only knew the whole congregation, but also knew the masses they attended. Her mother was familiar with the Ducharmes—the friendly woman with the thick French accent, her introvert husband, who had done some battle with the bottle, and their big, handsome son, who rarely joined his parents at weekly mass. Mrs. O'Hollaren thought that if Moose came to mass today with his parents to see her daughter, then that would be a positive sign, indeed.

Wearing her favourite powder-blue dress, matching bonnet, and white gloves, Sara was drawing the attention of many young men milling about, but she was clearly distracted. Standing outside, up near the large entrance doors, she scanned the crowd. At first, disappointment began to creep in when she did not see him. Moments later, however, she saw Maurice round the corner with whom she assumed were his parents. His big, athletic body was hard to miss. Wearing nice church clothes with his hair neatly combed made him look so handsome, it took her breath away.

She watched as he greeted people around him respectfully while he simultaneously scanned the crowd. As his search worked its way up the steps and towards the church entryway, their eyes locked. Pulses within both of them quickened. Moose continued to stare up at her with a nervous smile while he excused himself in mid-conversation and began working his way through the crowd. His mother was becoming more and more puzzled by his behaviour until the situation suddenly became very clear. After quickly ascending the steps, her son reached the entrance of the church and approached the beautiful young lady in blue.

"Good mornin', Sara...I wasn't sure what mass you might be at...you sure look pretty in that dress...I'm very happy to see you again..." Moose stammered as Sara smiled, enjoying his nervousness.

"Hello, Maurice," she returned, "I'm very happy to see you as well. I was worried I might not see you after mother told me that she only saw the Ducharmes' son at mass on special occasions."

Moose blushed but with growing confidence responded, "Well, Miss O'Hollaren, I guess I consider this a special occasion."

"I'm flattered, Maurice."

"Please, call me Moose. Everybody else does, on account of my size and my football days," he said.

Sara cringed. "Moose? Why ever would I call you that? It's not a very flattering name or image. I much prefer Maurice."

"Then Maurice it is," he said, feeling increasingly at ease. As the church bells began clanging loudly above them and parishioners made their way inside, he gathered up all his courage and asked, "Would you be interested in seeing me somewhere other than church? Could I talk to your father and ask his permission to maybe take you for a walk by the river one day? Or for a carriage ride around town?"

"That sounds lovely...and honourable, Maurice. But my father passed many years ago." Moose's reaction made her quickly add, "And my mother has full trust in my judgment, so I graciously accept your invitation."

Before they ended their conversation and were rushed into mass along with the remaining crowd, she told Moose where she lived, and they agreed on a day and time.

Their courtship lasted only six months before Moose was ready to propose and Sara was eager to accept. They had little in common but somehow seemed a perfect match. Clair, Sara's mother, saw the same humble, respectful man that Sara was drawn so strongly to. His limited education and financial prospects were of little concern: she could see that he was an honest, hard-working man who would surely make a good husband and father. Most importantly, she knew Sara truly loved him.

Marie Ducharme was thrilled with her son's finding such an intelligent and lovely young lady to wed. She had a flawless reputation and was from an upstanding, God-fearing family. Her husband offered no opinion in the matter.

In the spring of 1906, after a simple ceremony at their parish church, Maurice and Sara Ducharme began their life together. Sara followed the expectations of the day and forfeited her teaching position, resigning herself to be a good wife and future mother, while Moose settled into his role as provider.

No one could have foreseen that eight years later, he would be saying goodbye to his wife and children, climbing on a train, and heading for a war on the other side of the world, just as his own father had done many years before.

Moose's father, Henri Ducharme, was the second youngest of a very large French Catholic family living in southern Quebec in the latter half of the 1800s. Like most of their neighbours, the Ducharmes survived on prayer, hard work, and any additional income that their nine children could contribute once they were old enough. The small family farm grew some cash crops and had a few animals, but it was always a challenge to keep the large brood clothed and fed.

While his older siblings fell in line, sacrificing their education and any dreams they may have had to keep the family afloat, Henri had other ideas. A serious and withdrawn child—his own mother often referred to him as désagréable—Henri went about his limited schooling and chores on the farm in a begrudging fashion. At seventeen he met a pretty young girl named Marie from a nearby village; she was even more anxious than he was to get off the farm. After a year of courtship, Henri and Marie married in a simple service at the local church. Both families had little to offer the young couple, so Henri solidified his title as black sheep of the family by leaving his village, his family, and farming behind and moving to English Ontario. Marie's brother was a labourer in the growing community of Windsor, and he assured Henri that he could help him find work. The young couple took what little money and few possessions they had on a train, headed south, and started their new life together.

The struggles did not end once they left the farm. Steady work was more difficult to find than was promised, and even with Marie taking in some seamstress work with skills passed down from her mother, they still lived hand to mouth. Their limited English skills and the persistent undercurrent of anti–French Canadian sentiment in the area made matters even worse.

Their first child, Maurice, was born in 1885. There was little affection in the young marriage, and if Marie was expecting her husband's growing dependence on alcohol and increasingly withdrawn demeanour to change with the birth of their son, she was sadly disappointed. Three years later, they had another beautiful baby boy they named Pierre after Marie's father. Henri showed little love or even warmth towards his two sons, and even though he was often between jobs and claiming to look for work, he showed even less interest in helping raise them.

At four years old, little Pierre took sick with scarlet fever, draining the little savings the couple had scraped together to pay for a doctor before he died. Marie fell into a perpetual state of grief over the tragedy, and seven-year-old Maurice struggled to understand how the little playmate that he had grown so fond of was taken away from him. Henri withdrew even further into the bottle. It wasn't long afterwards that young Maurice began having to listen to and watch incidents of verbal and physical abuse that his mother endured stoically.

By the time Maurice was an adolescent, he and his mother had formed a loving, protective cocoon that helped insulate one another during those times when Henri came home early enough and drunk enough to conjure up some problem or misdeed. On several occasions, mother or son tried to step in and re-direct the anger and aggression towards themselves to help shield the other.

So it was a strange sort of relief when, in late 1899, Henri came home unusually early one evening and announced with a grumble that he had signed on with thousands of other Canadians to fight with the British Colonial Forces in a war in South Africa. He was being shipped out within days. Although the Ducharme clan back in Quebec considered Henri's enlistment in a British colonial war a betrayal to his French Canadian roots and the last step in his official estrangement from the family, Marie and her son had a quite different perspective. Once the news sank in and her husband was out of the room, Marie looked earnestly at her somewhat confused fourteen-year-old and whispered with a smile, *"C'est juste nous deux"*—"It's just the two of us."

Throughout the next three years, while Henri was away fighting in the Boer War against Dutch colonial settlers in South Africa and for a cause that many, including those outside of French Quebec, did not support, Marie and her teen-aged son were doing increasingly well. Money was still tight, but with Maurice old enough to start adding to a household income that was not being wasted on liquor, they were better off financially than they had ever been.

Maurice inherited a strong work ethic and had little difficulty finding temporary work for extra money. These jobs often involved some sort of physical or manual labour because by the end of his fourteenth year he had begun an incredible growth spurt, growing quickly into what had always been unusually large feet and hands.

Before he turned fifteen, he had left school, like so many others at the time, and began earning a steady income for the household. He was already well over six feet tall and had the lean muscle of the general labourers that were so common in their community. His size and strength caught the eye of a fellow worker who happened to belong to a local football team that played against American competition across the river. With his mother's blessing, he began training and practising with the Eagle Athletic Club team. It didn't take long for him to develop skill and passion for a game he grew to love.

Within two years, Maurice towered over most adult men in the community and was bigger and bulkier than most of the players he lined up across from on the gridiron. Tagged with the nickname "Moose", he became a fan favourite in the community and a much-feared competitor among opposing teams.

Then news came that the South African war had ended and Canadian soldiers would soon be returning. The news was met with mixed emotions at home. Despite the turmoil and struggles they endured before he left, Marie and her son both still had genuine love for Henri and prayed that he had changed and would come back a different man. Unfortunately, they found out quickly that he had not.

Henri's inability to secure steady employment and the late hours out drinking and staying in bed all morning resumed. A few weeks after his return, he came home relatively early one night, drunk and looking for conflict. Maurice was flipping through the most recent Eaton catalogue and his mother was sitting nearby sewing, letting out the cuffs on her son's trousers yet again, when their peace and quiet was interrupted. Upset about a meal that wasn't waiting for him and comparing it to how poorly he was fed while he risked his life in the heat of the African sun, Henri's anger escalated quickly. Just as he had done so many times in the past, he aimed his aggression towards his wife. Her side-eye look towards Maurice during Henri's tirade and her obvious dismissal of his complaints sent him into a rage as he stumbled aggressively towards her. Without hesitation or fear, Maurice jumped to fill the space between his father and his mother.

Standing tall, chest out and fists clenched beside him, he looked down, inches away from his father's face, and with his deep voice declared, "That's never happenin' again. You touch Mother, ever, and you'll have to come through me." The look on his father's face turned from rage to fear. "And then we'll throw you out on your ass. We don't need you around here anymore. You'll be on your own."

Henri was never a threat again. Instead, he withdrew even further into himself, completely emasculated and isolated. He stayed away most of the time and often didn't come home at night. Nobody asked or cared where he went. When he was home, he was a ghost. He rarely talked or interacted with his wife or son. His drinking subsided only after he took sick, and the doctor warned him that the bottle was slowly killing him.

Without the drink, what little social life he had came to an abrupt end. He spent most of his time at home, smoking and reading in the tiny makeshift bedroom they'd created, or he would be down in the dingy basement carving tiny British war-machine replicas out of scrap pieces of wood he scrounged. He attended family obligations when required, but did not engage anybody in conversation. Family, friends, and neighbours who were unaware of the troubles at home whispered about poor Henri and the trauma he must have endured on the South African battlefield.

By the time Moose was married, had children of his own, and was being given a send-off to fight his own war in 1914, the relationship between father and son was almost non-existent. Although he didn't like his father and certainly had no respect for him as a husband or a father, he could not help but love him. Deep down, there was something else—a desperate need for Moose to prove that he was so much better than what he came from. This innate desire seemed to tug at him uncontrollably with every important decision he made.

S ORRY ABOUT THAT, OL' BOY," MOOSE APOLOGIZED ON THE TRAIN as he extended his hand to the kid he had accidentally bumped to the ground. "I'm Maurice."

"Scotty McLuren," the smaller man said, looking up and returning the handshake. "You're a big lot, now aren't you? You signed on with the Scottish?"

Moose gave a nod.

"Well, I'm goin' to keep you close to me, ol' chap. I could use the protection from the likes of you."

Moose rolled his eyes and settled into the seat in front of Scotty, preparing himself for the hours ahead of them before they arrived in Toronto. He had never travelled anywhere beyond his own area, and seeing the big city, as well as parts of Quebec and eventually Europe, held some consolation for him despite his general uneasiness about the whole adventure.

During the two-day journey to Quebec City then north to Valcartier, Moose and Scotty killed a good deal of time reading, playing cards, and talking. Moose wasn't usually the chatty type, but he found Scotty interesting, engaging, and easy to talk to.

By the end of the second day, as they were just hours outside of Quebec City, Moose had already learned that Scotty was 22 years old, newly married to a young bride named Helen, whose picture he proudly shared, and worked with his father as an industrial painter's apprentice. He also revealed matter-of-factly that he never had a mother and was raised by his father. Scotty was a fellow Ford City boy, with all the grit, work ethic, and sense of pride that permeated the labour town. And he had dreams. "I'm not wantin' to be a bloody Rockefeller, you understand," Scotty rambled. "I just want a nice house, maybe on the river, a bunch of handsome little brats pesterin' me, and a decent job. One that'll pay me some good dough and let us get some nice things. Maybe even own my own shop one day."

"That sounds fair," Moose replied sympathetically.

"Throw in some respect for a war hero like me," he continued with a sly grin, "and everythin' will be right as rain when we come home in a few months."

Moose told him that he appreciated his youthful optimism, but he had seen a little more of life's challenges and disappointments. "And it's a good idea to prepare yourself for rough patches."

Scotty listened intently while Moose told him about his experience growing up. His great admiration and love for his mother was immediately apparent, as was the disappointment in his father. Moose was honest about the struggles with his father's drinking and lack of financial support. He even shared the details about the eventful night when he stood up to his father and finally ended the abuse. Scotty listened with growing fondness and respect for his new friend. Moose was pensive by the time he finished with, "Since then, he's been around and sober, but he's beaten down, a shadow of a man. He has no interest in finding a job and lives in his own little world."

"If your pop is as big as you and a mean drunk, I could have never of stood up to him like that. You were brave." Scotty acknowledged.

"I wasn't really brave. I had just had enough," Moose said, remembering those difficult days. "Sometimes a guy just has had enough, you know? You reach a point when you don't care what happens to you, you just need to stop others from getting hurt."

"You're my man for protection for sure then, Maurice," Scotty said with a friendly grin.

"Call me Moose. Only my wife and mother call me Maurice."

After a few thoughtful seconds, Scotty's eyes sprung wide with a sudden understanding. "Wait. Are you the Moose D that played football for the Eagles?"

"That'd be me," Moose admitted.

"Whoa! I used to read about you in the newspaper and heard all kinds of stories from my older brother and his friends. You're a legend!"

"A legend, am I?" Moose laughed. "Then why am I sitting on this train with the likes of you, and all these other sorry lots, heading to God knows where and God knows what?" He paused and turned to look out the train window. Rain was falling and creating angled rivulets on the window. His smile faded. "No, I'm just a working stiff like you who played on a good football team, got married, had kids, and now I'm putting it all on the line for king and country, ain't I?" Moose commented sarcastically.

This brief summary of their collective realities tempered Scotty's excitement, and they sat for a good while in silence.

By the time the train crawled into the bustling makeshift camp at Valcartier, Quebec, many hours later, Moose and Scotty felt they knew each other like lifelong friends. Had they not looked so different, one would have mistaken them for brothers in the way that they interacted. Moose stood well over six feet, carried a good deal of athletic bulk, and had a dark complexion that matched his dark hair and eyes. Scotty, on the other hand, was closer in height to the average five and a half feet of most recruits and was wiry thin and much fairer.

A cool, fresh breeze greeted the young recruits as they climbed off the train and began the march towards camp. They were joined in an impromptu parade by hundreds of horses and dozens of lorries full of equipment and provisions. The unfolding scene of uniforms, weapons, and units marching in column to the shouts of officers, along with the mud and manure everywhere, served as a stark welcome to their new reality and to a world they would have to endure for much longer than anyone could have predicted.

....

Private Ducharme and Private McLuren survived the three-month basic training despite it coinciding with the onslaught of snow and extreme cold that an early Quebec winter often brings. They, along with over 25,000 other recruits, learned to put up with uncomfortable cots in cold, drafty tents, food of limited taste and quantity, and the rigors of daily military exercises and marching.

Moose and Scotty, quickly dubbed the "Ford Boys" by the others, bunked together as part of the same regiment and grew even closer as the daily challenges pushed their limits. Intense training tends to reveal a young man's true character, and it certainly did with both of them. What Scotty lacked in physical strength, he made up for with effort and an innate perseverance that was recognized by many as the stubbornness of a mule. On a number of occasions he was dressed down by commanding officers for a variety of minor infractions, but the criticisms and occasional humiliations always failed to break his spirit. Moose, on the other hand, had little difficulty with the physical demands of the training and was heralded as an exemplary recruit. Even so, he often found the drills and combat simulations unrealistic to the point of being ridiculous. This was evident one day when he confided to Scotty, "If we're in the thick of it on a muddy battlefield, I'm not going to be too concerned about marching straight or holding my bayonet at a certain height. I'll be down low in the slop, protecting my ass." Then he paused, looked at his friend and added with a smirk, "And by the looks of it, probably your ass as well!"

Despite his private complaints about the training, by the end of their time in Quebec, Moose was already being singled out by officers for possible regimental promotion. His age, skills, calm disposition, and respect from his fellow recruits were all factors. Ironically, his size was the only thing that gave his superiors concern. As one officer noted, "The boys won't challenge that big lot, but the Huns will take his head off when it looms over the top of the trench."

It was with mixed relief and nervous anticipation that the soldiers heard the news that the local 21st Regiment Essex Fusiliers would be embarking for England in early March. They were going to be part of the Canadian 18th Battalion's plan for spring offensives. With only a day's warning, Scotty and Moose joined thousands of others transported to Quebec City, where they boarded ships headed up the St. Lawrence and sailed out to the Atlantic en route to England.

If the soldiers thought that their living conditions would improve once in southern England, they were sorely mistaken. The cold, wet, muddy camp at Shorncliffe, Kent, made daily drills and the simplest activities frustratingly difficult. What they didn't know, and any soldier who had been at the front would have gladly told the fresh Canucks, was that the terrible conditions they were enduring were the best training for what they were all soon going to be experiencing.

Few were surprised when Private Ducharme was promoted first to Corporal, then to Sergeant—advancements he didn't request or necessarily desire. The increase in pay, however, from one dollar a day to two, was enough incentive for him to accept. He felt a strange sense of relief mixed with uneasy responsibility leading a company that held many of the Essex Scottish boys from his area back home. As for Private McLuren, his feelings on the matter prompted a proud smile and put his superior at ease when he said, "I'll call ya Sergeant Ducharme and give ya a proper salute, all right, but I'm not gonna kiss your big French ass!"

As the weather warmed and March turned into April, the boys' growing eagerness to get out of the slog and "bring it to the Huns" was finally granted. Several thousand soldiers were shipped to the northern coast of France at Calais, and along with hundreds of horses and carts marched for two days to the Flanders region of Northwest Belgium. As the Canadians got closer and closer to the front, roads became sloppy, muddy ruts, trees in the patches of forest they passed were either cut down or blown to splintered stumps, earth-shaking shelling increased, and the pungent smells of war grew thick in the air. These were conditions they all would need to get used to as they crossed the border into Belgium and arrived behind the front lines at Ypres.

....

Whatever the young, wide-eyed Canadian soldiers expected out of war at the front could not have matched the realities. Although there was a good deal of indiscriminate shelling and sniper fire, the boys did very little actual fighting. When their rotation brought them to the front-line trench, they spent most of their days digging in soupy mud, cleaning their weapons, smoking, playing cards, and writing letters, all while trying to keep their feet dry. The daily demands on the soldiers depended on many factors, but none as much as the disposition of their commanding officers. In this regard, Scotty and the others felt lucky to be under the command of Moose, the name he allowed himself to be called as long as other officers were not within earshot. His leadership relied more on common sense and mutual respect for one another rather than on formalities or strict military regulation.

Although life in the trenches was brutal, after several months it offered a predictable routine that was occasionally broken by an easily thwarted attack by Germans across no man's land or by poisonous gas released into the incoming breeze. Scotty learned fairly quickly that staying alive was more about common sense than anything else. Always have your gas mask within reach, keep your head out of the scopes of enemy snipers, spend as much time in your dugout as possible protected from the water below and shells above, and be as slow as possible when ordered over the top for an attack.

Not all of the soldiers in Scotty's company and under Moose's command were able to avoid the dangers. The disease, injuries, and deaths that seemed to occur daily caused a fair amount of turnover in the two years prior to the third major offensive in Ypres that began in the summer of 1917, referred to as the Battle of Passchendaele. British High Command was putting increasing pressure on divisions to make significant advance into enemy territory around the same time that the U.S finally announced its entry into the fray. Several attempts had been made over the previous couple of months, and the brass demanded this one last big push, despite the obvious risks. They felt this would put nails in the German coffin. Moose, however, felt uneasy about the plans. He remembered well the stories he'd heard from other officers about prior attacks that HQ had devised and claimed as successful because the enemy trenches were breached. Nearly every time, however, a German counter-attack followed, pushing the British forces and their allies back to their original trench, all at the cost of horrific injuries and way too many young men's lives. Moose didn't want to send his boys into an attack without a clear advantage or allow them to be used as sacrificial lambs. But he had also learned that orders were orders.

He gathered the junior officers and explained, "Okay, boys. HQ says we're going over the top just before sun up, and so that's what we're doing. Get the boys ready. Full loads and masks. Forget the formal charge bullshit. Tell the boys to use the craters as much as possible for cover and stay in line. Hopefully we'll get lucky and break their trench, cause a retreat, and live to see another day. No goddamn heroes, you understand?"

The wide-eyed, blank look on their faces told Moose they realized the seriousness of the situation. He hated this part of his job: putting his men in front of a firing line and wondering how many would take some lead. He also knew that if he didn't do it, someone else would, someone who might care much less and sacrifice many more.

"And give the boys double rum rations before the attack."

As the meeting broke up, Moose ordered Scotty brought up from his dugout. He explained the unfolding situation to him and added, "I'm joining your platoon on this one, Private."

"Tryin' to go home a hero or in a box, Moose? Nobody expects you to get dirty. Why now?" asked Scotty.

"I've got a funny feeling about this one," Moose explained. "HQ thinks it could be the end for the Hun, especially with the Yanks coming. But I don't know. The numbers and the terrain don't look right, and I want to be out there to call it off if it gets ugly. So I might as well babysit you if I'm going."

"And what if I don't want babysittin', Moose?" Scotty said, annoyed. "Never needed or wanted it before."

"No longer your choice, Private," Moose finished while pointing to his Sergeant bars.

At oh-five-hundred the next morning, thousands of Empire soldiers quietly made their way from support trenches and tunnels, through the uncomfortably crisp November darkness and glue-like, icy mud, to the front trenches. Bayonets were fixed, ammunition checked, and rum rations consumed. As they waited for the whistles and flares to signal the beginning of the attack, best wishes and private prayers were being whispered. Moose made his way to the signalling area and, as inconspicuously as possible, made sure Scotty was nearby.

With his pocket watch in hand, Moose said a quick prayer and waited for the signal. Minutes later, the shrill of whistles echoed all down the line as flares shot high above no man's land, briefly illuminating the soupy mix of icy craters, mud, barbed wire, and human carnage.

With an age-old battle cry, thousands of Empire soldiers climbed up ladders and out of their trenches, beginning their slow advance through the slog. Moose did the same, respecting Scotty's wishes that he at least be able to lead.

Even with darkness and the poor visibility of an early winter fog, the German guns opened up. The cacophony of battle was unleashed—repetitive cracking of machine guns, deafening thuds of mortar shells, sharp whizzing of lead through the thick air, muted pops of bullets finding their marks—all mixed with the groans and screams of soldiers cut down in the sticky mud. The scene, repeated endless times over the past few years, was hellish.

Moose had never been in the thick of it like he was now. As a commanding officer, he was usually watching from a rear-guard position near his trench or getting updates from communication lines dragged into the battlefield. As unnerved as he was with the experience, he couldn't help but take pride in the way his boys fought with a fierce blend of bravery, blind devotion, and self-preservation.

As he forced his focus back to the task at hand, a mortar shell whistled loudly nearby, then exploded twenty meters in front of him. The force knocked him backwards as thick grey mud flew in all directions and smoke hung in the air. His ears rang as he slowly got back to his feet and surveyed the situation. Wiping mud from his eyes, he focused on a soldier lying in front of him on the edge of a fresh crater. It was Scotty. Moose made his way to his side and saw that he was conscious, but looked to be in shock. Yelling above the sounds of bullets and shells, Moose asked, "You doing okay, Scotty?"

Shaking uncontrollably, Scotty answered, "I'm in trouble here, Moose."

Amid the mud and water all around him, Moose noticed deep shrapnel cuts to Scotty's face and hands as well as crimson at the base of Scotty's left leg. His boot had been blown off, taking his foot with it. "You're going to be fine, Scotty-boy," he said as he struggled to remove his belt to use as a tourniquet.

"You're not followin' training," Scotty struggled to say, "you have to move on, sir. No wasting time on the advance."

"I'm your superior, Private. Stand down." Moose tugged the belt tight around Scotty's upper calf and looked around frantically to consider his options. His troops had made considerable advance, but Fritz was still lobbing shells everywhere, and the machine guns hadn't slowed. He knew what he was supposed to do. He had drilled it endlessly into his own men. An attack would not succeed if soldiers stopped to help fallen comrades. But leaving Scotty there for God knows how long to bleed out or get hit by another shell was not an option he could live with. "Listen, kid," he yelled over the mayhem, "I'm going to need you to grit your teeth and get ready for pain like you've never had. Do you trust me?"

"Of course," Scotty replied in a weak voice, "but I'm scared, Moose."

"So am I, kid, but here we go." Harnessing the strength and athleticism of his former football days, Moose took Scotty by his arms, heaved him onto his back, and began his slow and difficult trudge back towards their trench. With the uneven terrain, his feet sinking in the mud, and bullets whizzing all around him, the situation was perilous. Every step needed to be quickly and carefully planned and demanded a rebalance of the weight he was carrying. Scotty's painful grunts registered each stride. Just as he spotted a medic making a return trip out of the trench, a bullet caught Moose in the back of his thigh. He and Scotty both tumbled to the ground as a medic and stretcher-bearers headed their way.

....

The Battle of Passchendaele was a relative success in a war that measured victory by a few hundred meters of muddy farmers' fields. After months of fighting, four thousand Canadians were dead, and Moose and Scotty were among the twelve thousand injured. Scotty was stabilized at the field hospital, sent to Saint-Omer, France, for treatment, and finally transferred to No. 8 Canadian Hospital for rehabilitation before being shipped home. The war was over for him, but not for Moose. His wound was superficial, as the bullet had gone straight through his meaty thigh. More painful to him was his military demotion as a consequence of not following leadership protocol. He knew he should not have been part of the advance. He should not have compromised his leadership by trying to protect a subordinate, and he definitely should not have stopped his advance by bringing back a wounded soldier. HQ made it clear that he should consider himself lucky that he did not receive a dishonourable discharge.

....

Moose, now Private Ducharme once again, had little difficulty surviving the remaining year of the war, although he experienced a new level of loneliness with Scotty no longer there. The trench conditions and boredom remained challenging, but the Canadians were rarely called on for offensives due to the recent, substantial American involvement. Even though Moose lost his bars, he was still the de facto company leader and was looked up to by the others. The actions that caused his demotion by the brass were celebrated and respected by his fellow soldiers. Even the new sergeant saw little threat to his leadership, and often sought and was granted counsel from Moose.

By the fall of 1918, the Germans had shifted into survival mode. With U.S. might pouring in and failed advances at the front, the only way to avoid the invasion of Germany itself was a formal ceasefire, which they requested in mid-November. Months went by with no fighting, and soldiers on both sides continued with the miserable winter trench life while desperately waiting for news from Allied Command.

In the spring, Germany and the Central Powers officially capitulated and reluctantly signed a treaty to end the war. After more than four years of vicious fighting in sub-human conditions and the deaths of well over ten million people, military personnel from all over the world, including Moose, were finally free to go home. Or so they thought.

The Canadian government was overwhelmed by the logistical challenge of getting hundreds of thousands of service members back home with limited transport ships. As a consequence, Moose and many other Canadian soldiers were posted for months at English bases to wait for their tickets home; they grew increasingly restless and disgruntled. The bulk of the Canadians stationed there—

miraculous survivors of years of hellish conditions—were inclined to behave like the young, impatient men that most of them were. For their part, military brass wanted to avoid the inevitable drinking and carousing around the towns of Southern England, so they kept the soldiers on the bases, busy with standard daily training. Even though Moose was as bitter and frustrated as the rest, he avoided getting involved in the insubordination, drinking, and violent revolts that occurred.

In August 1919, Moose got the call. He was finally heading home to return to his wife, kids, and former life. Although his family was just as anxious for his return as he was, the community he had left and risked his life for would not be as welcoming.

AFTER DISEMBARKING IN HALIFAX AND TAKING NUMEROUS TRAINS over the course of several days, Moose stepped out into the bright late-summer sun and onto the same Windsor Station platform where he had waved goodbye to family and friends almost five years before. After what seemed like a lifetime filled with deprivation and death, he was finally home. The shaded platform area along the track was crowded and buzzing with anticipation as many families from the surrounding townships anxiously awaited loved ones. Straining necks, waving arms, and unrestrained hugging took over the crowd.

Blinded briefly by the bright light as he stepped off the train, Moose scanned the crowd for his family. With a mixture of relief and surprise, he spotted the head of his boy, Jack, hovering above the rest of the crowd. When their eyes met, Jack waved excitedly and pointed in Moose's direction. Jack led Sara, holding Annie's hand, along with Moose's mother and mother-in-law, towards him. Henri Ducharme, looking much older and frailer, hung back by the station doorway. By the time they navigated through and around the many joyful groups, Moose and Sara already had tear-filled eyes.

His long, strong arms embraced his wife and picked up Annie at the same time.

"Welcome home, luv," Sara said with a muffle as tears fell and her face was buried in Moose's chest.

Moose was too choked up to speak as he took in the sight of his little Annie, now eight years old, looking blankly into space and reaching for her mother. His focus then turned to Jack, who at thirteen years old was already looking very much like a man. Jack offered his hand to shake, but Moose put his large hand behind Jack's neck and roughly pulled him into an emotional hug, saying, "My son is a man. I missed my little boy growing up."

"Welcome home, Pa. We all missed you," Jack said in a voice cracking awkwardly from the onslaught of puberty. "Did you kill lots of Huns?"

Moose's bright, tear-filled eyes turned serious when he answered, "That part of my life is dead and buried, Jackie. It's over. I'm home now."

After greetings and hugs from his mother and Sara's mother, there was an awkward lull in the reunion when Moose saw his father standing at a distance by the station. Locking eyes briefly, Moose gave him a dim smile, and his father nodded back solemnly, his eyes misty. Sara ended the awkward moment by announcing, "Well, let's get you home where you belong."

He grabbed his bag and slung it over his shoulder. "That's something I've been dreaming about since—" Moose began to respond, but he stopped mid-sentence as he turned and saw Scotty standing, with the help of wooden crutches, near the corner of the station. Moose noticed he was a little heavier, looked much older, and his face registered evidence of a good deal of pain and suffering. As their eyes met, Scotty's face lit up with a gratifying smile as he began slowly negotiating his way over on his crutches. Moose was able to move towards him much more quickly before the two met in a powerful embrace.

"You survived, did you, you big lot?" Scotty asked as they stepped back to survey each other.

"I did. Wasn't the same without you, though. It's great to see you up and moving."

"Ya, I'm movin'. Just not very fast," Scotty joked and paused some time before adding, "It's sure nice to see you again, Moose. I was worried I might not. I've been feeling terrible about how—"

Moose cut him off, "You too? I just told my boy that we're not talking about over there any more. That part of our life is over. We're both alive and home. We have nothing but our futures ahead of us. C'mon, kid, let me introduce you to my family."

....

Days and weeks went by as Moose tried to reintegrate himself back into his former life. The cautious way Jackie and Annie initially interacted with him quickly turned to the kind of love and adoration that existed before he'd left five long years before. He also revelled in being back with his loving wife and sharing their warm bed, but comforting sleep did not come easy. Moose could tell everyone that the war years were over, but too many demons in the night suggested otherwise.

Many things had changed back home in Ford City during the war, none of them particularly kind to Moose and other returning soldiers. With so many men away fighting, women had convinced the government to allow them to vote during the war years, something they had been fighting for as part of the Suffrage Movement for decades. And with that kind of power now in their hands, women used their new-found political leverage for social change. Along with other progressive legislation, women helped religious organizations and the ever-present Temperance societies finally to pass laws to outlaw the sale, distribution, and consumption of alcohol.

The most immediate change that impacted Moose and many other returning soldiers, however, had occurred in the workplace. Labour shortages, caused by men leaving for war, were filled by women joining the workforce. Initial concerns that women weren't up to the task were quickly dismissed as employers realized that not only did women hold their own in most jobs, but they could also be paid much less. (Even Sara took advantage of the labour demand and started working a few days a week while her mother and mother-in-law helped with Annie.) As men returned from war, employers were reluctant to give up their much more inexpensive workforce.

Moose learned all about the challenges ahead of him from Scotty when they met up days after his return. Over a couple of beers that Scotty had stashed and brought over, the reunited Ford Boys sat on the front porch and considered their future. Scotty was lucky. His war injury didn't hinder his abilities in the paint shop where he continued to work with his father. In fact, business there was brisk due to the automobile industry's resurgence after the war. Unfortunately for Moose, his former wagon-works company, which was still building the popular Fords, had expanded to a point where Moose's few former colleagues that still worked there held little sway in the large corporation's hiring decisions. And with hundreds of other veterans from the area returning and competing for limited jobs, Moose didn't like his chances.

"I'd like to get you into our shop, Moose, but it's mostly a two-man operation," Scotty said.

"No, kid. Thanks anyway, but standing around on a line won't work for me. I've got to be moving," Moose offered while staring off. "We'll be fine for a little while. I'm still owed some soldier pay, and Sara's got her part-time work."

"Where is she working?"

"She's over at the Bell switching station. Most of the fancy homes around Walkerville have telephones now, and she connects their calls with wires and plugs on some kind of board. Boring work, I guess. And it's only women, so it's cheaper for the company," Moose explained.

Scotty thought for a while before saying, "You'll find something, Moose. Lots of businesses around here would be lucky to have a big, strong Frenchie like yourself." The two men smiled off into the street as they sat in comfortable silence—Moose concerned about work, providing for his family, and the night terrors that often stole his sleep, and Scotty about job prospects for a friend he felt an incredible debt to, one he feared he could never repay.

When the conversation turned more personal, Scotty struggled to admit to his friend that his home life and marriage were now in tatters. "Things weren't good when I came home," he confessed. "The missus had no time for me. She up and left."

"Why? What happened?" Moose said.

"Not really sure," Scotty said, his head dropping. "But I think it has a lot to do with this," he said as his hands wrapped around his wooden leg. "I don't think she saw me as a whole man anymore." He paused, giving thought to the situation. "We talked about things getting better and maybe having kids when I came back to a hero's welcome, but I guess we didn't count on me gettin' shipped back early, all cut up and missing a leg. I had trouble with sleep. Couldn't get past that day, Moose . . . it haunted me. Still does sometimes, if I'm bein' honest. She started staying away a lot and hardly spoke to me when she did come home."

His good friend's heartfelt admission was a gut punch to Moose. He didn't know how to respond.

"And I'm pretty sure she had another guy on the side," he continued. "So I decided I was just gonna give her a way out ...and I did. She left, and I didn't say a word."

"I'm so sorry." It was all Moose could think to say. He felt that Scotty was burdened with more than just the physical scars from his injury, and now he knew why.

Shaking himself out of his dark mood, Scotty looked up at Moose, forced a smile, and said, "Anyway, maybe it's all for the best. Fresh start and all that."

"Maybe you're right, kid." He put his hand on Scotty's shoulder. "Your fighting days should all be behind you now. You have a right to be happy."

Scotty nodded in agreement before lifting his empty beer bottle and saying, "You're so right, my friend. Another cool one of these will help with that."

....

Weeks later, as Moose was growing increasingly edgy and frustrated, Scotty dropped by his house with news of a possible job opportunity. He explained that Walkerside Dairy Company, less than a mile away, was looking for milk deliverymen. The company had hired his father's shop to paint logos on a handful of their new motorized delivery trucks, and a discussion with the manager revealed that they were in need of help.

"I talked you up, pal," Scotty said.

Although Moose was not particularly excited about the job prospect, he did like the idea of moving about town instead of the stationary dreariness of many local factory jobs. "How much does it pay?" he asked.

"Don't know. I would think it depends on your route and the number of customers. Maybe someone who wants to hustle and deliver to more customers could make good money."

Moose thanked Scotty for the tip and made plans to walk over to Walkerside first thing in the morning. When he went back into the house, he discussed the opportunity with Sara, who was very enthusiastic. She had been watching Moose's mood darken for weeks and was getting more and more concerned about his nightmares. Maybe a steady job and sense of purpose were what he needed.

"That sounds great, Maurice. You would be outside, moving about, and sort of be your own boss," Sara said as she wrapped her arms around his neck.

He looked down at her pretty face, their noses just inches apart. "I was thinking along the same lines. But I have to get the job first."

"A big, strong war vet like you? Who wouldn't hire you?" she asked as they both leaned into a kiss. Between the transition back to normal life after years at war, his lack of work opportunities, and the trouble he was having sleeping, there hadn't been many intimate moments between them since his return, and they both were enjoying this one. As the kiss lingered, Annie felt her way into the kitchen, calling for her mother, putting an abrupt end to the romantic moment. They both were smiling as their foreheads met.

....

Moose's visit to the dairy company could not have gone better. As luck would have it, he ran into the owner as he entered. He introduced himself, explained his war service and present situation, and made promises about hard work and responsibility if he was given an opportunity.

"Are you the same Maurice Ducharme that played the line for the Eagles?" the owner asked.

"I am," Moose replied.

"You sure dished out some pain in that championship game, son," he said as Moose's faced dropped, "so I know you're strong enough to handle the hard work."

"I sure can, sir," Moose said, encouraged, "if you'll give me a chance."

"You have it. I'm going to send you in to fill out some forms with my manager, and then I want you here first thing Monday morning."

Moose left the dairy with a sense of satisfaction and purpose he had not had since his working days before the war. The opportunity seemed like a good fit for him, the people he would be working for appeared nice enough, and he would be bringing home a steady salary.

....

After a week helping on another route and seeing the way the operation and deliveries worked, Moose began his own route, encompassing twelve-square-blocks not far from his home. His route, taken over from a retiring fellow and expanded to include new areas, included a mix of low-income homes like his own, some nicer homes mostly belonging to local Ford employees, some apartment units, and a few very wealthy homes surrounding Willistead Manor, which Hiram Walker's son Edward had recently built. This was the St. Mary's Gate district, where success and money were on full display: huge mansions sparkled amid manicured lawns and gardens, new automobiles gleaming in carports.

The job was simple enough. Just before sunrise each weekday morning, Moose would pick up and deliver quart or gallon bottles of cool, fresh milk to customers' porches or to milk boxes that were usually near a side door. Once a week, he would collect the money owed and take orders for the upcoming week. This was all done using the Walkerside truck, which Moose picked up at the company lot. As Moose explained to Sara, "You don't have to be a genius, just reliable."

Moose was a natural for the job. He was an early riser anyway; he enjoyed the physicality of loading, delivery, and unloading; he was able to be out and about throughout the day; and he enjoyed the interaction with his customers. His customers enjoyed him as well. Many felt a sense of pride that they got their milk from a former local football star and Great War veteran. With the steadily improving economy, Walkerside was happy to see increased customers and orders, but no route grew at the pace of Moose's.

When summer vacation came, Moose would bring Jackie along with him on his daily runs. He enjoyed seeing his son take to the hard work, and it lessened the workload at the hottest times of the year, but Moose continually stressed to Jackie the importance of his schooling to avoid being forced down a similar career path.

It was clear early on that Moose was not going to become rich delivering milk. He was making mere cents on the quart bottles and a nickel on the gallon bottles. After delivering to several dozens of customers each day, his weekly pay would amount to somewhere between seven and ten dollars. He struggled with the realization that this amount was less than he had made as a much younger man at the wagon-works company before enlisting.

The limited income bothered him much more than it bothered Sara. "We're doing fine, Maurice," she would say. "We've got each other, a roof over our heads, and you are earning an honest wage. We don't need all the other fancy things."

Her words always made Moose feel better, but he couldn't reconcile a reality that he was witnessing more and more around his neighbourhood and community. Many men had embraced opportunities to make what was being called "easy money" in the ever-expanding illegal liquor business. Fellows he knew or heard about who worked as labourers were suddenly wearing expensive clothes, driving new cars, or buying fancy homes. Nobody talked about how, but whispers told the story. With Prohibition in full swing and people with more money in their pockets, the demand for booze of any type had increased dramatically. Most people, including local officials and even law enforcement, disagreed with what they saw as draconian restrictions—and so they sidestepped the laws. And the irony was, one of the biggest whisky distilleries in Canada was only a few blocks away. Even more disheartening to Moose was the fact that the people who were taking those risks were making even more money by investing their profits into a sizzling-hot stock market that many were calling a sure bet.

....

Over the course of his first couple of years delivering milk, Moose's initial annoyance with his limited financial prospects grew into outright jealousy and bitterness. He felt frustrated that everyone else seemed to have hopped on an easy ride that he had missed. A growing moral dilemma was beginning to eat away at him, and Sara could sense something was wrong.

"Are you having the nightmares again, Maurice?" she asked one sunny spring morning.

"No. Why do you ask?"

"You're tossing, turning, and breathing heavy again in the night. It wakes me, and it worries me."

"The war's over, luv. So are the nightmares, for the most part, thankfully," he assured her. "I've got other things bothering me now."

"What is it?" Sara asked as she wrapped her delicate fingers into his large, callused hand.

"I'm missing the boat, Sara," Moose sighed after several moments of silence. "There are real opportunities out there for men who are willing to take them...willing to take some risks. But I get up every morning and slug milk bottles just so we can get by each week. And the future doesn't look all that promising. Annie's going to need expensive materials to keep on with her studies, Jackie's smart enough to go on in schools that we won't be able to afford, and more and more of my customers are buying those new electric ice boxes, so they won't be needing me every morning for much longer." He paused, then added with a hint of shame in his voice, "I wanted to be more than my father was, luv. One who is there for his wife and his kids and can provide them with everything they ever wanted."

A heavy silence filled the space between them. Sara knew her husband and the way he was raised well enough to recognize the demons he harboured about his father's drinking, abuse, and inability to earn a steady income. She turned to look deep into his dark eyes. "You are already so much more than your father, Maurice. Don't you see, honey? You are always trying to prove yourself, and you don't need to. You've done it your whole life."

Moose's eyes dropped from hers as he considered what she was saying.

She took his big hands in hers. "Think about everything you've done, Maurice. Working as a young boy to help put food on the table. Training so hard to become a star football player. Standing up and protecting your mother. Going off to war and risking your life." She lifted his face up to hers. "You don't have anything to prove to me, the kids, or anybody." As Sara pulled him in for a tender embrace, she felt a great release of emotion from his broad shoulders. When they separated, she reassured him with, "Things always have a way of working out, honey. The Lord provides. We just have to have faith."

His look said he was relieved and pacified, but it belied what he was really thinking. Moose did not have the heart to tell his wife that he couldn't change who he was. He could not stop trying to prove himself worthy of an incompetent father's respect. He couldn't tell her that he was tired of her blind faith in Providence—a faith he didn't necessarily share. He was tired of putting his future in the hands of some other power or force. And he was damn tired of busting his hump each week just to get by. As he looked into his wife's beautiful eyes, he was suddenly sure about two things: he still loved her more than anything in the world and would never hurt her or their family, but he was also done being a fool and grinding out each workday while those around him were reaping the rewards of a little risk. She deserved more. They deserved more. It was time for him to get off the sideline and into the game.

6

MOOSE ENJOYED A LITTLE HOOCH ON OC-CASION—A BOTTLE OF BEER, a shot of whisky, or some wine with dinner—but the impact that his father's love affair with the bottle had on his childhood, not to mention the extra money it would cost his young family, made drinking an activity that was not part of his daily life. But he knew it was a big part of many people's lives in the community. He often encountered men, from all walks of life and at any time of day, showing the effects of over-indulgence. He knew there were places around that people could go to buy liquor or clandestine establishments that offered a variety of drinks to those interested. He had also heard or read stories about dangerous gangs who controlled the flow of liquor and got very rich doing it. There was undeniable evidence all around him. The problem was, he didn't know how he could break into the business and make some of that money for himself.

But every venture starts with a spark of an idea. Moose was given that spark by one of the many loyal customers on his milk route one late Saturday morning during collection. He almost always did his collections on Saturdays, because unlike his deliveries, he could collect later in the day when most people were awake and home, and also because he could take the time that he didn't have throughout the week to chat with his customers. On one of these collection days, he was talking with one of his regular customers in his front yard. Mr. Dougall was an older gentleman with a dry sense of humour and a lot more love and affection for liquor than he had for his nagging wife.

"So two quarts on Monday and Thursday next week will make you a happy man, will it, sir?" Moose kidded.

"Sure would, Moose," Dougall replied with a sly grin, "but not as happy as it would if you could slip some whisky in one of them and some poison for my wife in the other."

They shared a wicked laugh as they shook hands and Moose turned to be on his way.

Late that night Moose was kept awake, unable to turn off recurring thoughts swirling around in his mind. Sara's patterned breathing next to him assured him that at least she was getting a good night's sleep. Mr. Dougall's remark from earlier in the day kept coming back to him. He had met Mrs. Dougall a number of times, and the idea of poisoning her was certainly understandable, but not something Moose took seriously. The whisky, however, was a different story.

What if he could deliver whisky right to a person's front doorstep along with their milk? Weren't business experts always talking about supply and demand and giving customers what they wanted? His mind was spinning with possibilities, complications, and questions. Knowing sleep was impossible, he made his way quietly down to the front parlour, turned on a dim table lamp, and using a pencil and the back page of his milk-collection ledger, wrote down some of the random thoughts bouncing around in his head:

> *Door-to-door liquor delivery.*
> *Where do I get large amounts of booze?*
> *How many of my customers would be interested?*
> *$$$ How much would it cost and how much*
> *could I make?*
> *Risks—police . . . job??*
> *Hiram Walker's?? Delivery on the sly. HOW??*
> *OPPORTUNITY!!*

His heart rate went up as he sat there in the quiet of the night staring at the last word. With no sound but the faint, rhythmic ticking of his pocketwatch lying on the table, he looked over the list and then slowly wrote and underlined one more item:

What would happen to Sara and the kids if I got caught?

His excitement dampened as he considered this last line. He knew Sara would never even consider such a scheme, so he decided just to make some inquiries, talk to a few people, and see if his idea had any potential.

There was nobody Moose trusted more than Scotty and his father. Moose and his wartime comrade were even closer now since Scotty was alone, abandoned by his young wife. Scotty's father, Thomas McLuren, owned a paint shop and was well connected in the community, but his younger years had left him with a reputation of being rough around the edges after fraternizing for years with men of questionable character. For Moose, this was the best place to start.

The next morning, Sunday, Moose was exhausted as the family made their way to mass at the local Catholic church, something Sara insisted they do weekly. Milling about on the front sidewalk afterwards, Moose spotted Scotty and made his way over to say hello and make arrangements to meet later that day. Knowing him as well as he did, Scotty recognized that Moose was preoccupied, and he was anxious to find out why.

"Lovely day today, fella," Moose said as he rounded the corner into his friend's backyard later that afternoon. Scotty was sitting on a lawn chair with his leg stump exposed and resting on a little wooden table.

"Sure is," Scotty agreed without turning around. "Why don't ya get us a couple of beers inside and come join me?"

As the two friends relaxed under the warm spring sun, sipping on cool ales, Scotty couldn't wait to ask, "So, Moose, what's got ya worked up and wanting to talk?"

Moose took a few seconds to organize his thoughts. "I've been doing some serious thinking about a business venture" He looked anxiously at his friend. "I know you're going to think I'm crazy, but I've got a business idea that's been bouncing around in my head, and I can't shake it. I think it just might work. I just need your help..."

"Why don't you just tell me what you're thinking," Scotty said, cutting him off.

Moose took a breath and let it all out. He explained his need to make more money and the reasons why and his idea of delivering booze right to the customer's door along his milk route. He outlined the questions he had about whisky availability and price and even admitted to the concerns he had about Sara finding out or him getting caught.

Scotty listened carefully, growing increasingly worried by what he was hearing.

"So, what do you think?" Moose finally finished, his face flush with excitement.

"I think I bloody well need another one of these," Scotty replied, looking down at his empty beer. After an awkward silence he added, "I'm not judging ya, Moose. I'm just . . . I just don't know what to say."

"Say you'll help me get some information, that's all. I just want to see if this idea has any potential. I was thinking your father might have some thoughts?"

Scotty looked him in the eyes for several seconds, slowly coming to appreciate the position Moose found himself in: a hard worker, war veteran, and honest family man who could not catch a break or get ahead. He couldn't help but agree to do anything for his best friend. Scotty was also sure that his father was the right man to answer some of the questions Moose had. What he also was quite confident about, and didn't want to tell Moose, was that his father would surely convince Moose that this idea of his was foolish and involved way too much risk.

Days later, Moose and the two McLurens met in a park down by the Detroit River. It was another banner spring day, and people were out and about, enjoying the fresh, cool air after a long winter. As the men sat around an old picnic table, Moose, once again, laid out his business idea and explained the questions and concerns that went along with it.

Mr. McLuren listened with little visible expression, which increasingly worried Moose. Scotty sat silently fretting about how his good friend was going to handle the disappointment after his father's rejection of an idea that Moose had convinced himself was so promising.

After several minutes of rapid-fire explanations followed by questions of concern, Moose anxiously inquired, "Well, what do you think?"

There was a tense pause while Scotty and Moose looked each other's way. "Well, young man, I've got to tell ya that home delivery of booze is a banner idea. The best I've heard in a long time," Mr. McLuren said as Scotty's head jolted up and his eyes widened. "But there are some things ya would need to work out."

"Dad! What are ya sayin'?" Scotty protested.

As Moose sat up with excitement, Mr. McLuren continued looking at Scotty and explained. "What I'm sayin, Scotty Boy, is that this young man has a Rockefeller idea here. Imagine getting hooch brought right to your door. Right under the noses of the police and liquor agents. Hell, they would probably be your customers, too. No more blind pigs down the street where prices are too high, the booze is watered down, and ya risk gettin' caught bringing it home."

He paused, thinking. "The local speakeasies are great if you're a young fella and feel like stepping out. But what about average folk who just want to enjoy some quality booze in their own homes?" He looked back and forth at Moose and Scotty. "I'm tellin' ya, I'm a business man, and this sounds like good business. Very good. But there are...issues."

"Like what?" Moose asked, clearly encouraged.

"You'll have the demand, I'm sure of it," the older man continued, "but supply will be a problem. Your best bet is whisky, and the best supplier would be Walker's, of course." They all looked west along the river as he spoke, eyeing the massive brick distillery only blocks away. "It's so close, and they got the best hooch around. But ya understand, ya can't just knock on Walker's door and buy barrels of whisky. These days they're only supposed to be exportin' the stuff." He looked at the two younger men and emphasized, "Supposed to be, ya hear. But they sell it under the table all the time. Ya just need to know someone connected who can get it for ya. Also, how do ya deliver the whisky without people around knowing what you're deliverin'?" He looked at Moose. "I assume you will deliver at the same time you deliver your milk?"

"That's what I was thinking," Moose answered.

"Early morning is good. Most people still in bed. That makes sense. And ya already have a truck for transport. But how do ya hide it? Can't be rolling barrels or hauling cases of bottles up to the front doors."

Scotty couldn't believe what he was hearing. "Have you two lost your marbles? You're talking nonsense here."

They both turned to Scotty, annoyed. "What we're talking here, son, if this young man is aware and willing to take some risk, is a great idea where lots of money could be made. Now pipe down and let us just talk out some details," the older McLuren ordered. Turning back to Moose, he continued, "Now ya understand, lad, that the booze business around these parts is run by a group who answer to their bosses, who have even bigger bosses, right? And these people don't play games."

Moose nodded. Like everyone else in the community, he had heard or read stories of local gangs, rum-runners and bootleggers, police busts, Al Capone in Chicago, contract murders, and all of that, but his concern was tempered because his plan would be a small neighbourhood operation, nothing more.

"But these people, and I know some of 'em, are business people first," Mr. McLuren continued. "Ya give 'em a way to make easy money, and they'll be happy to work with ya."

Moose looked at Scotty again briefly, then back at his father. "Can you help me meet someone like that? Someone who can maybe connect me?" he asked.

Scotty's head and shoulders drooped in defeat.

"Sure. It never hurts to sit down and talk." Mr. McLuren paused, looked out across the Detroit River and then added, "But ya have to understand something, Moose. These people will work with ya, treat ya fine, and help ya with your little . . . enterprise. But ya need to know who you're dealing with here. If ya get in bed with 'em, you're in deep. If they don't get their dough...If ya don't pay on time...If ya cross 'em... You'll get hurt. These people don't play games."

"But if my plan works?" Moose asked, ignoring his warnings.

"Then you'll be best of friends, and you'll proba-bly make lots of money together, my lad," he said as he stood up, ready to go. Scotty and Moose followed his lead. "Let me talk to someone for ya. Meanwhile, you've got to figure out a way to get that whisky to your customers on the sly, without anybody seeing it."

Moose's mind was racing as he stood and shook Mr. McLuren's hand.

As they began walking away together, Scotty suddenly stopped, turned, and with a strange look on his face said, "Ya know I'm not sold on this whole idea, right?" They both looked at him, curi-ously. "But what if the whisky was inside the milk bottles?" he asked.

"Pretty easy to tell whisky from milk, son," said his father.

"Not if the bottles are painted white, it's not," Scotty noted. The three stood there considering the idea's possibilities.

"Can it be done?" Moose asked. "Can glass bottles be painted?"

"We glaze glass with paint at the shop all the time," Mr. McLuren answered with a smile. "Easy as pie."

With heightened enthusiasm, Moose considered the magnitude of his next question, paused for a few moments, then, looking back and forth at the two of them, asked, "Would you do it for me, though? It would mean you both getting involved."

Scotty turned towards his father, both anxious and nervous to hear his response. On one hand, he hated to see Moose or his father get mixed up in something so risky, but he also respected his father's opinion, owed Moose his life, and if he was being honest, had to admit that the idea did sound promising.

"I would. Under very strict conditions," Mr. McLuren answered. "I've been in trouble with the law before, so if this operation gets movin' and you can find someone to supply ya with the booze, there can be no connection to me or Scotty. We could get the bottles ya need glazed, all right, for a price and some taste of the product, and that's it. We don't need to be knowin' what happens with your operation after the bottles are picked up. The less people involved, the better it would work for everyone. Do ya understand, lad?" Moose was nodding as Mr. McLuren continued, "And once ya have a plan that ya think will work, ya need to ask yourself if it is worth the risk." He looked for a reaction before he asked, "I assume the little lady has no idea of your plans?"

Moose shook his head.

"Keeping secrets from the missus and working with the type of people I will introduce ya to could wear on a man." He continued looking Moose in the eyes for a few seconds, waiting to see some hesitation or doubt, then smiled and said, nodding his head, "I like it, lad. I like it a lot. It could bloody well work. But I suggest ya think long and hard before jumping in. Ya just let me know if ya want to set up a meetin'."

With that, the three started back across Sandwich Street and headed towards home. Walking along the streets and sidewalks that he had come to know so well in his neighbourhood, Moose was lost in thought. On that first night, the possibilities had seemed limited and unlikely, like an idea or thought one gets and never gets a chance to act upon. But now he seemed to have the exciting opportunity to put a workable plan into action. He decided to take Mr. McLuren's advice and give the idea some careful consideration overnight, but deep down he was already feeling the adrenaline he used to love getting before big games—a nervous energy that got his heart beating a little faster, making it difficult for him to focus on anything but the challenge that lay ahead—a challenge where there was no guaranteed outcome. And it made him feel fully alive for the first time in a very long while.

By the time he laid his head down next to his sleeping wife's that evening, he already knew what he was going to do with the help of Scotty's father.

THOMAS MCLUREN'S LIFE WAS DEFINED BY RISK. He WAS THE third son of Scottish immigrants who made their way to Canada with two infant boys, little education, and even less money. On the advice of a distant cousin who had made the perilous trek before him, Thomas's father settled in Kent County, Ontario, with the dream of making a go off the rich, fertile soil.

Like so many before them, Scotty's grandparents abandoned the isolated, arduous, rural lifestyle soon after their third child, Thomas, was born. The family made its way south to the Windsor area, where a man could find labour jobs and not have his income depend on the often-fickle seasonal weather. Money remained tight, however, and an increasingly unhappy, unfulfilled marriage made for constant tension and dreariness in the home.

Years later, Thomas's two older brothers escaped the rigid and depressing household within a couple of years of each other. The oldest moved to Toronto to work in the railyards, and the other married young, bought some cheap land in the county, and took up farming.

At 13, Thomas was stuck as the only child left in a miserable, loveless home. He was doing poorly in school and running the streets with a misfit, culturally diverse group of neighbourhood delinquents who, like him, came from immigrant families. His parents blamed each other for their wayward son, threw their hands up in defeat, and essentially left him to his own fate. That fate included quitting school and getting part-time work with a friend's father, shovelling coal for home delivery around the city. The bulk of young Thomas's income came from crime, however. He and his neighbourhood group found a relatively lucrative enterprise in petty theft and the sale of stolen goods.

By the time he was 18, Thomas was well entrenched in a local crime gang, drinking heavily at local taverns, gambling regularly at illegal gaming houses, and spending a good deal of time with women of ill repute. "Tommy Mac," as he was known in his neighbourhood as well as to local police, spent a couple of short stints in jail, where he was able to network with other criminals. He was, at his core, a shameless opportunist.

When he was 21, however, three things happened that changed the trajectory of young Thomas's life. The first came in late winter, when he met a pretty young lady who swept him off his feet. Despite his own depressing family situation, Thomas convinced her to be his bride and that he would be a good husband and provider. Just before the wedding months later, the second critical event resulted from the highest-stakes poker game he had ever been involved in. Betting all he had in a final hand against another man who put up some property he owned as his wager, Thomas won the deed to a one-acre parcel of land a few miles east of Windsor, in an area that years later would be called Ford City. The land had a large abandoned garage on site. Thomas had no idea what he would do with the property, but he knew an opportunity when he saw one. Then, late in the year—just before he became a father for the first time—he found out, via a telegram from his brother, that both his parents had been killed in a tragic train accident on their way to Toronto. The train had derailed, and their passenger car's proximity to the steam engine and burning coal caused it to catch fire. Despite his estrangement from them, Thomas was affected by the loss. Weeks later, he was shocked to find out that between the value of the family home and a surprising amount of money his parents had managed to put away, he and his brothers were beneficiaries of a respectable inheritance.

Thomas was not particularly religious, but with a loving new bride, the birth of a healthy baby boy, an unusually large sum of money suddenly at his disposal, and property that he now owned in a developing area, he felt like some higher being was offering him a chance at a better life and to be a better person. He embraced the opportunity.

The young couple's first child, a boy they named Thomas after his father—to be known as Junior—was a handful even at two years old, when their second child was on its way. The McLurens' good fortune ended abruptly and tragically, however, with the birth of their second son. A complicated breach that the midwife was ill prepared for caused a long and torturous birth. After several agonizing hours, little Scotty made his way safely into the world just before his mother bled out and died.

Scotty's childhood was far from ordinary. A single father raising two young boys was most unusual for the time period. Even through rough patches, the small clan survived due to Mr. McLuren's dogged determination to be a better father than his own, as well as the growing success of the paint shop he opened on the property he had won years earlier. The income it provided allowed him to hire various inexpensive domestics, mostly young immigrant girls, who helped out and watched over the boys until they started attending school.

Like their father, Junior and Scotty did not have the patience or temperament for school. They were both easily distracted and showed little interest or ability in the rote learning and slate or sheet work that was often assigned. The sheer number of students and variety of grades in their one-room schoolhouse made independent learning essential for success. While teachers often reported that Scotty was a pleasant child with a good deal more energy and personality than intelligence, their concerns about Junior were much more alarming. Disruptive and sometimes violent behaviour made him a constant challenge for the young female teachers and shortened Junior's school experience considerably. He was thrilled when he was encouraged to stop attending around the time he hit puberty at age 13. Scotty, however, still enjoyed the experience and was anxious to get up every morning to go to school so he could be surrounded by, and play with, other children at recess and lunch breaks. Tension and conflict between his father and older brother got worse when Junior left school and resigned himself to running the streets with friends. As a result, Scotty's home life became more and more difficult. He often felt isolated and lonely, yearning for any kind of interaction with other kids. Unfortunately, close friends in the neighbourhood were hard to come by for Scotty. Parents were often concerned about their children consorting with "Tommy Mac's boy" or the "wild one's little brother."

What many people around them did not realize at the time was that the elder Thomas McLuren had taken great strides to make good on a promise he had made to himself years before—to live more responsibly and stay out of trouble. He did miss the excitement of the streets, the risky criminal lifestyle, and some of the people he'd done business with in the past, but more important to him now was the fact that he had a steady income, a solid roof over his head, and two healthy sons. He still harboured his demons, however. After his wife's untimely death, he fell back to a lifestyle of hard work, hard drinking, and carousing with a variety of women. He was never going back to a life of crime, but he would be the first to admit that he struggled to shake his need for the wicked combination of booze and female company.

By 16, Junior was already out of the house, working at whatever temporary work he could get to supplement his criminal lifestyle and in constant trouble with local police who knew him a little too well as "Junior Mac." He seemed to have no interest in his family or his future as he started slowly drifting from their lives. Many years later, Scotty and his father were saddened, but not surprised, to find out that Junior had died in a violent barroom brawl and left behind an estranged wife and young son living a good distance away, on the west end of Windsor.

Scotty, on the other hand, was already spending more weekdays in the paint shop than at his school desk by the time he was a teenager. He was learning a practical trade and becoming more and more helpful in what was now becoming a family business. He enjoyed transforming and giving new life to old, rusty, weathered objects, equipment, and carriage parts with the help of some elbow grease and a fresh coat of paint.

Years later, when Scotty was 19, he met the young daughter of a customer and fell instantly smitten. Although not remarkably beautiful, Helen Atkinson had a pleasant face and an easy, approachable personality. More importantly, she was one of the very few young women to ever show Scotty any interest. The youngest of a large brood, Helen had limited education and even fewer romantic prospects. Being restless, obstinate, and independent, she was anxious to leave the confines of her rigid household. Her father was even more anxious to hand her over to the first serious suitor and have one less mouth to feed.

A little over a year later, in 1911, Scotty and Helen married and moved into a rented duplex in the area that was already being referred to as Ford City, years before the village that contained the growing Ford Motor Company was officially given the title. Although Scotty was a happy and content newlywed, his young bride often seemed restless and distant despite the freedom she was enjoying away from her father. With no previous experience with girlfriends, sisters, or even a mother to draw from, Scotty was oblivious to the shifting moods and warning signs from his young wife. Remaining childless in the first few years of their marriage was no surprise, considering her detachment and how rare the moments of intimacy were for the young newlyweds.

A few years later, Scotty enlisted, succumbing to the excitement and pressure that came along with the announcement of war. Helen appeared indifferent to the decision. Scotty promised her they would continue their life together and begin their family when he returned months later as a decorated war hero. But when Scotty was boarding the train to ship out and was accidentally bumped by his oversized future friend, Helen was nowhere to be seen. She didn't bother to stay and watch the train roll out of the Goyeau Station because she was already making her way back home. She was excited to begin her new life, however temporary, of complete independence.

When Scotty was medically discharged and sent home from France three years later, the marriage that was already struggling was now hanging on by a thread. While he dealt with the overwhelming feelings of self-pity over a lost leg, survivor's guilt over dead comrades, and anguish at leaving Moose and his unit in the thick of the fight, he also now felt completely abandoned by Helen. She clearly had no desire to make the marriage work. She was rarely home, and when she was, she treated her husband with a dismissive chill. All these feelings threw Scotty into a mental state where he no longer cared—not about his wife, his job, or even himself. Not long after, Helen announced that she was leaving him and moving out of province.

For many months, Scotty struggled—not only physically, with lingering injuries and his cumbersome wooden prosthesis, but also emotionally. He often had trouble dragging himself in to work and was overcome with feelings of dread and loneliness in his empty house. When Scotty went to the train station almost two years later to welcome his dear friend back home, he felt like a dark chapter of his life could finally be coming to an end. As he leaned on his crutch and shook Moose's hand on the station platform, he smiled for the first time in a very long while.

....

The much-anticipated meeting took place on the following Tuesday evening. Mr. McLuren had sent word that someone who was "connected" was going to sit down with Moose and hear about his plan.

Telling Sara he was going to Scotty's to listen to a Detroit Tigers game on the radio, Moose picked up a brown bag tucked out of sight near the front door and began his fifteen-minute walk to a nearby park to meet his contact. He had no idea what to expect. Images of shady, trench coat–wearing gangsters filled his head. He pushed those images out and focused on his sales pitch. He had to be sure he was offering something they needed and couldn't get from anybody else.

As he entered the south end of the park, he scanned the area. A young couple was walking away from him with the soft, warm sunset in their faces. To his right, two older gentlemen were sitting across from each other on a park bench, smoking and using their hands dramatically as they passionately debated an unknown topic in an unknown language. Looking to his left, he noticed a sharply dressed middle-aged gentleman walking, newspaper in hand, to another bench nearby. With daylight fading and nobody else in the park, he headed in that direction. As Moose approached apprehensively, the slender blond-haired man said, "You must be Maurice Ducharme."

"I am," he replied, his deep voice cracking slightly.

"The name is Seamus Mahoney." He did not

offer a handshake. "I understand you have a business proposition."

Moose scanned the area nervously before answering. "Yes, I do." Then he fell silent.

As he eyed the brown bag suspiciously, Mahoney said, "Listen, Ducharme. We're not doing anything illegal here. We're just talking business. Why don't you sit down and tell me what's on your mind? We have a busy evening ahead of us."

"We?" Moose asked looking around. "There's someone else?"

"There's always someone else," Mahoney assured him with a sly smile. "I'm just here as a representative for my boss, to hear about an opportunity that I've been told can benefit both of us. Why don't you relax and explain it to me?"

Moose sat, removed his cap and took a deep breath, which helped calm him down before he began his pitch. While he ran his fingers along the top edges of the bag, he told Mahoney about his daily milk delivery job and his route. He explained that if he could get large quantities of whisky on a regular basis, he could sell and deliver it door to door along with the milk. He was sure his customers, many with very good incomes, would pay a premium to have quality whisky brought right to their doorstep.

"How do you plan on keeping the liquor on the sly?" he asked. "Big difference between milk and whisky."

"With these," Moose replied, as he took a glass quart bottle out of the bag. It was glazed white right up to about an inch from the rim. "With a normal milk cap on the top, you'd have to pour it out to know the difference from the others." Mahoney took the bottle, turned it around in his hands, and studied it closely. His long silence was beginning to be a concern, so Moose added, "And I can get as many of these as I need. I can even get gallon bottles painted the same way."

The silence continued until Mahoney handed him the bottle back. "Clever," he said. After some thought, he continued, "I assume you're going to reuse the bottles. How do you plan on collecting the empties? Won't they stand out next to the clear bottles?"

"Many of my customers have milk boxes, so that won't be a problem. Nobody looks in there. I'll tell the others to keep their glazed bottles indoors for me to pick up when I collect their weekly payments on Saturdays. And I can use a wooden crate to bring them back to the truck."

Mahoney remained quiet and continued studying the bottle, deep in thought. He then turned back to look Moose over once again slowly, with much greater scrutiny. As with any business opportunity, it was his job to assess the risk and reward. With the offer to bottle and deliver the product right to the doors of customers, the only serious risk Mahoney needed to consider was the young man sitting across from him. He was big and looked strong, but he was not like similar-sized men he had on his payroll. This fella was soft-spoken, nervous, and appeared very much to be what his men had reported:

an average, trustworthy working stiff with no known criminal connections.

The reward, on the other hand, seemed substantial. His organization was always looking for ways to give people what they wanted with little risk and effort, but maximum profit. They were in a literal cut-throat industry where if you weren't changing and adapting, you would get swallowed up. Standing still made you an easy target.

"So, what do you think?" Moose inquired meekly after a long period of silence.

Like a poker player who's just been dealt a flush, Mahoney hid his enthusiasm. "I think my boss might be interested. Of course, we would want a nice piece of the action. We could supply the product in bulk and provide other important..." He paused. "...services. But the final decision and terms of an arrangement will be up to him," Seamus said as he stood.

Standing with him, Moose responded, "Well, that's good. When will I hear? How will you reach me?"

"You'll hear very soon," he said, looking up at Moose, straight in the eyes. "Just keep this whole thing quiet. The less people that know, the better. You understand?" The lamppost that turned on behind Moose exposed Mahoney's dark eyes to him for the first time, and they gave him a chill.

"Should we set up a place and time?" he asked with his voice shaking.

"No. We'll come to you. We know where you live," Mahoney said as Moose's stomach dropped. "We like to know who we do business with, Mr. Ducharme," he continued, raising and pointing his finger, "and it's best that pretty little Mrs. Ducharme be kept in the dark as well." With that, Moose's prospective business partner handed back the bottle, put his hat on, turned, and walked away.

A GENEROUS PILLAR OF THE COMMUNITY. A SUCCESSFUL BUSINESSMAN. A loyal parishioner who led the church Temperance Society. A devoted husband. By all accounts, William St. Pierre was a community treasure in the town of Walkerville, which bordered Ford City to the west.

In his late 50s, with dark hair that was beginning to bald and grey, Will seemed taller than his average-sized frame, as he stood and walked with unmistakable confidence. In fact, many in the area would have agreed that the St. Pierres were as important to the community as the founding Walker family they lived a few blocks from. Indeed, before Hiram Walker's son, Edward, died suddenly ten years earlier, he and St. Pierre had been part of the same social circle.

This connection to the Walkers was fortuitous, considering that St. Pierre, who was also known by a very select few as The Saint, was also the head of a local rum-running syndicate that, among other enterprises, controlled the illegal sale and distribution of some of the best whisky in the world, Canadian Club from Hiram Walker's Distillery. He gained this control with intimidation and violence and with the backing of the deadly Purple Gang from Detroit, who themselves happened to be on the payroll of the infamous Al Capone from Chicago.

Although Capone visited the area on occasion, usually for clandestine business meetings with contacts at Hiram Walker's, St. Pierre never met him. This didn't stop him from feeling like he, too, was untouchable. Anybody in the area who was involved in the booming illegal booze trade knew you didn't cross The Saint.

Not that St. Pierre got his hands dirty. He kept his position a well-guarded secret in the community and had "his boys" take care of the day-to-day dealings. For organizing, negotiating, and bookkeeping, he had his trusted Irishman, Seamus Mahoney. Seamus looked like a numbers guy, wearing wire-rimmed glasses and nice suits and talking with an air of social standing that belied his background, but he could be cold and calculating. When a situation called for threats, persuasion, or violence, St. Pierre had a pair of very large, tough Eastern Europeans who lacked anything resembling compassion or morality. Boris Kaminski was an oversized Polish immigrant sent over from Detroit as a gesture of good faith by the Purple Gang. He struggled with English and rarely spoke, instead letting his actions do the talking. Called Wolf by virtue of his vicious way of handling situations and his unusually long eyeteeth, Boris was in charge of the messier part of the organization's business. His partner, Jakob Wojcik, was also a first-generation immigrant, but from Russia. His six-foot-six,

260-pound frame was capped by a huge bull-like head with an unappealing face carved by pain and suffering. As with Wolf, if "the Mad Russian" was involved, things had gone bad for someone. Backing up the brains and muscle of the operation were a large number of citizens who had specific roles or special skills that the organization could call on when needed.

Despite restrictions imposed by Prohibition, local law enforcement and government agents were understandably frustrated with their inability to put a dent in the booming illegal liquor business anywhere in Ontario, but especially in the Windsor area. To avoid job losses and lost tax revenue, the provincial government allowed the famous distillery in Walkerville to make their world-famous product as long as it was exported and not sold domestically. Even more challenging, the area was less than a mile across the river from Detroit, Michigan, a city with a thirst for quality Canadian whisky caused by the temperance laws American citizens were also suffering through. Combine these factors with a local citizenry who offered little support to what most thought were draconian liquor laws, police officers who often looked the other way or were customers themselves, and judges who were sometimes on the take, and fighting the lucrative booze operations often seemed hopeless.

That's not to say there weren't officials who were passionate about stopping the flow of illegal booze. Some local police did their best to enforce the laws, but their identities were well known, which limited their effectiveness. The Ontario government also had a team of dedicated local liquor agents, led by an inspector named Maxime Mousseau. A religious man who believed in the dangers of the devil's liquid, he patrolled the region, and especially the riverfront, trying to plug the flow. But he had a major disadvantage due to complicated Canadian legislation. As a provincial agent, Mousseau could enforce laws regarding illegal production, sale, and consumption of alcohol, but since federal laws covered importing and exporting, they were outside his jurisdiction. Many times Mousseau was witness to barrels and cases of whisky being loaded onto boats at the docks along the riverfront behind or near the distillery. He knew the shipments were destined for local rumrunners somewhere down the shoreline or across the river, but he was powerless to do anything about it—and those involved knew it.

Although Will St. Pierre would tell people that he had made his fortune in real estate and the stock market, that was only partly true. In truth, he'd made the bulk of his money as a wholesaler of illegal alcohol. Using his organization's ruthless reputation, Mahoney negotiated the best price with breweries and distilleries for large bulk shipments. Product would be loaded onto boats at their docks with the proper export papers to some foreign destination.

Federal agents were rarely around to check the validity of the documents. These shipments headed either down the river to LaSalle and Lake Erie locations, across the river to secret American docks for groups like the Purple Gang, or up the shoreline of Lake St. Clair to places like Tecumseh, Belle River, or Stoney Point. That's where St. Pierre's boys would often receive their beer and liquor before transporting it to secret storage facilities, ready to sell to their distributors.

Their supply of whisky was what Mahoney had in mind to supply Moose with, if his boss agreed to this new operation. He met St. Pierre in a local diner the next evening to discuss.

"This Ducharme fella's idea looks very promising for us, Saint. First, he seems like a stand-up guy. Football hero. War vet. Nice family. But he's bustin' his hump and making a pittance delivering milk. He's ready to break out, and his idea is not only promising, but it could change the way we do business," Seamus said.

St. Pierre looked intrigued. "I'm listening," he said.

"He proposes door-to-door delivery of our CC using his milk route. He showed me a milk bottle painted white to hold the hooch. It would be very difficult, even close up, to tell the difference. I think it would work. But he needs our supply."

St. Pierre was listening intently, looking for potential wrinkles.

As if reading his mind, Seamus continued, "This Moose fellow looks like he can be trusted. Word on the street is that he's a good man and has a family that could definitely be used to keep him in line. The risk to us is minimal because he does all the delivery and collection. And once we let leak that we're supplying this operation, he'll have little worry about customers snitching or stiffing him. Why would they? They're getting the product brought right to their doorstep. And I don't think his operation will put a dent in ours. In fact, I believe it will help our sales. There's a lot of fellas who won't go, or their dames won't let them go, to our joints in that area. So they'll pay top buck to be able to wet their beaks with our hooch instead of the watered-down shit they get from the blind pigs." He paused and finished with, "I've looked at this from every angle, boss, and it looks like a winner."

"What would our take be?" St. Pierre inquired.

"Well, that depends on the interest along his route. I figure we supply CC in barrels. It's cheaper, and there are no Walker bottles to tie them to the operation. We'll make dough off the barrel sale and work him for a percent of his take. He's green, and he's motivated. I figure we can name our price. He won't be able to get supply anywhere else."

St. Pierre leaned back in his chair and considered the proposal. He didn't know Moose personally, but he knew his parents and especially his mother-in-law from the local parish. They were all good people, and good people were easy to control.

After some thought, he said, "Let's set it up. Meet with him; set the barrel price so we make ten. I want to use one of our garages for shipment in an area where we own the beat cop and we can keep a close eye. Fleece him ten percent of the take for rent, delivery, storage costs, and any muscle he needs."

"Got it, boss," Seamus replied as he stood to go. At the door, he turned. "Oh, and there's two things this kid might need from us as well. He'll need some start-up dough for the bottles and the painting. And he's going to need a legit job as a cover to explain his work hours and all the extra dough he's going to start bringing in."

"Front the cash he needs at the usual rate. As far as a job, he can be added to the books as maintenance for one of my apartments," he offered.

Seamus nodded submissively. "I'll set the meeting, Saint."

....

A few blocks away from Walkerside Dairies, St.Pierre Real Estate Holdings owned an abandoned garage. In truth, it was payment for a defaulted business loan—a choice the owner had made over getting both his legs broken. This is where Moose met Mahoney the following week to hammer out the details of the new venture. To drive home the seriousness of the organization's expectations, Seamus brought along the Mad Russian, who loomed a few steps behind him in the garage, his arms crossed and his face as serious as it was ugly.

As Moose looked around the interior of the garage, Mahoney explained, "This is where you'll work the operation. It's our place, and we own the cops on the beat. This is where we'll deliver your supply. It will come in barrels with a spigot. Everything else, filling and cleaning bottles, orders and collection, will be your job." As he stood there listening intently, any thoughts Moose had had about this being his idea and his operation were fading. "And you'll pay us $45 a barrel for the product, plus twenty percent of your profits for our expenses."

The numbers took him by surprise. With the help of Mr. McLuren, Moose had done some research about the current prices of whisky from various sources. As Mahoney waited impatiently, Moose took out a notepad and pencil to do some quick math: approximately 50 gallons a barrel, which equals 200 quarts. Charging a competitive $1.25 a quart and $4 a gallon as suggested by McLuren, he would collect somewhere in the neighbourhood of $200 to $250 per barrel. Minus $45 for the booze and around $50 for their take, he'd be profiting between $100 and $150 per barrel—still a king's ransom compared to what he was taking home in his current job, but not what he'd been hoping for, especially since he still had bottle painting costs to consider.

He decided to push his luck and show Mahoney early in their partnership that he was not afraid to negotiate. "I can't do that," Moose protested. "I won't make enough on my end. I'd have to price the whisky so high that I'd scare off customers. The barrel price seems fair, but with all due respect, your take of the profits seems too high."

Mahoney stared expressionless as the Russian took a step forward. He raised his hand, stopping his large partner, and answered, "You've got some balls, Ducharme. I'll give you that." He paused for a few seconds, acting like he was being squeezed. "The boss may not like it, but we'll go to ten percent. No lower. Payment on time at the end of each month, or we charge interest."

Feeling a renewed confidence, Moose stepped forward offering his hand. "Then we have a deal."

Mahoney looked down at his hand, expressionless, but did not take it. "We do indeed, Mr. Ducharme. Just be sure you hold up your end. My boss isn't a very understanding man when terms aren't met." He dropped the key to the garage lock in Moose's awkwardly outstretched hand, then headed for the door; his enormous sidekick joined him, his eyes locked on Moose's the entire time.

Torn between the excitement of the new opportunity and the growing concern that he might have gotten in over his head with his choice of business partners, Moose stood alone in the middle of the large, empty garage. He jumped nervously when the heavy steel door slammed shut.

....

In the second week of September, 1923, Moose Ducharme, employee of Walkerside Dairies, began putting out feelers for his new venture. For months, he'd been using minor accidents and clumsiness to explain the loss of empty quart and gallon glass bottles, so he already had a good supply to give to Scotty for glazing.

"You sure were better holding a football than you are with glass, son," was the only comment from his supervisor at the dairy. When he brought the first load of newly glazed bottles to the garage for storage one Saturday, he found a full whisky barrel already delivered. The timely delivery of his supply was encouraging, but he was already uneasy about his business partners' access to the garage—something he'd have to live with.

What he needed now were buyers. He already had a short list of the most promising customers along his route, based on his instincts and their conversations on collection days. He worked on a subtle pitch to gauge interest. Beginning with his sure thing, Mr. Dougall, he would broach the subject with comments that criticized the current provincial liquor laws. If they expressed similar feelings, Moose would ask his customers if they were able to get booze when they wanted it. Trusting him, some would admit to frequenting speakeasies in the area or buying from friends, family, or neighbours who sold liquor on the side. This would open the door for his standard pitch: "What would you say if I told you that I could deliver Walker's famous Canadian Club whisky right to your door along with your milk?"

The interest from many was encouraging. Instead of concerns about breaking laws or questions about how Moose was able to offer this service, inquiries usually involved price. "The cost is $1.25 a quart or $4 a gallon. Any day of the week you want, right at your doorstep along with your milk," Moose repeated to several customers. To most, the offer seemed too good to be true. It was a fair price for a high quality whisky with the added benefit of home delivery.

If they took him up on his offer, Moose had to explain the use of the white-glazed bottles, warn against reselling the whisky for profit, and discuss precautions when returning empties and the importance of not discussing the arrangement with anyone. "And we'll never use words like liquor, whisky, or booze," he said. "When you order or we talk, this new product and the service will be called "Skim"—something extra on top of the milk you receive." Following Mahoney's instructions, he also included the veiled warning, "My suppliers do a lot of liquor business around here and take it very serious." That told them all they needed to know.

The first week he had a handful of Skim orders, and they were quickly filled and organized on a Saturday afternoon, ready for delivery. The following week, with bottles delivered as promised, the orders doubled. Then they doubled again. Some customers increased their amounts, and others heard whispers from neighbours and began ordering their own. Even people along his route who weren't regular customers sought him out and began ordering milk so they could be included in the Skim operation.

By early winter, Moose had just over half of his route ordering Skim. And many of his wealthier customers were ordering larger amounts, assuring him it was for large dinner parties or social events they were hosting. He far exceeded his original goal of selling a barrel of whisky a month, but his success came with challenges. More orders meant he needed more bottles and more bottles painted. Thankfully, Moose was able to order several dozen more bottles right from a supplier, and Scotty was more than happy to glaze them for his friend.

Other challenges weren't so easily handled. More orders meant more time spent cleaning and filling bottles. What used to be done in a few hours on Saturday afternoons after collection was now taking him additional time and forcing him to work some Sunday afternoons as well. As expected, Sara began asking questions, and Moose had to use Mahoney's suggestion and claim he'd been hired on as a weekend maintenance employee for St. Pierre Real Estate. He had never heard of the company and didn't know the connection to Mahoney's group.

"That's great you picked up the extra work, Maurice," Sara said one evening after he told her during dinner. "How did that come about?"

"One of my customers knew the company was looking for someone, and I showed some interest," Moose explained.

"Aren't you worried about more time away from me and the kids? Especially on weekends?"

"I'm home all week by lunch and sitting down to dinner with you every night," he explained as he walked over and pulled her into a hug, more to hide his face from the bold lying than to show affection. "Plus they are paying really well to do odd jobs that any stiff could probably do. And we could use the dough."

Seeming appeased, Sara asked, "And this is for Mr. St. Pierre?"

"I guess so. Apparently he owns lots of buildings. But I've never met him. I just answer to a supervisor, a guy named Mahoney." Moose was anxious to end the conversation. He hated having to be dishonest with his wife and wanted to join his son in the other room.

"You may not have met him, honey, but you've seen him plenty," Sara explained. "He's the sharp-dressed man who sits near the front pew at church every Sunday with his pretty wife. He's very involved with the parish council and Temperance group. Mother says he's very wealthy, but does a great deal for the church and the community."

"Can't say as I remember him. Maybe you could point him out on Sunday."

"I'll be sure to. And you better be sure that new job doesn't stop you from joining your family for mass on Sunday mornings," she warned with a smile as she left the embrace and began clearing dishes.

Moose nodded, pleased to have avoided a serious complication. He guided her handful of dishes back to the table and suggested, "Let's go join the kids in the parlour, luv."

Annie was dragging her finger across the page, trying to focus on reading her Braille book as Jackie listened to a prizefight on a Detroit radio station. Jackie motioned him over, and Moose obliged. As they sat beside each other, Moose couldn't help but notice the space that his son was now taking up on the sofa.

"Little" Jackie, just sixteen years old, already neared the height and bulk of his father. As they sat together enjoying the blow-by-blow broadcast from New York

City of the highly touted heavyweight championship bout between Jack Dempsey and "The Bull" Firpo from Argentina, Moose had an idea that would almost certainly help solve his Skim workload issue— but it would cross a dangerous line.

B Y ALL ACCOUNTS, MOOSE'S SKIM OPERATION WAS A RESOUNDING SUCCESS. By late spring, his customer base had plateaued at just over 40 homes along his route, going through one-and-a-half to two barrels of whisky a month, depending on the time of year. Christmas was a windfall, with almost a month's worth of Skim ordered over the two-week period. The Irish ordered heavily around St. Patrick's Day in March, as did almost everyone for Easter weekend. There were also upticks in orders among his loyal Commonwealth customers in May and early June for Victoria Day and George V Day. Another unexpected benefit he enjoyed was the generous tips the Skim operation generated, something he rarely got from his milk delivery. He wisely kept this stream of revenue out of the ledger that Mahoney inspected to verify his take at the end of each month. All told, Moose was now earning more than ten times his previous monthly salary, even with his required payments to Mahoney's people and the generous donations of product to the McLurens as they continued to keep up with the increased demand for glazed bottles.

With success came the need for more help. Besides Mahoney's people, the McLurens were the only ones who knew the internal workings of the Skim operation, but Scotty's bum leg and his father's prematurely aged body made them physically unable to help, even if they wanted to.

After weeks of internal moral debate, Moose decided to bring his son into the fold. Jackie was young, big and strong enough to handle the work, and one of the few people he could have absolute trust in. His biggest concern was not necessarily exposing the illegal activity to his son, especially since public consensus against liquor laws was increasing steadily. The thing that Moose struggled with most was voluntarily exposing his blatant dishonesty towards his wife and asking his son to join in it.

One evening when Sara and Annie were out enjoying an evening walk, Moose sat Jackie down, and with unusual earnestness, he laid it all out. He explained the details of the Skim operation, hoping Jackie would understand the situation and not judge him too harshly. "You see, son, I'm ashamed of having to go behind your mother's back, but to me, it's less shameful than a man not being able to provide a good life for his family. And keeping it secret is the only possible way it can be done. We both know your mother would never allow this."

Jackie's look of surprise was expected, but his grin wasn't. "How long have you been doing this, Pop?"

"Since fall. When you went back to school," he admitted.

His son sat there looking at him, somewhat puzzled, processing the situation. "And these guys you are getting the booze from, they don't worry you? I've heard stories from the guys at school that mobsters run the booze business, the clubs, and do the bootlegging. They're dangerous."

"Those are just stories, Jackie. Everybody loves a good gangster story, especially the newspapers. The guys I work with are business people. This is a business, and it's a good one—so good that I need your help. I didn't expect the kind of success I'm seeing, which is great, but filling all the orders on the weekends without being away from home too long is getting tough," Moose explained.

Without hesitation, Jackie answered, "How can I help?"

"Well, Saturday collection is basically the same as we've done, except we take in a lot more money and have to get those Skim bottles back," Moose explained. "The bulk of the time goes into cleaning, refilling, and organizing the bottles back at the garage. It's really become a two-man job."

Jackie felt a rush of pride hearing that his father considered to him to be a man and now needed his help. If his father—a football hero, a war hero, and his personal hero—thought this operation was a good idea and he needed help, Jackie would not hesitate. "I'll do whatever you need, Pops. And I'll keep it hush from Ma and Annie." He paused. "But how do we explain me being gone with you on weekends? I haven't really helped lately like I did in the summer."

"We're going to get you a part-time job, son," Moose answered, smiling. "We'll use the same work and boss I have now. Mr. St. Pierre could always use more help."

"That's the Mr. St. Pierre from church Ma was talking about, right? I've seen him." Jackie was quiet for several seconds and then, looking perplexed, asked, "Why would he agree to say someone who sells whisky works for him, when he's against booze? Ma says he's on that committee at church."

For the first time, Moose was forced to give that question more serious consideration. With all the other things going on in the past number of months, he had never really seriously considered the unusual connection between Mahoney and St. Pierre's real estate company. "I don't know, Jack. Maybe he's such a big shot he doesn't even know his own employees. Or maybe Mahoney has a friend who works for the company and is on the take. It really is a mystery." After more thought, he added, "But I've learned quickly, son, not to ask too many questions. And you shouldn't either. We just keep our heads down, do our job, and collect the dough."

"Got it," Jackie said with a handshake and a smile that made his proud father feel like he was looking in the mirror. "So when do I start?"

....

Sara found it unusually convenient that Moose was able to secure some weekend employment for Jackie as well in Mr. St. Pierre's apartment buildings, but Moose assured her that it wasn't unusual at all.

There were lots of little jobs that needed doing, they liked Moose's work ethic, and they could pay his man-sized kid a little less. When he was sure he had convinced her, instead of feeling relief, he felt a sense of profound shame once again. When they'd first married, he had a great deal of difficulty anytime he strayed from the truth. Now he was getting good at lying to her, and he didn't like it. But like a train going downhill, he couldn't stop it now, and he had to admit to himself that it was probably only going to get worse in the future. Moose found himself continually justifying the deceit, convincing himself that he was only doing what needed to be done so he could fulfil the promise to give his family the kind of life that his own father had been unable to provide.

Therein lay another major problem Moose could not overcome. The reason for his desire to get in the game and make more money was so he could give his family a more comfortable lifestyle. But how could he buy any of the things that he wanted to give them without raising questions or suspicions? Smaller, less expensive things like the home telephone, new radio, and small appliances that he had already bought were relatively safe. He had two jobs, after all. The first major extravagance—a tall, beautifully handcrafted grandfather clock Moose bought Sara for their wedding anniversary—was accepted, but reluctantly. So to purchase the new automobile he'd had his eyes on for months was going to be difficult. And the new house he figured he could afford in a year or so seemed like it was going to be next to impossible to explain. If he was going to spend big, he needed to convince Sara they could afford it. Moose needed advice from someone who might know about deception and explaining unexpected income. He thought he knew just the person.

....

"How's business?" Moose asked Mahoney awkwardly at the end of the month when they met in the garage to review his books.

He received a blank look that said, "I'm not interested in small talk."

Forging ahead, Moose said, "Can I ask you a question?" When Mahoney didn't even raise his head, he continued, "How do I spend the money I'm making without my wife getting suspicious?"

Nothing.

"I want to buy nice things, but they're things I wouldn't normally be able to afford."

Face still in the book, Mahoney was silent.

"I mean, does your wife or family know where your money comes from?"

Mahoney's head snapped up, his cold eyes telling Moose he had crossed a line. "My life and what I do or say is never your business. Understand? The only thing you need to know is how to keep your racket going and how much you owe us when I come to visit," he said, coldly.

Feeling like a scolded child, Moose apologized. "I'm sorry, Seamus. I just don't have anybody around me who can know what's going on and offer me advice."

Softening up only somewhat, Mahoney considered the issue. It was probably a good sign that this Ducharme fellow, so new to the business, didn't talk to anybody about the operation. "Listen," he said, "In my experience, most people don't care much where the nice things came from as long as they have them."

"Well, that wouldn't be my experience," Moose said. "You don't know my wife. She's never wanted the fancy life and doesn't think she needs or deserves it. She'll definitely want to know."

"So you need to convince her that you had a big payday." Closing his ledger book dramatically, like he was annoyed at being taken away from the task at hand, Mahoney went on. "Everybody's talking about the easy money in the stock market, right? People are getting rich fast. Tell her you've stashed dough into the market and you're hitting it big. It's not all untrue, you know. You've taken some financial risks, and now you're getting rewarded for them."

With that rare, brief departure from the business-only approach, Mahoney opened the ledger to finalize his inspection and make a record of the numbers into his own book. The message was clear: the collegial conversation was over. A few minutes later, he closed the book, stood, and put out his hand impatiently. Moose took an envelope out of his back pocket and handed over the operation's monthly payment. Mahoney slipped it into his suit coat pocket alongside several others and left without saying a word.

Even though it was going to require more dishonesty, Moose was inspired. The next evening while he and Sara were lying in bed, catching their breath after some passionate lovemaking, Moose tested the waters. "I've got a surprise for you, darling."

"Another one?" she giggled as her hand slipped under the sheet.

"That would be really surprising, luv," he laughed along with her. "No, this one involves money and something I've been working towards."

"Really? What's that?" Sara inquired, raising herself up on her elbow.

"I want to buy an automobile for us." As she sat up and began her expected protest, he shushed her. "Listen, luv, before you say anything." Her mouth closed and her shoulders dropped in submission. "What you don't know is that every extra penny I've been making in the last six months—the extra orders on the route, the tips, plus my weekend work—I've been putting into stocks on the market. My supervisor at the apartments has been helping me, and we've been making a killing."

"You did this without talking to me?" Sara responded, clearly annoyed.

"I had to," Moose replied. "We both know what you would have said if I had asked your opinion. 'I don't like risking our money.' 'We are doing okay, Maurice.' 'We don't need all those other fancy things.' Well, we could use and enjoy the extra things, luv. Things that my hard work and the hot market can provide."

Sara knew he was right, but turned away in disappointment.

"Listen," Moose said, lifting his large hand and turning her chin back his way. "What started out as under $100 has grown into several hundred, and it's still growing. I want to take most of it, not all of it, and buy us a Ford."

Sara seemed unconvinced. "But we could use that money for other things, Maurice. Annie's schooling and books…Jackie's education. Donations to the church."

"We still can, luv. I'm still working, and the market keeps printing dough," Moose explained. "At some point, Sara, you're going to have to trust me with the money I'm earning. I'm busting my hump, and I want us to enjoy the rewards."

Sara fell silent. She felt considerable guilt about questioning her husband's financial decisions, especially since he was the one who was working so many hours to provide such opportunity. A passionate kiss and snuggle into her husband's broad bare chest signalled her capitulation.

Sara slowly began not only to accept the improved lifestyle, but to enjoy it. Over the next several months, she came to enjoy splurging on more expensive meals, shopping for the latest popular household products, taking Annie out so they both could get new clothing, and especially increasing the charitable donations they made to the church and other causes. The poor conditions under which she'd grown up, however, innately compelled her to ask for her husband's permission before she made big purchases. Moose never said no.

....

Sara was looking and feeling particularly pretty when she wore one of her new dresses to church one warm and sunny Sunday morning in late May. The air smelled fresh from the overnight spring rain, and a light breeze was coming off the river as they walked to church. The original Lady of the Lake Church, where she and Moose had married and they'd attended weekly mass, had been destroyed years before in a fire. Now, rebuilt in a much grander scale, it was renamed Lady of the Rosary.

Even though they owned a new Model T, they didn't take it because Sara felt driving it to church was a show of avarice—a small concession Moose could live with for now. He was sure she would change her way of thinking once the cold winter hit.

Before mass started, Sara pointed out to her husband, as she often did, the sharp-dressed Mr. St. Pierre in his usual spot near the front. "There's our Golden Goose," she liked to kid. The view from behind at a distance was really the only encounter they ever had with the St. Pierres. The wealthy couple usually lingered after mass longer than Moose and the kids liked, then exited out a side entrance to their expensive car in the lot.

On this particular Sunday, however, Sara and her mother were very slow leaving the church, caught up talking to friends on the far side of the church. As usual, Moose and the kids were quick to exit so they could get home and enjoy the rest of their Sunday. As Sara was saying goodbye to a group of acquaintances, her family was milling about at the foot of the steep twin winding staircases to the sidewalk out front of the church. Moose and Jackie were watching the boats and ships on the Detroit River and Annie was holding her father's hand, swinging around him, and quietly singing her favourite hymns from the mass.

As Sara was turning to leave and join her family outside, her mother pulled her arm, saying, "Honey, I want to introduce you to Mrs. St. Pierre." She turned. "This is my daughter, Sara."

"Very nice to meet you," Sara said to the woman cordially as they shook hands.

"And you as well," Mrs. St. Pierre returned. "And what a lovely dress that is. The colour is striking."

Sara was taken aback, considering the compliment came from one of the wealthiest and most stylish woman in the parish. Blushing, she responded, "Oh my goodness, thank you. It feels so good to be wearing summer dresses again."

"Well, it is beautiful, indeed. Wherever did you find it?"

As Sara started to tell the woman about the little dress shop she'd found in downtown Windsor, her mother interrupted by saying hello over Mrs. St. Pierre's shoulder to Mr. St. Pierre, who stood away, seemingly intent on ignoring the group. His wife turned to her husband as well and said, "Oh, Will, darling. Don't rush away. Do say hello to Clair. And you must meet her beautiful daughter, Sara."

St. Pierre turned and flashed a well-rehearsed smile. "Well, my pleasure, young lady," he said, taking her hand. "Your mother is quite a lady. Her help on the parish council has been indispensable."

Clair flushed at the compliment. "Oh, I don't know about that, Will. You are the backbone of this parish, and you know it."

There were a few seconds of awkward silence, and St. Pierre was more than ready to end the encounter when Clair added, "And we both also want to thank you for giving Sara's Maurice and my dear grandson the opportunity to do some work for you. It has sure helped Sara and the family out tremendously."

Just as Sara was about to explain to her mother that Moose and Jackie had never actually met their distinguished boss, Mr. St. Pierre shocked her by smiling broadly and saying, "Well, Moose is a fine young man, alright. We hit it off right away. And his boy's a chip off the old block."

His comment threw Sara off so much that by the time she thought about what she wanted to say, the St. Pierres were already walking out the door bidding the group farewell.

"They are the nicest people, don't you think, honey?" Clair asked her daughter, who was standing there staring blankly and looking confused. "Sara? Are you not well?" she added.

"No, I'm fine, Mother," Sara answered as she turned, trance-like, and started making her way to the back of the church. Heading to the main doors, she was trying to reconcile an earlier conversation she had had with Maurice, when he told her he had never actually met Mr. St. Pierre.

As they stepped outside into the bright sun, Sara looked down at the sidewalk below to see her husband waiting impatiently and the kids holding hands and balance-walking on the curb. She had a sudden, nostalgic flashback to the time she and Maurice met at the same spot at the front entrance of the old church and planned their first date so many years ago. Looking down at her husband now, she began to wonder if she really knew him at all. The thought frightened her.

From the sidewalk below, Moose looked up and was ready to smile and wave Sara down to get going, but the look on her face told him something was definitely wrong.

"I GUESS I JUST FORGOT, LUV," MOOSE TRIED TO EXPLAIN TO SARA, WHO was standing there, arms folded, looking unconvinced. He was almost as confused as she was. Why would St. Pierre tell her that he had met Moose when he hadn't? Even though it didn't make any sense at all in his mind, Moose knew he had no choice but to continue the deception to protect the entire Skim operation. "It was probably a busy work day at one of his apartments a while back, so I don't remember."

"You don't remember meeting the wealthy gentleman who got you and your son a job and whose head you see the back of every Sunday at church?" she asked rhetorically. "It just doesn't make any sense, Maurice." Sara paused, still confused and growing increasingly upset. "Is there something you're not telling me?"

Moose was feeling the stress of being caught in a lie, something he was unaccustomed to and ill prepared for. He had to think fast, or his wife's doubts would fester. It did not help that he could see Jackie peeking around the kitchen corner listening to the conversation unfold. After some careful thought, he took her hand, looked her in the eyes, and said, "Okay, luv, I'll level with you and explain as best I can." He was scrambling. "I didn't tell you I met Mr. St. Pierre because...I was told not to." Sara's head tilted in a way that said she needed further convincing. "My supervisor, Mahoney—you know, the guy who helps me invest? He told me that if his boss gave a job to every chap who came asking, he would be out of business. So he says to me, 'Just pretend like you never met him.'" Sara was processing this explanation sceptically as Moose continued, "And what would happen if you knew I met him? You and your mother would tell your friends that I know big-shot St. Pierre and he's been very generous to us. Then what happens?" She shrugged her shoulders. "I'll tell you what happens. I'd be hearing 'Can you introduce me? Help me get a job there too?' And St. Pierre would be getting those people going to him and saying, 'You gave Moose Ducharme and his boy a job. Can you help me too?' Then what?" Moose felt like he was in a close football match again, his team grinding out an all-important first down yard by yard. "Then our Golden Goose, as you call him, will be upset with me, which threatens my job and our future."

Sara took several seconds to digest the explanation. Deep down she wanted to believe him. She figured it made some sense. But she could not shake the lingering doubt. Before she could ask anything further, Moose put an end to the conversation by saying, "Listen, luv. I already feel terrible breaking my promise. Not only do I need you to stop asking questions I can't answer, but I need you to forget what you found out today, too. And I need your mother to do the same. If we want to keep those jobs, we need to keep things the way they were," Moose finished.

Sara forced a smile, wrapped her arms up around his neck, and said, "Very well, honey. I'm sorry if I caused any problems today. I was just so confused. It caught me so off guard." She brought herself in, and they embraced.

"That's fine, luv. Now you know the whole story," he said, feeling an incredibly sharp sting of guilt as he looked over her head and saw his son standing near-by, looking at his father, expressionless.

....

At the end of the month, Mahoney was visiting the garage once again to check and record the Skim profits as well as collect the monthly take. As Moose stood nearby impatiently watching, the incident re-garding St. Pierre's comment to his wife was still weighing heavily on his mind. It took him a few min-utes to muster the nerve to say, "Seamus, can I ask you something about Mr. St. Pierre?"

Mahoney stopped what he was doing abruptly and with his head still down, his eyes looked above his reading glasses to meet Moose's. "I thought we under-stood each other about that topic, Mr. Ducharme."

"We do." Moose looked down, fidgeting. "But the strangest thing happened that I need to under-stand." He explained as briefly as possible Sara's en-counter with St. Pierre at church and the confusion that his wife and he both shared. "Why would he say that?" he inquired.

Mahoney's stare and expression did not change. He looked at Moose uncomfortably long before he responded. "Mr. St. Pierre knows many people and has many employees, Mr. Ducharme. My guess is that he didn't want to appear detached from people who are supposed to be working for him, or embarrassed not knowing who they are." Moose was nodding, but the explanation wasn't making sense. "It's best you don't give it any more thought. You handled it well with the little woman, and now it's done." His eyes turned back down towards his work.

"But..." Moose began, but Mahoney's dark eyes darted back up to his so menacingly he stopped short.

As happened every month, Mahoney carefully reviewed the Skim numbers, recorded them in his own ledger, received his take in an envelope, and left silently without a farewell. Moose latched the door. His confusion about St. Pierre still lingered after Mahoney left, but Moose's focus shifted as he turned around and faced the garage interior.

In front of him were many dozens of white quart and gallon bottles scattered in different areas. On the right, empty bottles ready for cleaning. Behind them the cleaned bottles sat drying upside down in racks near the large water basin, ready for filling. To the left, the filled Skim bottles were capped, placed in wooden crates, and marked for the day of delivery.

In the back left corner was a small area where a cradle shelf supported the whisky barrel currently being drained of its valuable contents. He walked over to the barrel, took one of the two coffee mugs off a nearby counter, and turned the spigot to pour himself some product. Leaning on the barrel and sipping on his drink, Moose thought back with a grin to when Skim first started and his attempts to hide the kind of business being conducted in the old garage. It seemed silly now, considering that anybody who stood within a stone's throw of the open door would know the nature of the operation inside immediately from the strong smell of whisky that permeated the area.

As he started organizing the mess around him, Moose began stewing over the payment he'd just made to Mahoney. After covering the wholesale cost of the whisky, he paid an additional $43 for the month of April, which was a little higher than average because of Easter. That was more than his monthly pay for the legitimate milk delivery he was still doing for Walkerside. As he was doing more and more lately, Moose questioned what Mahoney's people actually did for that $43. They delivered a barrel or two once a month. He and Jackie, by contrast, did all the bottling, delivery, collection and cleaning. As well, they also took all the risk of getting caught.

The question about the St. Pierre incident at church and his growing feeling of being taken advantage of by Mahoney's people caused Moose some sleepless nights, something that hadn't been a problem for a while. Reluctant to involve him any more than he already was, Moose, once again, sought the advice of Scotty's father, who if not a partner in crime, had certainly become his crime consultant. Taking a walk one sticky June evening, Moose explained to Mr. McLuren the confusion about Sara's introduction to St. Pierre.

"That's a puzzlin' thing, that is," he said. "What it tells me is that St. Pierre is more involved than ya think. Why else would he offer a lie to cover for ya?"

Moose let this possibility sink in then responded, "This is a God-fearing, charitable man. A leader in the parish." After a pause he raised his voice adding, "And he's with the Temperance people, too!"

"Don't act so shocked, lad," the older man said. "If St. Pierre is involved with Mahoney and his people, and I'm not sayin' he is, ya think he's the first fella to pretend he's somethin' he ain't? Do ya know how many rich folks around here—all upstanding citizens—have their paws in the hooch in some way?"

Moose considered the point.

"Ya only need to look in the mirror, son."

Moose turned to him, insulted.

"Ah, don't be lookin' like that now, lad. You're pretendin' to be a hard-working, law-abidin' milkman. And yet you're ass-deep in the business yourself. And in a way, so am I."

"I'm only doing it for my family—" Moose stopped mid-sentence, realizing who he was talking to and how weak the justification sounded as soon as he started.

They both continued walking without speaking as Moose considered the hard truth. If St. Pierre was involved with liquor in some way, who was he to judge? In essence, Moose was a bootlegger himself. The fact was a cold slap in the face, but he knew he still would not change any decision he had made. His life was so much better and his family so much better off now, there was no going back. He knew his moral compass could not be reset.

Mr. McLuren knew his words had stung Moose and tried to change the subject. "How's business these days?"

Moose refocused, answering, "Never better. We've steadied the number of customers, but orders have been rising. Jackie and I handle the load fairly well, and we're bringing in lots of dough, which means Seamus and his people are enjoying a good piece too."

"That's good," the older gentleman responded.

"Is it?" Moose questioned. "I mean, I wonder about the fairness of how the labour is divvied up. We do all the work, and they come in and take a good slice for doing a simple delivery."

McLuren stopped and pulled on Moose's arm, forcing the two of them to come face to face. With a hardened, serious look, he said, "That's where you're wrong, lad. You're not payin' just for the delivery. You're payin' for getting your hands on the best hooch around. You're payin' for the cops to leave ya alone. You're payin' for people not to cross ya and for those people to be taken care of if they do. That's the price of doin' business."

His perspective was sinking in and making some sense to Moose. "I guess you may be right."

"Not may be, lad. I am right," he insisted. "Ya best be remembering that. Any talk about unfairness or them not deserving their take is the kinda talk that can cause problems."

124

Moose nodded, put is head back down, and they continued their walk towards home. He knew Mr. McLuren had given him words of wisdom and experience, as he always did, and he appreciated it. But deep down, Moose couldn't stop thinking about a time in the future when he could expand his business and where he had all the control, free of the grip of Mahoney's people.

....

As summer turned into fall then to winter, the Skim operation was running like a well-oiled machine. With Jackie's help, Saturday collection and the Skim bottle cleaning and refilling went much quicker. Some Saturdays it went so well that the two of them had to kill some time after finishing for fear of coming home too early and prompting questions. They made a great team.

There were a few problems, however. On three separate occasions over a period of a few months, Moose had customers order considerably more than usual and he later found out they were reselling it for a profit. It was very tempting for them to make some easy money by selling marked-up quality whisky. Two of the offenders simply needed reminding from Moose about the rules of the operation, and they stopped. One, a Mr. Brownlee on Lincoln Avenue, continued, even after Moose gave multiple warnings. This was the first time that Moose had to report that kind of problem. When told, Mahoney seemed less concerned about customers making a few bucks off their liquor than he was about the operation potentially being exposed and threatening his revenue stream. As it was, there was already a fair amount of talk among neighbouring milkmen and their customers, wondering if the rumours of home whisky delivery were true. Mahoney assured Moose the problem would be handled.

During the following Saturday collection, Jackie made his way up to the Brownlee residence as usual for bottle collection and to take the next week's order while Moose stayed in the truck, organizing the paperwork. It took so long for the door to be answered that they thought no one was home. Then the door opened and Mr. Brownlee appeared in the doorway, leaning on crutches, with obvious bruises to his face. He made no eye contact with either one of them and simply gave his bottles and mumbled his order through swollen lips. When Jackie returned slowly to the truck and climbed in, they were both quiet and avoided eye contact. Mr. Brownlee was never a problem again.

Another more serious concern arose in early fall when on a number of consecutive mornings Moose noticed an automobile following well behind him while he did his route. When he turned around and headed back up one of the streets on his route, he passed the parked car. Inside, a gentleman sat behind the wheel pretending to be reading a newspaper. The car had an Ontario Government crest on the door. Reporting the incident to Mahoney at the end of that week, Moose was told to put the following week's Skim orders on hold. A liquor control informant on Mahoney's payroll had warned of upcoming searches by government inspectors. On Saturday's collection, Jackie and Moose explained the situation and apologized to their customers, assuring them that Skim would resume the following week.

As warned, on Monday and Tuesday morning, Moose spotted the gentleman walking up to the porches and inspecting the bottles he had just delivered. Following Mahoney's orders, Moose stopped briefly and walked back a few houses to confront him. Acting as innocent as possible, Moose said, "Excuse me, sir. Is there something you need help with? I'm working for Walkerside. Is there some problem with my deliveries?"

"Inspector Mousseau, Ontario Liquor Board," he answered, flashing an Ontario Government badge. "I'm just doing routine searches."

"Of milk?" Moose asked, looking as confused as possible.

"Well, yes. There have been some reports," Mousseau answered, not altogether confident.

"Reports of milk with booze in it?" Moose forced a chuckle.

"Yes. Well, not exactly," the agent was clearly perplexed as he held a quart bottle up closely. "There have been reports that this neighbourhood was getting liquor delivered, and we're checking out all possible sources."

"Well, I can assure you, sir," Moose said, smiling, "if there was booze in my milk, I'm not sure I could guarantee delivery."

The agent didn't see the humour in the present situation. Clearly frustrated, he returned the bottle to its crate and turned towards his car. "You will let me know if you see anything suspicious, won't you, Mr . . . ?"

"Ducharme. Maurice Ducharme." The name seemed to surprise the inspector. "Of course I will. But I can tell you that I've been delivering this route for years now and my customers are all good, law-abiding citizens."

"The devil's liquid is everywhere, Mr. Ducharme. Of that you can be sure," Mousseau said as he climbed into his car and shut the door.

As the car made its way down the street, colourful fall leaves flying up behind its generous bumper, Moose couldn't help but smirk and say to himself, "Yes, you're right, inspector. It is everywhere."

THE MEETING WAS SET FOR A MONDAY EVENING AT A RESTAURANT just a few blocks from the riverfront. The Saint didn't like meeting his associates in the same place too often for fear of authorities who might be watching, but this place, called the East Side Diner, needed some business taken care of anyway. Like many of his operations, the diner was not what it seemed. It did serve up some tasty family-style meals, especially its popular perch dinners sourced from nearby Lake Erie, but the restaurant's real money was made after hours. Like a number of local businesses during Prohibition, the East Side transformed its unusually large back storage area into a makeshift tavern three nights a week.

At this particular speakeasy, locals could get their hands on cool beer or a variety of liquors while listening to jazz either from a large radio behind the bar or live from a Detroit band on Saturday nights. The customers that frequented this gin joint did so with permission or by invitation only, gaining entry after a secret knock on the large steel back door, accessed from the alley. The regulars included a cross section of society, from small-time local gangsters, bootleggers, and rumrunners to area business owners, professionals, and even blue-collar labourers. Ladies sometimes came with husbands, and unlike saloons or taverns before Prohibition, single women could drop in for a drink or two without a male escort or concern about irreparable damage to their reputation.

The East Side was one of nine such drinking establishments that Saint had his hand in locally, and just as for Moose's operation, he supplied the liquor and muscle while also paying off the beat cops. Combined with his gambling operations, loan sharking and a couple of cathouses, the Saint had built himself a very profitable local empire. This revenue helped bolster the buying power in his legitimate real-estate business. But St. Pierre had his expenses as well, and they grew along with his empire. Payoffs took the biggest bite—to racetrack officials, liquor suppliers like Hiram Walker's, liquor agents, local police, and even a handful of judges. He also had hundreds of others on his payroll: maintenance workers for his own home and other properties he owned; business and real-estate managers who handled day-to-day operations; and truck and boat drivers who moved his product. They, along with small-time thugs, major muscle like Wolf and the Mad Russian, as well as Mahoney, his trusted accountant and right-hand man, all needed to be paid.

This particular meeting between Mahoney and his boss was like so many others. It was a chance to go over operations and numbers and to discuss any concerns or potential problems. With his leather briefcase by his side containing the ledger books they had just spent a good deal of time reviewing, the meeting was coming to an end when Mahoney reluctantly brought up the Ducharme Skim operation and the concern about St. Pierre's comment at the church.

"I've handled it with Ducharme, and he's handled it with his wife, as far as I can tell. My concern, as always, boss, is keeping William St. Pierre separate and far apart from the Saint, you see," Mahoney reminded him.

St. Pierre hated making mistakes or looking foolish, and when he did, he figured he paid people well to take the blame and clean up the mess. "You better have handled it," he said, mulling over the situation. "Our only problem is that bloody nosy bitch O'Hollaren. She never shuts her trap at church meetings, and now that she thinks I'm chummy with this son-in-law of hers, this...what do they call him?"

"Moose."

"...this Moose fella, she's going to be even more of a thorn in my ass. Can we do something about her?"

"I don't think so. Not without making it worse," Mahoney answered. "All she really knows is that you have been kind enough to employ her son-in-law and grandson. Not our biggest problem with the Skim racket right now, Saint."

St. Pierre's eyes narrowed, peered across the table and asked, "What are some of our bigger problems, then?"

"Well, Skim has been very successful for us. Maybe even too successful," Mahoney began to explain. "I mean our cut from him isn't huge, but it's a steady, easy take. We just have to deliver. And unlike our other operations, most of the clientele are law-abiding citizens, drinking at home, so it doesn't require a lot of our other resources. We've only had one customer issue and Wolf took care of it quickly." He paused. "But there's been more and more talk on the street about the operation, and somebody must have dropped a dime to local agents. It's Mousseau again. He's been sniffing around Moose's route."

"That bastard never gives up, does he? Did he find anything?"

"No. We had our inside guy tip us off beforehand, and Mousseau came up dry," Mahoney assured him, "Ducharme handled it well. But you know he'll be around again."

"What damage could be done to us if he exposed this Skim thing?" asked St. Pierre.

"Not much, really. We don't have fingerprints on this one. Ducharme knows me, and that's about it."

"Well, be prepared, just in case. If something goes down and that son of a bitch Mousseau finds something, be ready to serve up Ducharme to take the fall. Make sure he understands that his wife and kids may get a visit. I don't want him even thinking about fingering you," St. Pierre warned as he stood and dropped a wad of bills on the table.

"It's not going to be a problem, boss," Mahoney assured him.

"Good. Now, if you'll excuse me, I have to go do penance at another goddamned parish meeting," he said, looking down at Mahoney. "I swear these bloody things are going to kill me before anything else does." Putting his hat and suit coat on, he added dryly, "Remind me again why I waste my time at these."

Looking up as he was removing and folding up his eyeglasses, Mahoney forced a smile and responded sarcastically, "Because, boss, coppers don't waste their time with fine, upstanding Christian citizens. They want to pinch those nasty gangsters." He got up, grabbed his briefcase, and the two walked out the door together, turning in opposite directions once they hit the sidewalk.

....

As Seamus Mahoney was making his way back to his home several blocks away, where he lived alone in a somewhat run-down but comfortable two-story, and as William St. Pierre was in his car, heading reluctantly over to Lady of the Rosary Church for another weekly parish council meeting, Inspector Maxime Mousseau was in his tiny study at his home poring over a stack of files that lay in front of him. With five children and his active involvement in the local church and other Christian organizations, he had little spare time outside of work to spend on reviewing files on local bootleggers and rum runners or the operations they were involved in. Although he was paid fairly well by the province and given extraordinary powers to clean up the illegal liquor trade in Windsor and the surrounding area, he was growing more and more overwhelmed by the task. Frustratingly, every time he was able to secure an arrest or shut down an operation, others would spring up nearby. And people from every level of society seemed to be involved. Even local doctors got in on the action by generously doling out, at significant profit, prescriptions for liquors that patients claimed, conveniently, were remedies for everything from insomnia to pain relief.

Not that Inspector Mousseau didn't believe in the critical role he played. He was as dedicated to Temperance and the eradication of alcohol in society as he was to his faith and family. But with only a handful of men working for him and such a large, active area surrounding a major distillery just a mile across from the U.S. border, his job often seemed an exercise in futility.

The latest investigation in the Walkerville area was typical. He had reports from three reliable citizens that their friends or neighbours were enjoying home delivery of black-market Walker whisky. One even said he heard rumours that it was delivered by their milkman. But after several days of surveillance, inspection of the milk brought to customers' homes in the area, and even talking to the milkman on his route, Mousseau could find no reliable leads. He knew that if there was any kind of organized operation, it had to involve the distillery in some way and a group of local gangsters of which he knew very little. His people, with the help of the few local cops who he trusted weren't on the take, had made their share of arrests, but they were small time—public drunkenness, citizens operating blind pigs from their homes, after-hours speakeasies, or illegal liquor hidden in increasingly creative ways. But Mousseau knew what every other liquor inspector knew: to kill a snake you have to chop off its head.

Therein lay the problem. He knew local runners and thugs—big, tough guys with little education and limited opportunity or who were recent immigrants—who had been arrested on a variety of charges, but as a rule, they never turned on their bosses or named names. He encountered some of the middlemen who made deliveries or did collections, but they too would pay their fine or quietly do their time. He even knew a major player in the area, an Irishman named Seamus Mahoney, who had his hand in many of the operations, but without his name being offered up or any verifiable proof, a search warrant could never be secured, making him impossible to touch—and Mahoney knew it.

The biggest challenge, however, was finding the head, the boss, the one person who pulled all the strings. Mousseau knew the local operators well enough by now to know that whoever was running the show locally had to have a close relationship with people at the distillery and local breweries as well as some kind of connection with the big boys, the Purple Gang, from across the river in Detroit. All the area agencies knew the Purples used their connection with crime groups in Chicago, along with violence and murder, to control the movement of liquor on both sides of the border. Mousseau tried to explain whenever possible that the liquor business was not the victimless enterprise that many people claimed. He had witnessed the alcoholism, corruption, extortion, gambling, prostitution, and deadly violence first hand, and he made it his life's mission to rid his community of it all.

After going over the files from every possible angle, Mousseau came to the conclusion that he and his men had been spinning their wheels recently and that they needed to start fresh, beginning with what little facts they already had. The only thing the inspector was sure of was that the Seamus Mahoney character was involved in some way, so he decided to direct the limited resources he had in that direction, hoping for some carelessness or a lucky break.

B Y THE SPRING OF 1925, MOOSE HAD BEEN RUNNING HIS SKIM OPERATION for almost two years. In that short period of time, his increased income had helped his family transition comfortably into the growing middle class. They now owned a nicely appointed two-story home on a quiet street with a late-model Ford parked out front. Although Sara hated to appear to be putting on airs, their clothing also reflected the family's changing fortune. Jack, now 18 years old and even bigger than his father, was in his final year of private school, studying business administration at Assumption College in nearby Sandwich West.

Both he and his father considered his working partnership and increasing role with the books of the Skim operation on weekends as "on-the-job training." Annie, now an extremely bright fifteen-year-old, attended a private residential school for the blind called Ross Macdonald in Brantford, a four-hour train ride away. Although she initially struggled with homesickness, the independence of living away and the challenging academics of the unique school were helping Annie realize her incredible potential. She came home for special occasions, holidays, and summer breaks.

Under normal circumstances, the Ducharmes' rapidly improving standard of living would have raised eyebrows in the community, but with the booming economy of the mid-1920s providing a record number of good-paying jobs, the increased use of credit to purchase the many new products available to consumers, and the sizzling stock market where fortunes were being made daily, their much-improved lifestyle did not appear all that conspicuous.

Although his fortunes had changed dramatically from years before, Moose still harboured a good deal of discontent with what he considered unfair compensation based on the distribution of labour in his Skim operation. He continued to follow Mr. McLuren's advice, however, and resigned himself to the consistent, generous income that his arrangement with Mahoney and his people provided ...until opportunity knocked once again.

Although Moose was born and raised in the Ford City area, the Ducharme family had its roots in the province of Quebec. In fact, Moose's father, Henri, still had two estranged brothers who lived in the Port Alfred area in la belle province, two hours from the Ontario border. His uncle Louis and his cousin Alain ran a pulp-and-paper mill in the Saguaney Valley. After struggling for years with a depressed Canadian and international market, their fortunes changed dramatically when demand for paper products, especially newsprint, skyrocketed after WWI. The American cancellation of tariffs on Canadian newsprint in 1913, combined with the economic growth of the 1920s, created a huge market for their product. Despite the deep family chasm, Moose would often reunite with his cousin, Alain, when his truck travelled down through Ontario to Windsor. Alain's truckload of huge newsprint rolls was brought to the tunnel railway cars that rolled underneath the Detroit River before they headed for the markets in Michigan, Ohio, and Illinois. When Moose's family moved into a more spacious home, Alain began staying with them when he was in town instead of in the ramshackle boarding houses where he usually slept.

Before dinner during his most recent stay, Alain and Moose moved out to the front porch on a breezy cool evening to enjoy a cold beer and, it turned out, some surprising admissions. Despite his family's connection to Quebec and the years Moose trudged through French classes in school, Alain's English was still better than his cousin's French. After Alain lit up a cigarette and settled into the porch seat, he explained that the near monthly trips south to Windsor had proven a windfall for his family for a couple of reasons. Not only were they profiting well from the increased demand of their paper, but he confessed that they were making even more money because of Ontario's strict liquor laws. Quebec, always inclined to go against the Canadian grain, was the only province in Canada that had no liquor prohibition at the time, and it made the large, populous province to the southwest an attractive market for illegal alcohol. With the help of a distillery contact, Alain picked up large quantities of Seagrams VO whisky from Montreal, considered in the same class as Walker's CC, and sold it for more than double his cost to contacts in the Toronto area. The huge rolls of paper that surrounded the barrels from every angle on his large truck bed hid them easily.

"Easy money—" Alain said with his French accent, before stopping abruptly when Jack appeared suddenly and joined them on the porch, his own beer in hand. He went awkwardly quiet for several seconds as Alain looked from his cousin to young Jack.

"Looks like skirting booze laws runs in the family, Jackie," Moose joked, breaking the silence.

Jackie looked back and forth to the two men, confused. "What do you mean, Pops?"

Alain's concern regarding sharing the information about his illegal activities with young Jackie didn't last long once Moose explained to his cousin the workings of their own Skim operation. He went into detail about its connection to their own local distillery, the involvement of Mahoney's people, as well as the cat-and-mouse game they always seemed to be playing with the authorities. Moose even expressed his frustration at times of feeling that he was being taken advantage of. Alain found the story fascinating as well as concerning.

"You two take great risks with these people, no?" he asked.

"Not really. We make lots of money, and they do too. Our customers keep quiet because they want to keep getting their whisky, and most of the police in the area get paid well to leave us alone," Moose continued, speaking slowly to help Alain understand. "Our only worry are the liquor agents who come around once in a while, but they are very busy with all the booze in this area."

Nodding his understanding, Alain was intrigued. He asked more about the operational details, especially the costs and profits.

Looking proudly towards his son, Moose said, "Why don't you fill him in on the business end, Jackie?"

And so he did. Jack explained as clearly as he could about the wholesale cost of the whisky, the percent take for Mahoney and his people, the surprising amount of tips they received, the increased orders during holidays, and even the involvement and kickback of booze for their glazed-bottle suppliers. He further explained how the two of them used fictitious jobs and non-existent investing to explain the time-consuming but lucrative enterprise they ran. Looking over at his father, Jack finished with, "But Pops is thinking more and more that our partnership with Mahoney and his group is not really fair. He thinks we are being taken advantage of."

Alain gave considerable thought to the information he had just heard. After a long pause, he asked, "So, a new partner would be good, no?"

"No, cousin, you don't understand," Moose explained. "I probably couldn't stop Skim even if I wanted to. We're making lots of money, and our partners aren't going to let a good thing end. Besides, they control all the booze in this area."

"How about another operation, cousin? You use good Quebec whisky?" Alain asked. His shocking offer held their undivided attention. "I don't like driving into Toronto or the people there I do business with. I would be happier to end those deals and bring it here for my family—people I trust."

Moose sat quietly, mulling over the idea. While Alain was looking back and forth at the two of them, Jackie was watching his father closely, anxious for his reaction.

"A second operation is very tempting," Moose said, breaking the silence. "I already have the organization in place. Lord knows I have the customers, old and new, ready and banging on my door." Jack looked with some concern over at Alain while his father continued thinking out loud. "And I would still keep Skim going as usual so Mahoney and his people keep getting their money. They would never find out. But I would need to find another place. Maybe some more help—"

"What are you thinking, Pops?" Jack interrupted.

"I'm thinking that with Alain's product and a little more effort, we could make a lot more money. Striking while the iron is hot, as they say."

"But what if somebody talks? Or what about the police? More business means more risk. It could be dangerous," Jack pointed out.

Standing now and becoming excited, Moose seemed not to hear his son and continued. "This second one could be completely underground and off the books. With a different supply and different customers. We wouldn't be cutting into any of the other business." What Moose wasn't saying out loud—what he didn't want to admit to himself, but knew deep down—was that the risk of taking on this second operation had another driving force. It was yet another attempt to distance himself from a father who had failed to provide for his family or take any chances in life.

"They will like our whisky and pay much for it, cousin," Alain encouraged him with a smile.

Despite his misgivings, Jack was trying to let the offer sink in. His unwavering trust and respect led him to feel that if his father and his cousin, with their combined experience, thought this new enterprise was a good idea, who was he to disagree? He also considered what he was learning in school about successful businesses. Often they needed to expand when the market demanded it, or competitors would step in to fill the void. The booze business was no different. Jackie was as sure of the demand end as his father was. The risk, however, was unknown. "What kind of numbers are you thinking we could do, Pops?" Jack asked.

"Well, there's no reason why we can't move at least as much as we are doing now. I know of a few blind pigs along my route that have taken a hit because of Skim. They have reached out through some of our customers to let me know that they would love to get in on the action. Plus, I know two fellas on my route who are running little side gambling operations that are always looking for product and don't want to deal with Seamus' boys." He paused, thinking. "No, market is not the issue. A good and safe supply is. Quality supply like Alain's Seagrams. Supply that is out of sight and out of reach of our so-called partners. And the best part would be, because our customers already know about our connection to Mahoney, we will still enjoy all the same protection without paying extra for it."

Moose and Jack both turned to look at Alain, who was smiling and waiting for a sign that they had come to some sort of an agreement. Moose assured his cousin, "We would not want any special price. We will pay you the same price you're getting now." He looked over at his son again. "We won't have to give Seamus a cut on this stuff, so there's going to be lots of profit in it." After more thought he added, "And you know, Jackie-boy, with the extra money this is going to bring in, we might even be able to get out from under Seamus in a couple of years. Maybe offer them a payout and retire. How's that sound?"

"Sounds great to me, Pops," he answered with a smile.

Alain offered Moose his hand to shake, then reached for Jackie's, saying, "It's good, *mes amis*. I drive right by Toronto and come do business with my cousins."

"*Tres bien,*" Moose said, patting Alain on his back, then he and Jack shook hands as well with smiles all around. "Go in and get us three more, will you, Jackie? And we'll drink to a new partnership."

"Sure thing, Pops." As he reached for the front door knob, Jack stopped, lowered his voice and warned, "Remember, we've got to keep this quiet from Ma."

Moose's excitement about the new venture suddenly waned with Jackie's warning. He hated enabling his son's deception of someone they both loved and cherished so much. Next to him, Alain was nodding to show he understood.

....

It took only a few weeks to organize the supply chain of whisky from Quebec, but Moose's biggest hurdle in the expansion of Skim was his need for increased involvement from the McLurens. Because most of his new customers were running their own little enterprises and were not necessarily along his milk route, the mostly gallon bottles he supplied did not need glazing, but he was in need of additional space away from the Skim garage to run their new operation. The paint shop had plenty. Moose was fully aware of the magnitude of his request when he went to meet with Scotty and Mr. McLuren one evening at their shop after it closed.

With the older gentleman sitting at his office desk enjoying a cigarette and a glass of whisky while Scotty sat shuffling through paperwork at his own desk, Moose began his pitch. He explained the unique opportunity available to him: to work with a cousin he trusted and tap into a whisky supply far from the reach of local authorities and bootleggers. Yes, he realized that Mahoney and his people might be upset if they found out, but they would keep the Quebec operation quiet, and besides, nothing was going to change with the original Skim. Mahoney would still get his money. What he needed from them was garage space to work from. Yes, Moose realized that he was involving the two of them way more than he wanted to, but he had limited options and promised that with the increased revenue, he would make it a very profitable arrangement for them as well.

After several minutes of explaining the plan and their needs, Moose finished with, "Jackie and I are hoping you can help us out."

The two McLurens shared a look that Moose could not read. Scotty was torn once again. The plan sounded promising, and he really wanted to help his good friend out, but the risk was getting a little too close to home. He was sure, as well, that his father would have no part of it. Hoping to avoid having to reject Moose's request himself, Scotty passed the decision over to his father. "What do ya think, Dad?"

Mr. McLuren eyed his son then looked back at Moose before answering, "You know, lad, there was a time when I would've jumped at an opportunity like this. But those days are way past me now. I've tried to stay above board and avoid trouble with the law and the gangsters, ya see. I don't know why I would risk that all now."

There was a period of silence, and Moose's disappointment was palpable. Scotty considered the situation. He wanted more than anything to help a friend he owed his life to, and he had to admit to himself that he certainly would enjoy the extra money. He decided he would help Moose by going at his father from a different angle. "Dad, ya say it's a good opportunity, right?" Scotty asked.

His father nodded.

"But your days of taking risks are done?"

"That's right."

Scotty looked over at Moose, who was also wondering where he was going with the questions. He turned back to his father and continued, "Don't ya see, Dad? You were about my age when ya wouldn't have thought twice about getting involved in this kind of thing. Why not let me and Moose do the same? Why shouldn't we get a shot if we want to take it?" He could see from his father's expression that his point was hitting home. "And you don't have to have your hand in it, either. You can just stay clear of that corner of the garage."

Mr. McLuren could see some logic in his son's argument, but what was more apparent was Scotty's undeniable devotion and loyalty to his best friend. Because of the circumstances of the way his son was raised—motherless and with an estranged, now deceased, brother—the elder McLuren harboured guilt about the isolation Scotty had often felt when he was younger, the limited friendships he'd been able to make, and even the failure of his marriage. He did not want to jeopardize the most meaningful relationship his son had ever had. "You may be right, boy. You should have every right to throw your hat in the ring when ya want." He paused as Scotty and Moose eyed each other optimistically. "You boys can do your thing, but leave me out of it. Just make sure it doesn't cause problems with my shop business." The older gentleman was suddenly hit with an unusual feeling of jealousy over the excitement that illegal enterprises and easy money offered. "Lucky bastards," he thought to himself. With a half smile, he extended his hand and ended with, "And Scotty has to do this on his own time."

"Yes, sir," Moose said as he shook Mr. McLuren's hand enthusiastically. "Don't you worry about a thing."

In less than a month, everything was in place for the expansion. The new operation needed to be kept even more clandestine as they skirted not only the authorities, but anybody who could be connected to Mahoney's people as well. The new customers arranged delivery around the same time as his regular milk route, which now took considerably longer than it once had. Moose and Jack kept no business records for the second operation, however. They both agreed that it was essential to avoid any kind of paper trail. They paid Alain in cash when he made deliveries and demanded cash from their customers.

By the fall, the second operation was running as smoothly as the first and was equally profitable. With Scotty agreeing to help Jack out with the Quebec orders in the shop garage on weekends, the three processed all the orders in their two locations in almost the same amount of time as before. Tips from the new operation were not nearly as generous from the rougher customer base, however, and gallon bottles made less money than the more popular quart bottles on his milk route, but these losses were more than offset by lower wholesale barrel prices and the elimination of a monthly cut to Mahoney.

The additional income, however, was becoming more of a problem. Even though Moose opened another account at a local bank and made regular, generous deposits into a third account just for Jack, he knew they could not spend the additional profits of the two operations without drawing attention. Ironically, he solved this problem by doing what he had been lying to Sara about for quite some time. With the help of a customer on his milk route who was an investment banker, Moose opened ghost accounts to hide a good deal of his profits while at the same time investing some of his profits in the stock market. This made him even more money. Sometimes Moose would lie in bed at night and laugh about the fact that, years ago, he had lost sleep worrying because he had difficulty making money, and now he was having trouble sleeping because he was making so much money that he couldn't spend it.

....

One cool fall evening while Moose lay in bed, unable once again to fall asleep, Mahoney and Wolf were sitting quietly only blocks away in the corner of a small speakeasy. In the 20' by 40' storeroom of a local appliance store, a couple dozen patrons were crammed around a handful of tables and at a bar made of planks of lumber and empty whisky barrels for quick and easy dismantling. The bluish haze of cigarette smoke that hung in the air like a fog masked the pungent smell of liquor and stale beer. Voices from the mostly male patrons were loud, competing with the chatter around them as well as the radio playing jazz music behind the bar.

Mahoney did not want to be there. He was not a big drinker and had little patience for the type of clientele he was surrounded by, but there had been some problems recently with the owner. Johnny O'Connor's books didn't add up, and there had been increasing talk by some of his regulars about potential problems. The Saint was less concerned about lost profits than he was about one of his operations being run by someone who was not only watering down their quality liquor, but was also increasingly fall-down drunk and running his mouth off. Mahoney was here on the Saint's orders to see if the concerns were warranted.

Johnny was already so into the bottle when they arrived, he didn't notice Mahoney take a seat in a corner while his unusually large friend bullied his way to the bar to order a couple of beers.

It did not take long for them to see why Johnny was a problem. Matching his customers at the bar drink for drink, his deep voice carried over the small crowd gathered in front of him as he complained about his current situation. "...And how can I keep makin' a fuckin' livin' here when I got all those costs? And I'm losing more and more customers, too, because of these other goddamned operations. People around here are even gettin' their fuckin' booze now from the milkman, for Christ's sake! And I hear the same fella's been supplyin' other operations, too, with imported hooch. What am I payin' these bastards for if they can't control the supply of hooch?" he slurred loudly. The few patrons who were actually listening nodded awkwardly, looking a little confused. Mahoney and the Wolf looked at each other, concerned. Johnny took a long drag of his cigarette and exhaled skyward before throwing back a shot of whisky and continuing. "So I'm losing more and more money, but I still got to pay my fuckin' bills. Irish Shylock comes around wanting his pound of flesh no matter how shitty my month was. He doesn't want to fuckin' hear about tough times, he says. Says the boss wants what he wants." The Wolf was on the edge of his seat, looking like he wanted to pounce, as Johnny got even louder and more and more agitated. "And who's this boss?" he asked, looking across the bar with half-closed eyes at his small audience. "You guys have any fuckin' ideas?" They were shaking their heads. "Well, I do," he announced proudly, his head held higher, "I sure as hell do. And you fuckin' wouldn't believe—"

Johnny's drunken rant was violently interrupted by a thunderous crash behind his head as a heavy glass beer mug shattered the old stained mirror attached to the wall.

"Jesus Christ," Johnny was saying as he ducked late and looked around, trying to focus through the smoke to find the culprit. All heads at the bar turned towards the Wolf, who was standing fifteen feet away and staring down Johnny through the haze. All chatter stopped, and the only sound was the tinny beat of drum cymbals and piano coming from the radio as Mahoney got up, looked Johnny in the eyes for a few seconds, and headed towards the door. The Wolf turned and followed.

Despite his impaired state, Johnny's stomach dropped. He stared at the closed door for a few seconds while those around him waited for his reaction. Swaying, he said with liquid bravado, "Well, fuck them and their boss!" A few uncomfortable laughs from around the bar broke the silence before the chatter and drinking resumed.

....

Mahoney raced home and, with the Wolf waiting in his car, made an emergency phone call to his boss. Knowing that anybody working the switchboard could be listening and that private conversations were rarely private, he summarized the events at the speakeasy as best he could. "Our man was in rough shape, boss. Just like what was reported. Drunk, loud, and complaining about things that he shouldn't be. And he's saying he knows things he shouldn't know."

"What kinds of things?" St. Pierre wanted to know.

"Things about other operations and suppliers, but also things that could cause major problems for us—and especially for you."

There was a long, crackling silence from the other end before St. Pierre calmly responded. "Well, he needs to stop talking...tonight. You understand? Have your two friends help."

"Understood," Mahoney responded. Keeping the earpiece to his ear, he pulled down and released the receiver hook, rotated the side crank handle, and immediately asked the operator to put his next call through.

The Mad Russian met Mahoney and Wolf in the alley, several steps away from the back door of O'Connor's Appliance Store, and climbed into their car. The lone lamppost in the alley illuminated the back entrance. It was just before one in the morning, less than an hour since they had left the speakeasy. After some direction from Mahoney, the Wolf got out, walked to the big black steel door, and pounded, yelling in a thick Polish accent, "Cops! Raid!"

After some rustling of tables, clanking of glasses, and scraping of chairs across the floor, the few remaining patrons inside made for the exit, stumbling and tripping over each other as Wolf stood aside to let them pass through the doorway. He then poked his head in and gave Mahoney and the Russian the signal to join him. As they entered the speakeasy casually, locking the door behind them, they found

Johnny, still behind the bar, sitting on a stool in an alcohol-infused daze.

"Hello, Johnny," Mahoney said. Johnny strained to focus on him through the smoke and his blurred stupor. "How's business?"

"Been good," he slurred with a bobbing head, beginning to take in the other two very large men there. "What the fuck do these big goons want?"

"They want what I want and what the boss wants, Johnny. They want you to stop talking."

"Can talk if I want, for chrissakes," Johnny protested, barely able to keep his eyes open. "It's my place. I do what I want. You get your fuckin' money, you greedy mick. So leave me alone."

Mahoney reacted with a sly smile and looked briefly at his two associates. "That's not going to work anymore, I'm afraid." Directing Johnny's attention to the two men beside him, he added, "These gentlemen are going to help you stop talking. And because we like you, Johnny, we're not going to hurt those pretty daughters and that nagging wife of yours—not this time, anyway. They looked so comfortable in their beds back at your place tonight, so we just let them continue sleeping."

Johnny's eyes opened a little wider and he grew quieter as his dire situation began to sink in despite his condition.

"And we're going to let you live, too, Johnny, even though my friends here have other ideas." Mahoney moved closer as his sidekicks walked behind the bar from both ends. O'Connor tried to stand and attempted to begin defending himself, but he slipped and fell on the floor.

With his earlier liquid courage now drained, Johnny tried a different tack while being lifted up by his arms on both sides. "Okay, Seamus. I fuckin' got it. No more spouting off."

The men forced him down into a chair in front of the bar and the Russian pulled some rope out of his pocket. Johnny's eyes darted around as he pleaded, "Please, Seamus. I got the message. You don't have to do this. I'll . . . ." He broke off, watching his feet and hands being tied tightly to the chair.

"You're right. I don't. But they do," he responded as the Russian smiled, bent down, lifted his pant leg, and drew a shiny knife from a sheath attached to his calf. Johnny, now in full terror mode, began to scream. Wolf reacted instantly by pulling back and landing a solid punch dead center to his face, which quieted him down right away. As blood began streaming from Johnny's nose, Mahoney moved in closer and slapped his face to regain his attention. "Listen, Johnny, listen. Just let the boys do their job here, and we can all go home." Wolf got into position behind O'Connor and put on a pair of leather gloves as the Russian moved in closer, knife in one hand and two wine-bottle corks in the other. "You're going to live, my friend, for now," Mahoney concluded, "but you won't be talking any more."

Mahoney turned and began heading towards the door as Wolf grabbed Johnny's face from behind. Once he forced his mouth open as wide as it could go, his partner jammed a cork upright and far back between the upper and lower molars on each side, forcing his jaw open. Wolf then grabbed Johnny's hair, pulled his head back, and presented the Russian with the canvas he needed to do his artwork. Johnny's guttural screams turned to a loud, painful groan as the Russian's knife went to work.

As Mahoney got in his car, lit up a cigarette, and began waiting for his two associates to finish, a car further down the alley sat in the darkness, its lone occupant watching curiously.

THE FOLLOWING MONDAY MORNING, A BRIGHT, CRISP FALL DAY, Inspector Mousseau walked into O'Connor's Appliances, doing his best to look like a typical customer. It wasn't working well. He strolled up and down a few aisles, looked at a few price tags but was clearly uninterested. The young man behind the counter made the standard offer, "May I help you, sir?"

Mousseau, sizing up the youngster, asked, "Is the owner in? There's business I'd like to discuss with him."

Not sure how he should answer and looking back towards a curtain behind the counter, the salesperson replied, "Mr. O'Connor is not feeling well today. He is resting, and I'm not supposed to bother him."

"Oh, I'll be no bother, young man," Mousseau said, resorting to showing his credentials. "Just tell him an agent of the province is here, and if he wants to talk, he can come up here, or I can go searching back there."

Clearly rattled, the young man made his way through the curtain while Mousseau waited, listening. He heard the young man's voice in what seemed like a one-way conversation.

Moments later, Johnny O'Connor appeared behind the counter, looking to be in discomfort and sporting matching black eyes and a swollen nose. He looked at Mousseau, but did not speak.

Mousseau introduced himself and asked O'Connor if he could answer a few questions. Johnny shook his head and pointed to his mouth.

Sceptical, Mousseau asked, "What's wrong, Mr. O'Connor, cat got your tongue?"

Not amused, Johnny grabbed a pad of paper and a pen from the counter and wrote, "Hurt mouth. Can't talk."

Mousseau glanced down at the note and raised his eyes without moving his head. "That's unfortunate. Would this have anything to do with your visitors last Thursday night, Mr. O'Connor?" Johnny's eyes widened. "Because if it does, I can work with the law and bring charges. I saw who it was."

Along with the grimace from the obvious pain he was experiencing, Johnny's face now registered dread. He shook his head and scribbled, "Don't know what you mean."

"I think you do, sir. And I also think you have a room back there that may have products other than appliances. Products that could cost you pretty steep fines or even some time." Johnny was growing more agitated. "So, I'll ask you again about last Thursday night."

"Can't remember," he jotted down, calling the inspector's bluff.

"Okay, Mr. O'Connor. I'm going to call in my people, and we're going to help you do a real careful inventory back there," he said while Johnny's shoulders dropped in utter defeat. As the inspector turned to leave, Johnny grunted like he wanted to say something. Mousseau turned back to see Johnny's eyes begging and his mouth forming the word "please," while releasing a stream of bright red blood that slowly worked its way down to his chin. He wiped it away with the back of his sleeve.

"I see, Mr. O'Connor," Mousseau said, realizing now what had happened and feeling a sense of pity for the man. "Now you know these people mean business—enough to cut out the tongue of a business partner." Johnny was nodding slowly. Thinking for a few seconds, the inspector explained, "I'm not out for you or the other small-timers, you understand. I know Mahoney and his boys are the bigger catch, and they would do, all right. But there's someone else pulling the strings, isn't there, Mr. O'Connor? Someone big."

Johnny shook his head and shrugged his shoulders, knowing the value of that kind of information and the price he would pay if he were to provide it.

"You have to give me something, Mr. O'Connor. I can't leave here knowing you're breaking the liquor codes without exacting some kind of penalty or getting some information that will help me." The inspector paused and made his point clear. "You have to give me something."

Johnny considered his predicament. His eyes darted from the inspector out to the street and back again while his lips did their best to stop any pooling blood inside his mouth. He suddenly grabbed the pen and pad again, and while looking menacingly at Mousseau, slowly scrawled one word in large letters: "MILKMAN."

....

The following Saturday went as usual for the Ducharmes and their two operations. Moose and Jackie did their collections and orders, then separated afterwards at the two garages to do the cleaning and filling. Scotty was waiting to help Jackie. What was unusual that Saturday, the last one of the month, was that Mahoney did not show up at the Skim garage to inspect the ledger and collect his money. Moose had to consider if possibly he had his dates wrong or forgot about a change of plans, because in the years that Skim had been operating, Mahoney had never missed a collection day.

A few hours later, when Moose was done and the orders were ready for Monday morning, he got in his car and made his way to the McLurens' paint shop. As he always did in case he was being watched, Moose walked through the main doors of the shop and worked his way to the back doors, out into the loading yard, and then into their garage. With their backs turned, Jackie was moving about, and Scotty was organizing orders when Moose yelled loudly, "Cops! Reach for the sky!"

They both turned, startled. Scotty laughed, while Jack complained, "Pops! Don't do that. You scared me half to death."

"Sorry, Jackie boy. Too tempting." He glanced

around, seeing that everything looked in order. "Looks like you're good to go here. Ready to get home for some of your mother's favourite stew?"

"Sure am. Just let me lock up."

Moose looked at Scotty. "Want to join us again tonight, Scotty Boy?"

"Going to have to pass, Moose. Tell Sara thanks anyway. I promised Dad a night out for fried fish and a beer." Scotty said his goodbyes and headed for the shop office.

Moments later, father and son left the garage, and Jack rolled down the squeaky steel door before putting the padlock in place. They got into the car and drove the few minutes home, chatting about the big Tigers game against the league-leading Washington Senators on the radio that evening.

As they turned down their street and approached the front of their home, they both noticed the back of a well-dressed man standing with one foot on the first step of their porch, leaning forward and talking to Annie, who was sitting only feet away on the top step. Jack thought out loud, "I wonder who that is?"

Moose knew who it was instantly. He recognized his back. His chest tightened and his pulse quickened. As Moose rolled the car slowly up to the curb in front of their house, Seamus Mahoney turned his head slowly, saw Moose and Jack, smiled, and then turned back to continue his conversation with Annie.

Now recognizing him from monthly collections past, Jackie asked, "What is he doing here?"

Trying not to panic or appear concerned, Moose answered, "I'm not sure, Jackie. He missed the collection today, so maybe he's doing it now."

"But you don't have the book or the dough, do you?"

Moose shook his head slowly, deep in thought. "Listen carefully, son. Let me do the talking, okay? Just say your hello and that's it."

Now getting worried, Jack said, "Sure thing, Pops. Is this a problem?"

"I don't know yet," Moose answered, his eyes scanning the area with concern, as they both slowly climbed out of the car.

They walked up the sidewalk, approaching their house apprehensively just as Sara appeared through the front door, smiling and holding a drinking glass. "There they are, Mr. Mahoney. I knew they'd be along soon." Mahoney turned back again towards them, his forced smile a stark contrast to his dark, sinister eyes.

"Hi, Daddy," Annie chirped, standing up, her eyes off in the distance and feeling her way down the porch step railing. Mahoney reached out and offered his hand, which she took.

"Here you go, darling," he said as he walked her in Moose's direction, looking him in the eyes the whole way.

Struggling to mask his anxiety, Moose greeted him. "Well, this is an, um, unexpected visit." He didn't dare offer his hand to shake, instead picking up his daughter in a protective hug. He looked up at

Sara to gauge her feel for the situation.

"Is it, Maurice?" he said, still smiling. "You know we have something to talk about."

Moose's eyes darted back and forth from Sara to Mahoney, still unsure what might have been discussed with his wife.

Thankfully, Sara saved him. "Mr. Mahoney says you two have some unfinished business, dear. He was nice enough to drop by so you don't have to go out again tonight." She looked over at their visitor with a smile. "He says you need to make some important decisions about our future."

Mahoney kept his eyes locked on Moose when he added, "Yes, Maurice. You have some big decisions to make, indeed."

"Jackie, take your sister and bring her inside so your father and his friend can talk business, please," Sara requested. She handed Mahoney the cool drink and offered Moose the same as Jack took little Annie's hand and led her away. His eyes searched his father's for some sign or direction, but found none.

As the front door closed behind the others, Moose led Mahoney hesitantly up to the porch chairs. Mahoney took a seat, and instead of talking, just looked menacingly at Moose, creating a tension that was palpable. Unable to stand the awkward silence after several seconds, Moose acted disconcerted while asking, "What can I do for you, Seamus? Why would you come to my house? Is it for the collection you missed today? You know I don't keep the money or the ledger at home."

Mahoney purposely took his time to respond, sipping from his glass before answering, "No, Mr. Ducharme. That will be taken care of later. There were pressing matters today." He paused. "I'm here because we're having some concerns, and I need you to assure me that our concerns are unwarranted."

"What kind of concerns?" Moose asked, his heart rate increasing.

Without going into any details about the source or the pain the source had endured, Mahoney simply said, "There's been some talk about our Skim operation expanding without our knowledge or approval." As he spoke, Moose tried to look as confused as possible. "Now, I've gone over the books and the orders and checked our suppliers. It all looks on the level. But we hear people talking."

"I don't know what you're hearing and who's doing the talking, Seamus, but I can tell you it's not true," Moose responded, knowing full denial was his only option. As Mahoney continued looking for any hint of betrayal, he continued. "How would I run another operation? Where would I get the supply?" He paused. "I don't know who is telling you this nonsense, but that's exactly what it is." Even with his nerves on edge, Moose couldn't help thinking how his years of dishonesty to his wife were paying dividends now.

In his business, Mahoney wasn't inclined to believe anybody, but the lack of any tangible proof, as well as his general positive impression of Moose's character, caused him to re-evaluate his thinking.

"Well then. We feel the need to remind you again, Mr. Ducharme, how dangerous it would be if—"

The front door opened, cutting him off, and Sara appeared with Moose's drink. "Here you go, honey," she said. Looking at the two men, she added, "Sorry to interrupt, gentlemen. Is everything okay? Are you getting everything taken care of?"

"We sure are, Mrs. Ducharme," Seamus answered with a smile. "There was just a bit of confusion, I believe." He looked towards Moose and added, "But I think we understand each other better now. Wouldn't you agree, Mr. Ducharme?"

Moose was nodding his head in agreement when Sara said, "Please, don't be so formal. Call us Sara and Maurice. You've been such a friend and so good to us over the past few years, what with the jobs for my two men and all the help with the investing."

"Oh, you're too kind, Sara," Seamus smiled. "Your husband has worked hard and made most of the big decisions. We just hope he continues to make the right ones."

Sara appeared a little confused, asking, "We?"

"Just an expression, luv," Moose said as he stood and put his hand behind Sara's back, gently nudging her towards the front door. "I think Mr. Mahoney has probably had enough business talk for one evening. We're going to finish up here, and I'll be right in."

"Right. It was so nice meeting you, Mr. Mahoney." Sara was waiting for him to insist he be called by his first name as well; it seemed odd to her that it didn't happen. "Well...come back anytime."

"A lovely evening to you, ma'am," he returned, tipping his hat as she went inside.

Mahoney's friendly disposition changed quickly as he turned back to Moose, his face stern. "A lovely woman and a darling little girl, Mr. Ducharme. A family worth protecting, don't you think?" he asked.

The veiled threat to his family created a knot in Moose's stomach, but it also triggered an instinctual defensive reaction, causing him to lock eyes and take a step towards Seamus. Lowering his voice and gritting his teeth, Moose said, "I told you that this talk of another operation is a lie. I don't know why somebody would tell you that." Mahoney's smile instinctually returned with the mounting tension. "Now, we could have discussed this at the garage during collection. There was no need for you to show up here, trying to cause an uncomfortable situation or threaten me."

"Are you uncomfortable, Mr. Ducharme?"

"I don't like bringing my work home with me, you see. My wife asks enough questions as it is." Moose considered his next words carefully before adding, "And if my business is exposed, so are you."

This produced the desired effect. Mahoney's smile faded, his face reddened, and his eyes turned to darts. "Mr. Ducharme," he hissed, "the last thing you want to be doing is making threats to us."

Taking a page out of his adversary's book, Moose forced his own smile and calmly responded with, "I'm making no threats, Mr. Mahoney. All I'm saying is that there is no other operation. You and your people should not be concerned. I'm making money, which means you're making money. Why ruin a good thing?"

Seamus regained his composure, unlocked his eyes from Moose's, took a deep breath, and turned towards the steps. "Well, all right, then. We seem to understand one another. I will talk to my boss and assure him that—" Mahoney stopped suddenly, turned back around towards Moose, and said quietly, "Mr. Ducharme, look over my right shoulder. Do you see that Dodge parked across the street and down a ways?"

Moose looked and nodded.

"Is that the same car that you had following you on your route?" Seamus asked.

"It is. I recognize the door decal. Looks like the same gentleman, too."

Seamus continued to face Moose and took a few moments to consider the situation. "Interesting. The question is, then, which one of us is this bastard Mousseau tailing?"

"Does it matter? This is not good, Seamus," Moose answered, suddenly concerned that not only did the liquor agent know where he lived, but he now knew he had some connection to Mahoney. "It looks like your decision to come to my home may not have been a wise one."

Mahoney was thinking the same thing, but the look on his face showed Moose's criticism was not appreciated. He adjusted his hat, straightened his suit coat and tie, and declared, "I guess we're going to find out who he's tailing." He sauntered casually down the porch steps and took the sidewalk to his car, looking and smiling in the direction of Inspector Mousseau. Before climbing into the front seat, he looked back at Moose and warned, "I hope we understand each other, Mr. Ducharme." Moose went in his front door, closed it, and quickly made his way to the front window to look out through a gap in the sheer curtains. Even though the agent's car followed Mahoney as he sped away, Moose felt little sense of relief. Less than an hour ago, everything had seemed under control, and now he was feeling a threat from two opposing, very dangerous forces.

"What are you looking at?" Sara asked, standing behind him, hands on her hips. "What's going on, Maurice?"

Make that three, he thought to himself.

14

OW'D THE MEETING GO?" THE SAINT WANTED TO **know** immediately after they sat down across from each other at the back of another local diner that was on their payroll.

Mahoney explained the details of their conversation and said, "I think Ducharme is on the level. Says he doesn't know where the rumours are coming from. I would normally be sceptical, but I've checked all the sources around here, and nobody's supplying him. We would have heard about it. I'm thinking that O'Connor was just deep into the bottle and spouting off to impress his bar rats." St. Pierre stared off to the other side of the restaurant as he considered the update. "But we have a more pressing problem, boss." As St. Pierre's eyes shifted back his way, Mahoney continued, "Our friend Mousseau was tailing our meeting. We saw him parked down the street. He tried following me, but I shook him."

St. Pierre didn't like the news. "That was goddamned careless!" he said, raising his voice. "Now he's got a link between you and the milkman. Why did you have to meet at his house . . . on the fucking front porch?"

"May I remind you, Saint, that it was your idea to confront him at home. You said the threat to his family would be effective." St. Pierre was getting more and more agitated. "And I couldn't very well go into his house to discuss our business with the family there, now, could I?"

The Saint leaned forward until his face was so uncomfortably close to Mahoney's that he could smell the stale mix of whisky and cigar on his breath. With a low voice, the boss seethed, "Don't you ever question my directions or blame me for problems you caused. I made you, you Mick bastard." He leaned back and thought for several seconds. He cooled down as quickly as he heated up, offering nothing resembling an apology. "Now, I didn't get where I am by trusting people I do business with. We are going to make damn sure this Ducharme fella isn't playing us. We don't let anybody around here run an operation behind our backs. We lose money and it hurts our reputation...and it gives other two-bit operators ideas."

Mahoney was listening, obedient and expressionless, nodding in agreement. He had learned a long time ago that if he wanted to keep his position—a very lucrative one—he needed unusually thick skin; he couldn't take the Saint's frequent tirades and insults personally. It was just part of the job.

Saint continued. "Here's what we're gonna do. I want you to go have a talk with your contact who helped set up this whole Ducharme Skim thing—the paint-shop guy. See if he knows anything. I also want you to put a man on both Ducharme and his boy. See if they can sniff out anything suspicious. If they find something, I want to know. If he's dealing behind our backs and lied to you about it, we are going to have to send a very strong message."

Mahoney stood. "And what about Mousseau?"

"Just keep low for a while. Send your men for collections and meetings instead for three or four days. Drag that bastard around town...to the grocer, theatre, doctor's office...hell, bring him to church... anywhere to make him start losing interest. And I'm going to try, again, to find someone who might be able to grease his palms. That son of a bitch needs to get on board and stop being so goddamned right-eous." St. Pierre paused, stared off, considering other options. Thinking out loud, he continued, "I would love to have the Purples take him out, but that would draw way too much heat. For now, we have to try to manage him and what he finds out."

"Got it, boss." With that, Mahoney left the res-taurant through the back door, checked for a tail, and walked the three blocks to his car.

Moose had to continue his web of lies to Sara to get her to accept his unusual behaviour after his meeting on their porch with Mahoney. He explained that his relationship with this boss, who had been so good to him, had soured recently. He told her Mahoney was acting very strange and having severe mood swings. Sara listened sympathetically when Moose won-dered aloud if Mahoney was possibly having some kind of breakdown or hitting the bottle. "That's why

I watched him out the window when he left. I wondered if he should even be driving," he added.

"Poor dear," Sara said. "I didn't want to say anything about a friend of yours, but he was acting a little strange...the way he said things. Very unusual. How long has he been that way?"

"Been getting worse for a number of weeks now. But I'm sure everything will be fine," Moose assured her. "Sometimes guys just go through rough patches, luv. I see it all the time with fellas that served."

"Oh, you didn't tell me he was in Europe."

"He wasn't. But I think he's been going through some battles just the same. Just personal ones."

Sara reached out and took his hand. "Well, you should keep an eye on him. He's been very good to you and Jackie."

"I will," Moose agreed. "And I need you to let me know if he ever comes by again when we're not home. Maybe a telephone call. That kind of took us by surprise."

As Sara was nodding in agreement, Moose was thinking about the never-ending deception he was engaged in and how it was getting more and more difficult to keep all the lies straight.

....

That Sunday afternoon after church, Moose took the family for a drive out to an orchard in the county for some fresh apples. It was a sunny, cool day, and the four of them were in the car singing a popular song, out of tune, that they often heard on the radio. The windows were rolled down a few inches to allow into the car the fresh fall air, which blew Annie's hair about in the back seat. Moose loved these moments: just the family, enjoying a simple activity together far away from the work and the business that was becoming increasingly stressful. As the car made its way down a long, bumpy concession road, gravel dust flying up behind it, he was lost in thought. He remembered wanting so badly to get himself and his family out of the difficult financial situation they were in years ago so they could enjoy a better life. He had to ask himself if he was truly enjoying it now. The old saying "Be careful what you wish for" kept creeping back to him. As they turned off the road and onto the long laneway leading to the orchard, he was lost in thought about a possible change of course. He knew he had the money to end Skim immediately and have his family still live very well, but he also knew breaking ties with Mahoney would be even more difficult than the suspicion and threats he was dealing with now.

"Are you coming, Maurice?" Sara asked after he parked the car, shaking him out of his trance. She was slipping on a sweater as Jackie was helping Annie from the back seat.

"Yes," he answered, snapping back into the moment. "Let's go clean this orchard out." As he climbed out of the car, stood up, and adjusted his jacket, he glanced over the roof of his car and saw other cars lined up alongside him on the grass beside a large red barn. Turning to join his family who were heading towards the barn to get baskets, he realized he had seen something familiar. He stopped and looked back at a car that had just parked after him, dust from the laneway still settling gently around it. It was the same government car, with the same crest and the same liquor agent sitting in the driver's seat. His hopes for a relaxing afternoon came to a sudden end.

Not wanting to appear guilty or provoke questions from his wife, he turned back and continued towards the barn. They picked up baskets, found a little wooden cart, and made their way into the orchard.

They all enjoyed fall apple picking, but none more than Annie. She had made a special trip home from school for the weekend so she could revel in the annual outing that always provided her with a sensory overload. The warm sun and fresh crisp air of fall, the sweet smell of rotting apples littering the tall grass, the sound of families chatting and children running about, all combined with buzzing insects and the feeling of Jackie lifting her to tug the smooth, cool apples from the branches, made this annual family tradition one of her favourites.

As Jackie and Annie drifted to a different row and Sara was searching for the section of Cortlands, which she claimed made the best pies, Moose was wandering, distracted and deep in thought, down a deserted row.

"Hello again, Mr. Ducharme. Inspector Mousseau. Do you remember me?" came a voice from behind.

Startled, Moose turned and answered, "Yes...

well, hello." He offered a handshake. Gaining his composure and thinking about the situation, he added, "What brings a liquor agent out to an apple orchard on a Sunday afternoon?"

Hands now buried in his suit pockets and looking down at his dress shoes shuffling the tall grass, Mousseau answered matter-of-factly, "You." Moose's smile faded as he was considering how to respond. The inspector didn't give him a chance. "Listen, Mr. Ducharme. I don't know how an upstanding citizen like yourself got mixed up with the likes of Seamus Mahoney and the kind of people he runs with, but you are in way over your head. Believe me. I've been in this racket for a time now, and they are nothing but bad news for you and your family."

Moose was searching to find the right reaction, one that could mask the guilt, concern, and stress he was often feeling lately. He couldn't find it. "I appreciate your warning, inspector," he mumbled, emotionless, looking around for Sara. "But I don't know what you are talking about."

The agent's shoulders slumped in disappointment. "You're swimming with sharks, sir, and you may not even know it. I've seen what they are capable of." Mousseau looked over Moose's shoulder and saw Sara heading towards them from the far end of the row. Moose followed his glance, saw her as well, and became jumpy. "Don't worry. I'm leaving," he said. "But I'm going to say this just once. I'm throwing you a lifeline, Mr. Ducharme. You've got one chance to grab it. If you don't, I'm afraid you're going to drown." He shook Moose's hand like an old acquaintance, slipped a card with his personal telephone number on it into his hand, and looking towards Sara, added, "And maybe even pull the people you love down with you." With that he turned away, hands still in his pockets, watching his steps carefully to avoid the rotting apples hiding in the tall grass.

"Who was that, Honey?" Sara asked as she approached. "He's awfully well-dressed for apple picking."

"Oh, just one of my customers," Moose answered, staring off into the trees thoughtfully.

....

With Moose and Jackie together on the family outing on the same bright fall Sunday afternoon, the two men who Mahoney had following each of them seemed like wasted resources. Instead, one ended up sitting in his car at the entrance to a county apple orchard while the other took advantage of the Ducharme family home being empty for a few hours. Parking his car at the end of the block and working his way through the alley, he entered their backyard and was pleasantly surprised to find the back door unlocked. Unsure of what he was looking for and in no particular hurry, he wandered through the rooms, casually looking around for anything that could please his boss. The kitchen at the back of the house, front living room, and hallway that led to the front door yielded little. On a small hallway table under the telephone was a short stack of mail—a couple of bills and some personal letters. One letter was from a friend in Toronto catching up on news about their growing family; one was from an Aunt Gillian in Michigan who missed her darling Sara dearly; and another was from a Ducharme relative in Quebec who seemed to have a little bit of trouble writing in English. The intruder assumed that the letter would make more sense to its intended recipient than it did to him.

Losing patience combing through their mail, he headed upstairs to the bedrooms. The first, on the right, was clearly a girl's room and had a suitcase sitting on the bed, clothes hanging over its sides. On a nearby table were some strange-looking books with no writing, just page after page of thousands of tiny bumps. He had heard of these kinds of books for the blind before, and he spent more time than he probably should have sitting on the edge of the bed and running his fingers slowly over the lines on different pages.

Across the hall, the next room had a much larger bed and demanded much closer inspection: the parents' room. Searching carefully through bureau drawers and the nightstand, he considered how boring they were when he found nothing incriminating or even embarrassing. The small closet yielded little more than hanging clothes and a couple of shoeboxes, one filled with letters and postcards, the other with military letters, uniform patches, and even a medal. "A war hero?" he thought to himself as he fondled the intricate ribbon and steel medallion, examining it more closely.

At the end of the hall was the last bedroom, clearly belonging to a young man. Sports magazines, business-school textbooks, and a mix of dirty and clean clothes littered the room. Searching stacks of magazines, he was disappointed to find none of the girlie ones that he enjoyed so much. On a small table next to the bed was a stack of the popular Great War comic books. The one on the top had the cartoon image of Canadian ace pilot Billy Bishop, from nearby Owen Sound. He was waving from the cockpit of his biplane as destroyed German aircraft and pilots lay burning, decimated and defeated, in the background. Sitting down on the desk chair, he flipped through the pages, amazed at the quality and detail of the sketching. Returning it to the top of the pile, he began to dread the thought of reporting back to Mahoney that he was unable to find anything useful.

As he turned and surveyed the room one final time, he noticed a thin white booklet wedged between two textbooks. Carefully sliding it out, he read the purple lettering on the cover: "Assumption College School Calendar 1925–26." Flipping through the pages, he learned about the kid's class schedule that semester, his homework and study group meetings, as well as the assignments he had due. A short list of girls' names were written inside the blank front cover page, with one named Maria Dario underlined with a few little hearts drawn around it. Continuing his inspection, he flipped through the monthly calendar pages and found the two squares at the ends of each row, Saturday and Sunday, had the word "work" written on them. This was repeated every week, but he noticed as he turned pages that every third weekend, the added words "Alain delivery" appeared, followed by a time, usually in the afternoon. Although he wasn't privy to the Skim operation details, he often helped with the delivery of Walker whisky to the garage. He grew more suspicious as he realized the dates didn't seem right, the times were much later in the day than their early-morning delivery routine, and he sure as hell never heard of anybody in the organization named Alain.

Relieved to have found something, he tore the two October pages out and returned the booklet to its original place between the textbooks. Heading down the stairs slowly while looking over the sheets, the name Alain was nagging at him. When he glanced down to the hallway below and saw the mail on the small table again, he made the connection. Opening the one from Alain Ducharme from Port Alfred, Quebec, once more, the numbers written at the bottom of the letter suddenly held much more meaning. Holding the calendar sheet in one hand and the letter in the other, there was an obvious correlation. Where the letter had a random O24-5 written, the school calendar had "Alain delivery 5 p.m." marked on Saturday, October 24th. That was only six days away. With a satisfying smile, he folded the letter up with the calendar sheet, stuffed them into his jacket pocket, and made his exit through the back door.

....

Moose's tail had been parked and watching the Skim garage from a distance for hours on the following Saturday afternoon, October 24th. At the same time, the man assigned to Jack was also sitting patiently across the street from the paint shop, ordered not to go in and unable to see the yard behind the shop.

At four-thirty, Moose appeared from his garage, locked up, and headed for his car. Within minutes, he was in the paint-shop parking lot and walking through the front door, while both of Mahoney's men were now watching curiously from a distance. Five o'clock came and went, and there was no sign of the Ducharmes or any unusual activity. Thirty minutes later, just when one of the tails was going to leave and report to Mahoney that there was nothing to report, a newer-model pickup truck with "McLuren Paints" emblazoned on the side drove loudly down the street towards them. The vehicle slowed to a crawl and had to wait only seconds before the side gate was opened; then the truck made its way into the yard. The gate was closed quickly behind it.

Both of Mahoney's men got out of their cars, lit up cigarettes, and considered the situation. After some discussion, one climbed back into his car while the other crossed the street and began rounding the corner, trying his best to look like an average pedestrian on a stroll. As he passed slowly in front of the yard gate, he peered through a gap between the fence posts and watched the activity in the yard carefully. His timing was perfect. While a man with crutches stood nearby, two men pulled back a light-coloured tarp. Ducharme and his son dragged a heavy-looking wooden structure behind the truck. The four men then rolled three large oak barrels down the makeshift wooden ramp and guided them into a garage in the corner of the yard.

Seeing all he needed to see, the tail returned to his car in a hurry, tossing his cigarette aside before he sped away, his partner following close behind.

After spending ten minutes driving around in all directions and even exchanging cars in an alley with one of his men, Seamus Mahoney was sure he was not being followed. He had important business to attend to.

Thomas McLuren used Monday mornings to catch up on the paint-shop paperwork, pay bills, and organize jobs for the week. While sitting at his desk just after eight o'clock, he was caught off guard by Mahoney standing in his office doorway. Even though they knew each other and went way back, they weren't friends. The unexpected visit caused immediate dread.

"Seamus Mahoney. What brings ya to these parts so early on a Monday morning? Shouldn't ya be home countin' your money?" he said, forcing a smile.

With no change in his serious expression, Mahoney answered, "Business, unfortunately, Tommy." McLuren's smile faded quickly. Mahoney took off his hat, walked slowly into the office, and sat down with a huff before continuing. He looked around the office slowly, like he was in no hurry to talk. Finally, he swung his gaze across the desk, then dropped his head and said, "You know, Tommy. We all appreciated you sending the Ducharme operation our way. So did my boss. We've all done very well with it. But now we know all about him, and your son, expanding the operation and freezing us out."

McLuren's body stiffened and his heart raced. He knew better than to try to lie, so he stayed silent. This told Mahoney all he needed to know. "We know it's happening, all right, and we know it's happening here. We just don't know the details." He leaned forward in his seat, looked down into his hat, and let out an exaggerated sigh. "You know, Tommy, we go back, you and I, so I convinced the boss that taking everyone out would be too messy. I told him that just because it's at your shop doesn't mean you're involved. I told him that Tommy Mac was smarter than that and that your running days were behind you." McLuren nodded, disoriented. "The boss always thinks violence first, which I believe would not be in our best interest this time. I'm paid to think about financial opportunity, and that's what we have here." McLuren took a deep, anxious breath. "So what we're going to do is take over the action. And you're going to help us do that."

Expressionless, McLuren was thankful that some lives were going to be spared. "So my boy is good? No payback?" he asked apprehensively.

"He'll be fine as long as he cooperates," Mahoney assured him. "But things are going to change now, you understand. We're going to run this new operation." He repositioned himself in the chair, crossed his legs, and leaned back a little too casually. "So I assume the whisky is coming from Quebec?"

Feeling numb, McLuren nodded. His mind was racing, wondering about what this shocking development was going to mean for everyone involved.

"That's good. The boss has been looking to branch out from under the thumb of Detroit for a while anyway, and this will give him the opportunity he's been looking for."

Silence enveloped the room while the two men studied each other. "So what do you want me to do?" McLuren asked nervously.

"Nothing for now. We're going to wrap up the month, make our deliveries and collections, and get a feel for the Quebec thing. Let Ducharme relax and sort of show us this new operation without even knowing it." Mahoney stood and put on his hat. "And of course your silence is expected, Tommy. I can't save your sorry Scottish ass twice."

McLuren nodded, understanding. As Mahoney headed for the doorway, McLuren impulsively blurted, "What's gonna happen to Ducharme?"

Mahoney turned, looked at McLuren with his dark, menacing eyes from under the shade of his hat brim, and answered matter-of-factly, "I think you know the answer to that question."

THE SUBTLE WARNING MOOSE RECEIVED FROM MAHONEY, and the less subtle one from Inspector Mousseau, had been weeks earlier, and nothing had come from either. It was business as usual with both operations, and they were running as smoothly as ever. The mounting stress Moose had felt earlier had subsided considerably. It was a Monday in late November, and the bright, crisp, warm days of autumn were long gone, replaced by the cold, wet grey of early winter. The first snowfall of the season was already blanketing Ford City in white.

With Jack almost halfway through his final year of college, Annie doing so well at her private boarding school, and the family finances in better shape than ever, Sara and Moose had been enjoying a sense of peace and contentment recently. They didn't live the lavish lifestyle of some of the wealthy families who lived nearby, but they had all the comforts and conveniences that they had ever wanted.

On this particular evening, the cold, snowy weather outside prompted a discussion about the upcoming holiday season. Sara and her mother were on the decorating committee of the church, which made them both anxious to get an early start on their own

Christmas decorating. As they were sitting at the dining room table after dinner and Jack was in his room doing schoolwork, Sara was applying the pressure.

"All I'm saying, luv, is that it seems a little early, but I'll pull out the decorations from the basement if you want," Moose said. The white winter wonderland on full display out their dining room window supported Sara's request.

"That's all I'm asking," she responded. "If I have them out, I can work away at them when I want. At my own speed."

"Uh-huh," was Moose's only response while smiling her way. They both knew she would have the decorations up within days. It was another thing he loved about her: Sara had an unbridled enthusiasm for holidays, especially Christmas.

As she stood to begin to clear the dishes, the telephone on the kitchen wall rang. Because they were only one line on a party line of four neighbourhood houses, they both looked towards the telephone and paused, waiting to hear the ring pattern. The three-ring sequence indicated that the call was indeed for them, so Moose pulled himself out of his chair to answer it. Sara was at the sink, listening to one side of the conversation.

"The Ducharmes'...Yes, sir, it's me." There was a long pause. "Tonight?" Moose's voice lowered while his eyes watched the back of his wife's head. "It's late, and it's snowing heavy out there...Well, I see. Okay, okay. I'll be there." Moose hung up the telephone, already preparing his explanation to Sara.

"Who could possibly want you to go out on a night like tonight, Maurice?" she asked, not bothering to turn around.

"That was Mr. Mahoney," he answered. "Apparently the snow has caused some problems at the apartments. He could use my help." He was not being totally dishonest. The caller was Mahoney, but his sudden demand to meet remained a mystery to Moose.

....

Around the same time that Moose and his wife were finishing up their dinner, Scotty and his father were stuck at the shop, trying to get ahead of clearing the snow in their back lot and around the gate entrance. The early darkness brought on by the shorter November days was not making the job any easier. The next day was sure to be busy, with four cars being delivered by a local business for decal painting and two Model T's being picked up, both repainted after minor collisions. More importantly, the next Quebec liquor shipment was due to arrive in the afternoon, and the last thing they needed was the truck getting stuck in the snow, drawing unnecessary attention.

The unusually early heavy snowfall was the least of Mr. McLuren's concerns, however. It had been almost a month since Mahoney had indicated that the takeover of the Quebec operation from Moose to his own people would take place before the next shipment. He knew from an earlier conversation with Scotty that the delivery was happening the next day.

McLuren knew Ducharme's fate was sealed, and he had no way to help or warn him without risking his own life as well as his son's. The strain of knowing the pain and anguish it was going to cause Scotty, as well as all of Moose's loved ones, was an unbearable weight that seemed to be slowly crushing him. He was spending sleepless nights trying to find a way out of the mess, but to no avail. Even the bottle he was hitting hard as of late wasn't tempering the anxiety. McLuren couldn't reason with Mahoney's people. It was all business to them, and they had already shown unusual restraint in sparing McLuren's son. He now looked back on helping Moose get involved in bootlegging with Mahoney and not stopping him from starting a second operation with the kind of regret that would eat away at him for the rest of his life. With no options available to him, all he could do was let the scene play out, feign shock and disbelief, and then help his son through what was surely going to be a very difficult period of anger and grief. His guilt was already becoming unbearable.

While shovelling aimlessly in the growing darkness, the stress and uncertainty of the tragic situation became more than McLuren could stand. Shouting to Scotty on the other side of the yard that he would be back in a few minutes, he trudged through the snow and made his way into his warm office. He pushed the door closed, but it didn't catch, so a long sliver of brightness was cast into his office from the flickering hallway light. Sitting behind his desk, knees bouncing nervously, he poured himself another drink. He took a small booklet from his top drawer and flipped through a few pages, straining to read in the limited light. Finding the number, he brought the bulky black handset of the telephone to his ear and tapped the cradle to get the operator. He turned his chair away from the door and in a hushed voice gave the number to be connected to Mahoney's residence. He did not hear his son come in to use the bathroom. As Scotty limped by his father's office, he heard whispers and stopped, straining to hear the conversation. His presence cast a shadow on the door's frosted-glass window.

"Seamus. It's Tommy," the elder McLuren said hesitantly. There was a long pause. "I know. I know. I'm sorry, but this thing has got me turned inside out."

Scotty leaned in closer to the door crack.

After more silence, McLuren begged, "Can ya just tell me if it's happenin' tonight? The shipment is due tomorrow."

Scotty, completely intrigued now, pushed the door open a few more inches.

"Got it," he whispered somberly. After a few more seconds, he added, "Ya, I know. It's my son that's got me worryin' so. It's his best friend, for Christ's sake. They served together, after all. Ducharme saved his life."

Scotty pushed the door open fully, no longer caring if he was seen.

"Ya. I understand...I won't call again," Mr. McLuren finished. His hands were shaking as he leaned forward, and his head dropped. He spun around slowly in his chair to hang up the telephone and was startled by his son standing in front of his desk, looking confused and concerned.

"What about my best friend?" Scotty demanded.

....

Jack was at the desk in his bedroom, trying to focus on a business management paper he was writing, but he was finding it very difficult. A young Italian beauty named Maria whom he had met months earlier, combined with the first snow of the season falling heavily outside his bedroom window, were causing too much distraction. Convincing himself that it was Friday night and he had the rest of the weekend to finish the assignment, he gathered up his pages, closed his books, and headed downstairs.

"Where's Pops?" he asked his mother while entering the kitchen.

"He just left, Jackie. Had to help Mr. Mahoney with some problem at the apartments," she answered. "He called a few minutes ago."

"I heard the ring," Jack said vacantly, his mind drifting off. He took a few steps back towards the stairs, wondering why they would call his father out at night? They never did that. And on a night with the first winter storm of the season brewing outside? It was all very strange. Then Jack remembered that the next day was also their next Quebec shipment, but he couldn't recall the time. His eyes swung over to the hallway desk where the recent mail sat. He walked casually over and fingered through the few envelopes in the stack, but he didn't see Alain's letter. His concern intensified. Hoping that his father had the letter for some unknown reason and not wanting to prompt questions from his mother, Jack was deep in thought as he went back upstairs to get the delivery time from his school calendar. As he entered his bedroom, he scanned the various stacks of books looking for the white booklet. Being so deep into the semester and knowing his schedule by heart, he didn't use it nearly as much as he had weeks ago. It took some searching and shifting of textbooks, but he eventually found it buried beneath his business ethics textbook, sat on his bed, and opened it. Flipping through the pages, his unease turned to dread as Jack turned over September—and a page with a ripped edge slipped from the booklet and fell to the floor.

"What the . . . " he whispered to himself as he held half of the November page in his now shaking hand. His mind was frantically rifling through possible explanations. Nobody ever used his calendar except him. Hell, he could barely find it most of the time. And he never ripped pages out, especially ones with shipment information on them. The more he considered the mounting circumstances, the more terrified Jack became.

Panic drove his oversized body out of his room, down the stairs, and into the kitchen. Doing his best to appear calm despite his agitated state, he inquired, "Hey, Mom. Do you know where Pop was going tonight?"

"To work, dear. One of the apartments, I think. Why?"

Jack's eyes gave away his frightened thoughts as he considered the possibilities.

"Why?" she asked again, turning around from the counter. "What's wrong, Jackie? You look a fright."

"Nothing, Ma," he said as he darted down the hallway to the front foyer closet. "I'm just thinking that maybe he could use my help." His heart was jumping out of his chest as he struggled to throw on his coat and slip into his shoes at the same time.

"What in the Lord's name are you doing, Jackie?" Sara demanded as she watched from the kitchen entryway. "You can't go out on a night like this. With those shoes on. It's snowing like the dickens—"

The front door slamming behind Jack cut her off.

....

Scotty was beside himself with frustration as he tried once again to call Moose. "Goddamned party lines," he yelled into the telephone.

His father was still sitting behind his desk, head in hands, nervously considering the dangerous situation they were in. After what his son had overheard, he had no choice but to come clean, which McLuren now felt was probably for the best. The knowledge of Moose's fate and keeping it a secret from the one son who had shown unwavering love and devotion to him was not something he could live with anymore. Tonight, Scotty's best friend was going to pay the ultimate price for his betrayal. Scotty resigned himself to the fact that he might very well be next.

After the local operator failed several more times to connect him with the Ducharme residence, Scotty slammed the telephone handle down and shouted hysterically, "Where would they do it, Dad?"

"I don't know...I didn't...He didn't say..." McLuren stumbled, now clearly rattled as well.

Scotty aggressively approached his father, grabbed his coat, and leaned in, inches from his face.

"Think, Dad. Where? "

Taking a few seconds to calm down, his father's eyes widened and he answered with some renewed hope, "Maybe the river. They always say the bad shit happens along the river. That's where people disappear or they find bodies."

Limping over and grabbing his keys in a rush, Scotty asked, "Where at the river, Dad? Is there a place?"

McLuren thought for a moment. "Has to be near Walker's. Or the Island View . . . down at the docks. Lots of business gets done down there," he responded. "But ya can't go there, Scotty. Please. You'll end up joining Moose—"

His son cut him off as he rushed for the door. "I owe Moose my life, Dad!" he yelled. "Don't you understand? I have to try."

As his son turned down the office hallway in an awkward limping jog, his father still sat frozen in his chair, overwhelmed with both fear and regret. He called out behind him, "I'm sorry, Scotty-boy. I'm so sorry."

....

The large, blowing snowflakes, combined with the darkness, made it very difficult to see as Jack ran as fast as he could towards the only place he could think of—the Skim garage. The leather Oxford shoes that he'd thrown on in such a rush couldn't gain traction in the heavy snow, and he slid and slipped repeatedly. Snowflakes clung to his hair and eyelashes, his face was dripping wet, and his eyes watered as he weaved his way down sidewalks and through intersections.

As Jack crossed a street only a couple blocks from the garage, a speeding car came to a sliding stop in the snowy street, just making contact with his outstretched arms. The headlamps shone on his panicked face briefly as he attempted to regain his footing and continue. The car door opened. "Jackie. Wait!"

Jack slid to a stop and looked back. It was Scotty. "I've got to get to Pops!" Jack cried out.

"I know. Get in. I think I know where he is," Scotty shouted from the open door.

He trudged back through the slush carefully and climbed into the car. Scotty pulled his door shut, and using his left hand to force his wooden leg to control the floor clutch pedal, he shoved the stick shift into gear, causing the tires to spin before they grabbed.

"I think Pops is in trouble," Jack said, looking over with a frightened look on his shimmering wet face.

"I know, kid. I've been trying to call and warn him, but I couldn't get through," Scotty told him as he strained to look out the front windshield while manipulating the automobile's levers and pedals. Visibility was down to only feet in front of them as the car's two weak headlamps illuminated the oversized snowflakes coming at them.

As the car grinded, skidded, swerved, and bumped its way down several blocks before turning onto Sandwich Street, Jack was in a state of panic, asking what Scotty knew and where they were headed.

Trying not to make the situation worse, Scotty explained, "Dad says Mahoney's people often have meetings down by the river, in the parking lot of one their places. It's outside, away from anyone listening, and tucked away behind the building." He looked briefly over at Jack, who was shaking uncontrollably. He couldn't tell if it was from being damp and cold or from sheer terror. "How did you know he was in trouble?" Scotty asked.

"I thought it was just strange that they would call a meeting so suddenly, especially on a night like to-night," Jack explained. "Then I noticed a letter from Alain missing and a page from my school calendar ripped out. From up in my bedroom!" He looked over at Scotty, suddenly overwhelmed by guilt. "I was so stupid to put the deliveries in there. Pop warned me not to keep records." He paused for a few seconds as the car bounced its way in and out of the snow ruts and cable tracks on the road. "They must have searched our house. Who are these people? They must know about Quebec."

"They do, Jackie," Scotty said. "We just have to hope they are meeting your dad to give him a warning or force him to get them in on the operation. They know the next delivery is tomorrow."

The car began to slow as they got closer to the Island View Roadhouse, which sat on the river's edge near an intersection that was unusually quiet on this stormy night. The parking lot and docks sat beside and behind the two-story building. Like many such establishments dotting the area shoreline, the Island View existed officially as a restaurant, but made its real money in illegal liquor sales, while the docks in back served as a distribution point for rumrunners moving their product and money back and forth between Detroit and the Walkerville area.

As Jackie pulled on the brake lever and they slid to a stop across the street, the building was barely visible from the blinding snow. "Listen, kid. Let me go see if anything's happening first," Scotty told him as he adjusted his hat and buttoned up his coat. Jack began to protest, but he was cut off. "If I need you, I'll come back for you, I promise. No good us both taking a risk."

Jack nodded, his eyes giving away his uneasiness.

As Scotty negotiated his way slowly across the snowy street, occasionally having to use his hands to help pull his wooden leg out of the deep snow, he couldn't help flashing back to that unforgettable day during the war and the vivid memory of Moose dragging him from what surely would have been his muddy grave. Since that time, he had endless dreams of returning the favour—pulling his large friend from a raging fire or saving him from drowning in the river – but no scenario he'd envisioned ever involved rescuing Moose from murderous gangsters.

As he rounded the east side of the tavern and made his way along the dark red-brick wall, he began to make out headlamps from two cars. Approaching the end of the building, shielded from the blowing snow by an entrance alcove, he could see outlines of people and hear parts of a conversation. Through the blowing snow, he could see Mahoney standing beside another well-dressed gentleman, and they were both facing a much larger fellow. Even with his back to him and the poor visibility, Scotty knew instantly that it was Moose. He moved a little closer.

" …know I screwed up…let me make it up to you… give me another chance… " Moose was pleading.

"Maybe we can work something out. What do you think, boss?" Mahoney asked his partner.

Boss? Scotty realized at that moment that Moose's fate was already sealed. Not only had he crossed some very dangerous people, but he now knew the identity of the man who ran the organization and whose identity had always been a well-guarded secret. That would only happen if Moose was no longer going to be alive to divulge that information. His nerves were at a breaking point as he considered his next move. Although he was never much of a street fighter and his bum leg would prove a serious disadvantage, with the poor visibility and the element of surprise, he could be by Moose's side unexpectedly, and if Mahoney and his boss didn't have weapons, it would be a fairly even match. It was a risk he had to take.

Just as Scotty summoned the courage to begin his move towards them, two extremely large men appeared from the opposite side of the lot, walking up behind Moose. Scotty retreated and froze. As the older gentleman was saying something about being sorry that they couldn't do business together any longer, one of the men behind Moose raised something with his right hand and brought it down full force on the back of Moose's head. The sickening, clanky thud of what sounded like a metal object froze Scotty where he stood. Moose's bulky body dropped to the wet, snowy ground in a heap.

Feeling very much as he had years ago in the chaos of an attack during a battle, Scotty began having an out-of-body experience. Suddenly the wind settled down and the clearing skies allowed him to see the events unfolding more easily. His body was numb, and everything seemed to be happening in slow motion. The boss barked some orders, and the two thugs struggled to pick up Moose's massive body and shove him into the driver's seat of his own car. The boss stepped towards the car, took a long swig to finish the last of a liquor bottle, and tossed the empty casually into the car. One of the thugs struggled to lean into the cramped driver's side and start the car before working his leg towards the floor clutch and engaging the gearshift. With a loud grind and sudden jump, the car jolted forward violently, causing the man to fall to the ground and the door to slam shut as the black sedan rattled loudly and bounced towards the water.

As Scotty watched in disbelief, Jack startled him by appearing suddenly with him in the alcove. His height allowing him to look easily over Scotty's head, he took a couple of seconds to focus on the scene and comprehend what was happening. Seeing his father's automobile heading for the river's edge, shock took over, and Jack instinctually leapt into action. Scotty caught the back collar of his coat and struggled to pull him back and around to face him. "Jack, no!"

"I've got to help Pops. They're trying to kill him," Jack said in a panic.

"And they'll do the same to you, kid, if you let 'em."

A loud grinding sound drew their attention back to the car. As it bumped and rolled in the snowy gravel to the water's edge, it hit some large rocks that lined the shore, forcing it to the right, where a gap in the wooden dock caught the front right tire. The back wheels were still turning, spinning in a mixture of snow, loose stones, and gravel. A glimmer of hope rose in Jack and Scotty as the four gangsters trudged through the snow towards the stuck automobile. The older gentleman shouted and pointed, and the three others worked their way to the wedged car. Mahoney and one of the thugs pushed from behind while the largest man went to the edge of the dock, grabbed the front steel fender, and lifted. After several seconds of grunting and swearing from the men, the Model T lurched forward, hit the edge of the dock with a thud, and bounced down the rocks into the icy-cold river.

"No!" Jack began to yell before Scotty could cover his mouth with his hand. While the three other men stood at the shoreline brushing snow from their long overcoats and pant legs and watched the car slowly sink out into the water, the boss turned slowly towards a sound he thought he heard coming from the side of the building. Scotty's hand was still over Jack's mouth as they stood frozen before slowly backing into the shadow of the alcove. The restaurant's lone dim lamp hanging from above threw just enough light out to illuminate the older gentleman's face. Even though Jack was struggling with the shock of the events unfolding before his eyes, he recognized the face of the older gentleman instantly.

"Mr. St. Pierre?" he muffled loudly from under Scotty's gloved hand.

"We need to get outta here, kid," Scotty said, shaking him.

The Saint continued to look towards the building for several seconds before he turned, walked over to his men, pointed towards the restaurant, and ordered them to go and investigate. Scotty used the brief opportunity of St. Pierre's turned back to pull Jack quickly towards the front of the building and across the road.

At the same time that they were climbing into the car, Mahoney and the two others were following the fresh trail of footprints in the snow from the building's side door alcove back towards the street. As they rounded the front of the building, Scotty was nervously trying to shift into gear while Jack sat next to him silently in a state of shock. Just as the two big thugs heard the puttering car, spotted it across the street, and began running towards it with revolvers in hand, the car jolted forward. Spinning its back tires in the snow, it bounced clumsily over the low curb and the streetcar tracks before straightening and driving away from the gangsters down Sandwich Street.

When Mahoney and the two men met back up with St. Pierre, the boss was rattled. "Who in bloody hell was that?" he demanded.

"Don't know, boss. There were two of them." The Russian and Wolf were nodding in agreement. "We didn't get a good look. Couldn't even see the plate."

St. Pierre thought for a few moments while his anger subsided. "I hate goddamned loose ends." He looked at his men menacingly. "Who knew about this meeting? Did anyone let slip where they were going tonight?"

While the two large men shook their heads, Mahoney immediately thought about his conversation with Tommy McLuren hours earlier. Knowing the repercussions that confession would bring, he simply answered, "No, boss."

The Saint looked suspiciously at all three before giving them their orders. "You two. Take a ride and see if you can find them. The roads are empty tonight...maybe we'll get lucky. Call me if you have them." He turned to Mahoney. "You go make a call and find some of our coppers on duty tonight to call this in. We don't have time to wait for it to be found now. This thing's got to be an accident and wrapped up fast. Make sure they understand. Tell them if they do any serious digging, it's going to cost them. Got it?"

"Got it, boss," Mahoney answered, and they all headed towards their cars. As St. Pierre climbed into his luxury sedan on the other end of the lot, Mahoney pulled the other two men aside and altered their instructions. "When you're out looking, take a drive by Tommy McLuren's shop. You know the place, Wolf." The big Pole nodded, hesitantly. "Let me know if you see anything suspicious, like the kind of Ford we saw tonight, and if it's been on the road in the last half hour."

The men headed out of the lot while Seamus walked in the snow the short distance to his car. Along the way, he gave more thought to the situation. Nobody could have known about the meeting location tonight, not even McLuren, despite the earlier telephone conversation. The chances were good that the footprints belonged to a couple of people out for a joyride in the snow and stumbled upon the scene. If that was the case, Mahoney was very confident that nothing would come of it. Everyone in the area knew better than to get mixed up in anything that might be connected to local crime groups.

While Mahoney's people were leaving the scene of the crime, Jack was begging Scotty to return to it. "We've got to go help Pops. We can't just let him die there," he kept repeating, on the verge of hysterics. He was shaking, and the sweat and flowing tears made his anguished face shine in the intermittent lights hitting the vehicle. Scotty didn't need much convincing to go back and possibly help his friend. He drove west for a while, then turned down some side streets before curling back east towards the restaurant. As they slowly approached from a road that led right into the lot, the better visibility, as well as their car's headlamps, revealed that the dock area now appeared empty. Scotty slowed the car a good distance away in the darkness. He wanted to be sure they would be safe to approach. Jack could not wait. He jumped from his seat just before the car rolled to a stop and began running towards the intersection across from the lot. He had only taken a few frantic strides, struggling to keep his footing in the snow, when he suddenly slid to a halt. Scotty had just exited the vehicle to join him when he froze as well. They stood, looked at each other, and listened to the increasingly loud, wailing sound of an approaching police car using its hand-cranked siren. When the patrol car pulled into the restaurant lot and made its way back towards the docks, Scotty and Jack retreated to the car and watched anxiously.

"They're going to save him," Jack said with a weary smile, a glimmer of hope in his voice.

Scotty glanced over and then back out the front window. He did not share Jack's confidence. Scotty knew immediately that the quick police response, such a short time after the event, was not a good sign. "Something's not right, Jackie. This is not good," he said. "We're the only ones that know about this. They must have called the police themselves."

"Why would they do that? It doesn't make sense. Let's go talk to them . . . tell them what we saw." Jackie was confused and rambling. "Maybe we can help—"

Scotty dropped his head, feeling defeated and

helpless. He cut him off. "Don't ya see, kid? These cops are working for them."

Jack looked at Scotty, dazed and baffled, before looking back at the police, who were now standing in front of the patrol car's headlamps, talking and looking down towards the water's edge. "What are they doing? Why aren't they going in after him?"

Jack's eyes filled once again as he began to accept what he already knew. Through his sobs, he asked, "What if you're wrong, Scotty? What if they're the good guys?" Hands shaking, he grabbed the door handle to leave. "We know who they are. I want those bastards to pay."

Grabbing his opposite arm and looking at his best friend's son with tears forming in his own eyes, Scotty struggled to calm him. "Listen, kid! I'm sorry. I really am, but I need ya to think right now, Jackie. Think!" He slapped Jack across his wet cheek to get him to focus. The only light coming into the car was reflecting off the bright snow from a street lamp at the intersection. "What if you go over there and they're not on Mahoney's payroll? You report what we saw, right? Then what happens?" Jack's eyes dropped. Scotty didn't let him answer. "Then everything your dad worked for is for nothing, and the amazing father and war hero becomes another dead bootlegger in the news." Hearing the word "dead" caused Jack to start weeping uncontrollably again as the reality of the situation sunk in. "Then we're in trouble, too, because we were in on it. And your poor mother..." He waited to regain his attention. "And if the coppers do go after 'em, they'll have all kinds of fancy lawyers, and we'll need to be witnesses, and we'll be in danger." He paused while they stared out in horror at the officers still standing idly by, now sharing a laugh. "And that's if they're the good guys, kid," he continued, looking back over at Jack. "What if these coppers are on their payroll? We go out there and both of our lives, and our families, will be in danger. They would have to get rid of us, don't you see? It's your dad and my best friend. We've seen too much and—" The tragically surreal circumstances he was explaining suddenly gripped Scotty in despair, and he couldn't continue.

Next to him, Jack's eyes were wide, staring straight ahead. He rocked forward and back in his seat, his arms folded, trying to deal with the physical pain of the unbearable grief. "We have to do something," he moaned.

"We will, Jackie boy. That's a promise on my life." Scotty started the car, slowly pulled away, and headed towards home in agonizing silence.

PART 2

The best way out is always through.
ROBERT FROST

J ACK AND SCOTTY WERE SITTING IN THEIR SHARED OFFICE on a Friday evening, getting warm and enjoying a glass of whisky after a busy week of work. It was February 1930, only a few months since the good economic times of the 1920s had been brought to an abrupt, unexpected halt.

Months before, many investors and most businesses had watched their fortunes sink along with the stock prices on the market. Locally, nationally, and around the world, people who had amassed great wealth on paper watched helplessly as their fortunes faded, big companies and corporations lost the capital they relied on from investors, and a large portion of the working class saw their jobs disappear as businesses struggled or went under. The town of Ford City was representative of the economic decline. With depleting household incomes, demand for new automobiles dried up quickly. Ford Motor Company, the largest local employer, was forced to lay off or let go a large portion of its labour force. The resulting community decline was painfully gradual, like a tooth slowly decaying in a healthy mouth. Over time, fewer new automobiles were on the roads. Retail stores became less crowded, as did neighbourhood grocers, who were seeing more and more customers struggling to pay for their basic necessities, many eventually relying on government relief vouchers to put food on the table. For those who were able to hold on to their homes, keeping them updated was becoming more difficult; their chipped and fading exteriors, combined with overgrown gardens and lawns, pointed to the financial struggles within. The proud people of the town fought together to survive the downturn, but Ford City's amalgamation into Windsor in 1928 was the only thing that allowed the devastated town to avoid bankruptcy.

....

Fortunately for business partners Scotty and Jack, McLuren Paints in the heart of the town was insulated from the devastating economic downturn. Since Scotty's father had died three years earlier from a sudden heart attack brought on by a lethal combination of smoking, drinking, and unbearable regret, the paint shop had done very little actual painting. Just enough jobs were done each week to keep up a realistic façade. The bulk of the shop's income continued to be generated by one of the few enterprises that had proved depression-proof—the importation and distribution of illegal whisky. Their very successful but loathsome partnership with Mahoney's people, which now included the Quebec operation as well, continued after Moose's death.

To minimize risk, Scotty and Jack had only two young employees on the payroll. Joey McLuren was the

17-year-old son of Scotty's wayward brother, Junior, and the wife he'd managed to hold on to for a couple of years before she ended the abusive marriage. Joey wasn't built for physical labour. He was short for his age and so thin that his threadbare clothes just sort of hung off him. His difficult childhood in a dysfunctional environment made him desperate to get out and be given a chance to show he had some worth other than the wasted life his father had lived, dominated by unemployment, alcohol abuse, and petty crime. When his uncle Scotty offered him a job at the shop and a room in his home, Joey and his mother both jumped at the opportunity.

Jack and Scotty were thrilled to find out quickly that Joey's work ethic and reliability more than made up for his unusually slight stature. And the arrangement turned out to be a godsend for Scotty, as well. Young Joey gained some much-needed independence and was making an income for the family during tough economic times, while Scotty benefitted not only from a great employee, but from an injection of life and youthful energy into his lonely and depressingly quiet home. Within months of living and working together, they began forming a bond not unlike a father and son's.

Johnny Burns, the big, lumbering 18-year-old son of a Ducharme family friend, was Joey's sidekick at the shop. He came from a dirt-poor family that had only become poorer after the crash. Johnny wasn't very smart, but he was trustworthy, and his raw natural strength often came in handy. He and Joey both enjoyed working for their bosses and had no concerns about getting involved in the illegal liquor business. They knew they were very lucky to be earning a good, steady income when more and more working-class men of all ages around them were unemployed.

With his business degree, a reliable young workforce, a loyal partner with an inherited paint shop, a large customer base, and the protection that Mahoney and his people offered, Jack was now running a very lucrative enterprise. His impressive education and years of experience in the illegal liquor trade were proving invaluable. He was now 24 years old, but the trauma he had secretly endured over the circumstances of his father's death, along with the challenge of holding his grief-stricken family together afterwards, now gave him a maturity and seriousness that belied his age.

Light did break through the darkness, however. After over a year of dating a local girl whose family had emigrated from Italy after the Great War, Jack married Maria Dario in 1928. He and his young bride moved into a duplex just down the street from his mother and Annie. His proximity allowed him to fulfil his role as man of the house in both residences. A little more than a year later, they welcomed a healthy boy they aptly named Maurice, but lovingly referred to as "Little Mo." Like his father, Jack took to marriage and fatherhood naturally and was determined to give his young family the comfortable lifestyle that he had come to enjoy as a result his own father's risk-taking and hard work.

Jack's mother, Sara, was never the same after her husband's death. Although she remained a loving mother and constant companion and aide to Annie, and she revelled in being a granny to Little Mo, she now had an unshakable vacancy about her. Her adventuresome spirit and sense of humour died with Moose. What was left was a loving, dutiful, and faithful woman, but with a void that could never be filled.

Annie, now 19 years old, lived at home after graduating from her private school with honours. It gave her mother great pride that Annie forged a career as a private tutor for other blind children from all over the county, most of them from well-heeled families. With the severe economic downturn, however, the number of pupils and the number of hours she spent with them were decreasing, along with her clients' incomes. She inherited Sara's natural beauty, but her prospects for marriage were limited due to her disability, and after her father's tragic death she resigned herself to the reality that her place would forever be with her mother.

Three years earlier, in 1927, the provincial government had finally realized the futility of Prohibition. They saw the immense potential tax revenues being soaked up by growing organized crime groups, so they repealed the liquor laws and set rigid standards for the sale and distribution of alcohol within the province of Ontario. Unfortunately for the newly created Liquor Control Board and its local inspectors like Maxime Mousseau, black-market liquor and moonshine around the Windsor area were still a major problem,

and rum running actually became an even more lucrative industry because Michigan and the rest of the
United States were still dry. The repeal created a Wild
West atmosphere where everybody saw opportunity
selling marked-up Canadian liquor across the border.
The really big money was being made by only a handful of local players, however, and vicious turf battles
over territory often occurred.

It was in this climate of competition that Mahoney
demanded that Jack and Scotty reorganize the Skim
and Quebec operations they continued after Moose's
untimely death. Skim home delivery became unnecessarily risky with the repeal of the liquor laws, so the
Saint ordered it ended. Black-market Hiram Walker
whisky was still in high demand and was combined
with expanded importation of whisky and other spirits
from Quebec. Jack used his cousin, Alain, to organize
transportation of ever-increasing amounts of out-of-
province booze to their area, free from the control and
high taxes of the Ontario government. The paint-shop
yard, its chain-link fencing now lined with black tarp,
became a busy distribution hub. Liquor was brought
in, organized, stored, and prepared for runners to pick
up and deliver to local customers or, more commonly,
to the shoreline for transport across the Detroit River
or Lake St. Clair and into Michigan. In this way, St.
Pierre did like many successful businessmen: he diversified. He had his Walker liquor and all the related
operations that were under the costly protection and
watchful eyes of the Purple Gang in Detroit, but he
also had his Quebec operation, a profitable but much

more dangerous enterprise. The Saint knew better than anyone the potential cost of doing business behind the back of the Purples.

For Jack and Scotty, Skim never really ended. Using Jack's business savvy, they fine-tuned a system of minimizing graft at every level of the supply chain and pocketed it themselves. They negotiated lower bulk prices at the distilleries and breweries and cut costs wherever possible. This money, which was above and beyond the profits from selling their wholesale booze, was not recorded in their official ledgers, which Mahoney still demanded to see monthly. Over time, this money—which they fittingly continued to call "Skim" as a tribute to the man who started it all—grew into larger and larger amounts and was hidden away in a safe location that only the two of them knew about. Combined with the small fortune passed down from Moose's original operation years before, the partners had no concerns about their financial futures. They both looked forward anxiously, however, to a time when they could free themselves from the grip of the organization and the stresses of the illegal booze business, settle into legitimate careers, and enjoy the fortunes they had risked so much for.

Even though they were separated by a number of years and life experiences, a solid partnership and profound friendship developed between Jack and Scotty. Jack respected and looked up to Scotty like a big brother. Scotty saw a great deal of Moose's admirable qualities in his young partner. But their relationship went even deeper. They shared a common bond of love for a man they had both revered, as well as profound trauma and grief over the violent circumstances of his death. Scotty suffered through an extended period of indescribable anger and melancholy after the murder of his best friend, and he often felt deep regret over not attempting to save him when he had the chance. The effect on Jack was, not surprisingly, even worse. The combined factors of losing a father he loved and adored at such a young age, being an eyewitness to the crime, and feeling responsible because of his careless note keeping—along with the difficult challenge of having to keep the details of his father's death a secret—drove young Jack into an emotional tailspin. For several months, he drifted through stages of loneliness, depression, and seething rage. Forced to continue a working partnership with the source of all his pain, he found his situation almost unbearable.

Over time, Jack and Scotty learned to survive by helping each other through the darkest days, the days when they were suddenly overwhelmed by the immensity of the gaping hole in their lives that Moose's absence caused. Especially challenging were the days when business dictated that they couldn't avoid having to meet face-to-face with Mahoney. Thankfully, there was something that always helped during those most trying of times, another thing the two men shared: a deep-seated thirst for vengeance, no matter how long it took, no matter the cost. They vowed they were going to make Mahoney and St. Pierre pay for the loss of the most important person in their lives.

LONG WITH HIS IMMENSE BODY AND HAND-SOME FEATURES, including dark hair, dark eyes, and a chiselled jaw, Jack soon inherited his father's difficulty sleeping as well. Instead of the war memories and financial worries that so often kept Moose awake, his son's nightmares stemmed from the trauma of witnessing his father's murder.

Awake once again in the middle of a cold night in late February, Jack quietly made his way to the kitchen for a tea. He rarely had to worry about waking Maria. She slept soundly through almost anything, a trait that was thankfully passed down to their son. The winter wind was whistling outside as Jack buttoned up his favourite sweater. Settling into his well-worn armchair in the corner of the parlour, a space he used as his makeshift office, he began the ritual of trying to veer his thoughts away from the painful images that once again were racing through his mind. A few minutes of deep breathing, which began to relax him, ended abruptly as he spotted the article poking out from behind the grainy photograph of his father pinned on the wall beside him. Jack slipped the newsprint clipping out, clicked on the table lamp, and stared into the dark eyes of his father. The Border City Star news story, written two days after that traumatic night more than four years before, used a photograph of Moose, looking young and handsome in his army uniform before being shipped overseas. Fully aware of the emotional reaction it was going to illicit, Jack began to read through the article, as he so often did, looking for some form of catharsis that never came.

STORM LEADS TO DEATH OF LOCAL GRIDIRON STAR AND WAR HERO

The season's first snowstorm on Monday evening caused the tragic death of a local Ford City hero, police confirmed yesterday.

Maurice Ducharme, 39 years of age, of St. Luke Road, was a football star at Windsor Eagle Athletic Club from 1902–1905 and later a member of the 21st Regiment Essex Fusiliers during the Great War, where he was unofficially credited for conspicuous acts of valour.

Police report an automobile with his body in the driver's seat was found submerged in the water late Monday night along the Detroit River shoreline east of Walkerville. Further investigation revealed a significant head injury. This evidence, combined with the poor visibility and road conditions that evening, led police to classify the tragedy as a motorcar accident.

After serving in France and Belgium between 1915 and 1918, Mr. Ducharme spent many years in the employ of Walkerside Dairy Company on Argyle Street and was regarded fondly by colleagues and customers alike.

He was a parishioner of Our Lady of the Rosary Catholic Church.

Mr. Ducharme is survived by his wife, Sara, and two children, Jack, 18, and Anne-Marie, 14, as well as his parents, Henri and Marie Ducharme.

....

Once again, Jack flashed painfully back to the night of his father's murder. He remembered Scotty driving him home; he remembered walking into the house, wet, cold and in a state of shock. He threw off his coat, went straight to his bedroom, and closed his door, trying to conceal his condition and state of mind from his mother.

Seconds later, she rushed into his room to check on him. "Where have you been, Jackie? I've been worried sick." He lay on his bed with his back to her, shaking uncontrollably. She sat down next to him, put her hand on his shoulder, and asked in a calm, concerned tone, "What's wrong, dear? What's got you so worked up?"

With his chest tightened and having trouble catching his breath, Jack struggled to answer. Finally he was able to murmur, half into his pillow, "Pops is out there. I couldn't get to him, Ma."

"Oh, Jackie. It was just a storm, and it's over now," she assured him, baffled as to why he was so worried. "Your father has been out in far worse. He'll be home soon, you'll see." She stayed for a while with her hand rubbing his back. After some deep breaths, he fell into a more normal breathing pattern and appeared to have fallen asleep. She slipped out of the room with an unexplained anxiety building inside of her.

As night faded into early morning with no sign of her husband, Sara grew increasingly frantic and began thinking that Jack's concerns the night before might have been prophetic. After searching Moose's desk for numbers, she tried to call the only person she could think of, despite the ungodly hour. Her emotional state only worsened when Mahoney did not pick up. Soon their home became crowded with concerned family and friends. A very weary-looking Scotty was the first to arrive. Later, her parents, Moose's supervisor from the dairy, and a couple of concerned neighbours all gathered and tried to convince her and the kids that everything was going to be alright. Jack and Scotty sat together through it all, still in a state of shock, knowing it wouldn't.

The group grew uncomfortably quiet mid-morning as a police officer made his way up the snowy sidewalk to their front door. Jack was helping to hold his mother upright by her arm when they were given the news in the front hallway. The assembled group in the front parlour couldn't help but overhear, heads down and tears beginning to flow. Even though he knew the truth already, the officer confirming the news that morning gutted Jack all over again. He wanted to scream out, "I know who did it! I was there!" but he knew he couldn't. The risk to his freedom and possibly his life, not to mention his father's good name, was too great. Shaking uncontrollably with tear-filled eyes, his mother begged the officer for an explanation, and he coldly provided limited details. Slippery roads. Poor visibility. Possibly speed. Motorcar sank in the river. The officer waited a few seconds to add one more detail while looking squarely at Jack, emotionless. "There was also an empty liquor bottle found in the automobile, ma'am. But we're going to keep that out of the papers. Just thought you should know."

Jack remembered seeing his mother's eyes turn from profound sorrow to utter confusion with that piece of information. "But...Maurice didn't drink, at least not like..." she struggled to explain.

After a few moments of awkward silence, the officer put his hat back on and tipped it in Sara's direction, then turned to leave, repeating, "Just thought you should know, ma'am."

At that time, Jack couldn't imagine that his hatred for Mahoney and St. Pierre could have grown any more intense, but this little extra twist of the knife was unbearable. Despite the fragile emotional state they were in, Jack and Scotty both realized immediately that the liquor bottle was an insurance policy against the family's demanding a more thorough and public investigation from police who they knew were being paid to bury the incident. They knew nobody would dare tarnish the memory of Maurice Ducharme.

The visitation and funeral mass days later were well attended and befitting the great man that his father was, but Jack, along with his mother and Annie, wandered through the formalities in a suspended state of shock and disbelief. Mahoney's brief presence at the wake was understandable given the work relationship with his father, both real and fictitious, but Jack slipped out of the room while Mahoney was paying his respects to the widow, aware how difficult it would be to mask the rage festering inside him.

Jack and Scotty struggled to contain their rancor the following day at the funeral mass when they spotted Mr. St. Pierre in the congregation. His presence, strongly encouraged by Mahoney, was not unexpected from a sympathetic fellow parishioner after such a tragedy. Sara's mother made the esteemed community member's attendance even more painful for Jack when she saw the well-dressed gentleman and whispered a little too loudly to her daughter before the service, "Oh, look, dear. William St. Pierre is here. What a kind gesture. He did say he really liked your Maurice."

The only light moment during those darkest of days happened at the beginning of the funeral mass. While most of the people waited solemnly inside the warmth of Our Lady of the Rosary, the immediate family and pallbearers were outside standing in the freezing winds whipping off the river, readying for what Jack felt was an unnecessarily morbid procession into the church. The large, dark casket was rolled from the hearse parked along the curb out front, and the pallbearers positioned themselves beside it. But when the six men went to lift, there was a collective grunt. Even though the under-taker had removed Moose's shoes to squeeze his long frame into the modest casket Sara had insisted on, his planning hadn't taken into consideration the potential strain on those having to carry such a load. They strug-gled up the curb and shuffled precariously through the slippery slush and ice to the foot of the steep, winding stairs. While all six gazed up at the prospect with a look of awkward concern, Jack could not help but find the scene amusing. Thankfully, a funeral-home employee at the top of the stairs quickly assessed and solved the problem by enlisting the help of two very large former football teammates of Moose's from the back of the church. They each took an end and helped the other six struggle to the top. Jack's anguish returned full force, however, when he saw Scotty at the top of the stairs, in full dress Empire uniform, saluting, his eyes red and brimming with tears. Once they were beside the casket trolley and inside the church entranceway, the eight men needed a moment to catch their breaths and use their handkerchiefs to wipe their brows before the ser-vice could begin.

....

In the weeks that followed, the family tried to settle into some kind of normalcy despite the gaping hole in their lives. Annie reluctantly returned to school to finish out her term, and Jack had no difficulty convincing Walker-side to let him take over his father's milk route. The loyal customers, many of whom came to the funeral, were devastated by the news, but also secretly relieved to find out that the Skim operation would continue.

At the next end-of-month collection at the garage, several weeks later, Mahoney was all business. Jack found it almost impossible to be in the same room, let alone look at the man, afraid he would reveal the venom held deep inside. He got through those visits by avoiding eye contact and busying himself while his boss went over the books. It was similarly painful when the family joined his mother and grandmother for Sunday mass and Jack was forced to stare at the back of the esteemed and dapper Mr. St. Pierre. "A wolf in sheep's clothing," he often thought. The vivid thoughts of violent retribution that built up inside him while in a place of love and worship caused so much inner turmoil that he would at times become physically ill—dizzy, shaking, and sweating.

....

Considering the unexpected circumstances, it was a blessing that Jack's father had given him equal control and signing authority on the multiple banking and investment accounts that had been created with the Skim proceeds. Jack remembered the pride he had felt when his father informed him of his new authorizations, shook his hand, and told him that he was now a full business partner.

The amount of money in the accounts surpassed anything Jack could have imagined. Clearly his father could not have spent most of it without drawing the attention of authorities, or even worse, his wife, so most of the money sat untouched, earning interest. And unlike most of the *nouveau riche* of the 1920s, Moose was uncomfortable investing too heavily in stocks, so the sudden market collapse in 1929 had minimal negative impact on his wealth. Jack had felt then—and still did, despite the emotional trauma he experienced—a great sense of relief and gratitude that his family would never have to struggle financially.

As time went on, Jack slowly climbed out of the dark days of grief and anger by embracing the love of family and friends, as well as focusing his energy on three critical goals: to be a model partner and employee, avoiding any conflict with Mahoney and his people; to be vigilant, remaining one step ahead of the police and liquor inspectors when doing business; and, most importantly, to be patient and look for the perfect opportunity to exact vengeance on Mahoney and St. Pierre.

THE SAINT OFTEN FELT THE NEED TO REMIND THOSE ON HIS PAYROLL, especially Seamus Mahoney, that they were indebted to him for the organization's success and for the comfortable lifestyles they all enjoyed. But the truth was that other than his proclivity to dress in expensive suits when doing business, Mahoney lived very modestly. Like everything else he did, this was calculated. Unlike St. Pierre and others in their employ, he was keenly aware of the unwanted attention conspicuous wealth could bring, so he lived alone in a small, run-down home several blocks from his boss and drove an older-model Packard. Although he had a sizeable bank account and some investments, his paranoia, combined with his lack of trust in any institution and people in general, caused him to keep the bulk of his wealth in cash. Large bundles were stacked in a simple cardboard box in his basement, not far from where he kept his organization's ledger books. The only entry to the basement was through a heavily fortified steel door, secured with a padlock, whose only key was always hanging around Mahoney's neck.

Even though he lived meagrely, Mahoney liked money as much as the next guy—even more, considering he'd grown up a dirt-poor orphan. His mother had died of tuberculosis not long after he was born and his father, an abusive drunk, had died in a street fight when he was only six. An estranged uncle, seeing an opportunity for cheap labour, had taken him in, not sparing the rod when demanding hard work both on the farm and in his schoolwork. Young Seamus Mahoney had excelled in mathematics. When he was 17 years old and had had enough indentured servitude and abuse, he ran off. His toughness, street smarts, and bookkeeping skills gave him the opportunity he needed in town with a budding local gangster named William St. Pierre. His timing was perfect, rising up the ranks as demand for illegal liquor became big business with the onset of Prohibition.

Mahoney's natural good looks and the expensive, stylish clothes he liked to wear made him popular among the ladies he met while on the streets or working with St. Pierre. Most were prostitutes or women who were willingly passed around among wealthy gangsters. Others were flappers, independent-minded young women, restlessly looking for their next fix of booze and a good party. Although he took full advantage of such opportunities, he really only ever had romantic interest in one stunning and bright young woman he met when he was 21. She was the daughter of a business associate of St. Pierre's, and she showed initial interest in him until her father ordered her to keep her distance. Unfortunately for the father, Mahoney overheard him when he ordered her to "stay away from those greasy gangsters, darling. They're good to make an easy buck, but they're not the kind of people you want to associate with." The insult cut him to the core, partly because he knew it would end his chances with the young beauty, but mostly because he knew the warning was true. Instinctively, Mahoney sought retribution by leaking her father's illegal financial dealings to the right sources, and within six months he was struggling to stay in business and out of jail. Over time, Mahoney resigned himself to his work and convinced himself that marriage would not be compatible with his profession or lifestyle. His occasional physical needs were fulfilled by well-paid, high-class professionals who didn't stick around until morning and knew the risks if they didn't keep their mouths shut.

Today, Mahoney knew something important was happening. It was the second week of May, and the bright morning sun hinted that summer was on its way. Instead of sitting and enjoying a coffee in the warmth of the sun streaming through his back kitchen window, however, Mahoney was rushing out the door, late. The Saint had ordered him to gather the ledgers and join him for an important meeting. As a rule, he tried to avoid having the books with him unless absolutely necessary. The details in them were enough to send him and the Saint away for a very long time. The thought of having all of them in his possession today was already making him unusually jumpy. He quickly made his way to retrieve the black leather briefcase from its secure location in his dingy basement fortress, headed outside to his car in the backyard detached garage, and sped away.

"I've decided on some operational changes," the Saint announced abruptly as a greeting when Mahoney walked in. He sat down across from his impatient boss at a large wooden table in the basement of a local banquet hall that they controlled. For meetings of this importance, especially with the incriminating records involved, the Saint liked this location because the labyrinth of various-sized rooms made a raid difficult, and its many exterior doors made for a quick and easy exit. The Wolf and the Russian, still on the organization's payroll, were strategically positioned outside for security.

As Mahoney opened his briefcase and began taking out the ledgers, he asked, "And what changes are you proposing, Saint?"

"Let me ask you," his boss began. "With this huge market opened up across the river, where can we expand? How can we get a bigger slice?"

"Well, we both know that will be difficult . . . and dangerous," Mahoney answered. "The Purples are controlling most of that action. We'd have to sit down with them and—"

"You see!" The Saint raised his voice, cutting Mahoney off. "It's those bloody Jew gangsters. We pay them for Walker connections and dock operations over here. We pay them to move product over there. And with more and more of their Jew pirates on the water, we're even paying them with stolen product."

"What are you suggesting, boss? We can't go to war with them. We wouldn't last a day," Mahoney warned.

Looking ahead, straight through Mahoney, St. Pierre calmed down and responded, "No. No. We wouldn't, would we?" He thought some more. "But I'm getting goddamned good and tired of always paying and getting less and less return."

Mahoney had heard this song before. "We could ask for a sit down with one of the Bernsteins and try to negotiate a better deal. Maybe ask to have his boys keep their hands off our shipments," he suggested.

St. Pierre's eyes narrowed and focused back on Seamus. "Think, you dumb Mick!" he shouted, agitated once again. "They're not supposed to know about some of those shipments! The Quebec ones. They find out about those, we're done." Raising his hand to stop Seamus from speaking, he took a few seconds to settle again before he explained his plans. "I've been thinking about changes, and they both involve Quebec." Mahoney searched, found the right ledger book on the table, and located a pen while listening. "First, we need to take full control of it. We have to get rid of those two fellas. Not the same way as we did that Moose fella. Something different. If they're out of the picture, we get rid of the added costs and can set our own price with the suppliers." Mahoney had his eyes and his pen on the book in front of him, but he was cringing at what he was hearing and unsure what to write. Head still down, his eyes came up and looked across at his boss, concerned about this new plan of action. St. Pierre continued.

"Second, we set up a whole new distribution system into Detroit. Bypass the fucking boats. They're too damn costly. We can use the bridge now. Get creative with the shipments. Pay off the border people." Mahoney started jotting notes. "I've even thought about reaching out to Diesbourg in Belle River. 'King Canada,'" he sneered. "Maybe we could have him move our stuff across in his airplane, too, like he does for the Purples and Capone . . . like a side deal. It would be good for both of us." The Saint paused, waiting for a reaction.

"Are you talking about keeping all this out of the Purple's reach?" Mahoney wanted to know.

His boss looked at him and nodded, somewhat hesitantly. "That's what I was thinking."

Mahoney always struggled to be the voice of restraint and reason with his boss, so he was quiet, thinking carefully about how he was going to respond. After some consideration, he said, "Well, boss, while those changes will definitely bring in a good deal more dough, they will also increase our risk considerably. We don't like risk. We've always done better expanding when we put that on someone else." He thought for a few moments. "Taking the Quebec operation over wouldn't be too difficult. McLuren and Ducharme are nothing. Patsies. They would fold easy and probably not talk, but I could see problems with taking them both out. Why make a mess when we can keep it clean?" St. Pierre's expression showed at least he was weighing another option. "As far as turning to land transport across the bridge, that's going to take some planning and some big up-front costs." He paused again, choosing his words carefully. "And the idea of reaching out to Diesbourg in Belle River? The ties seem pretty tight to the Purples. That seems like a huge risk that could backfire. You know how that surly bastard feels about us."

St. Pierre digested the response. He hadn't gotten where he was without making bold moves and taking a risk here and there, but on the other hand, his success over the last number of years also was due, in great part, to listening to Mahoney, who considered every angle before making calculated moves. "So how can we do this with less risk?" he asked.

The two sat quietly, Mahoney gently tapping his pen on the page in front of him and St. Pierre looking up and out the basement window, watching the Wolf's legs pace back and forth outside near the back entranceway. Mahoney suddenly broke the silence with a question. "What if we put all the risk on our two Quebec boys?" This name that they'd given Jack and Scotty was being used more and more recently because of their connection to the out-of-province liquor. Without moving his head, St. Pierre's eyes shifted back across the table. "If you can live with them still running the operation, we could lean on them heavy to expand," Mahoney went on. "Make them start using the bridge with their delivery trucks from Quebec. Avoid the boats. We could also make arrangements for them to meet King and make an offer."

He had his boss's attention. "If it all works out, we make more money and expand our market. If the

Purples get wise, we give the two of them up and let them take the fall. We say we weren't involved, that they were making a play behind our backs. Then they'll be taken out, which you wanted to do anyway." He paused. "Sacrificial lambs, like in that Bible of yours," Mahoney added with a sly smile. While the satisfied look on St. Pierre's face told his partner that his idea had hit the mark, Mahoney couldn't help but feel that he always seemed to be saving his boss from himself and the way he conducted business.

....

Even though they were successful partners in crime, there was very little in common between St. Pierre and Mahoney, both in personality and in background. Mahoney was calm, calculating, and pragmatic, while his boss was anxious, impulsive, and often illogical. Growing up, Mahoney had endured the tragedy, struggle, and abuse of an orphan being raised by a virtual stranger and the unforgiving streets, while St. Pierre was born into a life of wealth and privilege, enjoying all the advantages afforded the upper crust of society in the second half of the 19th century.

William St. Pierre's father had French bloodlines, but married well into an English aristocratic family in Toronto who were making a fortune on land speculation in a rapidly growing city. The elder St. Pierre stepped seamlessly into his in-laws' family business and made his own fortune. He and his wife had two children, William being the younger, but their lifestyle and social calendar afforded little time for their children, who were raised by nannies and domestics.

When young William graduated from a private boarding school at age 17, he left the Toronto area unceremoniously to make his own mark in the real estate world with little more than a handshake and a generous amount of seed money from his father. He chose the Windsor and Walkerville area, where a successful distillery and expanding industries were increasing the demand for property. At the age of 19, he married a young woman from a well-heeled family in what was more like a well-executed business deal rather than the result of attraction, romance, or love.

Throughout his twenties and thirties, St. Pierre positioned himself socially with local wealth and power. When the Great War required the sacrifice of so many young Canadian men in 1914, he was already in his forties and was quite happy to be considered too old to enlist.

St. Pierre liked his drink and loathed the growing Temperance movement that had begun in the region and across the country many years before, but he came to realize that political pressure to outlaw alcohol could provide a very profitable business opportunity. So in 1916, when the Province of Ontario officially prepared to bring in Prohibition laws, he already had a basic structure in place for the illegal delivery, distribution, and sale of marked-up Hiram Walker whisky in local establishments. Then he used his liquor profits to secure his dominance of the local real-estate market. As both enterprises grew larger and more profitable, St. Pierre began buying off local authorities and bringing in characters of every sort to work at every level of his expanding organization. He eventually struck up a mutually beneficial working relationship with a large and violent group of criminals from across the river called the Purple Gang. Although St. Pierre would never admit it, bringing Seamus Mahoney into the fold in 1918 to manage the ever-expanding operations was critical for turning a wide variety of profitable, albeit disorganized, enterprises into an impressive local empire.

Having never been shown true affection or love when he was younger, St. Pierre was ill equipped to form any loving relationships as an adult. His wife tolerated his indifference and occasional drunken abuse because she enjoyed the social standing and lavish lifestyle he provided her. The fact that they were childless prompted a good deal of talk, but it was no surprise considering the absence of intimacy that began immediately after their wedding.

And unlike so many of the power brokers he knew and looked up to, who used their money and influence to indulge themselves in a variety of extramarital sexual escapades, St. Pierre remained, for the most part, asexual. Not consorting with the women who could be made available to him had the unintended benefit of helping St. Pierre successfully live the double life that helped insulate him. The only passionate longings he ever experienced—but never dared act upon, knowing the social repercussions—involved handsome, well-dressed young men who smelled of wealth and power.

St. Pierre had many employees, business acquaintances, neighbours, and fellow parishioners, but no true friends. The older he got, the more the Saint convinced himself that he didn't want or need to be loved or even liked—just feared.

Now, ten years after they first met, St. Pierre and Mahoney were settled into a very successful, albeit unlikely and tenuous, partnership. They didn't like each other, but they needed each other.

19

NSPECTOR MOUSSEAU WASN'T NAÏVE ENOUGH TO BELIEVE that when the provincial Prohibition laws were repealed in 1927, his job would get any easier. In fact, in many ways, his job was tougher now than ever before. Enforcing the many rules regarding distribution and consumption of alcohol seemed more difficult than enforcing an outright ban. Making the situation next to impossible was the continued Prohibition in the United States. That ever-increasing demand swelled just across a narrow river, now spanned by the new Ambassador Bridge above and the even newer motorcar tunnel below. Rum running across the border was at a fever pitch by 1930, and Mousseau was well aware that current estimates put eighty percent or more of that activity in his area. Illegal liquor flowed into the States across the Detroit River, Lake Erie, and Lake St. Clair. And it wasn't just the big boys anymore. Mousseau was getting increasingly frustrated with the number of average citizens, men and women alike, who were lured into making a quick buck by transporting booze in more and more creative ways. But the small timers weren't the ones involved in extortion, prostitution, gambling, and murder. Such scourges of society were caused by the cancer of organized crime in the area, and almost all of those gangs had some connection to the notorious Purple Gang in Detroit. These local groups and the gangsters they worked for were the people Mousseau and his men used their limited resources and time to go after.

On the top of that list was a local organization he had been after for many years, but one he could never bring down because of a lack of concrete evidence. He knew the face of the group was still Seamus Mahoney, but even after almost a decade, Mousseau still didn't know the person who was really in charge—the one who was pulling the strings. Raids and investigations continued to yield very little. The inspector was well aware that many local police officers were still on the take and that any street-level players they arrested would refuse to talk.

Five years before, Mousseau thought he finally had an opportunity to put Mahoney and his people away for good. He was sure that the death of Maurice Ducharme, a well-known and well-liked local war veteran, was caused by his involvement with Mahoney. The police were uncooperative, however, and labelled the death an accident, quickly closing the investigation. He had even warned Ducharme that he was in over his head, but like so many others, Ducharme claimed he wasn't involved. Now, years later, he was sure that Ducharme's son was working with the same group, and this provided some hope for a new opportunity to get at Mahoney.

Finding Jack Ducharme was easy: his residence was only a few houses away from his mother's, and he walked between them a couple of times each day. Some digging revealed that Jack continued his father's milk delivery route for a couple of years after Mr. Ducharme's untimely death, but was now using his business education to help run a local paint shop. One of Mousseau's men who surveilled the property for days reported the paint shop to be somewhat suspect, given that vehicles of every size and purpose came and went throughout the average day, but very few looked to have benefitted from a fresh paint job.

After walking around the shop property himself on a drizzly, warm Friday in May, Mousseau decided it was time to pay the younger Ducharme a visit. Walking into the front doors of McLuren Paints, he was met with the distinct smell of industrial paint and solvents. With no one at the front desk, Mousseau felt justified in poking his head around corners and looking through door windows.

"Can I help you, sir?" A voice came from behind him as he was looking down a long hallway towards an office.

"Uh, yes," Mousseau responded, unrattled. "I'm looking for Jack Ducharme. I understand he runs this place."

"We both do, sir. I'm Scotty," he limped over and extended his hand. "Scotty McLuren. Who's asking for him?"

This point in every unannounced visit Mousseau made involved a calculated risk. He could lie, pretend to be an ordinary citizen, and see if he could get information through casual conversation. On the other hand, flashing an inspector's badge gave him the chance to watch closely for a telling reaction. The approach he was going to use was almost always decided upon once he sized up the person who greeted him. This McLuren fellow was getting the badge. "I'm Inspector Mousseau from the Ontario Liquor Control Board," he said as he flashed his credentials.

"Nice to meet you, Mr. Mousseau," Scotty replied with no discernible change in his demeanour. "I think I've seen you in the Star. Going after the gangsters, are you? That must be exciting stuff, I bet?"

Mousseau was thrown off by the casual, unexpected friendliness. In his experience, even citizens who had done nothing wrong, or had no connection to running booze, would tense up and get a little nervous talking to him. He took a few moments, wondering if this McLuren was just not bright enough to understand the situation, had nothing to do with illegal liquor and therefore had no concerns, or was just a really smooth operator. "Not as exciting as it sounds, unfortunately. We just try to protect the community from the evils of liquor." Looking around, he added, "Is Mr. Ducharme here?"

"He is. Let me go see if he can talk. He gets in his books and loses himself sometimes," Scotty said, limping towards the hallway.

Watching his gait curiously as he walked away, Mousseau asked, "Bum leg, Mr. McLuren?"

"The Huns took a piece of it in '17," he answered out of habit. He paused slightly before opening the door, not sure if that was information he wanted to share. As the door closed behind Scotty, the inspector was satisfied to confirm what he had already suspected: a war connection between this McLuren and the deceased Maurice Ducharme fellow.

Before going to their shared office, Scotty poked his head onto the shop floor and asked big Johnny to keep the inspector company at the front counter. "And don't get chatty. Just pretend like you got some sort of business up there. Don't let him poke around. And you don't know nuthin'. You just work here painting cars. Got it?"

The young man nodded his understanding as Scotty headed to the office. He walked in and closed the door behind him, causing Jack to look up from his books. "You got a visitor, partner," Scotty said. "Liquor agent. The big gun, Mousseau."

Jack dropped his pen, leaned back in his chair and considered the situation. "How did you play it?" he asked.

"Nice as pie. Told him I think his job is really somethin'. I played it real dumb and innocent."

"Good," Jack said. "He doesn't have a warrant or anything, does he?"

"Nah, looks like he's just fishin'. Probably wants to get a feel for the place," Scotty offered. "We don't have much stuff here now, anyway, and it's tucked away good. If he had a warrant, he woulda showed me."

Jack considered the situation. Mousseau was well known by runners in the area, and Jack's father had told him many times about the inspector and his unrelenting perseverance. The truth, the older Ducharme explained to his son, was that Mousseau was smart and probably knew all about the people and operations he was investigating, but was handicapped by authorities who were on the take, so he had trouble getting solid evidence to make arrests. "We're not going to help him, either, Jackie boy," his father would say.

The memory of his father stirred up the same emotions it always did. Jack shook off the approaching gloom, put both hands on his desk, and stood. "Well, we knew this visit was coming eventually. It's probably time, don't you think, partner?" He made his way slowly to the door, grasped the knob, and looking back, said, "Let me go see if he can maybe help us." As Jack headed through the door, Scotty's look gave away his concern.

"Well, hello, Inspector," Jack welcomed Mousseau as he walked into the front of the shop.

"Mr. Ducharme," he responded with a handshake. "I wonder if I can take a few minutes of your time?"

"Sure. That would be fine. Please, call me Jack. What can I help you with?" he asked.

The inspector knew this meeting was going to require a special touch. Here was a respectable, well-educated young man who he was sure had been involved in moving liquor with his father, a man Mousseau was convinced had been murdered by the very people his son was now in business with. A unique case indeed. He decided on being brief and direct.

"I'm going to save us both a lot of time and trouble, Jack," Mousseau said, pausing and searching for the right words. "I know that your father was running liquor with Mahoney and his boys, and I know you were, or still are, involved." Jack's expression did not change. "And I know the business has expanded somehow beyond local suppliers, but I don't know how. I also believe that your father's tragic accident was no accident, and that you might know that as well." He waited for a reaction and noticed Jack's eyes get a little misty. He continued. "But I have very little interest in you and your partner, Jack. Our interest lies in Mahoney and especially his boss, the one heading the whole operation. We want them so bad that we'd be willing to make a special deal with you and your partner that would help us achieve that. And I'm thinking you just might like to see them taken down as well and pay for what they did."

Jack was silent, listening carefully.

"So what will it be?" the inspector continued. "Am I going to spend my valuable time tailing you and your partner, talking to your family and friends, and work on getting a warrant to bust up your operation, or will you take the opportunity to get away clean while you can and allow us to get at the people who were probably involved in your father's death?"

Mousseau knew what to expect. Denial. Ignorance. "Thanks inspector, but . . . " Jack's answer shocked him, however.

"We'd like to take that opportunity," Jack said, "but it has to be on our terms and timeline."

Mousseau was so thrown off balance that he was momentarily speechless. "You...you want to help?"

"We want to do more than that, Inspector. My partner and I can hand you Seamus Mahoney and his boss, whom we know, on a silver platter. But we need to do it our way and at the right time."

Instincts told Mousseau that he was being played. This was too good to be true. He needed some assurances and some deadlines. "Well, that's good. Very good. And I'm willing to work with you and your partner, who I'm assuming is the McLuren fellow I just met." Jack's reaction confirmed his suspicion. "But how do I know you fellas can be trusted, Jack? I need some guarantees."

Jack looked around nervously, lowered his voice, and finished with, "You don't, Mr. Mousseau. I have nothing to give you but my word and my partner's word." He thought for a moment. "But it's the word of two people who have been looking to get out for a while, and who have vowed to see these bastards pay for what they did. What we're asking for is a little time and cooperation to let us work on a plan and get out clean."

Inspector Mousseau was so far outside his comfort zone with the direction of this conversation that his head was reeling. Under normal circumstances, he would never consider taking the word of a bootlegger or agreeing to such a deal. But other feelings at play, besides this young man's apparent sincerity, struck a deep chord in Mousseau. Not only were Jack's grandparents transplanted Quebecers like himself, but the inspector's mother also happened to be a Ducharme. They were no relation, according to the research he'd done, but still, it softened something in him. "Patience I have, Jack. I've been working for years to get at these fellas," Mousseau said. "Trust is something else entirely."

"From where I'm sitting, Inspector, you don't have many options if you want the big players. We know who and where they are," Jack assured him. "Just give us a couple of months to make sure we can get what you need to bring them down and also keep ourselves and our families safe."

Mousseau knew Jack was right. He gave the proposition some thought. "What if I gave you until the first of July?" he responded. "That gives you almost seven weeks." He reached into his pocket and gave Jack a small card. Eyeing him with both sympathy and suspicion, he added, "Here's my personal number, son. Call it anytime you can give me developments. I'm going to give you fellas some space. But if at any time up to that point I think we are being played, I'm coming after you, your partner, and this shop with everything I have. I don't take kindly to being made a fool, you understand?"

Jack looked him in the eyes, trying unsuccessfully to mask his sudden anxiety. "Understood," he said as he shook the inspector's hand and turned back towards his office.

FOR YEARS JACK HAD WATCHED HIS FATHER STRUGGLE with the stress of keeping his clandestine business dealings a secret from his wife. He decided early, even before he married Maria, that he was going to be honest with her despite the possible repercussions. It was with great relief, then, one evening years ago after a dinner at his then-girlfriend's house, when Mr. Dario sat Jack down to share some homemade grappa and hear his incredible story, almost all of it translated by his daughter. The potent homemade liquor, combined with the several glasses of wine he'd had with dinner, made Maria's father very talkative and animated as he told stories about his former life in Italy. Some of it Maria was hearing for the first time; she asked lots of questions.

Jack did his best to appear to be enjoying the toxic drink he was sipping as Mr. Dario reminisced fondly about his childhood and coming of age in Italy towards the end of the last century. Like so many others in their tiny village in Sicily, the Darios were a large, loving, and close-knit family who thrived despite poverty, political upheaval, and the ever-present organized crime in their area. Maria's grandfather was an olive farmer, and other than his involvement in olive-oil sales to criminals on the black market, he avoided direct involvement with the gangs. Enrico, his eldest son, did not.

Even though Enrico Dario was speaking in Italian, Jack could feel the sense of regret in his voice as he described how as a boy he was a disappointment to his parents because he did very poorly in school and showed no interest in the family olive farm. Like so many other boys his age, he watched the young men of the powerful crime gangs, the Cosa Nostra, parade around his village with swagger and confidence, wearing nice clothes and jewellery, with pretty girls on their arms and guns on full display. His first involvement in the group was as a spotter to warn of the presence of the local *polizia*. Later, his role within the organization grew. As she translated, Maria's eyes widened occasionally as he described his participation in what he called *alcune cose molto brute*—some very bad things. She appeared somewhat bewildered at one point as she turned to Jack and said, "This was when I was just a little girl."

Dario went on to explain that although he avoided any trouble with the police, as he climbed the ranks of the organization, rivalries and conflicts arose between some members. He told them about one man in particular who was jealous of his growing influence and who had tried to set him up to get killed. When Dario confronted him and challenged him as a matter of honour, serious threats were made to Dario's young family.

When Dario discussed the danger his family was in at that time, the energy and tone in his voice changed dramatically. Collecting himself, he sat up straight, took a deep breath, turned towards Jack, and in his limited English said, "We comma here to starta new." Recounting the past, some of it dark, while answering his daughter's many questions, all while under the influence, tired the middle-aged gentleman out. With a weary smile and sigh that signalled he was finished, he gulped down the last of his drink, ran his hand down his daughter's long hair, stood, and abruptly excused himself for the night.

Jack watched him leave the room, enthralled by Enrico's story and disappointed that it had ended so suddenly. He turned back to Maria and begged her for more details.

"As it was explained to me, Poppa was like most men in the village," she said. "They did what they had to do to make money. Anybody who said no to those people or, God forbid, reported them to the police, weren't around very long. You have to understand, Jackie, involvement meant survival."

"So what happened with this enemy of his? Why did your father have to leave?" he asked.

"Momma told me once about the threat made to his life. She said that Poppa wanted to confront him man to man, but when he found out that his whole family had a price on their heads, too, he gathered up all the cash he had, and with the help of a good friend, snuck out of town one night with all of us and booked steam passage from Palermo. I don't remember all the details, but I remember the long boat ride."

"So he was a hero? Saving all of you."

"No," Maria responded with tears forming in her eyes. She reached for Jack's hand, causing his pulse to quicken. "He's always seen himself as a coward. In that culture, one of *l'uomo duro*, the tough man, sneaking away was considered cowardly. He wanted to stay and fight, even if it meant dying. But he had to swallow his pride to save his family."

Jack was as mesmerized by her exotic beauty as he was by her amazing family story. He caressed her hand, and they both leaned in for a brief but passionate kiss. Feeling emboldened by her father's story and the connection to his own situation working with local criminals, he asked, "So the regret I saw tonight isn't about any crimes he might have been involved in? It's only about the damage to his pride and being considered a coward?"

"That's right, as strange as it sounds. You see, Jackie, to Poppa, a man is someone who provides for and protects his family, no matter the risks," Maria said, adding, "But he's got a whole new life here with us and some of his friends who came from the old country. Some of them lived a similar life with those gangs in Sicily . . . now they're just memories that are whispered about over morning espresso or afternoon vino down in Little Italy."

Mr. Dario's story was a lot for Jack to take in, but he realized that it was the perfect opportunity to come clean about his own situation, the group he was involved in, how he was brought into the illegal business by his own father, and how he wanted desperately to get out. As he held her hand and explained his present situation in detail, Maria's expression never changed. He looked towards the floor with a hint of shame and finished with, "I don't want to be a criminal any more, Maria."

Smiling and bringing her other hand to wrap around his, she responded with, "What is a criminal, Jackie? The government sells booze now that was illegal a few years ago. Are they criminals? My father makes his own wine and grappa down in our basement. Is he a criminal? What about the rich people who live in luxury off the backs of the poor or the immigrants? Aren't they criminals?" She stopped, looked down, and seemed to be gathering her thoughts. Her eyes suddenly opened wide and came up again to meet his. "Jackie, did your father's death have anything to do with the people you were doing business with?"

Jack didn't have to respond. His eyes lowering again and his shoulders slumping told her all she needed to know.

Still holding his hand, Maria leaned out of her seat and wrapped Jack in such a loving embrace that he started to weep. "Shh, shh," she whispered in his ear.

Despite the sudden rush of emotion, Jack realized right then and there that he was going to marry this girl. She clearly loved him, understood his situation without passing judgment, and now was the only one other than Scotty who knew the truth about his father's death. Collecting himself after a few moments, he wiped his eyes and looked into hers. "You can't say anything to anyone, Maria. Nobody but Scotty and I know." He took a deep breath and added, "We were there."

Maria pulled him back into her. "Oh, Jackie. How terrible." After some time of blissful contact and silence, Jack's tear-filled eyes opened suddenly over her shoulder when Maria said, without emotion, "I hope you're going to make them pay for what they did."

....

The week after Mousseau's visit, Mahoney was in Jack and Scotty's office going over the books for the month. As always, he spent several minutes with his head down, going over every line. These times were the most difficult for Jack. As he stared at the top of his neatly combed head each month, he often fantasized about crashing heavy objects over it, using a knife to slit his throat from behind, or his favourite, using a lamp or telephone cord to strangle him slowly while he explained why he was exacting his revenge. He knew, of course, that he wasn't a killer and that should he kill Mahoney, the Saint would inevitably rain down swift, vicious retribution that would almost certainly include his family. The only thing that made these visits bearable was the thought of the vengeance that had been planned and was presently in the works.

On this particular visit, at the end of May, Mahoney wanted to meet with both Jack and Scotty after finishing with the books. Scotty was rounded up out in the yard, came in, and sat in a folding chair because

Mahoney was in his desk chair and showed no intention of giving it up. Mahoney loved those little displays of power. The alpha male, Jack thought to himself with disgust. Once Scotty settled in, Mahoney began. "Gentlemen, our boss has decided to make some changes in our operations, ones that will give us more of a market share and protect more of our product."

Jack and Scotty looked briefly at each other, both concerned about what the changes could mean for the present operations, but even more importantly, about the impact they might have on their own covert plans.

Mahoney continued, "We're going to open up two new avenues of distribution that will allow us to get more of our Quebec product into Michigan and maybe even beyond." He paused for effect. "With the new bridge as an option now and some of the border people in our pocket, we'd like to start sending our trucks right across to new contacts."

Jack and Scotty stole another look at each other before Jack asked, "New? Meaning not the Purples?"

"That's right," Mahoney replied.

Looking back at his partner nervously, Jack continued, "You know that's going to put our drivers at risk, right? If they get caught, they—"

"Not your concern, kid. This is what the boss wants, so it's got to happen. Just put up the product prices and pay your drivers more. We'll call it hazard pay," Mahoney said with an evil smile that Jack wanted to slap violently from his face.

Scotty, trying to ease the tension, asked, "You said changes. What others?"

Refocusing, Mahoney answered, "The boss also wants you guys to reach out to the King in Belle River. He's been moving some big numbers across the lake using his own airplane. He's got a landing strip on his farm. We want you to convince him to move some of our Quebec product over there for us. I'll set up the meeting."

Mahoney knew that Jack and Scotty had both heard of the legendary exploits of Blaise Diesbourg, also known as King Canada, out in the county. According to several sources, he was one of the few area rumrunners who actually met with the infamous Al Capone from Chicago, which meant he had very strong ties to the heads of the Purple Gang across the border.

As the two men sat there contemplating their orders, Mahoney made a few notes, closed his ledger book, and placed it back in his black case. "Well, gentlemen. That's about it. I'll set up the meeting with Diesbourg. We're expecting to hear significant developments about both changes by the end of next month at the latest," he said. Walking out the door and without stopping or turning around, he added, "Don't let the boss down."

It took a few minutes after he left for Jack and Scotty to look at each other and begin discussing the situation they now found themselves in. Scotty broke the silence. "They want us dead, don't they?"

"It looks that way, partner. They're both suicide missions," Jack reasoned. "But what I can't figure out is why. And why now?"

"Could they know what we're up to?"

"I don't think so. If they knew, we would have been visited by their goons or be dead already," Jack answered. "No, I think St. Pierre wants a bigger piece of the pie, and he's using us to get it for him without him taking any risk. The greedy bastard is playing with our lives."

"What are we gonna do, Jackie?"

Jack was deep in thought, considering the new developments.

"Jackie?" Scotty repeated.

"Ya," he answered, snapping back to reality. "Well, it looks like our timelines just got bumped up. Now we're down to just weeks."

"Is that even possible?"

"Well, a lot will depend on what's happening right now with Joey," Jack said as they looked at each other anxiously.

....

A couple of months earlier, in late March, Joey McLuren was brought into the paint-shop office and faced two very serious-looking bosses. He thought he was being fired. To his surprise, Mr. Ducharme and his uncle explained that they were in serious trouble and needed his help. They needed to find out where their boss, Mr. Mahoney, lived. They knew that having someone follow him home in their car would be too conspicuous and potentially dangerous, but they believed that a kid—or in this case, a young man who looked like a kid—on a bike could use shortcuts and alleys to follow him and go unnoticed.

"We know he doesn't live far, Joey. My dad once told me he was local . . . lived around here some-where," his uncle told him. "But we're pretty sure he takes different ways home in case he's being followed, so it may take a few tries on the days he leaves here."

Although Mahoney organized the day-to-day transfer of product from the shop to their distribu-tors and customers, he still kept a very low profile. Jack and Scotty saw the group's deliverymen and even the two thugs much more often than they saw Mahoney, other than during his end-of-month visits.

Joey was both nervous about the assignment and excited for the opportunity to be able to help two men that he respected and looked up to. "How do we even know he goes home from here?" he asked.

Jack was impressed by the astute question. "We don't," he answered, "but the book he brings here with him has information that could destroy him and the group. We're guessing he would want to get it back to a safe location as soon as possible. And knowing Mahoney, who doesn't trust anyone, safe probably means staying with him."

Starting on a cold, windy day at the end of March, Joey was on his bike and down the street as Seamus wrapped up his business, got his money and headed out of the shop. The ball cap and tattered, oversized coat Joey was wearing on his small frame made the 17 year-old look like a young boy. He was able to track the big, elongated vehicle for several blocks, but lost him when he turned at a busy intersection nearby.

A month later, during the April visit, Joey rode down to the same intersection and was waiting when Mahoney turned the corner and headed east into a less affluent area than he expected. He watched carefully as the back of the car made a quick turn before Joey lost sight of it, only to have it re-appear at the same corner minutes later. He had done a complete circle around the block. Mahoney then made his way to Sandwich Street before turning south again while Joey was pedalling down a parallel alley. The numerous stop signs Mahoney hit at street corners along the way helped Joey keep up. As the car turned onto Moy Avenue, Joey lost ground quickly, but watched it slow to a crawl a couple blocks ahead before it disappeared.

Now, in May, as Jack and Scotty were in their office contemplating the new operational demands that Mahoney had suddenly announced, Joey was already in position a couple of blocks down from the river on Moy, waiting. His patience paid off when Mahoney's Packard drove towards him. The car turned down a side street and rolled slowly into the nearby alley. Joey hung back and watched. Ahead, the car stopped. Mahoney got out and scanned the area before opening a large, steel garage door. Joey was off his bike a distance away, pretending to have an issue with the bike chain. Several minutes after the car was in the garage and the door was pulled shut, Joey walked his bike slowly past the back of the property and made a mental note of the features so he could remember the house. After hopping back on his bike at the end of the alley, Joey rode the mile or so back to the shop, smiling and whistling along the way.

....

At home with Maria and his son that evening, Jack's mind was racing. He needed to be called to dinner three times before it registered. As he made his way to the kitchen table, patting Little Mo's head on the way, Maria could tell he was lost in thought. He sat down.

"What's got you in dreamland, Jackie?"

"Mahoney was in today doing his end-of-month," he said, looking up at her. "Seems the boss wants to go in a different direction." He paused while his wife studied his face. "They're wanting us to expand into Detroit behind the Purples' backs."

"*Merda*," Maria swore. "Why would he do that?"

"We think he wants to get rid of us—streamline the business." Jack thought for a few seconds and added, "It's going to rush our timelines."

Maria's eyes gave away her concern, but then she said, "Maybe that's a good thing, *Caro*. Maybe it's time."

As she moved towards the stove, he reached out, put his arm around her waist, and pulled her into him. "You may be right. Even though there's still a lot that has to happen, we made some great progress to-day," he told her. He explained how Joey did so well, finally finding Mahoney's residence, and how they now needed to find out if he secured the valuable ledger books somewhere in his house.

"I don't know who we can trust for that," Jack said. "Scotty and I can't be seen hanging around there, that's for sure. And it's too risky for the boys, especially if Mahoney's goons are around," he continued.

Maria was listening attentively and deep in thought while she was feeding Little Mo. She fully understood the seriousness of the situation that Jack found himself in, but also understood the risk to him and their family if he did nothing. Jack was quietly considering his limited options when Maria surprised him by putting down the spoon, placing her hand on his arm, and looking him in the eyes before saying, "Jackie, I know just the person for the job."

Jack and Scotty stalled as long as they could to act on Mahoney's order to start using the bridge for shipments. The potential increase in pay for a few extra miles seemed attractive to the drivers coming in from Quebec, but they didn't understand the full extent of the dangers they would be facing. If anyone connected with the Purple Gang caught wind of large shipments of booze coming in from Canada without their group's approval or involvement, the shipment and the drivers would not be around very long. So their plan was to try to make Mahoney believe that they were putting some kind of operation in place, but to drag their feet long enough that they would never have to.

Of more immediate concern was the upcoming meeting that had been arranged with Blaise Diesbourg. This could not be put off. One of Mahoney's associates reached out and set a date and time for the meeting, so they had little choice. Neither Jack nor Scotty knew what to expect. They were fully aware that the meeting was some kind of dangerous set-up. Since they could not deny their bosses' request to meet, and since the success of their covert plan relied heavily on somehow making contact with the leadership of the Purple Gang, this Diesbourg character would be their best option, especially given their shortened timeline.

It was a hot Friday morning in mid-June when Scotty and Jack made their way in Scotty's new Model A out to Belle River. Using the paved roads along the waterfront to drive east, they soon were on gravel and eventually bouncing down dirt roads as they followed the Lake St. Clair shoreline into Maidstone Township. Their long drive out into the county ended with a dusty drive on a gravel road that led to a large farm along Duck Creek. At the end of the laneway that led up to the farm, there was a muddy Ford pickup truck with a fellow sitting and smoking in the driver's seat. As they approached, the man got out, dropped and rubbed out the cigarette butt in the fine gravel with his dirty boot, and walked up to Scotty's window. "What's your business here, boys?" he asked as he surveyed the new automobile with disdain.

"We have a meeting with Mr. Diesbourg at 10 o'clock. Under the name Ducharme," Scotty answered.

Giving both Scotty and Jack a slow once-over, the man said, "Wait here". He walked back to his truck casually and jumped in. The truck made its way up the long laneway to the farmhouse as they waited with growing anxiety in their car.

"I don't like this one bit," Scotty said, breaking the silence after a few moments.

Jack looked over. "Me either, but we don't have any other option from what I can see." Before the truck came rumbling back towards them minutes later, he added, "Just remember. Let me do the talking,

Scotty. I'm hoping my being a fellow French Canadian will work in our favour." This was only partly the truth. Jack's request to be the point man had more to do with his concern about Scotty's lack of business savvy and his habit of carrying friendly, casual conversation too far. One of the many things his father had taught him, and Jack had learned himself in his own business dealings, was that keeping business meetings short, clear, and direct worked most effectively.

Returning to his position at the end of the laneway, the driver simply waved them through, and they turned and rolled slowly towards the big white farmhouse. After stopping and parking along the shaded side of a large barn, the two men got out hesitantly and looked around for some direction. A middle-aged man, looking like the quintessential farmer in a stained light-coloured short-sleeve shirt that was unbuttoned over his generous belly and battered green pants held up by a pair of suspenders, waved them over. He led Jack and Scotty to the back of the farmhouse, where they expected to be introduced to the local legend, King Canada. But when they rounded the edge of the house, there was only one large young man standing by the back door. Numerous lawn chairs sat empty in the shade under a huge weeping willow in the yard.

When the three got to the chairs, the farmer turned and with a slight French accent said, "Well, boys, you have ten minutes. What can I do for you?"

With no formal introductions and the short timeline announced, Jack was already thrown off his game plan. Looking sideways at Scotty, he said, "Uh, we're here to meet Mr. Diesbourg."

"You're looking at him, kid," he said while he fished a cigarette out of a small case in his chest pocket and felt around for matches. "Now sit down and make sure I'm not wasting my time, because whoever set this up told me you boys have a deal to offer me."

Scotty and Jack both sat, hats in hand, feeling the tension of the moment. Jack mustered some nerve and began, "Mr. Diesbourg. Nice to meet you. My name is Jack Ducharme and this is Scotty McLuren. We're here today to discuss with you—"

Diesbourg cut him off. "I know who you boys are, for Christ's sake, kid. I only took this meeting because you're Moose Ducharme's boy. Now spit it out. What do you two want from me?" he asked.

Jack was thrown by the fact that Diesbourg knew his father, but he tried again, nervously. "On the record, we're here to request—. uh, inquire as to your interest in—improving your profits . . . uh, making money by helping our group distribute some of our product to your people across the lake, but out of reach from your Detroit people and—"

"*Tabernac*!" Diesbourg cut Jack off again. "On the record?" Diesbourg was raising his voice, annoyed. He took a long drag on the cigarette while eyeing Jack with squinted eyes. "What the hell does that mean? Nothing is on the record." He paused. "All I'm hearing so far is you asking me if I'd move your product," he continued sarcastically, "out of sight from my Detroit people? What the hell are you talking about?

I don't know you. I don't know your product. You better start making this worth my time, or we're done here, boys."

Still flustered, Jack began again. "We have product that we're supposed to try to arrange with you to—"

Scotty cut him off this time with a loud clearing of his throat. "Mr. Diesbourg," he began more deliberately, as Diesbourg's eyes shifted his way suspiciously. "With all due respect . . . we are here because we don't want you to move our booze." Jack's head dropped and his shoulders slumped in defeat. Diesbourg looked at him, confused. "We are only here because we were ordered to be here. We don't want to get involved with what you got goin' on out here. But our boss, a Mr. Mahoney"—Diesbourg's eyes tightened on hearing the name—"and his boss sent us out here on a suicide mission. They know you won't do business with us, especially behind the back of the Purples." He now had Diesbourg's full attention. "What me and Jack are really here for, what we really want, has nothing to do with you moving our hooch."

Diesbourg was still confused, but intrigued, as his eyes looked Scotty over slowly. The bottom of Scotty's pant leg was up high enough to reveal a portion of his wooden prosthesis, which caught the older man's gaze. "What happened to your leg?" he asked, now distracted.

Looking down, surprised by the question, Scotty answered, "Lost part of it in Europe."

"You serve with the Scottish?" he asked.

"Yes, sir. Sent me home in '17. And I'd be dead

if it wasn't for this boy's father," Scotty explained, looking over at his partner. Jack lowered his eyes.

"Ah *oui*. Yes. We know all about Maurice Ducharme," Diesbourg said. "He made nous *les Franco* proud." He took notice of Jack's emotional reaction.

With the sudden shift in the conversation, the tension lifted, and Jack sat back in his chair, trying to gather himself.

"What field hospital did they send you to?"

The question threw Scotty off. "Well, I was pretty much out of it when they took me from the line. I ended up in the Number 8 Canadian for months before I was shipped back. Why?"

Diesbourg smiled. "I have a cousin who was there. Maybe you heard of him. Do you remember a doc named Paul Poisson?"

"Doc Fish?" Scotty said with surprise and a little too much excitement. "Everybody remembers him. He helped save my life. Got me through a really rough stretch over there." He turned to his partner. "Talk about war heroes, Jackie. This Poisson won the MC, the Military Cross, in Passchendaele, the same place I lost my foot."

"That's right. He was the pride of our family . . . still is," Diesbourg explained.

Scotty and King Canada sat there for several minutes talking about the war, family and friends who served, and those who didn't make it back. Jack remained quiet and feeling somewhat awkward because he couldn't add to the discussion. He was also humbled by the fact that he had wanted Scotty to keep quiet while he handled this rum-running legend, yet it was Scotty who was now saving the day.

After several minutes of friendly conversation, Diesbourg reached in his pocket, checked his pocket watch, and announced, "Well, boys, it has been good chewing the fat about the past, but I need to be somewhere real soon. You're going to have to give me a better idea about what you're looking for from me."

Scotty turned to look at Jack, handing the job back over to him. Jack explained everything, as briefly as possible, with more detail and honesty that he ever thought he should. He told Diesbourg all about his father's Skim operation and its connection to Mahoney's group, and he fought back his tears as he described his father's murder. After taking a few moments to regroup, Jack went on to explain their new enterprise and partnership with certain Quebec suppliers and how they were now being set up by Mahoney and his people, even though all they really wanted was to get out of the business.

Jack was unsure whether he was getting any understanding or sympathy from Diesbourg until he added, "And because my partner and I witnessed the murder, we now know what only a handful of people in our area know. We know who is really running the whole operation around there," Jack said.

Diesbourg sat up straighter, intrigued.

"So what we are looking for, sir, shouldn't be too difficult, and we think it will benefit both of us greatly. We need your connection to the Purple's leaders to help set up and bring our bosses down," Jack explained, his stomach sinking at the thought of what he was asking. He knew this request could get them killed. Diesbourg was listening intently. "In return, we'll give up our boss's identity, you'll have the first opportunity to fill the market they will leave behind when they are taken, and most importantly, you'll be seen as a hero to your connections over in Detroit for exposing a traitor."

There was an extended silence after Jack finished while the two partners waited in anticipation for Diesbourg's response. Although King Canada was well known as a major rum runner in the area and had strong alliances with some ruthless gangsters over in the States, he was also a loving family man, loyal to the people he worked with, and fervently proud of his country and his French-Canadian roots. Even though he appeared expressionless, as Diesbourg looked at these two younger men in front of him, he was moved. He felt a sense of indebtedness to this young, disabled veteran who had risked his life for his country and who had formed a strong connection to his beloved cousin. He also felt sympathy and respect for the young Ducharme kid, who had the misfortune of losing his father so horribly at a young age, but who survived, thrived, and now wanted to settle what Diesbourg saw as a well-justified score.

Finally Diesbourg took a long last drag from his cigarette and stood abruptly. Scotty and Jack followed suit. He dropped his cigarette into the grass, rubbed it out with his manure-caked rubber boot, and brought his eyes up to stare Jack down.

He offered his oversized farmer's hand to him, and Jack shook it. He then turned to Scotty and did the same, saying, "I like you boys. You've got some balls, I'll give you that. I think we can help each other out." He turned serious, looking back at Jack. "But you can't forget the people we're dealing with here. There can't be any problems. Get me your proof without getting caught or killed, and make sure it's good enough for me to take the risk. If it isn't enough or anybody gets wind of our little deal, I never met you and you're on your own. Understand?"

"We understand, Mr. Diesbourg. We really do. And we appreciate your help." Jack answered, looking over at Scotty. "But we hope you can understand that we're already knee-deep in a deadly situation. We're just hoping you can help pull us out and maybe save our lives."

....

A few weeks had passed since Mousseau's meeting with Jack at the paint shop, and he was growing more and more impatient. He wanted to trust the young Ducharme fellow, but instead of bringing some hint of progress or information about how to get at Mahoney, his men, or the operation, the past couple of weeks had produced nothing. In fact, although his men couldn't tail them all the way, he was sure that a drive out to the county by the two partners on the Friday before might have been for rum-running business. Even though he was the most senior inspector of the local liquor control and made all the operational decisions, Mousseau realized that if Ducharme and McLuren were playing him, he would be humiliated—and could possibly even lose his job. There were agents on his watch who had been ordered to ease up on surveillance and investigations into the paint-shop operations and who knew crimes were being committed under their noses while their boss promised them a big payoff down the road.

By the third week of June, over a month since their meeting, Mousseau felt the need to make contact and get some assurances. It was a bright, warm Saturday afternoon, and Mousseau had followed the young Ducharme family to an area park. While his wife pushed their little boy on a swing nearby, Mousseau surprised Jack by sitting down beside him on a park bench. "Nice day, isn't it, Jack?"

Irritated by the intrusion and concerned about being seen with Mousseau in public, Jack looked around and answered curtly, "What do you want, Inspector?"

"Just looking for some progress, Jack. It's been weeks, and even though my boys tell me you've been busy, I've seen and heard nothing."

As Jack watched his smiling wife and child enjoying themselves, he said, "I asked you for patience, Mr. Mousseau. We've got things in the works, but it's going to take a little more time."

"How much time? July is right around the corner."

Jack was losing his cool with the added pressure. "You think I don't know that? The things we have in the works are so dangerous I'm not sleeping, Inspector. I have trouble eating. I sit here watching them," he looked out towards Maria and Little Mo, "and wonder if we're all going to make it through this. You think there's pressure on you?" Jack was near tears.

Mousseau felt his anxiety. He suddenly wondered if his unscheduled visit was a mistake. Trying to salvage something to ease his concerns, Mousseau asked, "Can you give me anything, Jack? Something to ease my mind . . . a show of good faith?"

Desperate to appease him, Jack decided to give him a scrap that might interest him and keep his agents busy. "The bridge," he said. "They want to start using the bridge as their main supply line. They say they have border people on the take."

Content with the information, Mousseau replied, "That's good, Jack. You see? I can work with that." He looked over sympathetically at the mother and son enjoying the swing, got up, put his hat on, and casually walked away.

As Maria looked over with concern, Jack hung his head and ran his fingers slowly through his hair.

....

Mahoney was returning from another busy day that ended with an evening meeting with the Saint. His boss was looking for an update about the Quebec boys, Ducharme and McLuren, but he had little concrete progress to report. One of their drivers reported they were working on the logistics of the bridge supply line but needed more time to organize the Quebec truckers. More encouraging, the boys had used the contact Mahoney had given them and had met with King Canada the week before. They were still both still alive, in good health, and continuing their business as usual. Mahoney was unsure how to feel about that update.

"I'm going to see them next week for the month's end, so I'll get the details then," Mahoney explained. St. Pierre seemed satisfied until Mahoney added, "But we've got a couple of concerns."

"What concerns?" St. Pierre said, sitting up straighter.

"For starters, our guy inside liquor control says that Mousseau is pulling some guys off the paint shop. Says there was no explanation. Then one of Wolf's men says he spotted Mousseau talking to Ducharme in a park earlier in the week." St. Pierre's silent stare meant he was processing the news. "And then yesterday, one of our border guys at the bridge says he's getting nervous because agents are hanging around asking questions and doing background inquiries." He stopped for a response. Nothing. "I guess it could all be explained or possibly coincidences," Mahoney suggested.

"I don't believe in fucking coincidences. You know that. Something's happening. Could they be making a move?" St. Pierre asked.

"Highly unlikely, Saint. Unlike a lot of our guys, they've got smarts. They both have too much to lose, too . . . especially the Ducharme kid. He would never put his family at risk. And they're making good coin. I just don't see it."

St. Pierre took several moments to consider the situation and was growing more and more agitated, while Mahoney capped his pen and closed his book, assuming the meeting was over. "This meeting ain't over til I say it's over!" St. Pierre shouted. "Open that goddamn book and make a note." Without reaction, Mahoney methodically opened his ledger and prepared his pen. He had been through so many of these little tirades that they no longer had any affect. "I want inquiries made. Everybody we have on the payroll at liquor control and at the bridge. I want to know what's going on, and I want it soon! And if we hear that they are playing us or rolling over for Mousseau, I want them gone!" He stood up, pointed a finger at Mahoney, and added, "Remember, you're the one who convinced me not to take them out like I wanted. Anything happens here, and it's on you!" With that, he marched out and slammed the door behind him.

Letting out a big sigh, Mahoney made some final notes, packed up his things, and headed out to his car. He was deep in thought as he made his way home, along the way considering the possibility that he may have underestimated Ducharme and McLuren. Even though he was completely distracted by the recent events and his boss's threat, Mahoney still took a long, convoluted way home. He had been doing it for so long it had become a habit. A short time later, he drove slowly down his dark alley and parked his car in the garage. Coming out from its side door carrying his case, he locked the garage and made his way to the side entrance of his house. The light that was turned on inside at the landing darkened quickly as the door was shut. Another light, this time from the basement, lit up two very narrow windows less than a foot off the ground at the back of the house. From outside one of the windows, Mahoney's muted figure could be seen through sheer curtains putting some kind of briefcase inside a dark cupboard sitting along a bare cement wall. His outline went out of view, but his footsteps could be heard clearly as he made his way back up the wooden stairs, as could the slamming of a heavy-sounding door, followed by the clank of a padlock.

The illuminated, weathered face watching from outside suddenly went dark as the basement light was turned off. In the darkness, one last long bright glow of a cigarette ember was the only thing visible before it was dropped and stomped out. The figure then made its way casually back to the alley, out of sight.

I T WAS A BRIGHT, SUNNY THURSDAY MORNING IN LATE JUNE, and the summer humidity that locals loved complaining about was already building. Mahoney was looking forward to finding some respite from the stress of the previous day, so he decided to take a walk to the riverfront and read, something he rarely had time for lately, it seemed. Checking twice that his side door was locked, he made his way towards the alley behind his house. As a rule, he avoided using his front door, front porch, or any part of the front of his house—another precaution to keep his comings and goings less conspicuous.

Walking down the side of his house and into the backyard, he surveyed the area. Many of his neighbours were first-generation immigrants and took great pride in their small backyards with meticulous lawns or beautiful vegetable gardens. Not Mahoney. Because of his garage, his yard was tiny and mainly featured long, patchy wild grass with an abundance of weeds that took hold in early spring and weren't letting go.

Something caught his eye on the ground right behind his house. The heavy dew from the previous night helped reveal an area of trampled grass and dandelions close to one of his back basement windows. He moved closer. His heart rate increased as he bent down to inspect the area. Nestled there in the flattened area, wet and shimmering, was a lone cigarette butt. Crouching, he picked it up and looked around warily. Any hope of a relaxing morning vanished as Mahoney made his way back into his house. He instinctively started to replay the previous evening over in his mind. Nothing of note came to him.

He made his way to the basement door, removed the thin rope he kept around his neck, and used the attached key to open the heavy lock. After descending the creaky, steep steps, his eyes searched the basement and found everything as he had left it. He went to the back awning window, reached up, and looked under the dusty curtains to check the window latches. A few cobwebs stretched and snapped, while dust floated in the air, hanging suspended in the morning suns' rays. All secure. Only somewhat relieved, he sat on a nearby stool and considered the situation. Instinctively, he was much more concerned about the books than he was about the large cardboard box of money sitting nearby. He could always make more dough, but the books were a potential threat to his freedom and even his life. This was especially true due to the fact that tucked behind the official set of ledger books that he used for his daily operations and meetings was another book that held no accounts receivable or payable. Instead, this book contained the detailed breakdown of the entire St. Pierre organization as well as the roles and contact information of everyone on their payroll. At the top, with tentacles branching out like the roots of a tree, was William

"The Saint" St. Pierre. It included major suppliers, both local and in Quebec, names and addresses of the biggest and most profitable operations, as well as all the business leaders, police, judges, and other public officials who were either major customers or were on the take. He had just recently updated it with the names of some bridge border guards. Although Mahoney liked working for the Saint's organization and was rewarded handsomely for it, he was no fool. St. Pierre could behave erratically; Mahoney wasn't always sure he could trust him. Hence the need for self-preservation.

Under normal circumstances, he would have been quick to report the incident of a potential intruder to his boss, but considering the Saint's mood and the threats he'd made the night before, Mahoney decided against it. His money and books were secure in his personal fortress, and he had no further evidence to go on. He decided instead that he would institute a new precaution immediately by having the Wolf or the Russian keep an eye on his place whenever he was away.

Satisfied that everything was in order and would remain that way, Seamus went back upstairs to make the call to meet with his men and set up their new security measures.

....

That same evening, Jack and Maria welcomed her parents, the Darios, as well as Scotty and Johnny for dinner. Just like he had with Moose and Sara years before, Scotty looked forward to visits with the Ducharmes and was treated like one of the family. He appreciated it even more now, since the death of his own father. The Darios never declined an invitation to spend time with the family either, showering affection not only on their daughter and grandson, but on their son-in-law as well.

After a typical Italian feast that Mrs. Dario insisted on helping prepare, the group refreshed their wine and retired to the front parlour while Maria's mother took Little Mo upstairs for a bath and to put him down for the night. She knew the rest of the group had very important issues to discuss. After devouring enough food at dinner to impress even Mr. Dario, Johnny obeyed Scotty's earlier request and thanked his hosts before leaving them, as well.

Despite the casual atmosphere of the evening, tension was growing as the guests found their seats in the parlour and prepared to talk about the situation the partners were now in. Maria sat next to her father on the large chesterfield so she could help translate anything he might have trouble understanding. Mr. Dario was enjoying a cigarette with the homemade wine that Jack was abundantly supplied with but rarely drank. After a chair was dragged in from the kitchen for Scotty and everybody seemed settled,

Jack looked anxiously over at his wife, cleared his throat, and began with, "Well, let's get to it." He paused, looking for the right words, then simply stated, "It seems Scotty and I are in some pretty serious trouble. We all know about our boss's new demands and why we think he is making them." He looked towards the floor and added, "We believe the organization's leadership want us killed." Just saying the words made Jack stop and consider, once again, the dire reality they found themselves in. Looking back up at Scotty, he continued, "We have our regrets about the people we have been in business with, and that's why we have been trying for a while to find a way to end it with them. But we realize that with these people, that's impossible. We can't just walk away." After a quick, whispered translation, Mr. Dario nodded in agreement, clearly appreciating the situation they found themselves in. "So we've been working on a plan for months that could save us and get us out. The problem is timing. Because our boss threw us this curveball a few days ago, our timelines are now very rushed. Now we basically have until Monday, when Mahoney will want to have proof that we did what he demanded. We have no idea what will happen then. That gives us only four days."

Maria was whispering to her father, trying to find the right translations for the words "curveball" and "timelines," when Scotty added, "And it all depends on us getting our hands on our boss's ledger books. The way we see it now, our freedom—maybe even our lives—depend on those books."

Saying the words out loud while looking in Maria's direction made Scotty pause briefly to contemplate the magnitude of the situation for Jack and his young family. He realized that the risks they were talking about had so much more consequence for all of them. The thought made him shudder.

Jack's tone changed when he looked next to his wife and added, "But thanks to Mr. Dario, we know exactly where they are now. We just have to go get them."

"Well, we know how we might be able to get them, but it could be a problem," Jack explained. "Because Mahoney's basement is locked up tighter than Fort Knox, and the only way in is through a very small window. Right?" he asked, looking over at the older gentleman.

"Itsa small," Mr. Dario announced after his daughter's translation, using his hands, one on top the other, to show a height of only about ten inches. "Bigga thissa way." His hands showed a width of well over two feet.

"Too small for almost anybody to go through," Jack added.

"Almost?" Maria asked.

Jack looked at Scotty and then scanned the faces around the room before answering, "Well, we do know somebody we think will fit." He paused, then told her with some reluctance, "We're thinking about Joey. Scotty's nephew—"

"Oh, Jackie! He's just a kid," Maria interrupted. "That would be so dangerous. There's got to be someone else." She looked over at her father for some agreement, then turned back to Scotty. "Are you okay with this?"

"No, not really," Scotty replied. "But we can't think of anyone else who we trust and who'll fit. We don't have any other way in. Joey's rail thin, and when your father saw him, he agreed that he'd probably fit." Dario was nodding. "Besides, he's already involved in our business, and we know he would do it." He considered what he was proposing and justified it with, "He's not really a kid, either, Maria . . . he's 17. Jack's father and I fought in the trenches with boys that age who lied to sign up."

The group sat quietly, digesting the idea of putting Joey into such a potentially deadly situation. Maria broke the silence by asking, "And do you send him in there alone? How frightening. What if Mahoney's home or comes home and catches him?"

"No, no. Listen, Maria," Jack answered attempting to calm her. "Scotty and I are going to arrange a meeting tomorrow night, make up some emergency to get Mahoney out of his house to come meet us. It's important we're with him when it happens so he doesn't think we're involved. Your father said there was no one else there last night, right? He must live alone, so we know the house will be empty. Joey slips in, grabs the books, and gets out." Maria was processing the plan and getting even more anxious because it needed to happen the very next evening. Jack looked to Mr. Dario and hesitated, then added, "And your father will be with him."

Maria turned quickly to face her father, sitting next to her, and reached out for his hand. "*Oh Gesu,*

Poppa." She turned back to her husband, looking uneasy. "I don't know, Jackie. Snooping around is one thing. This is much more—"

She was cut off by her father suddenly patting her leg and interjecting, "Maria, Maria. *Dici sul serio, Maria?*" he said, asking if her objections were serious. "Poppa wasa playing theesa games backa when I wasa younga thana Joey. This isa *niente*," he continued, dramatically waving off her concern. "Nothing."

Her father's reaction did little to ease Maria's anxiety. Although Mr. Dario seemed completely untroubled by any potential danger as he took a long drag from his cigarette, Jack and Scotty shared a common feeling of unease about what lay ahead. Moreover, they felt profound guilt for having to involve loved ones in a risky plan to get them out of the deadly situation they found themselves in.

For Maria, it was suddenly clear to her that the plans being discussed tonight had already been decided by the three men well before they all sat down. She was also sure that Jack wanted to make her feel like she was involved and could have some input, something that her father and other men his age in their Italian culture would not be the least bit concerned about. Although Maria had serious misgivings, especially about the role that a young kid and her own father would be playing, she appreciated Jack's gesture.

With detailed plans firmly in place, the night ended with farewells out on the front porch. The mild, breezy evening was changing with gathering clouds and humidity beginning to roll in. As their guests made their way down the front sidewalk and out of sight, Jack's arm was over Maria's shoulders, and she locked her hands around his large torso possessively as if refusing to let him go. As Jack enjoyed the embrace, he couldn't help thinking with dread about the long, sleepless night that lay ahead.

....

Around the same time that the Ducharmes were bidding farewell to their guests, Inspector Mousseau was at home at the west end of Windsor, sitting in his study and making plans for simultaneous raids on McLuren Paints and the Ducharme and McLuren homes. There were only a few days left in June, and the closer the end of the month got, the less confident Mousseau felt about the arrangement he had made with Jack Ducharme. He knew he needed search warrants if the raids were to happen, and they could take some time, especially over a weekend. He decided to get the ball rolling in the event promises weren't kept.

He wanted so badly to trust the Ducharme kid, but there was growing evidence that he was not going to deliver. The tip that Jack had given about the bridge border guards yielded very little and felt like a wild goose chase. Then earlier in the day, he heard from a fellow agent out in the county that the reason for Ducharme and McLuren's ride out to the Maidstone area days before was to meet with Blaise Diesbourg, a big-time rumrunner from the area whom

Mousseau had been trying to arrest for years. Enough was enough. He wasn't going to be humiliated and lose his job because he trusted some young bootlegger.

It was too late in the night to make calls, but the next day, Friday, he would gather his men to make the necessary plans and fill out the warrant applications. He was a man of his word, however, so he would keep it. Ducharme and McLuren would have until Monday, but if there were no developments, then on Tuesday morning, the first of the month, the simultaneous raids would be executed.

23

WITH PLANS FIRMLY IN PLACE AND THEIR LIVES potentially hanging in the balance, Jack and Scotty had a very long and anxious day at the paint shop on Friday. Try as they might to keep everything business as usual, they both found it hard to concentrate and were a little jumpy. Three liquor pickups were scheduled throughout the day, and an old Ford that was repainted on Wednesday was being prepped for pickup by its owner after lunch. Dark clouds to the west continued to threaten rain, which could slow down the work ahead.

The first time Jack saw Joey that day was when the shiny Ford drove out of their yard in the early afternoon. After saying hello casually, Jack studied the kid for some sign of hesitancy or nervousness and found none. As Johnny left the two of them and walked back into the shop, Jack caught up with Joey and asked, "Everything good, kid?"

"Sure, Mr. Ducharme. Just have a busy afternoon. Supposed to be a big order being picked up soon, and it looks like rain." Joey answered. "How about you?"

His calm threw Jack off. Either he was hiding his anxiety really well, or he wasn't fully aware of the risk he was going to take that night. "Yes, well, um, I'm fine, Joey," he responded. "Just a little worried about tonight. Thought you would be too."

"Nah, not really," he said. Then his head dropped, and with some degree of embarrassment he admitted, "Uncle Scotty probably told ya I've done some break-ins before. When I was younger. Not too proud of it now."

Jack nodded. He knew Joey's story through Scotty, and it wasn't a happy one. Joey's father Thomas, who everyone called Junior, was two years older than Scotty, but couldn't have been more different from his younger brother. Where Scotty was a hardworking, honest, and loyal friend as well as a proud war veteran, Junior was a petty criminal and a loner who was rarely employed for long due to absenteeism and drinking or fighting on the job. Junior married a young woman with a tainted reputation whom he got pregnant. It was a literal "shotgun wedding"—his bride's father had one loaded and waiting nearby—but Junior was as poorly equipped to be a good father as he was to be a good husband. The short time he was around while his son was growing up was fuelled by alcohol and violence, until his wife managed to throw him back to the streets, where months later he was found dead in an alley under suspicious circumstances. Thankfully, what Joey's mother was unable to provide in material needs, she more than made up for with love and support as he was growing up. Like the male McLurens before him, Joey struggled with school. As he got older, he often found himself in the company of questionable characters who helped him become well known to police. Once he was old enough, however, Scotty took him under his wing and gave him an opportunity to work, have some responsibility, and earn some money. This seemed to bring out his true character. Although he had been in some trouble in the past, Jack saw Joey as a good kid who just wanted to be loved and respected.

Joey continued, "I've even broken in a couple of times when people were home." He thought for a moment. "There'll be nobody home there tonight, right?"

Jack nodded again.

"And Mr. Dario will be with me, right?" Joey continued, almost enthusiastically. "Is it true he was in the Mafia in Italy?'

Jack continued nodding, this time with a smile he couldn't suppress. "Many years ago," he answered, "but I'm sure you're in good hands."

"So, there's nothing to worry about, right?" Joey was assured by the smile on his boss's face. He started putting his work gloves back on and was turning to head back to work when he stopped, turned back to Jack, and said, "Ya know, it's actually kind of funny, Mr. Ducharme."

"How's that?" Jack wondered.

"Well, I've always been told by ma to eat more to put more meat on my bones, and kids always made fun of me, calling me names or picking on me because I'm so skinny. It really bothered me, and I'd get angry and want to fight when I was younger. But now, I get to be a hero and help you guys out because I'm the only one who's skinny enough to do the job. I guess everybody has some sort of purpose, eh?"

"That's true, kid," Jack answered, but the smile left his face as he stepped closer to Joey, adding, "But we wish we didn't need you, kid. Your uncle and I both feel terrible that we need to put this job on you. And we appreciate it so much."

"I'm glad you need me . . . makes me feel important," Joey responded. Before walking away, he finished with, "Relax, boss. You and Uncle Scotty will have those books in your hands tonight."

The thought of Mahoney's books and the impact they could have on so many lives did nothing to ease Jack's growing anxiety.

....

Later that evening, Seamus Mahoney was relaxing and reading in his easy chair after another quiet meal by himself. The sun was setting behind even more gathering rain clouds, over the roofs of his neighbours to the west, as he peered out the living room window.

He had resigned himself to the freedom and solitude of bachelorhood years ago, knowing his line of business did not work well with marriage. He did not want to share a life with someone under the shroud of lies like his boss and others he worked with—that was just too messy. But after all these years, he still found eating dinners alone to be a bit depressing. He was never much for talk, but having someone sit across the table while he ate seemed appealing to him. Even when he was out at local restaurants, unless it was a business meeting, he would sit alone at a table for two, at times making him feel pathetic. It was on these occasions that he often made a call and had one of a variety of young women on his payroll join him to eat and then fulfil his needs afterwards—something he considered just another business expense.

As he was lost in thought and feeling a little sorry for himself, the telephone rang. He turned and looked at the nearby table where it sat. His reluctance to get up had nothing to do with laziness or listening for the right ring sequence. For security reasons, he had spent the extra money years earlier to have a dedicated line to his home. The fact was that Mahoney had another habit. As an additional safeguard, he always let the phone ring at least ten times before answering. Business associates and people who knew him personally expected to sit through that many rings before he picked up, while most others would lose patience.

On the eleventh ring, he got up, walked over, and put the heavy receiver to his ear. He said nothing for several seconds, then, "Why tonight, Mr. Ducharme?" He quietly listened for a while longer, staring at a plaster crack on the wall. "I don't seem to understand the urgency. Couldn't we meet tomorrow?" After a good deal of convincing from the other end of the line, Mahoney ended the call, saying, "Very well, then. This better be important. We will meet in twenty minutes at the pavilion in the park on Assumption. Rain is on its way, so don't keep me long." He put the receiver back on its cradle carefully while he continued staring off, deep in thought. It was critical for him to be prepared for any situation that might present itself or any delicate questions that might be posed. He went to a credenza near the front foyer, opened a drawer, and took out his revolver. Stuffing it in the back of his beltline, he walked over and checked that the front door was locked, even though he never used it.

Despite the imminent rain, he decided to walk, which he always preferred. Mahoney grabbed his light trench coat and hat, along with his umbrella, for the fifteen-minute walk to the park. He was on his way out the side door when he suddenly remembered something he had forgotten. He leaned his umbrella up against the wall of the side landing and went back to the living room to make a very important phone call.

Jack and Scotty were waiting nervously for Mahoney under the pavilion at the park. As it grew darker, the only light was cast from the electric street lamps nearby. Underneath each light, the misty rain that had begun minutes earlier was now heavier and slicing down on an angle. Thunder cracking in the skies over the Detroit River told them that the weather was only going to get worse, and very soon. The two men were quiet, both of them wondering if their boss would actually show up despite the oncoming storm, both of them contemplating the impact that the next hour would have on their collective fates.

The rain picked up, and the first flash of lightening revealed a figure with an umbrella walking from the sidewalk up to the pavilion. Jack and Scotty looked at each other, and after taking a deep breath, Jack exhaled and mumbled sideways, "Here we go, partner."

Mahoney approached the men, studying them both closely without saying a word. The annoyed look on his face said, "This better be good."

"Thanks for coming to meet us, Seamus," Jack began, talking loudly over the sound of driving rain pattering the corrugated steel on the pavilion roof. "We have something very important to talk to you about."

"So talk," was the curt response.

Jack looked over at Scotty briefly. The intermittent illumination of each man's face by the swaying street lamps and the flashes of lightning combined with the jolting thunder created an intense atmosphere. Jack's elevated heart rate jumped even higher, and he had difficulty swallowing. "I'm . . . uh. I mean, my partner here and I . . . well, we're worried, Seamus."

Mahoney tilted his head, waiting for more.

Jack pushed through more confidently now, sticking to what they had rehearsed. "We have always done everything that you and your boss have asked. You know that, right?" He was waiting for agreement from Mahoney, but none came. "And after this last request, we started to plan the bridge shipments and even met with Diesbourg, but neither operation looks promising." Jack stole a glance at Scotty, who was nervously running his fingers over the edges of the hat that he was looking down at in his hands. Mahoney still remained silent, his eyes tightening to a suspicious glare, so Jack continued. "You see, if we start up either of these operations, we are going to be targets for the Purples, and we think—uh, we wonder if maybe—you and your boss know that."

Mahoney finally spoke. "What are you saying, Mr. Ducharme? Are you saying we don't know what we're doing? That we want you two to fail or meet some untimely tragedy? Is that what you're saying?"

"No, Seamus. Well . . . maybe. We just wonder if you thought through all of the potential problems, is all we're saying," Jack answered.

"Who's we? I only see one person talking here, Mr. Ducharme," he said, looking menacingly at Scotty.

"I . . . I feel the same way, Mr. Mahoney," Scotty almost shouted over the sounds of the intensifying storm. While Mahoney stared at him, he continued. "I feel like I did in the trenches when our C.O. would tell us that we're goin' over the top and there seemed to be no good in it. Nothin' to gain. And we knew guys were gonna die." The limited light on Mahoney's face showed he was unmoved. "It just isn't making sense, is all we're sayin'." He paused, then gathered all his nerve to say, "It feels like you people are tryin' to get us killed."

An uncomfortable silence followed; you could have cut the tension with a knife. Jack and Scotty looked at each other, waiting for a response. Mahoney read each of the men's faces carefully for several seconds, then put his head down, seemingly gathering his own thoughts. "First," he stated with loud authority over the sound of the storm, "it is not for you to question the direction we go. Just like you didn't question your C.O., Mr. McLuren. You get an order, and you follow it. Secondly, gentlemen, if we wanted you two gone, you'd be six feet under already," he explained. "It doesn't make much business sense to get rid of employees who are making the organization money, does it? We're in the moneymaking business, gentlemen. We're not killers."

Considering the trauma of witnessing his father's murder, this statement caused an uncontrollable reaction in Jack as his eyes shot up and met Mahoney's with an intense hatred that was hard to hide.

His look, caught in a bright flash of lightning, caught Mahoney a bit off guard, and he instinctually slipped his right hand behind his back slowly as he said condescendingly, "Mr. Ducharme. A look like that will not serve any purpose here tonight."

Jack took a deep breath and turned his gaze away from Mahoney in an attempt to subdue his rage. He found it much easier to calm down with the satisfaction of knowing what should be happening at that very moment at Mahoney's house.

Scotty attempted to ease the tension as well. Looking over at Jack, he struggled to speak loudly over the driving rain. "I guess what we're askin' here is for some guarantees about these two operations. What happens if they can't get off the ground? If they're not possible or we need more time? Will St. P—uh, will your boss give us more time?

Mahoney's eyes flew open wide and looked from Scotty to Jack. Jack stifled his reaction. "What did you say?" Mahoney shouted.

Scotty recovered quickly, acting like he hadn't just made the most deadly mistake of his life, and answered, "I'm asking if your boss will give us a break or more time."

Mahoney looked at both men suspiciously, not sure if he had heard what he thought he had heard. The roaring noise all around them from the storm and the pelting on the pavilion roof made it difficult to hear anything clearly. The expression on both of their faces gave him no reason to force the issue, but his patience had clearly run out. He had little experience with subordinates questioning orders, and the foul weather darkened his mood considerably. "That's not an option. It's an order, gentlemen. From the boss." He made a point of looking at Scotty when he said the word boss. "So instead of dragging me out in this bloody storm and wasting my time with your goddamned whining, you should be figuring out a way to make the operations work." He put on his hat, opened his umbrella, and turned to leave.

Jack and Scotty looked at each other, both realizing they could not drag the meeting out any further. Concerned about buying time for Joey, Jack reached into his coat, took out his father's treasured pocket watch, and tried to find a splash of light so they could check the time.

Mahoney began walking away, preparing himself for the storm he would encounter once he left the overhead protection of the pavilion. He was lost in thought as he second-guessed himself about what he thought he had heard from McLuren and questioned the urgency of the meeting that just took place. His uneasiness intensified seconds later when he looked back briefly from under his umbrella in the pouring rain and in a bright flash of lightning saw the two men looking down and straining to see the time on Ducharme's pocket watch.

....

Earlier, the darkening sky and distant thunder had promised rain was on its way as Joey sat with Mr. Dario in a dark-blue Buick a distance down the alley behind one of Seamus Mahoney's neighbours' houses. They had been waiting less than thirty minutes, but to Joey it felt longer. He tried casual conversation, but Joey had trouble understanding most of what was said, and the older man seemed content to sit silently and smoke one cigarette after another, dropping the butts out a thin crack in his window. Joey wanted so badly to ask the older man about his days as a gangster in the old country, but he could see that wasn't going to happen.

Just when the extended period of silence was becoming uncomfortable, they spotted Mahoney coming from the side of his house. They both crouched instinctively. With umbrella in hand, Mahoney looked north to the skies over the river, pulled his collar up, adjusted his hat, and began walking away from them down to the other end of the alley.

As he exited the far end and disappeared from sight, Joey went to grab the door latch, but Mr. Dario put his hand and forearm across his scrawny chest. Unsure what they were waiting for, Joey let go. Soon large raindrops began tapping and pinging against the windshield and the thin metal of the hood and roof of the automobile. The rolling thunder in the distance grew louder.

Joey's patience was almost at the breaking point when Dario announced, "*Andiamo*, Joseppi. Let-sa go." They both exited the vehicle and closed the doors quietly. Joey pulled his coat up over his head with one hand while the other held a flashlight and a small burlap bag. Mr. Dario casually put his old, ragged cap on his balding head while they both walked quickly towards Mahoney's backyard. A dog in a nearby yard barked as the heavy raindrops drummed off the roofs of nearby garages and garden sheds. Flashes of lightning illuminated the sky for brief periods as the storm clouds overhead turned early dusk into a premature nightfall.

As Joey and the older man reached one of the two small windows at the back of the house, Mr. Dario kneeled, took the burlap bag from Joey, and wrapped it around his right elbow and forearm. Leaning on the house with his left hand, he froze and looked up to the skies. After an uncomfortable amount of time with his partner just waiting there in the pouring rain, Joey's patience was being tested once again. Suddenly, another bright shock of lightning lit up the sky. Dario dropped his head, cocked his wrapped arm, and when a crack of thunder followed only seconds after, he threw an elbow punch that shattered the window. The move impressed Joey. Dario reached in, unlocked the awning window at the bottom latch, and pushed, swinging it up into the curtains. As he held the window frame open, he grabbed the flashlight from Joey and signalled him to crawl in. Once his head was inside, Joey used the inside bottom corners of the window frame to pull his shoulders through. Although it was a tighter fit than he'd expected at his shoulders and chest, Joey shimmied his way past his waist, at which point his body weight brought him down hard to a table below with an umph. After standing and getting his bearings, he reached up and was handed the flashlight and bag. *"Presto, Joseppi. Goa fast,"* he was instructed loudly over the noisy rain.

Mr. Dario crouched and watched flickering beams of light bouncing around through the shroud of thin curtains as Joey negotiated his way in the dusty old basement. Following the directions he was given, Joey made his way to the wall where he knew he would find the old cupboard. Moving quickly, he used the flashlight to look behind several squeaky doors. Some were empty, while others held a variety of items that he was not going to waste time investigating. He knew what he was looking for. When he opened the bottom right door, Joey smiled and said, "Gotcha," as his light shone on a black leather briefcase. With his flashlight tucked under his arm, he pulled the case out, slid it into the bag, and went to close the door when the bouncing beam of light caught something else at the back of the shelf. He put the bag down, shone the light in again, reached back, and pulled a dark envelope out. Looking inside, he found another leather-bound book. He added this to his bag and was making his way back to the window when the beam of light passed over a lone, large cardboard box sitting in the nearby corner. Knowing he had completed his task in record time and unable to resist his curiosity, he put the bag on the table below the window and went to investigate. He unfolded the top flaps of the box and shone the light inside. The sight took his breath away. The box was three-quarters full of elastic-bound stacks of money piled in a variety of denominations.

Joey could hear the driving rain outside, and the occasional thunder was preceded by flashes that lit up sections of the basement for a split second at a time, like two large rectangular spotlights being turned on and off quickly. Despite knowing that he was committing a crime and breaking into the home of a dangerous gangster, Joey had not felt any hesitation about the endeavour; in fact, he had been excited about being involved in such a bold plan. But now, staring down at what he knew was more money than he would ever see in his entire life, anxiety crept in. His initial instinct had him thinking about ways to get the contents of the large box through the small window. Then he considered the job that his uncle and Mr. Ducharme had sent him to do; stealing cash was not part of it. His greed was overpowered by the fear of disappointing the people that had put so much trust and faith in him. He reluctantly left the box as it was and headed back for the window.

Outside, the rain was now coming down in a steady torrent and pelting off the back of Mr. Dario's coat and hat as he remained crouched and looking towards the basement window. The darkness, the rain, and his position facing the window made it impossible for him to see or hear the large figure slopping through the wet ground and coming up behind him.

Jakob Wojcik, the Mad Russian, had received a call from Seamus less than an hour before, ordering him to watch his place while he went out for a short meeting. The late notice and stormy conditions caused some delay; the Mad Russain had arrived on foot from the dark alley only moments before. Through the heavy rain he saw flashes of light from his boss's basement window, and the recurring flashes of lightning revealed a lone person huddled in front of it. Staying out of the crouched intruder's sightlines, he inched his way up the back lawn and removed a short steel pipe from inside his trench coat.

In the basement, Joey was negotiating his way onto the table below the window. With the flashlight slid into his jacket pocket, he handed the bag up through the curtains and out the opening. Once Mr. Dario had it and placed it beside him, he got on his knees and struggled to push the window frame back up towards the ceiling with one hand while he offered the other to Joey to help pull him out. When Joey's arms and head made it far enough out, he let go of his partner and used the outer windowsill to shimmy himself through the rest of the way. The rain began pelting him as his hips were clearing the opening. A smile of success that was forming on his face as he glanced up towards Mr. Dario suddenly turned to a look of horror as a bright lightning flash illuminated a hulking figure standing behind the older man, the figure's raised hand brandishing a blunt object. Joey's expression caused a split second of confusion for his partner as the object came down with a thud so loud it could be heard over the storm. Mr. Dario's sudden dead weight dropped to the side, the outline of his face landing hard and splashing in a muddy puddle only feet from Joey.

In a sudden state of shock, everything began happening to Joey in slow motion—straining to see Mr. Dario's face as his eyes adjusted to the darkness; flashes of light reflecting off the water Mr. Dario's head lay in; two big, strong hands grabbing Joey's coat and yanking him the rest of the way from the window opening; being lifted off the wet ground by his jacket collar and staring up into the outline of an evil-looking face; a large mouth moving and loud shouting that made no sense.

A violent slap across Joey's face snapped him back to the grave reality he found himself in. "Who you worrk forr?!" the Mad Russian was shouting in a thick accent as rain ran down his face and streamed off his chin.

"I...I don't work for no one," Joey yelled, his eyes wide with fear.

"One morre time or pain," the Mad Russian threatened. "Who you worrk for?"

Joey was regaining his wits, but was in a panic. "Just myself, mister. I break into houses."

"Wid him?" the giant asked sarcastically, looking down at Dario's motionless body.

"We work as a team—" Joey began, but was cut off.

"*Nyet. Nyet.* You lie, little man," the Russian argued. He removed one hand from Joey's collar, still easily holding him up on his toes, and reached into his own coat. He produced the same object he had struck Dario with, pulled Joey close enough to smell liquor and cigarettes on his breath, and demanded, "Tell trruth now or die."

The Russian's strength allowed him to easily spin Joey around and bring the cold, wet steel pipe up against his throat. Joey instinctively brought his hands up and curled his fingers around the pipe where it made contact with his neck. The Russian leaned back, increasing the force to the point where Joey's feet were kicking wildly off the ground.

"Trruth now?" he repeated as Joey's windpipe reacted to the pressure, causing him to choke and sputter.

Joey forced out some garbled words and his feet touched the wet ground again as the Russian relaxed some of the force. Clearing his throat, he managed a loud but raspy, "We're...just ...thieves."

The Russian's patience came to an end. "You die," he said matter-of-factly. He applied even more force on the pipe than earlier as Joey's thin, frail body was jolted off the ground once again. With his hands still helping cushion some of the pressure, Joey began contemplating the reality of his imminent death. As his airway began collapsing and his breathing became laboured, the rush of thoughts weren't about his young life ending so early, but were strangely focused on the disappointment of letting his uncle and Mr. Ducharme down. A profound sadness overtook him as he resigned himself to his fate.

Suddenly, as his grip on the pipe began to give way and he could feel his windpipe being crushed, Joey felt something slide across the back of his head and a rush of warm liquid trickle down his back. In an instant, all the force ended, sending him falling to the ground. As he lay there bewildered, another flash of light revealed the face of the Russian lying next to him in a darkened puddle, his evil, vacant eyes open. Joey's throat was searing with pain as he looked up to see Mr. Dario casually using the top of the burlap bag to wipe a long knife clean.

MAHONEY'S DARK MOOD ONLY WORSENED AS he trudged home in the storm. His pant legs and shoes were uncomfortably wet. He was tired and beyond annoyed not only at Ducharme and McLuren, but also at himself for agreeing to such a useless meeting on such a miserable night. Making matters worse, the meeting had raised more concerns that he would have to deal with. The boys clearly understood they were being set up with the new operations that Saint was demanding. But something else about the meeting was gnawing at Mahoney, and his instincts for trouble were usually right.

As he entered his alley, the storm began to subside. The worst of it was moving to the south, and only a gentle wind and light rain remained. He dodged puddles even though his shoes and wool socks were already soaked.

As he made his way around the back of his garage, into his yard, and to the back of his house, he was alarmed at the scene that slowly came into focus. A dim light from the next-door neighbour's back porch revealed a body propped up against the brick wall next to his basement window. Mahoney scanned the area well before getting closer to investigate.

His pulse quickened as he recognized the Russian's ugly, rugged face, drained of any colour, and the near-black-stained shirt collar and coat below his deeply gashed throat. The Russian's favourite weapon, a sixteen-inch steel pipe, sat on his lap, soaked in blood; looking around the body, Mahoney spotted some broken glass on the ground. The curtains of the narrow basement window next to the Russian were fluttering in the breeze.

Mahoney always prided himself on his calm and cool disposition, but the sight of the dead Russian and his breached fortress threw him into a full panic. He made his way quickly into the house via the side door and pushed the buttons on the wall to bring light to the landing and basement. His hands were shaking so badly that he struggled to get the key from around his neck and insert it into the padlock, whereupon it fell open with a clack.

The first thing that caught Seamus' eye as he got to the bottom of the stairs was the open cardboard box in the corner, but that's not where he headed first. With an increasing feeling of dread, he went immediately to the cupboard by the wall and opened the only door he used on a regular basis—the only one that mattered. Hoping his eyes were failing him, he reached in and felt around. Empty. His knees felt weak as he considered the implications of losing not only the books that recorded his organization's day-to-day business transactions, but also the more important one that named names. This one critical book, which he had spent years putting together and which he updated regularly, was supposed to be the ace up his sleeve if ever the Saint or the Purples put a price on his head; it would have been his most valuable bargaining tool with the authorities if his freedom was ever threatened.

Mahoney's legs were growing weak as they carried him slowly over to the opened cardboard box. Peering in, he was surprised to see that most if not all of the money was still there. Giving in to his wobbly legs, he leaned his back against the bare wall next to the box and slid down until he was sitting on the dusty cement floor. His head was reeling.

His first instinct being self-preservation, Mahoney began considering when and how to report the theft to the Saint. He had worked under St. Pierre long enough to know that the death of the Russian would be of minor consequence. The Russian had no family here and, given his line of work, no true friends. Filling his vacancy with another ruthless, desperate immigrant wouldn't be too difficult. The loss of the books, however, was a threat to the organization, which meant a threat to himself and the Saint.

He knew he needed to act quickly. He went upstairs and immediately made a telephone call to the Wolf. He needed to take care of the Russian's body and secure his basement while it was still dark.

Once the call was placed and an old blanket was thrown over the body in the backyard, Seamus sat at his kitchen table while waiting for help to arrive. Despite his justifiable anxiety about reporting the incident to St. Pierre, his thoughts inevitably turned to who might be responsible. Although there were many unanswered questions about possible suspects, there was one thing Mahoney already knew: two or more people had to have been involved. He was absolutely sure that any person who was small enough to squeeze through his narrow basement window could not have been strong enough to murder the Russian. There weren't many people who came to mind . . . except . . .

Mahoney's instincts and his common sense were at odds. His gut was pointing to the unscheduled and unproductive meeting he'd been called to earlier and how it coincided with the theft and murder. His common sense, however, argued that the timing must have been an unbelievable coincidence because he felt certain that Ducharme and McLuren lacked the skills, nerve, and brutality to have been involved.

Thinking like a police investigator, Mahoney began considering motive. Who would want the books? Liquor agents and police, for sure, but their weapons of choice were warrants and arrests, not a knife across a gangster's throat. He also couldn't see anybody in his own organization, or the Purples for that matter, being involved, especially considering that his box of cash had been found, but not taken. None of it made any sense.

A single rap on his side entrance door jolted him back to the task at hand. Without needing to say a word, he joined the Wolf outside and began the first, and no doubt the easiest, step in cleaning up a very big mess.

....

As Joey lay on the couch with an ice pack on his throat, Jack, Scotty, Maria, and Mr. Dario sat silently in chairs around the Ducharmes' parlour, staring at the wet, muddy burlap bag sitting on the hardwood floor in front of them. Even though the group had agreed that securing the books would be the only possible lifeline for Jack and Scotty, having them there now and knowing the repercussions if they were ever caught was making all but one of them anxious and tense. All except Maria's father. He was sitting, holding an icepack to his swollen and bloodied head while his other hand held a cigarette, a little confused at the sombre mood in the room.

When Dario and Joey had appeared at the front door minutes before, Maria was near panic mode. Her husband and Scotty had been back from their meeting with Seamus earlier than anyone had expected, and they were all concerned that the two thieves might have run out of time. Then came the sight of her father, caked blood surrounding a massive bump on the side of his head, helping Joey, whose own head and jacket were covered with darkened blood, up the porch to the front door. It proved to be both a relief and a shock.

"Oh, Poppa. What happened?" Maria wanted to know as they came through the doorway.

Mr. Dario handed Joey over to Maria before he swung the burlap bag, partly stained with blood as well, onto the foyer floor and with a sly smile said, "*E fatto.* Itsa done."

Jack and Scotty, standing back with wide eyes, shifted their gaze from a dazed Joey to the bag on the floor in front of them and then over to Maria's father, standing proudly by the door. Although they all were desperate for a recap of the events, Joey was unable to speak. Scotty helped him out of his blood-stained jacket and shirt, while Jack left to find him something else to wear. The oversized shirt he returned with made Joey look even frailer; he was given an old throw blanket and helped to a nearby sofa to lie down. Mr. Dario stood expressionless, smoking a cigarette and silently watching the others tend to Joey.

Once Joey was comfortable, Maria looked at Jack, then guided her father to the other sofa, saying, "Poppa. Tell me what happened. *Cos'è successo?*"

As they all sat, her father began a rapid-fire explanation in Italian to his daughter. His rising and falling intonation and theatrical gestures with his hands, along with Maria's occasional gasps and hands over her mouth in a display of horror, had Jack and Scotty on the edge of their seats. Jack attempted a couple of times to get an update, but Maria's reactions told him to be patient until her father was finished. At one point, Maria interrupted to ask him something, and Mr. Dario reached down under his pant leg and presented a long, deadly-looking knife.

Minutes later, her father's flurry of Italian ended abruptly and his hands dropped back into his lap. Maria continued to look at him wide-eyed before she slowly turned towards her husband and Scotty, whose anticipation was making it difficult for them to sit still. Even Joey leaned up on his elbow, anxious to hear the details of his own near-death experience.

She organized her thoughts and began to translate. "Poppa says that the plan was going very well, but it was a terrible storm. He says that Joey got through the window, even though it was a tight fit, and found the briefcase along with the other package and handed it out to him. But when he was helping Joey back out the window, Poppa was...*eliminato*..." She looked at her father, who was demonstrating, using his hand to hit the back of his head, then continued, "knocked out...with a steel pipe by a very big man." With tears forming, Maria looked sympathetically at Jack, who was already staring off, lost in the painful memory of the similar cowardly attack on his father years before. Scotty put a supportive hand on Jack's shoulder as Jack insisted she continue.

"Poppa doesn't know how long he was out, but when he came to, he saw the man lifting and trying to choke Joey with the pipe." All eyes turned towards Joey on the couch. Joey leaned up further, put his hand to his throat, and tried to speak, but the grimace of pain that accompanied an inaudible rasp caused Scotty to raise his hand and demand he stop. The room fell quiet as Maria turned back towards her father, seemingly unsure how to continue. As tears ran down her cheeks, she went on, "Poppa said the man was *cosi grande,* so big, that he could not stop him, so he used his knife." She paused, looking down. "And cut his throat. He's dead." Jack and Scotty looked at each other in disbelief, while Joey leaned back onto the sofa and stared at the ceiling.

Mr. Dario looked around the room, a little confused, like a kid wondering if he had inadvertently done something wrong. He broke the silence with, "Itsa good, no? Hava da books. Noa more *bastardo cattivo!*"

Scotty stood and attempted to change the dark mood that hung in the air by saying, "Yes. Yes, Mr. Dario. It is good. You and Joey did very good." He looked at Jack and added emphatically, like he was trying to convince his best friend, "And that man deserved to die."

Maria wiped the tears from her face and put her arms around her father as Jack stood and made his way towards them. He reached out to his father-in-law with his right hand and extended his left to Joey on the sofa. "Gentlemen," he said with profound sincerity and tears welling up in his own eyes, "We owe you our lives. Thank you. *Grazie.*"

Scotty made his way over to Mr. Dario also and shook his hand, putting his left hand over his heart. He then turned to Joey, put his hand on his nephew's head, and said, "I could not be prouder of you, kid. I'd go into battle with you anytime, young man." Despite the obvious pain he was in, a proud smile lit up Joey's face.

Mr. Dario brought a sudden end to the serious atmosphere by looking to the floor and saying, "Whatsa ina da bag?"

Minutes later, Dario was using his knife to break into the leather case as Jack wiped off the leather-bound book he took from the wet, muddy envelope. Then Jack gathered them together and dropped them with a low thud on the coffee table. "Our freedom and our lives now depend on these," he announced.

....

Early the following morning, well after Mr. Dario had made his way home to his wife, Joey had fallen asleep on the sofa, and Maria had made her way to bed, Jack and Scotty were still poring over the books. Keenly aware of their importance and the unlimited and potentially deadly resources that would be used to find them and get them back, the two men moved to a small table with a desk lamp, far away from any windows. The rest of the house was dark. While Scotty was shocked by the vast assortment of the names of the people and places with direct ties to the organization, Jack was more interested and increasingly impressed with the complicated financial structures that

Mahoney had set up and maintained. The operations being run and the profits they were pulling in were beyond anything he could have imagined.

Although the financials found in the ledgers inside the briefcase would be a treasure trove for liquor control, the police, and court prosecutors, the two men agreed that the additional book, the one found in the envelope, could prove to be the most valuable for their plan to succeed. They understood why it was not with the others. Clearly Mahoney had other, more personal intentions with that book.

By late morning—a beautiful, bright Saturday—Jack and Scotty were exhausted. With all of them involved in the dramatic events of the previous night, they had little choice but to call Johnny and have him come by for the keys to open the paint shop. The request was a first for Johnny, and although he welcomed the added responsibility, he worried about running the place alone on a busy Saturday morning.

Before Scotty and Jack could drag themselves to work for what was destined to be a very tiring day, they needed a plan for the books. They both agreed that the books should not be at either of their homes or the shop. They knew once Mahoney discovered the theft and murder, he would be enraged and in a desperate state, using every resource he had to find the culprits and the books. Their homes and shop could become targets of a search if Mahoney had any inkling that they might be involved—a real possibility after the less-than-convincing emergency meeting they'd requested the night before. They agreed the books also needed to be nearby, where they could access them as part of their normal routine, in case they were being watched. Despite Jack's misgivings, they both knew the best place was a few doors down at his mother's house. After some discussion, Scotty eased his partner's concerns and brought a smile to Jack's face when he pointed out that his dear friend Moose's house was the perfect place to hide the evidence that would help bring his murderers to justice.

Less than an hour later, while Scotty was at the shop fighting off the exhaustion from a sleepless night, Jack was making a stop at his mother's house on his way to work. His mother and Annie were in the kitchen when he let himself in the front door, carrying a small cotton pillowcase that held the books. He dropped in so often that the ladies greeted him from a distance.

"What are you girls up to today?" he called from the foyer while scanning the hallway and front parlour for potential hiding places.

"Making a mess," Annie teased from the kitchen.

"Oh, Annie. Stop it," their mother said. "We're doing our strawberry preserves. Not at work today, dear? Is everything alright with Maria and Mo?"

Distracted by the task at hand, Jack answered while searching, "Heading over there now. Everybody is good, mother." Crouching down to get a better angle nearer to the floor, his eyes fell on a potential spot. He wanted it close to the front door for quick, easy access, but as inconspicuous as possible.

Jack walked into the parlour, looking more closely at the elegant grandfather clock, his father's anniversary gift to his mother during the height of their Skim success years before. Thinking of his father, especially now when they were risking their lives to bring him justice and themselves some peace, tugged that much harder at his heartstrings. Like so many other nice things that Moose bought his wife, Jack recalled his father having to convince Sara, yet again, that she should enjoy some of the finer things in life. Jack could still hear her saying, "Oh, Maurice. It's stunning, but so ritzy for us." By that time, however, his father had honed his skills at salesmanship and explained that not only was she indeed worthy of such a grand gift, but Annie would also benefit from the beautiful chimes that announced the time of day each hour.

Using a small brass key he located in the nearby coffee-table drawer, Jack opened the ornate wooden door at the bottom of the clock, where the shiny silver and brass mechanisms churned and clicked with precision from the once-a-month winding. Sliding the white pillowcase in, Jack found that the space between the lowest wheel and the base was just big enough to fit the flat stack of books.

Jack closed the door, locked it with the key, and was startled by his sister standing behind him when he turned to go. Looking blankly in his direction, Annie asked, "What are you doing, Jackie?"

"Oh...well...just adjusting the clock. I noticed the time was off when I walked in. It needed to be wound," Jack replied, looking nervously for his mother in the direction of the kitchen.

"That's odd," she said. "It was just done last week, I think." She felt around, and when her hand made contact with the arm of the nearby sofa, she took a side step towards it and sat down. "Is something on your mind, Jackie? You don't sound like yourself."

Jack was always amazed at his sister's innate ability to pick up on someone's state of mind based on subtle changes in their voice and tone. When they were younger, Annie used to report to him the kind of mood each of their parents was in after eavesdropping on conversations. It came in very handy when either of them wanted to ask for something. "Everything is fine, Annie. I'm just a little tired, and I'm late getting to work," he answered, very conscious of the way he said it. His sister seemed unconvinced as he stood up and forced a change in the subject. "How is mother? Is she sleeping better?"

"Same as always," Annie answered, fully aware of his tactic. "She's still up in the middle of the night, and I still hear her crying sometimes in the kitchen. Even more lately, because their anniversary is coming up again. I've tried to sit and comfort her, but she prefers to be alone. The curse of a broken heart, I guess."

Jack now regretted diverting Annie towards that subject. His mother's continued grief was painful to witness over the years, but it also helped fuel his desire for retribution. Because his mother had so many unanswered questions about her husband's death, Jack was in a constant state of internal struggle about telling her the truth. He truly felt, however, that the enormity of the truth—her husband's murder, their involvement in illegal activities with a crime group, and his quest for vengeance—would be more than she would be able to understand or endure. He looked forward to a day, very soon he hoped, when St. Pierre, Mahoney, and their people were destroyed and he was a free, legitimate businessman. Then he could have a long-overdue talk with his mother and Annie.

"Jackie?" Annie broke the silence. "Are you sure there's nothing you'd like to talk about?"

"I'm sure, kid," he responded, standing up and slipping the brass key into his pocket. He reached for her hand and kissed her on the top of her head, saying, "I've got to get to work. We'll talk later." With a goodbye call to his mother, still working away in the kitchen, Jack made his way out the front door.

"What did Jackie want, Annie?" her mother asked after Annie felt her way back to the kitchen.

"I'm not really sure, mother," she answered, deep in thought.

JOHNNY, THE MOST JUNIOR EMPLOYEE AT McLUREN PAINTS, was unaware that he was the subject of such great interest as he opened the shop first thing Saturday morning. He felt a certain pride as he made his way up the shop's sidewalk, unlocked the front door, and then made his way out back to the yard to take the chain off the gate. He didn't notice that he was being watched by two separate cars parked adjacent to one another on the opposite street corner. In one car were two liquor agents assigned the job by Inspector Mousseau. One of those men, an Agent Simmons, had been on Seamus Mahoney's payroll for a couple of years, ready to tip him off if there was any talk of raids or arrests. He knew that although a search warrant for the shop was being processed and was planned for Tuesday, Mousseau was getting increasingly nervous about Ducharme making some kind of move or skipping town beforehand.

In the other car, sitting in the shade of a large maple tree, was a lone and much more inconspicuous gentleman, a freelance gangster hired by the Wolf, who was given the simple instructions to stake out and report. His window was rolled down, and he sat and smoked while reading the Saturday morning paper.

Well over an hour after the shop opened, Mousseau's agents and the Wolf's man left their posts briefly at different times to get to the nearest telephone and call in a similar report: although a few customers had come and gone through the front door or driven a car into and out of the yard, the two bosses and the other kid who usually ran the shop were nowhere to be seen.

....

When the Wolf called to say that the Quebec boys were a no-show at work, Mahoney ordered his trusted goon to have his people move their stakeout to Jack and Scotty's homes instead. They had clear instructions to remain unseen and call in a report before noon about anything even remotely suspicious. The last thing he wanted was to spook them, in case they did have the books or knew their whereabouts.

Any doubts that Mahoney had about Ducharme and McLuren being involved in the theft and murder at his place the night before were evaporating quickly. The Saint's words, "I don't believe in fucking coincidences," kept coming back to him and forced him to face the dangerous prospect of having to report the mess to his boss before he could clean it up himself. Time was not on his side. Mahoney knew better than anybody that the longer he waited to report this unprecedented threat, the greater the wrath he would face from St. Pierre. He decided to go see the Saint at noon, right after an update by the Wolf.

The Wolf received his reports just after 11:30 a.m. One said that the McLuren fellow had made his way to work as usual, but was two hours late. There was nothing suspicious about his appearance or his demeanour. The other call was much more interesting and promising: Ducharme had left his house around 10:30, carrying a white bag while looking around nervously. He stopped briefly three doors down at his mother's place before going to work. The package he was carrying must have been left there. The Wolf knew Mahoney would be even more interested in what his man witnessed as his car began following Ducharme to work only minutes later. The skinny kid who worked at the shop appeared from his boss's house nearby and was being helped down the front-porch steps by Ducharme's pretty wife. She had her arm around his waist as he walked gingerly, one hand holding a bulky bandage around his neck.

Armed with these updates, Mahoney reluctantly headed to meet St. Pierre. The midday sun beating down was not the only thing making him sweat. Because of the sudden and urgent nature of the meeting, they ended up meeting in St. Pierre's backyard, a place where they had met only once before. Seamus was careful to park a block away and to slip into the Saint's yard using the back gate.

"This better be important," St. Pierre warned, scanning the neighbours' backyards as Mahoney approached. He hated any situation that caused his two separate lives to converge.

Mahoney looked down nervously towards his hat. The men sat under an ornate pergola adorned with the flowering vines of mid-summer. On the ground around him, sunrays were dancing on the ground. Mahoney fully expected his news would be met with an uncontrollable tirade and personal insults about his incompetence. He wasn't disappointed. His boss's face reddened and he became increasingly agitated as Mahoney explained what he found when he came home from the meeting with the Quebec boys the night before, his suspicions about their involvement, and what the surveillance from the morning had revealed.

With his wife nearby in the kitchen and neighbours' homes close by, St. Pierre avoided his usual loud, profanity-filled bluster and leaned in, quietly snarling, "What the hell have you done, you stupid fuckin' mick? How could you let this happen? These two-bit choirboys played you for a goddamned fool. They could ruin us!"

Mahoney absorbed the jabs like a seasoned prize-fighter and waited to respond. As he watched his boss seethe across from him, he couldn't help thinking what would happen if St. Pierre knew the whole truth, about the other, more damaging book that was taken as well. After letting St. Pierre unleash, he said, "Listen, boss. We both agreed my basement was the best place to stash them. I don't know how or who could have got through that window. It would have to be a child or an unbelievably skinny—" he paused, suddenly realizing the connection to the injured kid reported earlier by the Wolf. It had to be McLuren's nephew who had gotten in, the one Mahoney had seen around the shop.

St. Pierre watched Mahoney fall deep into thought, piecing something together across from him. "What?" he asked angrily.

"I think I know who lifted the books for them," Mahoney said. "But somebody else had to be there. There's no way that kid could have taken out the Russian alone."

"I don't give a damn about him. Another dead Ruskie. Who cares?" the Saint said, waving his hand. "What I do care about is our business being out there for sale," Mahoney's boss made clear. "And make no mistake, that's the only reason anybody would want them."

Seamus was digesting the possible explanations, but was confused. "Why would the Quebec boys want to risk that? Throw us and themselves at the law?"

"They must have made a deal with that Mousseau bastard, for Christ's sake," Saint pointed out.

Mahoney was still piecing together his thoughts, staring out into the Saint's yard. "I don't think so, boss. Our guy inside liquor control was doing the tailing this morning. He's telling me that they are planning a raid in a couple days. Says Mousseau has it out for the boys now."

"Maybe they know about the raid...maybe they're going to use the books as their bargaining chip."

Mahoney shook off the idea, saying, "That's assuming they know about the heat on them and the raid. How could they know that? You're giving them too much credit. They can't be that smart."

Mahoney's assessment of the situation pushed St. Pierre's self control past its breaking point. The boss stood up in a fury, knocking his chair over as he leaned forward, pointing a finger and shouting, "Too much credit? Jesus Christ! The problem here, you dumb limey, is that you underestimated them!" Mahoney was looking around as the yelling continued, his boss's spit flying and catching bits of the sun's rays splashing through the pergola. "You keep telling me you trust them. 'They're just two-bit runners, not that smart. They wouldn't risk a good thing. They have families...' Bullshit! I'm saying you've been played for a goddamned patsy. Your carelessness has put everything I've worked for in jeopardy, for Christ's sake!" St. Pierre suddenly realized the scene he was creating and looked towards the house and around the neighbours' yards before sitting back down and taking a deep breath. He paused for a few moments, then looked up at Mahoney, leaned in, and quietly said through his teeth, "You caused this fuckin' mess, you bloody fool. So you're going to clean it up. I want those books back. Now. I don't care what it costs or who needs to be rubbed out, you understand?" Mahoney's eyes told him he did. "They are back in your hands by this weekend, or we're having a much different conversation on Monday morning."

....

A busy Saturday afternoon at the shop dragged into the evening as Jack and Scotty finally got to the work that their late arrival had left unfinished. Despite the long, stressful day, Johnny stayed to help as well. When everything was done and ready for the following Monday morning, Jack and Scotty sat in their office, still in their coveralls unbuttoned to the waist, ready to discuss the next step in their plan. In the heat of summer, they often kept cooler by climbing into the coveralls with just their boxers underneath. As they poured themselves a much-needed drink of whisky, Johnny wandered by the office on his way back from locking the yard gate.

"Hey, kid!" Scotty called as he walked by. Johnny poked his head in the doorway reluctantly. "Good job today. We're glad we could count on you." Jack was nodding in agreement.

"Sure thing, boss," the big, awkward teenager responded with an unusual look on his face that Jack had trouble reading. He went to leave, but his hand held the doorframe, and he turned back. "If you don't mind me askin'—is everything all right? I mean...are we in trouble or something? And what about Joey? Is he okay?"

After their unusual and sudden request that Johnny run things on his own that morning, the partners had expected some kind of inquiry from him. Jack fielded the question. "Everything is good, kid. We had a bit of an emergency last night, and Joey got injured helping us out, but he'll be fine. Don't you worry about him."

Johnny's eyes looked down, curious for details he knew he wasn't going to get. "Yes, sir."

Before he went on his way, Jack added, "And Johnny . . . things need to be even more secure around here for a little while. It's important you don't talk to anyone about anything. It's just business as usual, you understand?"

Johnny's eyes shifted back and forth nervously to both bosses. "Yes, sir." He stood there for a few seconds, unsure about what he should do next. "So...can I go now?"

"Yeah, get outta here, kid," Scotty said with a smile.

Johnny left with Scotty following to lock the front door behind him. He returned to the office, plopped down in his chair with a loud sigh of exhaustion, looked at Jack, and asked, "Now what?"

"I think the tough part is over, partner," Jack said with more than a hint of sarcasm. "Now we've just got to get the right books to the right people at the right time."

Johnny left the paint shop as the sun was fading and began walking his usual route home. As he turned the corner a few blocks from the shop, he looked back nervously and ducked beside a garage at the end of an alley. As he stood there shuffling his generous weight anxiously from one foot to the other, a shiny new Chevrolet slowly rolled towards him from down the alley. As it approached the young man, the passenger window rolled down and the Wolf smiled at Johnny, his menacing eyes and long eye-teeth causing him to look more like a rabid wild animal.

While the Wolf just stared, the driver said, "Hey, Johnny boy. What do ya got for us?"

Johnny, now sweating profusely, looked around and stammered, "Well...I...I asked them about being late and about Joey. They said there was some emergency last night ...and Joey got hurt. They didn't say anything else, I swear. And I went through their office desks and their shirts and pants and stuff...like you said...when they were out in the yard. I...I didn't find books, a bag, or nothin'. Just...well, I found their wallets, but I didn't want to steal—"

"C'mon, kid. We didn't ask you to steal dough. We've got lots of that to give you later. Did you find anything else? Anything?"

"I was rushing, you know? Scared of getting caught," Johnny continued. "But I did find this."

He held up a small key, the little remaining light sparkling off its shiny brass surface.

The Wolf reached for it and held it up for inspection.

"Do I get paid now?" Johnny asked.

"Sure, kid. Of course," the young driver answered. "But we can't do it here. Get in. We'll take you to get the cash and drop you close to home."

Johnny's heart began racing even faster. The two gangsters already made him nervous, and he certainly did not want to get in their car with them. Fearing their reaction to a refusal, he said, "Maybe you can get me the money another time. I only did it because you promised not to hurt my family."

The Wolf's smile did not leave his face as he looked at Johnny, making sure the youngster saw the revolver he slid from his waistband and held in his lap with his left hand. With his right, he reached behind him to pull the handle of the back door. The door swung open and in a deep, thick Polish accent he demanded, "Get in."

....

Jack and Scotty were a few drinks deep by the time they mapped out a timeline for the next couple of days. They were beyond exhausted, both mentally and physically, as they sat in their office chairs, still in their coveralls. From the small window behind his partner's desk, Scotty noticed the sun had recently set, prompting him to pull himself up from his chair and begin getting ready to leave. Jack followed suit.

The two men dropped their coveralls and reached for their pants and shirts, which hung on hooks behind their desks.

"Be nice to get a good night's sleep tonight, before I head out to the county in the mornin'," Scotty said, reaching for his clothes.

Jack looked wearily across the room, "Sleep? Really? This whole thing has made sleep impossible for me. I just want it all to be over."

"We're close. One last push, kid," Scotty replied.

Jack pulled up his trousers, zipped up, and buckled his belt. After slipping on his shirt and buttoning up, he put his hands into his pockets and froze, the colour draining from his face. He felt frantically around his pockets again and with a look of panic announced, "The key. It's gone."

Scotty stopped his buttoning and looked over with concern. "You sure it was in your pocket? Could you have put it somewhere else?"

"No...No...I'm sure it was right in this pocket," he answered. "I remember when I came in and hung my pants up. I double-checked just to be sure. I wanted to make sure where it was...those books are too important."

The two men stood there for a while, taking in the gravity of the situation and considering the possibilities. "We were the only ones here all day," Scotty pointed out, "and nobody woulda been near the office."

Seconds later, both men came to the same conclusion simultaneously. "Johnny," Jack stated with a look of bewilderment.

"But why would Johnny want it?" Scotty asked. "He wouldn't even know what the key was for."

"Nobody would. But somebody must have got to him and wanted him to start snooping—somebody that he couldn't say no to."

This new development was a gut punch to both men. Not only did they now realize that Mahoney and his goons probably knew they were involved in the previous night's activities, but there was also a chance they now had the key that could get them back their books—Jack and Scotty's only hope for the freedom they longed for and the justice they so desperately wanted.

Jack's mind was reeling, trying to absorb the situation they found themselves in. If Mahoney knew they had the books, they and their families were in grave danger.

Scotty was thinking the same thing. He was already picking up the telephone on his desk and anxiously making a call to make sure Joey was safe. While he was asking the switchboard operator to make the connection, Jack was pacing, mentally putting more pieces of the puzzle together. It did not take long before he came to the conclusion that the key piece, the piece that held their lives in the balance, was the books. If Mahoney and St. Pierre knew they were involved in the theft and murder, they should be dead—except for the books. Mahoney was too smart not to realize that the organization's survival—and because of his one tell-all book, his life—depended on getting the books back. Killing the only two people who knew where they were wouldn't help him do that. Thanks to Johnny, however, they might have the key, and if so...

Jack was brought back into the moment by the clunk of Scotty's telephone handset being dropped back on its cradle. "Everything is good with Joey," he said. "I told him to find somewhere else to spend the night. Now call Maria."

Jack made the call from his desk and was relieved to hear all was well at his home too. Trying not to scare his wife, he instructed her to gather up Mo and spend the night at her parents' place. He apologized for rushing and not being able to explain, telling Maria that he needed to make one more very important call. After a unusually heartfelt I love you, Jack tapped the telephone cradle repeatedly until he was connected once again with the switchboard, and then he asked to be connected to his mother's house.

"Hello, the Ducharme residence," Annie answered.

Trying not to raise any concerns, he said, "Hi, Annie. It's Jackie. What are you and mom up to tonight?"

"Mom's out at the church. The committee is setting up for the Sunday social after mass tomorrow. She'll be home later. Why?"

Jack searched for the right words. He couldn't ask his blind sister to go somewhere else all alone, and he didn't want to frighten her. "Annie. Listen carefully. I want you to do me a favour. I'm a little worried about—"

The conversation was suddenly interrupted when he heard a loud bang on his mother's door through the telephone. "Oh, goodness. One minute, Jackie. Someone's making an awful racket on our door," Annie said loudly, over the pounding.

Jack tried to yell over the commotion on the other end of the line. "Annie? Annie? Don't answer that...Annie?" He listened closely, helpless, to the sound of a door being forced open, his sister's muffled screams of protest, deep voices barking orders, heavy footsteps making their way to the kitchen, and finally the loud click of the telephone being hung up.

"Jesus Christ! They're there!" Jack cried out as he grabbed his car keys and flew in a panic out of the office. Scotty finished getting dressed as quickly as possible, gathered up his things, and rushed out to join him as fast as his limp could carry him. As he was locking the front door behind him, he could hear Jack's profanity-laced shouting from the seat of his car, parked out front.

"What's wrong?" Scotty asked as he approached.

"Bloody car won't start! Won't even turn over," he said in near hysterics.

"We'll take mine. Hurry!" Scotty rushed to his car nearby, climbed in, reached over to unlock the door for his partner, and turned the key. Nothing. Not even an ignition click. He looked blankly through the passenger window at his partner. He climbed out, and with Jack beside him, unlatched and folded up the side panel of his hood. With an expression of dread, both men stared at a handful of thick, black electrical wires cut and dangling uselessly from the car's firewall.

Jack's arms went up and his hands ran through his hair in a state of despair. "What do I do, Scotty? They're at Ma's. My sister—"

Scotty grabbed him by the arm, forcing him to make eye contact. "Go, Jack. You can get there in minutes."

Jack didn't hesitate. He turned and began running towards his mother's house, just over a mile away. His large frame sprinted through intersections, ran over lawns, and cut through alleys. Pedestrians jumped out of the way, people watched in the limited evening light with curiosity from their porches, and cars screeched and beeped as he covered the distance like a fugitive running for his life. His frenzied state of mind shifted from concern about his sister's safety to a flashback from nearly six years earlier when he was in a similar situation, running through the snow-covered darkened streets, fearing for his father's life. He prayed that this time, things would end differently.

....

Minutes later, dripping with perspiration from the evening humidity, his lungs burning from overexertion, he turned out of an alley only a few blocks from the house and raced across a darkened street. At that moment, a car's headlamps lit up Jack's light-coloured trousers as it skidded to a stop and slammed into his hip, sending him flying onto the dark, grassy boulevard.

Jack had no idea how long he had been unconscious, but gradually the loud humming sound in his ears subsided and was replaced with muffled murmurs from strangers hovering over him. His head felt like it was being squeezed in a press. A throbbing pain shot from his hip down his right leg. Even with his eyes closed and his body slowly registering the trauma it had just encountered, Jack returned to thoughts of the danger his sister was in.

As he opened his eyes and began to test various limbs for injury, he could hear the people surrounding him making hushed comments like "He's alive," "Are you okay, son?" and "Don't try to move." Using his skinned elbows, he pushed himself into a sitting position as those around him moved back with concern.

"Hey, mister. You should just lay down until a doctor sees you," one young man suggested. Others around him agreed.

"I've...got to get...home," Jack stammered slowly as he swung his legs over the curb, sending a bolt of pain through him. His bloodied face winced.

"He's delirious," a woman commented. "He can't go anywhere."

Even though there was concern for his well-being among the small group of strangers around him, his intimidating size as he struggled to stand, as well as his bloodied face and arms, gave him a frightening, monstrous appearance, which prevented anybody from trying to stop him. At first a little unsteady, he got his bearings and began limping in the direction of his street. Once he was well away from the startled group, who were still partially illuminated by the car's headlights, he slowly worked himself into a steady, but very painful, limping jog.

A short time later, he turned onto his block. Street lamps revealed nothing unusual as his mother's house came into view. Slowing to a walk as he neared the front sidewalk, Jack noticed the light coming from the front window and the front door was ajar. All was quiet.

As he pushed the front door open nervously, he called for his sister. Fear crept in when there was no response. He made his way into the foyer. Everywhere he looked, things were in disarray. Items of every kind littered the floor, furniture was turned over, and drawers and cabinet doors were open. His eyes instinctively swung towards the grandfather clock, now shattered across the hardwood floor of the parlour. The clock's bottom door was flung open, revealing nothing but the shiny pendulums and gears lying sideways. Any hope that Jack had had of achieving his longed-for vengeance, of breaking free from the grips of the organization, or even of staying alive vanished with the sight of that empty compartment. He felt utterly crushed.

Unconcerned now about his own safety, he focused on his sister. He limped towards the kitchen, calling loudly, "Annie! It's Jackie...Annie?" The door to the basement was open slightly, and as he moved by it, a stair creak from below stopped him in his tracks. He reached around the corner into a kitchen drawer and slid out the first sharp object he found, a well-worn boning knife his father used to use to cut up the various bits of meat when he made what he famously called "trench soup." Another creak came from the darkened basement as Jack stood next to the doorway, knife in hand. His heart was threatening to pound out of his chest.

Another creak was accompanied by, "Jackie? Is that you?"

Jack pressed the button to light the basement landing. Standing there was Annie, cautiously staring in his direction. "Yes, Annie, it's me," he answered in a hushed tone as he relaxed his iron grip on the knife and placed it on the counter. "I'm right here." He took a couple steps down and reached for the hand she was using to feel her way up the walls. They hugged.

"Oh, Jackie. Thank God." They separated and she faced her brother with a worried look. "Are you okay? You're soaking wet."

Jack was startled when the lone light bulb above them in the stairwell revealed that the side of her face was glistening with a combination of his sweat and the bright-red blood that continued to run down from the top of his head. "I'm fine. Just a little sweaty from work," he lied as he led her up the top few stairs and into the kitchen. Annie knew he was being dishonest as he guided her to a chair and searched for a hand towel in the nearby drawers. He found one and wiped her face and the side of her neck. When he finished, he unfolded the towel to wipe his own face and his head wound. Looking down, he couldn't help but be struck by the irony of the dark reddish-brown blood streaks running across the powder-blue *fleur-de-lis* motif on the white towel that cousin Alain had given the family as a gift from Quebec years ago.

Holding the towel back on his head, Jack turned his attention back to his sister. "Are you alright, Sis? Did they hurt you?"

"I'm fine, Jackie," she assured him.

To cover his connection to the break-in, he added weakly, "I wonder what they wanted."

Annie got up from her chair, faced his direction and said matter-of-factly, "I think you know what they wanted, Jackie." She could not see, but she could feel her brother's shame and regret as she felt her way back to the basement stairs, disappeared briefly, then returned with the same white cloth bag her brother had attempted to hide that morning. "They came for these," Annie said.

26

"OH MY GOD, ANNIE, YOU JUST SAVED OUR LIVES," Jack said to his sister as he stared in disbelief at the bag she was holding. He caught her by surprise with another sudden embrace, using his free arm, the other still holding the towel to his head wound. Despite the stress and terror of the home invasion she had just experienced, a smile lit up her face over his shoulder. Stepping back, he stammered, asking, "How did you? ... I mean, where did you? When?—"

Annie's smile turned to a light chuckle. "Sit down, Jackie. I'll explain. It really wasn't some courageous thing." He sat, and she offered tea. As she felt her way around the kitchen with the confidence of familiarity, carefully closing drawers and cupboards left open from the earlier search, she continued. "When you left today, I knew something was wrong. I could feel it. Later, mother was upstairs resting, and I was in the parlour. It was quiet, so I could hear a faint, unusual sound along with the ticking of father's clock. I went closer to listen, and there was a rubbing sound coming from the bottom of the clock, so I opened it to find out what was making the sound—"

"But I had the key," Jack interrupted.

"I don't know where that key came from, Jackie. There must be an extra. We always keep the key on the clock ledge so it's easy for me to find. I'm the one who usually winds it."

Jack wasn't particularly religious, but he couldn't help feeling that the spare key he'd found in the drawer was some kind of divine intervention, as if his father was involved in some way.

Annie went on. "I felt something in the clock cabinet that was rubbing against the wheel mechanism. I knew then that whatever it was, you had put it there earlier when you were here. I knew you were acting strange and that if you hid something, you must have had a good reason. So I just moved it to a different place so the rubbing would stop. I planned on telling you when you came over tomorrow."

"Good lord, Annie. I can't tell you how glad I am that you did," he said, pausing and considering the consequences if the bag had been found by the intruders. "Where did you hide it?"

"The milk box at the side door," she answered. "I'd love to say I gave it great deal of thought, but the truth is it was the first place, and the easiest place, I could think of. I figured because we don't use it anymore and there's no handle on it, it's easy to miss. Besides, our raincoats are hanging in front of it."

The irony of the family home's milk box helping to hide the evidence that just might bring his father's killers to justice was not lost on Jack. It brought a smile to his face.

Annie had the cups on the counter and the kettle heating up on the stove when she came back to the table, sat down, and continued. "These two men stormed in, one of them shouting about getting something back that was stolen. Looking for a cabinet that needed a fancy key. I knew exactly what they were talking about from your visit this morning. I was cooperative, but I told them I didn't know what they were talking about. They weren't rough with me at all, and one of the men didn't say a word. People are always a little uncomfortable around the blind...maybe criminals, too." She smiled. "They gave me the key and asked what it opened, and I showed them. When they found it empty, they got angry, destroyed the clock, and went searching through the house. I sat in the kitchen and prayed they didn't search the basement stair landing and look behind the coats ...and they didn't. They kept asking me about you and some package, and I kept telling them that you don't live here anymore, and anyway, I don't know your business. I even played up my sad situation and asked them what I'd be able to see anyway, considering my situation," she finished with a sly smile.

Jack reached out and took his sister's hands in his and said, "You're so brave, Annie."

"Not really," she disagreed. "When people tell lies, it's mostly the eyes that give them away. I don't have that problem." Annie got up and returned to the counter as the kettle on the large cast-iron range announced with a loud whistle that the water was boiling. With her back to her brother, she turned the stove dial to off and paused. Although Jack was seeing her with a newfound admiration, she turned and revealed a sober expression as her head and shoulders dropped before admitting, "You see, Jackie, I know about the business you and Scotty are in." She gazed vacantly in his direction. "And I knew father was involved in the same kind of thing, too." She could sense the surprise registering on Jack's face. "People with sight don't realize that we hear everything. We have to. Whispered conversations. Telephone calls. Discussions behind closed doors."

Jack felt an overwhelming sense of shame. "How long have you known?" he asked, needing to know.

"Oh, for years. It started with the visit from cousin Alain years ago. Do you remember? I was in the parlour, and I overheard your conversation on the porch. I was young and didn't really know what it all meant, but over time bits and pieces came together...like a puzzle. " She anticipated what his next concern would be.

"Don't worry. Mother has no idea. I've even helped make excuses or explained things away for you and father at times. I'm not passing judgement on either of you, and I realize many of the things we enjoy have come from that business. But I worried, Jackie. I still do."

Jack was growing agitated, thinking that if Annie knew about the business, she probably had lingering questions about her father's death. Considering what she had just been through and what she already knew, he decided she deserved to finally hear the truth. After they both had a fresh cup of tea in hand and she was sitting back down at the kitchen table across from him, the white bag containing the books placed between them, he recounted in detail the night that changed him forever and still haunted him. Annie listened, enraptured by the tragic story and staring straight ahead with tears in her eyes. She occasionally nodded sombrely and asked questions for clarification. Reliving the events of that night still cut Jack to the core, and he was shaking by the time he finished describing the horrific event. "So Scotty and I made a vow years ago that we would work to eventually get out of this business and make sure St. Pierre and Mahoney pay for what they did. And those books you hid are our only chance."

They were still both in tears afterwards, but Jack was anxious to secure the books and make a couple of very important calls. He stood up, gathered himself, and went to the telephone while Annie sat at the table, running her hands gently over the cotton bag while still processing what she had just heard. Like her mother, she had always felt like there were unanswered questions about the sudden, tragic death of a father she adored. Although Annie was relieved to finally hear the truth, her heart ached for her brother and Scotty, who had to witness the death of someone they both also loved so much. The fact that Mr. St. Pierre was leading a double life and was involved in her father's murder seemed incomprehensible and enraged her. She couldn't help but think about the respect and near reverence given to St. Pierre by Grandma O'Hollaren and her church friends.

Fearing someone might be listening in on his calls, Jack kept them both very brief and cryptic. After hanging up, he crouched next to his sister, who had a look of concern on her face. He took her hand and said, "Annie? Everything is going to be okay now. We're going to put the books back where you had them, clean up this place as well as we can before mother gets home, and figure out what to tell her about the clock." His sister was nodding slowly as Jack took her by the hands and added in a serious tone she was not used to him using, "But I have to ask you to do one more thing for us, Annie. If you would, please. It's a simple request, but very important."

"What is it?" she asked as she turned her face towards him.

"I need you, mother, and Grandma O'Hollaren to take Maria and Mo to church tomorrow."

....

Seamus Mahoney was in his kitchen in an uncharacteristically agitated state; the Wolf and his new partner sat watching Mahoney pace and listening to him rant. The Wolf was a man of very few words, partly because he was quiet—a man of action, not talk—and also because he spoke very little English. His new partner, nicknamed Babe, did enough talking for the both of them—a little too much talking as far as Mahoney was concerned. Babe was a big, bulky former street kid, an up-and-comer in the organization who'd gotten his nickname because of his skilful brutality with a baseball bat and his love of the New York Yankees. He had learned at an early age that getting ahead not only required violence, but also opportunity, and the Mad Russian's sudden death had provided him with a great one.

Summing up the events of the day, Mahoney's disappointment and increasing anxiety were clearly evident. "So we know that the Quebec boys have the books somewhere. And the kid couldn't give you anything useful except a key to an empty clock cabinet." He turned and looked back and forth at them and asked, "You worked him over hard for more information before you took him out?"

"He had nothing to tell, boss, believe me," Babe assured him with an evil smirk while rubbing his bloody, swollen knuckles.

"And you turned the bastard's mother's place upside down, and it was clean?"

The Wolf stared at him without reaction while Babe nodded and answered, "Yes, sir."

He gave the situation some thought. "They've sent their families away, so they know we're on the hunt," Mahoney continued. "But we can't take them out, can we? We'll never get those god-damned books or know who they might have given them to." He seemed to be talking to himself, as the two men watched curiously. "If I could just figure out why they're doing it. What's their motivation? Why risk the operation and their lives? That's the mystery." Mahoney paused, hands on the back of a kitchen chair, looking down. "Maybe I should contact them and try to negotiate—"

The Wolf's baritone voice interrupted suddenly with, "Da boss say no deals," as he sat up straighter, folding his arms across his barrel chest.

"Yes, Boris, I know. I'm just considering alternative options," he responded. The Wolf's blank look caused him to simplify his response: "I'm thinking of other ideas." Mahoney's lack of trust in his colleagues applied especially to the Wolf, who displayed an unwavering loyalty—blind devotion, really—to the Saint that Mahoney could never understand. St. Pierre did give him a steady, good-paying job when nobody would even consider the intimidating-looking Polish immigrant who couldn't speak English, but he also treated him, and all the other muscle, even worse than he treated Mahoney. He started pacing again, planning out his next move. After a long period during which the only sound was his own footsteps creaking across the linoleum floor and Babe's knee bouncing impatiently, Mahoney announced, "Boys, there's one person left who we might be able to use. I want you to find that McLuren kid who works at the shop. He lives with his uncle, but I'm thinking he's been told to hide out. He's involved, I'm sure. Who knows? He may even have the books." The two large men got up loudly, their chairs scraping across the floor, and were heading to the side entrance when Seamus added, "If you find him, do what you have to do to get something out of him about the books...but keep him alive. Then bring him to me."

After locking the door behind them, Mahoney went back to his kitchen table. His mind was racing. As he sat silently, fumbling with an empty coffee mug, he had to admit that he was as completely baffled as he was worried. As a person who took great pride in planning everything out methodically, he was having trouble comprehending how, all of a sudden, his freedom and possibly even his life were now under threat.

A few hours later, Mahoney received the second unexpected telephone call in as many days from Jack Ducharme, requesting another meeting at the same location the very next day. Unlike the night before, Mahoney was looking forward to this one.

I T'S LOVELY THAT YOU TWO ARE JOINING US THIS MORNING, MARIA," Sara Ducharme said to her daughter-in-law as she picked up her grandson for a hug in the foyer. It was Sunday morning, and even though Maria and her son had spent the night at her parents' place, they'd been dropped off early at home and then made their way over so Maria could follow Jack's instructions and accompany his mother to mass.

"Good morning, Mrs. Ducharme. Jackie said you wouldn't mind if we tagged along with you today."

"Of course not, dear. We were thrilled when we heard you were coming," she answered as she reached for her grandson.

"I hope the good Lord will forgive us for not making it every week, but here we are," Maria said. She scanned the front parlour. "Oh, there's the clock. What a shame. Jack told me about poor Annie and her accident last night. I hope she's not hurt."

"She's fine, dear. Just an unfortunate incident. We're just blessed it didn't come down on top of her," her mother-in-law explained. "She is usually so sure-footed."

"We are blessed, indeed," Maria said. "But Jackie is determined to have it repaired. He told me it was a special gift from Mr. Ducharme."

"It was," she replied, looking away with tears welling up in her eyes. "And Annie and I have grown so accustomed to my poor Maurice's hourly chimes that—"

Annie's sudden appearance at the bottom of the stairs interrupted her mother and the emotional path she was headed down. "Good morning, Maria," Annie said. Her blank gaze searched as she asked, "Where's my little Mo?" Her mother placed the chubby little boy in her arms and then used her free hands to wipe her cheeks. "There you are," Annie cooed. She ran her free hand methodically over the little boy's face and head as she stared off with a bright smile. She then turned in Maria's direction and said convincingly, "So, mother no doubt filled you in on my near-death experience last night."

"She did, and so did Jack. I'm so glad you are all right. He was raving about how brave you were," she went on slyly, "when the clock fell."

An extended silence prompted Mrs. Ducharme to move towards the door and announce, "Well, we should get going. Mass starts in thirty minutes, and Mother will be waiting."

Annie handed the baby over and joined her mother, who was slipping into a light sweater and adjusting a summer church hat in the foyer mirror. Maria was already making her way out the door with the little boy, an uneasiness growing inside her. It was a warm summer morning, and the three women walked to church, pushing Little Mo's pram along with them.

Although Maria did not attend Sunday mass as regularly as she felt her mother-in-law and Grandma O'Hollaren wished, she did find comfort and community when she did appear. This morning was sure to be much different. She was on edge as they entered the church, torn by two overwhelming sensations. On one hand, Maria felt a desperate need to pray as never before for her husband's safety and the success of his and Scotty's dangerous plan. On the other hand, she was tense about her critical role in their plan, which relied on the monster who had haunted her husband for years, Mr. St. Pierre, keeping his regular routine. So it was with a strange sense of nervous relief when the four of them sidestepped into the pew near the back of the church to join Mrs. O'Hollaren and Maria spied the well-dressed man sitting in his regular spot towards the front of the church with his wife. Her heart rate increased further.

To Maria, the hour-long mass seemed much longer today. Before the priest gave the final blessing, the choir began its final hymn, and the procession made its way back down the centre aisle, the chair of the fundraising committee took to the pulpit to remind the congregation of the social in the church hall after the mass and of all the charitable works the money raised would go to help. The announcement was met with a buzz among the congregation. Maria could not keep her eyes off of the St. Pierres, while her mother-in-law held Mo, asking him playfully if he was looking forward to some sweet ice cream.

There was a festive atmosphere as they entered the ornate hall attached to the church several minutes later. Loud voices filled the large room as adults stood and exchanged pleasantries while children ran about unattended or lined up impatiently for ice cream. As Annie's mother and grandmother made their way around the room like hosts of a grand party, Annie held on to Maria's arm, sensing her anxiety. "Do you see him?" Annie asked, somewhat overwhelmed by all the chatter.

"He's here," Maria responded. "With his wife. Over by the coffee area behind you, talking to another couple."

"Well, let's get the ladies back here and have them bring us over before they decide to leave. He doesn't linger at these things very long, especially when his wife gets chatty," Annie suggested.

Maria picked her son up and used him like a magnet to draw her mother-in-law back to them. She made eye contact with the older ladies as they were chatting with another committee member towards the middle of the room, then used her son's little hand to wave adorably. It had the desired affect. The two women excused themselves and worked their way back to fawn over the little one once again.

"Grandma," Annie announced when they rejoined them, "I was just saying to Maria that it would be nice to introduce your great-grandson to the St. Pierres. They were so fond of Father. They would love to meet his grandchild, don't you think?"

"A lovely idea, honey," Mrs. O'Hallaren answered, already scanning the room, holding her daughter's arm.

"There they are," Annie's mother said excitedly as she reached for Mo and they began to make their way over.

Annie heard her mother's voice trailing off as she turned and said with a smile to Maria, "Never too difficult to get them to go and show off the little one." She leaned in and whispered, "Are you ready?"

Maria clutched her hand tightly, took a deep breath. "I'm ready." They followed Sara over to the St. Pierres.

"Well, hello, William," Clair O'Hallaren said, as she approached from behind.

St. Pierre seemed to be caught a bit off guard as he turned to greet her and eyed the large group of women with her. "Well...good morning, Clair," he said with what Maria clearly recognized as a pained smile. "Who do we have here? The whole family has joined you today, I see."

"Yes," she answered. "You already know my daughter Sara and her daughter Anne-Marie." The ladies nodded appropriately to the esteemed couple. "But I don't believe you've met my grandson's young wife and their beautiful little boy." She turned and encouraged Maria to come closer.

"This is Jack's wife, Maria, and their son Mo."

"How lovely," Mrs. St. Pierre commented as her husband strained to keep smiling and feigned interest. "And what an original name for a little boy."

"It's short for Maurice. You remember my son-in-law, Maurice, don't you?" she asked. Annie squeezed Maria's arm uncomfortably tight at the question.

"Yes, of course," he responded. "A fine young man. And what a beautiful family he started. Such a shame the Lord called him home so soon." As Clair and Sara instinctively reached for each other's hands, Maria studied the gentleman with a feeling of hatred unlike anything she had ever known.

"Yes, it was, indeed," Clair agreed, her eyes finding the floor.

"Let me see this little man," Mrs. St. Pierre announced to relieve some of the awkward silence that settled upon the group.

As Sara moved to bring her grandson closer, Maria stepped in, and with her back turned to him, blocked Mr. St. Pierre from the rest of the group, who were now huddling, fussing over the little boy. There was an unusual moment of awkwardness as St. Pierre stood there with nobody facing him.

Being unaccustomed to the social slight, and wanting to get away from the Ducharme group anyway, he turned to wander away just as Maria turned and caught up to him a few steps away from the group. Her stomach was in knots as she nervously said, "I'm so sorry. I was being rude."

He stopped reluctantly and faced her. "Quite all right, young lady."

Maria checked around quickly to be sure they were out of earshot, then turned her eyes back on him, took a deep breath, and said, "I wanted to thank you personally, anyway, Mr. St. Pierre . . . or should I call you Saint?" St. Pierre's forced smile faded instantly as he looked around the room uncomfortably. The group of ladies were several feet away still fawning over Little Mo. "We are all so relieved that your man Mahoney and my Jackie are going to meet this afternoon and come to an arrangement. It's for the best, really," she explained as he stood there speechless, an evil scowl slowly forming. "Jackie tells me that your man is ready to make a deal. Seems he wants to save himself," Maria continued, then leaned in closer and whispered, "Now would be a good time for a Christian man like yourself to beg forgiveness for all your sins—especially the murder of the father-in-law and grandfather we never had a chance to meet."

Maria turned back towards the ladies, shaking. As she slid back next to her sister-in-law and reached protectively for her son, Annie latched back on to her arm and could feel her racing heart rate.

Only seconds later, the ladies were back in full chatter mode when St. Pierre, red-faced and clearly flustered, interrupted abruptly, and while looking menacingly at Maria, grabbed his wife's arm, saying, "We are going...now!"

....

Around the same time that Maria was in mass praying for the success of a daring and dangerous plan that was already underway, Scotty was doing his version of the same, by himself in his car, driving out to the county to meet once again with King Canada.

Earlier that morning, Scotty had made his way over to the Ducharmes' to pick up the one and only book that Jack felt the Purples would need to see. Following instructions from her brother, Annie waited until she heard her mother upstairs getting ready for mass before she signalled to Scotty using the back porch light. Knowing Mahoney probably still had people watching the house, he came up from the backyard, opened the stubborn milk box by the side door, and grabbed the Quebec operation ledger book that had been separated from the rest and was now waiting for him. With a quiet "good luck" through the passageway from Annie, he closed the door, stuffed the book into his waistline underneath his jacket, and was on his way.

Although Jack thought they both should make the trip, Scotty insisted he could handle the meeting alone. He reminded Jack of the rapport that he and the King had developed during their first meeting due to the connection to Diesbourg's cousin. He assured his partner that they both weren't needed to simply hand over the ledger for Diesbourg to deliver. Jack didn't need a great deal of convincing to stay back for several reasons: the threat to both of them made it unwise for them to be together; he wanted to stay close by his family while they were staying at his in-laws'; and he wanted to be sure he was on time and prepared for what was surely going to be the most critical and stressful meeting of his life.

....

The meeting between Scotty and Diesbourg could not have gone any better. Unlike at their first meeting, the King welcomed Scotty graciously. When handed Mahoney's Quebec ledger, he sat down and leafed through it briefly, clearly interested in seeing how a competitor's operation was being run.

After taking a few minutes to scan some of the pages, Diesbourg closed the book, shook his head dramatically from side to side and said with a grin, "*Merde*! They're not going to like this." Scotty felt reassured, and the tension that had gripped him all morning began to lift. Diesbourg stood and excused himself. "I don't like having this here. Could be dangerous. So I'm going to deliver this little gift *tout de suite*. I like to fly across sometimes during the day with no shipment anyway. It frustrates the bastards to no end when they track me and come up empty handed," he explained. He held up the book, put it in a leather bag, and announced, "The Purples should have this in their hands within the next couple of hours."

"We can't tell you how much we appreciate this, Mr. Diesbourg," Scotty said. "You are saving our lives here."

"Glad to do it, *mon ami*, believe me. You know, this is going to be very good for us, too," he said with a smile and a handshake. Before Diesbourg climbed into a waiting old-model Ford that would take him out to a landing strip nearby, he added, "There's someone waiting in my backyard to say hello." The car puttered away down the long, dusty laneway.

Having a good idea who Diesbourg was talking about, Scotty limped quickly around to the back of the farmhouse and was thrilled to shake hands and re-unite with Dr. Fish, his doctor and friend from what seemed like a lifetime ago in France.

The two men caught up quickly as they sat and reminisced about the war, sharing the unique experiences of comradeship and sorrow that only veterans could understand. However, it wasn't long before Scotty was pulled back to his present precarious situation when they were interrupted by the sound of a small airplane engine roaring overhead, heading north across the lake.

....

Mahoney was already waiting when Jack walked up cautiously in the early afternoon to the same pavilion where they had met on Friday night. The sun was high in the sky, and no clouds were around to offer reprieve from the hot sun. He scanned the surrounding area to be sure his boss had indeed come alone. As expected, there were others using the park on a lovely Sunday afternoon—a young couple enjoying a picnic and some kissing under a tall oak tree; a young family letting their two toddlers run around and wrestle in the grass; an elderly couple enjoying an ice cream cone at a picnic table; and an older gentleman sitting on a bench, smoking and reading the paper—but Mahoney was the lone person under the tired but shady wooden structure.

It seemed impossible to Jack that it had been less than 48 hours since he and Scotty had unleashed their perilously bold plan. For years they had been talking and dreaming about the opportunity to break free and exact vengeance on their bosses, and now the time had finally come. So much was different today. On Friday night, his trepidation in the face of Mahoney's power and potential brutality had rendered him apprehensive and near helpless. Now, as he approached his boss, his large frame moved with unmistakable confidence and strength. As usual, his boss was in his business attire: a white shirt and brown tie with his tan suit jacket folded over his arm. Jack's light, short-sleeved shirt and baggy trousers offered considerably more comfort in the stifling heat.

There were no formal greetings as they met in the relative cool of the shade under the pavilion, each examining the other's sweat-glistening face for any hint of weakness. While Jack's face remained expressionless, Mahoney's narrowed eyes and pulsating jawbone gave away the rage that was festering inside of him.

Mahoney was the first to break the silence when he looked Jack up and down with disdain and hissed, "Mr. Ducharme, you are playing a very dangerous game." Jack held his stare. "You know by now that I could have you, your partner, and your families eliminated anytime." He paused, took a breath, looked around, and added more calmly, "Now, you've made a big mistake, kid. I don't know why you would do it, but it's nothing that can't be undone. You have something very important to the organization, and if it is returned, we can move on from this. Get back to business as usual—"

"Listen, you heartless bastard," Jack interrupted, standing tall over him and looking down. "We're tired of your demands, your threats, and your thugs that creep around doing your dirty work." Mahoney was caught off guard by Jack's threatening tone. Although he tried to respond with his usual evil smile, Mahoney could only manage a grimace. "It's time we told you how things are going to work, if you want to stay alive." Jack waited for a reaction that did not come, so he took a deep breath and continued. "First, you know we have not only the operation ledgers, but we also have your secret bestseller that I'm sure many people would love to read—the police and liquor control for starters, but I'm sure St. Pierre and maybe even the Purples would be very interested in that one." Mahoney's eyes suddenly gave away his concern at the mention of his boss's name. "Yes, sir. We know who is running the show...and not just from the book you put together. We've known for years who your boss is. And you want to know how we know?" Jack's voice grew louder and angrier as he stepped closer to his boss. "Because we were there, you see. I was there...the night you animals called my father to a meeting and your thugs murdered him at the docks."

It took great effort for Mahoney to mask his surprise and concern. Looking back on that night, he now knew where the mystery footprints in the snow had come from. His response did nothing to help the fury building inside Jack. "He broke a code, kid. Your old man knew the risks. He betrayed us."

Jack fought off the impulse to strike. "Like the way you and St. Pierre are betraying the Purples now? How is that any different?" There was no response as Jack fought to regain his composure before adding, "So we figure that maybe your people in Detroit should deliver the same kind of justice to you and the Saint."

"So that's what this is all about. Revenge? You want to sacrifice it all—the money, your freedom...maybe even your lives...for what? For revenge? It doesn't make sense, kid." Seamus' disposition changed dramatically as he looked over Jack's shoulder. His evil smile returned before he added, "What you fail to understand is that we have plans, too. And unlike you two amateurs, we don't cry over people getting hurt." He looked Jack back in the eyes, daring him with, "We had to set an example with your old man." Jack's blood was reaching its boiling point. He stepped towards him, fists clenched. Mahoney was enjoying being on the offensive again, where he belonged. "And the big kid at your shop. Johnny, was it? Nice young man—not very bright—but another necessary sacrifice."

The emotionless, cold-blooded confession sent a shockwave through Jack. He thought about Johnny, the gentle giant of a kid. He didn't want to believe what he was hearing, but the teenager's connection to the missing key, the search for the books, and the potential risk to his bosses made him easily expendable. "You bastard!" Jack shouted, as he leaned back and landed a hard blow to Mahoney's face, knocking him to the ground.

Mahoney sat in the fine gravel, his hair askew and his hat thrown a few feet away. Leaning on one hand, his other came up slowly to wipe below his nose. He looked down at the bright blood on it, then up at Jack with a grin and said, "Be careful, Ducharme. You're about to lose the other one."

Jack was standing over him, heart racing, feeling his loss of control. He was having difficulty processing his boss's threat. Then Mahoney's eyes forced his attention behind him and towards a car parked a short distance away along the curb. Jack stepped back and turned. Sitting under the shade of one of the park's large maple trees was a shiny brown Chevrolet. Leaning casually against the backseat door was a big, tough-looking kid, the newest thug in Seamus' stable. He was wearing grubby work pants and boots along with a white sleeveless undershirt that accentuated his generous upper-body muscle. Even from a distance, Jack could see what looked like dark blood stains on his shirt. Looking in his boss' direction, Babe was holding the handle end of a baseball bat and swinging it playfully just above his feet. When he was sure he had Jack's full attention, he slid his body forward casually towards the driver's door—and there in the backseat of the car was Joey, his gagged and bloodied face pleading wide-eyed up against the window.

"So you see, Mr. Ducharme, if you are determined to go down this path, you're going to continue losing more people along the way." Mahoney stood with an exaggerated sigh, brushed off his trousers, ran his fingers through his hair, and bent over to pick up his hat.

"Are you really going to kill more people before you get what's coming to you, Mahoney?" Jack asked.

"Scorched earth, kid," he responded. He casually reshaped the dents in his hat and put it back on his head. "So what's your play? Are you going to return the books and we'll see if we can work something out? Or do I have your kid here join Johnny before I send my new boy here for others... maybe even your family?"

Jack stood there, looking towards the car and Joey in utter defeat and fearing for his loved one's lives, when they both noticed an older gentleman, the one who'd been reading the paper earlier, walking slowly and carefully with a cane down the sidewalk towards the car. He had a hat pulled over his brow and a light jacket on despite the hot day. Babe looked over at Mahoney for some direction, but none came. On the contrary, Mahoney found dark humour in the moment—this clueless old man walking into a scene where life-and-death drama was unfolding. As the gentleman came within steps of the front of the car, Babe slid back over to block the back window of the car again and called out, "Hey, old timer. Walk the other way." There was no reaction. "Hey, fella. Beat it!" he said louder, gripping his bat with more purpose.

The gentleman raised his head slightly and looked up at Babe before putting his hand to his ear and walking even closer. When he was only a few feet away, the large kid lost his patience and moved towards the intruder. In a flurry of movement, the gentleman brought up his cane and swung it across Babe's head, sending him flying to the ground. Dazed, Babe lay beside the car, struggling to get his bearings. As he reached for his bat, the older man swung his cane down with surprising force on his arm, then adjusted his weight back before kicking the kid's head full force, knocking him unconscious.

Jack and Mahoney stood there and watched the action play out in something faster than real time, like the moving picture show down at the local theatre. Joey, on the other hand, had a front-row seat to the action, and his swollen eyes grew even wider as he took it all in.

The older gentleman stepped over the bloodied thug, opened the driver's door, reached in, and unlocked the backseat door. He opened it and helped Joey out. He untied the gag in the younger man's mouth and the rope binding his wrists behind his back.

Wiping his eyes of the sweat and drying blood, Joey looked more closely at the man and exclaimed, "Mr. Dario? How did…" But he was overcome with relief and lunged forward to lock the older gentleman in an embrace.

"Joseppie, I alaways sava you," Dario replied with a smile when they separated. He looked over at Jack, standing dumbfounded near Mahoney, and nodded. Dario reached down, picked up the bat, and looked menacingly at Mahoney as he began walking towards them. Mahoney swallowed hard and took a couple of unsteady steps back.

Jack threw up his hand to stop Dario's approach, turned to his boss, and said, "We're not killers like you, Mahoney. I only came here today to make sure you knew why we're doing what we're doing. My father was a brave and honourable man that made you good money, and you people ripped him from our lives. There's a price you're all going to pay for that. The books will make sure you do." Jack turned to leave, checking around to see if anybody had seen the violent drama unfold. The only witnesses around, the young lovers and the family playing in the shaded grass, were already making their way quickly out of the other side of the park.

Mahoney, relieved to be spared and already considering his next move, stood there and watched Jack walk away with reluctant admiration.

While Jack and Dario helped Joey cross the street and out of sight, Mahoney headed towards Babe just as another car pulled up right behind the Chevrolet. The Wolf climbed out. "Where in the hell have you been, you big, useless Polack? You were supposed to be here with the kid too," Mahoney shouted.

As always, the Wolf was silent as he approached. The look of contempt Mahoney saw on his face only made him angrier. "C'mon, get him in the car," he growled, indicating Babe. "They know the Saint is running the show, and he's not going to be happy. We'll bring this piece of shit back to my place and decide our next move."

The Wolf struggled to lift the big kid from under his arms and drag him into the backseat. After considerable effort, Babe's feet were still hanging out of the doorframe when Mahoney watched Wolf reach into the driver's door and grab the key from the ignition. He walked back behind the car, opened the trunk, and scanned the surrounding area carefully.

"What are you doing?" Seamus asked. "We're not throwing this goddamned lug into the trunk now. Just help me slide him in the rest of the way."

As Mahoney bent down towards Babe's feet, the Wolf came up behind his boss, put his left hand over his mouth, and with his right, thrust a long knife violently into his abdomen. He pulled his boss's head back next to his and whispered, "Dis from da boss," before he dragged the knife slowly up to Mahoney's ribcage. His left hand relaxed, and the small, limp body folded forward before Wolf dragged it quickly to the back of the car, dumped the body inside, and slammed the trunk shut.

....

Scotty did not know the dramatic events that had unfolded at the park when they all met back at the paint shop late Sunday afternoon. After scanning the mostly empty streets and locking the front door behind him as he entered, Scotty made his way to the office. He was shocked to see Jack standing with a wet cloth over his nephew, who was sitting in his desk chair, badly beaten. Mr. Dario lounged in an armchair across the room, looking casually through some of the latest automobile colour catalogues.

"What the hell happened, kid?" Scotty asked as he took in the scene.

Jack described the events at the park, and Joey added details occasionally with his sore, raspy voice. Dario continued flipping pages, expressionless, speaking only once, when he held up a page with a deep-red drawing of the newest sleek Cadillac and declared with a smile, "Thatsa *bello*."

After the recap of the events at the park, Scotty dragged a folding chair over towards Joey, sat down, and while looking at his bloodied nephew, tried to wrap his head around their present situation. As happy as he was about the way things turned out that day, he was feeling incredible guilt about the pain and suffering Joey had endured once again. His life had nearly been cut short—twice—all because he was helping solve a problem not of his making. And his life would have ended both times had it not been for Mr. Dario. Looking across at the older man, seemingly unaware of the dangerous game he was involved in, he wondered out loud, "How did he know where Joey was . . . or where they were taking him?"

Joey looked up at both men, shrugged his shoulders, and Jack answered, "We both have no idea." All three looked towards Dario, mystified. "But what I do know is that Mahoney is going to be out for blood. He knows that we know about St. Pierre and that we plan on using the books to bring them down. I'm not sure that the ledgers will protect us anymore." He thought for a moment. "It's probably best to keep our families tucked away for another day or two, until the books get into the right hands."

Thinking over their plan, Jack suddenly realized that he had neglected to ask Scotty about the other, very crucial element. "I'm sorry, partner. It's been such an unbelievable day that I forgot to ask about your county trip. How did it go with Diesbourg?"

Scotty was still looking towards Mr. Dario with a combination of admiration and confusion when the question was posed. He was deep in thought considering this man—a recent immigrant who could barely speak English and whose daughter was now caught up in a life-and-death drama—who had been not only his nephew's saviour, but also the only reason their plot against St. Pierre's people was still even possible. He then thought about his dear friend Moose and the pride he would have had in the man that Jackie had become. He would have loved his young daughter-in-law as well as her devoted immigrant family. And he surely would have been over the moon about his beautiful grandson. It all seemed a damn shame to Scotty that that was never to be.

"Scotty? Hey, partner?" Jack repeated, trying to get his attention. "How did it go in Belle River?"

"Uh...ya...great," Scotty replied, coming out of his trance. "Diesbourg was great. Said Detroit would have the book this afternoon and we'll have to wait and see what they do with it. We even saw his plane when he took off. Flew right over us. Brought us both back to the Front and the Empire's flyboys."

"Who's 'us'?" Jack wondered, suddenly distracted by the thought of now involving the notoriously powerful and violent Purple Gang.

"Diesbourg had his cousin there. Dr. Poisson. Remember?" Scotty began recounting, again, the connection between the two of them from the war years, but his audience could not have been less interested. Mr. Dario understood almost nothing of what he was hearing; Joey was battered, bruised, and clearly in pain; and Jack was too deep in thought about the next move that needed to be made in the life-and-death game that was rapidly nearing its conclusion.

"We better stay here tonight, where it's safe," Jack announced. "They'll be watching our places." Joey and Scotty considered the suggestion, looked at each other, and nodded, but Mr. Dario was clearly confused. Jack looked over at his father-in-law and said louder than necessary, "Sleep here tonight," while he pointed down and made a sleeping gesture by cupping his hands against his tilted head.

"No, *grazie*," Dario responded while standing. "*Sto tornando a casa*...I goa to homa. *Proteggerò la famiglia*. Noa body seea me."

The others looked at each other as he stood up decisively and began to leave, knowing they could do little to stop him. Jack actually felt some relief knowing that his wife and little boy would be in safe hands at his in-laws' home.

They all stood, a struggle for Joey, and shook the man's hand with sincere gratitude before Jack led him to a side door. "Be careful," he warned as Mr. Dario put on his hat and slipped out into the early evening, looking around casually.

When Jack locked the door and returned to the office, Joey was leaning back in the chair, trying to fight off the pain, while Scotty was making his way to the garage storage area to find anything they might be able to use for beds, blankets, and pillows. All three had already resigned themselves to the fact that there would probably be very little sleep. It was going to be a long, nerve-wracking night.

Once settled into their uncomfortable accommodations, Jack and Scotty discussed their next move. They agreed that Diesbourg's delivery to the Purple Gang was now out of their hands, and they needed to focus on the part of the plan they could control. "It's time to bring Mousseau into the picture," Jack said as he fished the liquor agent's card out of a concealed part of his desk drawer. Looking down at the number then back up at the other two, he added, "We need to get the rest of those books back here and into Mousseau's hands first thing in the morning. I don't think we're going to be safe until that happens."

Jack picked up the telephone handset and gave the number to the switchboard operator. It took uncomfortably long for the line to connect, and all three of them felt the tension increase when Jack finally spoke into the receiver: "Mr. Mousseau? It's me. Yes, it's time."

....

"That's him, the son of a bitch," Babe said loudly as he and the Wolf watched Mr. Dario enter the sidewalk from the opposite side of the paint shop, carrying a cane and scanning the area. The left side of Babe's face was scraped and swollen, and he was sporting bandages on his left shoulder and hand, the same arm that was in a makeshift sling. "I'm taking him out," he said as he reached with his opposite hand for the door handle.

Wolf grabbed his injured arm to stop him, sending a searing pain through his partner. "Da boss say no. We follow," he said in his deep voice.

As Dario walked the half-dozen blocks back to his home, the large automobile followed, rolling slowly at a safe distance. When he came to the sidewalk that led to his front porch, Dario stopped and looked around carefully. A full block away and out of sight, the Wolf tucked the Chevrolet in behind a parked car, small stones and gravel crunching under the tires. Dario made his way quickly to his house, entered through the side door, and locked it behind him. He hung the cane and his jacket on a hook, moved quickly to the front foyer, shushing his relieved family on the way. He watched the street from the small window next to the door for a few minutes before going to greet his family in the kitchen.

After waiting for what seemed to his young partner like much longer than necessary, Wolf pulled slowly back onto the street, drove past the Dario house, eyed the address, and headed to a nearby telephone.

28

I T TOOK ALL OF SCOTTY'S SKILLS OF PERSUASION To CONVINCE JACK TO agree to let him be the one to retrieve the ledger books during the night and bring them back to the paint shop. Generally easy-going, he was never one to be pushy or cause conflict, so Jack was taken aback when Scotty announced, "I'm going, kid. No discussion! We're not sendin' Joey back into harm's way, that's for sure. And there's no damn way you're goin'...not with the little woman and family at home needin' you." When Jack opened his mouth to protest, his partner cut him off, continuing more calmly and passionately, "I can't risk losing another best friend, Jackie. Do you understand? I didn't take the chance I should've before we lost your father, and it still keeps me up nights. It's not happenin' again. And let's face it, kid, I have the least to lose if somethin' happens." He caught Jack's subtle but concerned glance towards his prosthetic leg pointing out at an awkward angle below his trousers. "Don't worry about the bum leg, either. This job isn't about speed, kid. We have all night. It's about stayin' out of sight, in the shadows, which I can do much better than a big, clumsy lug like you," he finished with a grin.

Jack was touched by Scotty's sincerity and loyalty. He reached out and shook his partner's hand with a nervous smile. "But we're going to plan this out, okay? I can't lose you, either, and if you don't make it back here with those books, we're all in danger."

Scotty had learned from his war experience that the best time for a raid was early morning, just before daylight, when the enemy had been sleeping for hours and darkness still shielded the advance. So at 4:30 early Monday morning, Scotty slipped out the side entrance of the paint shop wearing a hat and dark coveralls. He walked at a slow but determined pace, his steady limp carrying him through the darkness towards Jack's mother's house. The anxiety of the task was heightened because of the eerie early-morning silence. With most people still in bed and no automobiles on the road, the only sound breaking through the stillness of the dark morning was the wind rustling through the trees. The bouncing shadows cast by the full moon and streetlights above the dancing leaves made him jumpy. Scotty's heart was racing and his senses were on high alert. The feeling brought not-so-fond memories back from many years before, when he was sent crawling out into no man's land towards enemy trenches. Here he was, negotiating his way through yet another no man's land, moving through a life-and-death environment, exposed and vulnerable to an unseen enemy.

Twenty minutes later, he was back in the alley behind the Ducharme family home and making his way slowly up the side of the house. The angle of the street lamp in front of the houses provided a protective shadow as he struggled to see the outline of the milk box next to the side door. Jack had refused to call the house and warn Annie about the visit before Scotty left, worried that waking his sister and mother so late in the night would bring too many risks. Now, as Scotty scanned the area around him one last time and reached for the small steel door handle, he prayed the books were still there. A sense of overwhelming relief surged through him as he opened the small door, reached in, and felt the soft cotton bag.

....

Not long after the sun rose on the same cloudless Monday morning, Mr. Dario was already up and heading out to do the watering and weeding in his backyard garden. Just like his father and his grandfather before him back in the old country, Dario took great pride in his garden and cared for it meticulously. It provided the family with all the onions, peppers, tomatoes, and herbs they needed for their traditional meals, as well as peaches and pears from small fruit trees sitting beside three healthy rows of grape vines, already stretching to eye level on homemade wire trellises.

As he dragged his rubber hose out into the middle of the yard and began spraying down the thirsty plants, he spotted a large man standing by the last row of grapevines inside the back fence gate, near the alley. Appearing unfazed by the intrusion, Dario turned the hand nozzle off, put down the hose gently, and took a few steps to pick up a small spade shovel that was leaning against a pear tree. He turned and began making his way towards the intruder, who was now smiling at the actions of the older gentleman with menacingly pointy eyeteeth.

As Dario came within striking distance and raised the shovel, the intruder opened his suit coat to show he had no weapon before raising both hands and saying, "No. No. We talk."

Dario lowered the shovel, took a few seconds to scan the area, and then looked the man over dubiously. He knew immediately whom the sharp-dressed visitor was working for, and the thought of these people knowing where he lived and being a potential threat to his family infuriated him. "Youa go," he ordered, waving his free hand, then stepped closer, putting both hands back on his spade handle threateningly.

Suddenly, there was a sickening thud as a wooden bat came crashing across the side of Dario's head from behind, dropping his body into the tomato plants beside him, crushing them.

Standing tall over him with a bat in his right hand while a sling secured his left arm was Babe. "Let's see Ruth do that with only one fuckin' arm!" he said excitedly.

He raised the bat again, anxious to finish the job, but the Wolf snatched the bat effortlessly. "Get rope," he demanded, and Babe stomped angrily like a spoiled child back to their car, parked nearby in the alley.

Moments later, Babe watched with a pout as the Wolf tied Dario's hands and ankles with rope and gagged his mouth with an old rag before dragging him into the small garden shed Dario had proudly built the first summer he was in Canada.

Watching the drama unfold from two doors down, hidden from view behind vines that had taken over his elevated back porch, was Mr. Lapari, another middle-aged Italian immigrant and a very good friend of Dario's.

With the remaining books hidden in their office safe, the bright morning sun rising in the east, and the paint shop locked up securely, Jack, Scotty, and Joey anxiously awaited Inspector Mousseau and the authorities. A sign on the front door informed customers that the shop was closed unexpectedly for the day. There was nothing they could do but watch the slow-moving clock. The tension in the air was thick, having its effect on all three.

Shortly after 9 a.m., a loud knock came from the front glass door. They eyed each other nervously and made their way towards the front. Scotty went out to the lobby, and looking tentatively through the front glass door, saw one of their regular customers using his hand over his eyes to peer in. Scotty pointed to the handwritten piece of paper and shouted through the door that they were closed.

Less than a minute later, another loud knock caused their hearts to jump again. Scotty went back to the door and saw the same customer there. "I said we are closed today, sir," he shouted through the door. Jack and Joey headed back to the office—another false alarm. The customer looked bewildered through the dirty glass, put his hand to his ear, and shouted back, "What?"

Scotty got closer to the door and yelled, "We're closed!"

"But I have to talk to you," the man shouted back through the door. "Just for a minute."

Exasperated, Scotty reached for the deadbolt and turned it before unlocking the door handle. He pushed the door open just enough to put his face into the opening to say impatiently, "I'm sorry, sir, but we are not open today. You have to come back tom—"

In that split second, another fellow's foot came out quickly from beside the customer, forcing its way into the gap of the doorway. He leaned into the door, forcing it open, then stood defiantly in the entrance with a smile. Scotty recognized the balding, older gentleman in the expensive tailored suit instantly, and his heart sank. "Good day. Mr. McLuren, I presume?" William St. Pierre said calmly. "I see you're closed, but we have some important business to take care of." Scotty looked around in a panic to find anything he might be able to use for a weapon as the Saint stared at him, reaching deep into his pocket. Still smiling, St. Pierre pulled out a thick wad of folded bills and handed several to the customer, who was still waiting in the threshold of the front door. "Now beat it," he ordered, and the man was happy to be on his way.

"What do you want?" Scotty asked, his voice catching nervously.

St. Pierre's expression turned to a scowl as he hissed, "I think you know what I want." He reached into his suit coat and pulled out a gun. Pointing it at Scotty, he demanded, "Now call out the boys."

Scotty called loudly, and Jack and Joey appeared at the hallway door. While Joey's eyes registered shock at the sight of the gun in the stranger's hand, Jack eyed the Saint with a combination of fear and uncontrollable rage. He was also shocked that the older gentleman was not flanked by Mahoney or the Wolf.

Considering it a positive sign that St. Pierre felt the threat significant enough to risk exposing his real identity, Jack said, "Hello, Mr. St. Pierre. Where are all the goons that usually do your dirty work?"

"I think you'll find I'm quite capable of getting my hands dirty, young man," St. Pierre answered. "Now be a good employee and go get those books for your boss, and nobody will get hurt."

"I'll tell you what I told Mahoney yesterday. The books are hidden in a secure location," Jack responded. "If any of us were to get hurt, or if we mysteriously disappeared, they would be delivered to just the right people who can bring you and your whole operation down."

The Saint seemed unfazed by the threat. "And why would you do that, kid?" he asked, almost mockingly. "We gave you every opportunity to make lots of money. The product. The protection. And then you bastards had to go and get greedy, for Christ's sake." The gun stayed pointed in Jack's direction as the Saint's anger was building. "Just like your old man!"

The mention of Moose from the man responsible for his death was an unbearable sting to both Jack and Scotty. They both instinctively moved towards St. Pierre. They stopped when the gun was raised and aimed.

Years of intense hatred for this man, too many sleepless nights to count, and endless hours of planning all seemed to have come to this one, critical moment. Jack took a fearless step forward, looked St. Pierre in the eyes, and said, "I'm sure Mahoney told you that we were there when you and your men killed my father. We both saw you." The Saint masked his surprise well, staying stone faced. "And we're going to make you all pay. Even if you kill us right here, you're going down and taking all your people with you."

"I see you're upset, kid," St. Pierre said, condescendingly. "Let me bring you up to speed before you lose your head." He paused, enjoying the dramatic moment. "First of all, Seamus didn't tell me nothing. Dead men don't talk, kid. He paid the price yesterday for double-crossing me. I didn't agree to that meeting with you. You see, I don't negotiate, especially not with the likes of you two-bit amateurs. Secondly, you might not care what happens to you, but I think you'll care about what happens to your lovely family."

The mention of his family sent Jack into a panic. He searched St. Pierre to find any hint of a bluff. "Threaten our families," Jack said, shaking, "and we'll deliver the books to the right people."

The Saint looked at Jack, then at the other two, who were standing behind him watching the dangerous volley of threats go back and forth. "Well, I'm happy you still have them. That's good," he said with a smile. "You can still save your pretty little chippie and that baby boy." St. Pierre revelled in these moments when he gained the upper hand and could watch his adversaries crumble. Jack's face could not hide his palpable fear. "I think you need to call your beautiful wife, kid."

Jack stared at St. Pierre, then turned and looked at his partners. His legs were weak from dread as he moved to the front lobby counter, reached for the phone, and gave the operator the number to connect him to the Darios'. As the connection was being made and the number rang, he turned his back to St. Pierre silently reciting a prayer of hope.

After the third ring, Maria answered in a state of alarm. "Jackie?!"

"Yes, honey. It's me. Are you okay?"

"We're fine, Jackie. Little Mo and Momma and me are okay. But they say they killed Poppa!" She was near hysterics. "They say we're next if you don't give them what they want."

He didn't think his hatred for this man could get any more intense, but Jack was mistaken. He looked St. Pierre's way and thought about his father-in-law and his family. The proud Italian man had come of age in the rough-and-tumble Sicilian countryside, risked everything to bring his family to the safety and security of a new country, and even risked his own life for his new son-in-law. The unbearable loss would surely crush his wife and drive a wedge between him and the Dario family. That thought, and his seemingly hopeless situation, left him with no other option. "Then I will, Maria," he said, looking back again at St. Pierre, whose smirk had turned to a victorious grin. "He's here. I'm going to get them for him right now." He held the telephone away from his ear for a few seconds, thinking, then brought it back up. "Maria, listen carefully. Don't hang up. I want you to give the telephone to one of his men there. Do you understand?

"Yes, Jackie. Okay. Are you going to be alright?"

"Don't worry. Everything is going to be fine, Bella," he answered, even though he knew it wasn't true.

He listened carefully to the other end of the line, and after some indistinct chatter between two men, one of them deep-voiced and foreign-sounding, the receiver on the other end rattled and crackled. A young man's voice said, "I'm here. I want to speak to my boss."

Jack turned around to face St. Pierre, held the receiver out towards him, and said, "I'll give you the ledgers, but you need to call your dogs off first. No books unless they leave and my family is safe."

St. Pierre reached for the handset, keeping the gun pointed with his other hand. He put the phone to his ear, and looking at Jack with an evil smirk, ordered Babe, "Unless you hear from me, you stay. If I'm not back on the line in five minutes or if this line goes dead, I want the whole family taken out." He watched carefully for Jack's reaction when he added, "Maybe even save the pretty little wife for the end and have some fun with her."

Scotty had to grab his partner to stop him from lunging at St. Pierre. Jack's eyes were wild with fury.

The Saint was enjoying the moment. He had learned years ago to find an enemy's weaknesses and use them to his advantage. He glared at Jack. "You're on the clock, kid. Get the books," he said.

Jack yanked himself out of Scotty's grasp, looked St. Pierre in the eyes as he straightened his shirt, then put his head down in defeat and headed for the office.

"Stop," St. Pierre demanded suddenly. "Come here, kid," he ordered Joey, waving the gun towards him. Jack and Scotty watched Joey move towards him slowly, nervously. When he got close, St. Pierre grabbed him, spun him around to face the other two, and brought the gun up to Joey's temple. "Anything but those goddamned books comes out in your hands and you're going to lose someone else," the Saint informed them.

Jack turned back towards the hallway door. His fear and fury were clouding his thoughts, making it difficult for him to think about his next move. Entering his office, he saw no option but to give up the books. As his mind cleared from making the decision, he realized he had a dilemma. Although he could hold back Mahoney's tell-all book that St. Pierre knew nothing about, he only had four of the other five ledgers. The Quebec operation book was already in the hands of the Purple Gang, and it appeared too late now for that to be of any help.

Jack went to the office safe, and with hands shaking turned the dial back and forth until the small steel door unlocked with a click. Checking the office door first, he pulled the white bag out, removed Mahoney's betrayal book from the others, and returned it to the safe. He locked the safe, stood holding the cotton bag, took a deep breath, and headed back out to the lobby.

As Jack returned from the hallway with bag in hand, St. Pierre concealed a great sigh of relief. As much as he wanted to inflict violent retribution on these amateurs who had the nerve to challenge him and threaten the very existence of his organization, he realized that at this point it was critical for him to secure his financial records and not create another mess that would be very difficult to clean up—especially without Mahoney to help out. He would have to be content knowing all three would pay a heavy price later.

With the gun still pointed at Joey's bruised and swollen head, St. Pierre reached out with his left hand and took the bag roughly from Jack. He pushed Joey back to his partners, and looking down briefly into the bag, inspected its contents. He looked up, confused, and back down again, a little more closely. Jack swallowed hard as Scotty looked his way with concern.

"What are you tryin' to pull here, kid?" the Saint demanded, raising his gun towards Jack. "There's one missing."

"There's only four left," Jack explained. He looked at Scotty to back him up when he added, "We got rid of the Quebec book. We burned it. We didn't want any record of our operation when it ended up in the law's hands."

St. Pierre considered the situation and didn't like it. "The deal was all the fuckin' books. I want that book or your family will pay!" he yelled as he headed for the telephone.

As Jack went to speak, Scotty cut him off loudly and abruptly, with a newfound fearlessness. "Stop! It was me that destroyed it, you see. Jack didn't even know I did it at first. I was afraid of the connection to my family business." As St. Pierre stood near the telephone thinking, Scotty took a bold but awkward step towards him and continued. "Listen, that book would only hurt us if we kept it. Why would we do that? We'd be diggin' our own graves." Scotty pointed at the bag in St. Pierre's hand. "Those are the only books that could've helped us, and now you have 'em." He waited a few seconds before adding with more confidence, "C'mon, Mr. St. Pierre. You need to call off your men. You don't want more blood on your hands." Scotty took another unsteady step towards him, and with all the courage he could muster, added, "Because if you don't call them off, you're going to have to kill us, too." Jack was emboldened by Scotty's threat and moved to the opposite side of the foyer to create separation among the three of them. Joey's knees felt like they were going to buckle as he watched the standoff unfold. "If that order is given, you'll have a battle with us right here, right now," Scotty continued, "and there's no guarantee how it'll turn out. We have nothin' to lose now, do we?" He waited, heart pounding, barely able to breathe, while St. Pierre mulled over his situation, swinging his gun back and forth between the partners on opposite sides of the room. "You have what you came for. Let's not do this."

The Saint stared down Scotty for several more moments, turned his head slowly, and did the same to Jack. He moved towards the counter, took the bag with his gun hand, and slowly reached for the telephone with his other. Before bringing the handset up to his face, he declared, "You boys have twenty-four hours to get out of town. You understand? I take over this shop and the whole operation. You disappear by tomorrow and keep your goddamned mouths shut. Nobody crosses me . . . ever! And if you show your faces in my town again, you will all end up like that Johnny kid and that goddamned dago father-in-law of yours," he warned, looking towards Jack.

Because of the strain of the life-and-death scene he was suddenly a part of, it took Joey a few seconds to figure out exactly what it was that St. Pierre was saying. He then came to the realization that St. Pierre was admitting that Mr. Dario, the man who saved his life twice, and Johnny, his workmate who had become one of his best friends, had both been murdered. Joey felt an overwhelming wave of weakness and nausea. With the colour drained from his face, Joey looked over at Jack for some sign that what he was hearing couldn't possibly be true. Jack could only look over at the distraught teenager briefly before he lowered his eyes towards the floor in a combination of sorrow and regret.

"Do you understand?" St. Pierre repeated louder.

"Yes, sir," Jack and Scotty said in unison. Joey stared straight ahead in a daze, still trying to absorb the news.

As St. Pierre began to raise the telephone receiver to his mouth, they all jumped at a sudden, loud knock on the glass front door only feet away. The partners looked at each other curiously, then at the Saint for some kind of direction. St. Pierre put the telephone down on the counter again and eyed Jack threateningly.

Another loud knock was accompanied by a gentleman trying to peer in and shouting through the door, "Mr. Ducharme? It's Inspector Mousseau. Mr. Ducharme?"

"Expecting a visitor, were you, kid? Did you have something for him?" St. Pierre asked sarcastically. He had little time to react to this new threat. If the inspector was not let in, he could bust in with agents, arrest him, and get his ledger books. However, he was sure that this Mousseau character, the inspector he had heard so much about, couldn't possibly recognize him. St. Pierre looked over at Jack and said quietly but coldly, "Let him in. Everything is normal here. I am just a customer using the telephone. Nobody leaves. Nobody whispers. Any hint or sign about what's happening here or who I am, and I'll whisper the order into this telephone and your family will be taken out before anybody can possibly get to them. Got it?"

Jack nodded, shaken by the thought of his family and the traumatic circumstances that they were facing at that very moment.

As Mousseau knocked loudly again, St. Pierre pocketed his gun, tucked the bag of books into his waistband, buttoned up his suit coat, and brought the handset back up to his ear. He slowly turned his back to the door before turning his head slightly and ordering, "Let him in."

On the other end of the telephone line, Babe was sitting in a wooden chair that straddled the kitchen and small dining room of the Dario house. As he sat straining to hear his boss's conversation in the lobby of the paint shop, the Wolf was in the adjoining front room sitting casually in Mr. Dario's easy chair, across from Mrs. Dario, Maria, and her baby boy. The two women were staring ahead in a state of shock and grief, tears flowing. Little Mo, hungry and unable to crawl about and play, was cranky, fidgeting in Maria's arms.

Less than an hour before, the two men had stormed in the back door of the house and demanded the family all sit in the front room and not move. When Maria and her mother exhibited some defiance and looked with anticipation at the back of the house for Mr. Dario, the Wolf used some of the few Italian words he knew, informing Maria in his deep, emotionless voice, *"Padre è morto."*

Now everything seemed to be in a state of suspended disbelief. The Wolf was just sitting and growing increasingly impatient and annoyed at the restlessness of the child. Babe was leaning back on the chair, smoking a cigarette and waiting on the phone for instructions from St. Pierre. Although he considered himself as ruthless and violent as any of the thugs in the Saint's stable, deep down he secretly had misgivings about the thought of having to kill an entire family—especially a baby. He secretly hoped that order never came.

Just when Little Mo seemed to be settling down and an uncomfortable, grief-filled silence filled the room, a loud knock came from the front door. The noise startled the little boy, and the women jumped nervously, looking at one another. The Wolf leaned back from his seat and saw the figure of a man through the white lace curtain in the front-door window.

Babe stood, leaned into the hallway, and whispered loudly to his partner, "What should we do?"

"Stay. Talk to boss," was his response. After more knocking, Little Mo began crying. Annoyed by the noise and the disturbance, the Wolf pointed to Maria and directed her with his hand to answer the door. As she stood and walked by, the Wolf yanked the little boy out of her arms, held him uncomfortably against his chest, and put his right index finger up to his lips as a warning to her.

Trembling, Maria unlocked the front deadbolt, pulled open the heavy oak door, and faced the Darios' trusted neighbour, Mr. Lapari. *"Ciao, Signor Lapari,"* she said, shaking and barely able to get the words out.

The neighbour's eyes darted from her to inside the doorway in a way that told her he knew their situation and was there to help. Trusting the two intruders would not understand, Lapari spoke in a rushed Italian that was even difficult for Maria to completely pick up. Given the baby's loud crying, it was hardly necessary. In less than twenty seconds, he explained that there were men there to help them. He just needed her to get one of the intruders to the front door.

"No, no, Signor Lapari. Poppa is not home," Maria said nervously in response.

Little Mo was now in full tantrum mode—scared, screaming, and trying to wiggle out of the Wolf's uncomfortably tight grasp. The Wolf's impatience, combined with the crying child and the unknown conversation that was taking place at the front door, threw him into action. He stood, tossed Mo roughly over to his confused Nonna, and moved in behind the partially opened front door. "No more. Goodbye," he said in a low voice to Maria as he started to close the door. Maria backed away as it was closing on her, but just as the door was about to meet the frame, the long barrel of a rifle halted its movement. Before the Wolf could react to what was happening, the door was kicked open with enough force to throw him back a few steps. Mr. Lapari stormed in and pointed an old rifle at the Wolf, who instinctively smiled and put his hands up slowly. Lapari was followed by another middle-aged, rough-looking man carrying a pistol.

At the same moment, Babe jumped from his seat, letting the telephone handset drop and knock against the wall as it dangled. As he faced the two older men and their weapons in the front hallway, another man who came quickly through the back door was upon him from behind. A long knife was drawn and brought against his throat, its sharp blade given enough pressure to begin drawing a slow stream of blood.

When both of the captors were neutralized, Maria instinctively ran to her screaming son and took him in her arms. She sat on the sofa next to her bewildered mother and was shushing her little boy when a fourth man, a bloodied white bandage around his head and dried blood caked along one side of his face, came in from the kitchen and entered the front room.

"Poppa!" and "Enrico!" were shouted simultaneously as the two women jumped from their seats and hugged Mr. Dario. A flurry of Italian words of love and comfort followed as the three were locked in a family embrace.

Mr. Lapari, rifle still pointed at the Wolf, ended the reunion by asking Dario in Italian what he wanted them to do with the two men who had made the cowardly attack on him and then threatened his family.

Dario stared menacingly at the Wolf, who was struggling to hold his wicked, eye-teeth smile. He then looked at Babe, his eyes wide with fright, a knife cutting into his throat and blood dripping down his chest. He moved towards the telephone handset dangling against the wall near the young thug, picked it up, and put it to his ear. He heard nothing but the steady breathing of someone on the other end. While slowly hanging up the telephone, he looked back at Lapari and replied coldly, *"Falli sparire."*

Making enemies "disappear" was something all four of these men had some experience with from another, more violent time of their lives back in the old country.

....

Considering the sign on the door, Inspector Mousseau was surprised to find the lobby of the paint shop so busy when he was finally let in. Since Jack's late phone call the night before, the inspector had been trying hard not to get too optimistic about the opportunity to finally get what he needed to help him bring down a local operation that he had been chasing for years. Not only had Mousseau dedicated his life to fighting this moral war on alcohol—even banishing his own son to Chicago because of his involvement in rum running—he also knew a successful bust of that magnitude would be great for his legacy at the end of a long career.

"Mr. Ducharme," he said as he took off his hat and greeted Jack just inside the door. As the two shook hands, Mousseau scanned the room. He recognized the McLuren fellow right away and was pretty sure the young kid standing with him, looking a little worse for wear, was another employee. On the other side of the lobby at the counter, a well-dressed man who had his back to the door was using the telephone.

"Good morning, inspector," Jack answered, his voice unsteady.

A period of awkward silence followed, and Mousseau was already sensing some unknown tension in the air. When Jack stayed silent and appeared unusually uncomfortable compared to their last meeting, the inspector began. "Well, Mr. Ducharme. I'm here as you requested. Should we go somewhere to speak privately?"

Jack looked sideways towards the back of the lobby, then his eyes dropped before answering louder than necessary, "Sorry, Inspector. We have nothing to talk about."

Mousseau's instincts were suddenly on high alert. His disappointment at Jack's response was tempered by a feeling that something important was happening at that very moment. The two other employees were standing near the hallway door doing nothing, also looking uncomfortable and out of place in their own shop. The gentleman at the counter kept his back to them, but his head was turned slightly as if eavesdropping, which was altogether possible given the fact that the telephone handset was well away from his ear and Mousseau had not heard him speak a single word.

Instead of forcing the issue, Mousseau simply said, "That's unfortunate, Mr. Ducharme. I won't waste any more of your time, then. You know how to reach me if there's anything important to discuss in the future." He looked around the lobby one last time, lingering at the stranger standing by the counter, before giving Jack a reassuring look.

"Good day, gentlemen," the inspector said before he turned and made his way back out the door.

....

St. Pierre was having difficulty listening to two critical events happening at the exact same time. In the lobby, Jack was following the Saint's instructions to get rid of the inspector, but there was also drama unfolding on the other end of the telephone line at the Dario house. Just as the inspector was bidding farewell, St. Pierre brought the handset back up to his ear in time to hear Babe on the other end exclaim, "What the bloody hell..." There was some loud thumping as if the telephone was dropped, then muffled conversations and women shrieking. The line crackled briefly, and there was some heavy breathing. Someone had picked up the handset and was listening. Then the line went dead.

Jack, Scotty, and Joey's eyes fell on St. Pierre as soon as Mousseau left the shop. The look of confidence and control he had on his face earlier had changed to something resembling confusion. For several seconds after Mousseau's departure, St. Pierre kept the telephone to his ear while he looked in Jack's direction, but did not say a word until he slowly lowered the handset and put it on its cradle.

"Well, gentlemen," he said as he brought his gun back out. "You've done the first part. Now you have a day to get the hell out of town, as agreed."

Something in his tone had changed, but Jack's first concern was for his family. "I didn't hear you call your goons off," he said. "Are they safe now?"

"Of course, kid." St Pierre's wicked smile and sarcasm suddenly returned. "Are you saying you don't trust me?"

Jack's escalating concern now turned to a full panic. "No, I don't!" he said boldly. "You don't have a problem if I call them to be sure, do you?" he said as he moved towards the counter.

The Saint looked with feigned disbelief at Scotty and Joey, who were equally shocked by Jack's brazen tone. He turned back towards Jack, raised his gun, and answered, "You got some balls, kid. I've got the gun. I've got the books. You have nothing but your life . . . for now. I suggest you back off."

The contest of wills lasted for a few moments as Jack stared down his boss before his gaze dropped and he moved slowly back to his partners.

"Smart move, Mr. Ducharme," the Saint said as he backed his way towards the door, gun still pointed, carrying the bag. As he awkwardly pushed the door open behind him and slipped outside into the bright sunlight, St. Pierre couldn't resist adding with a smile, "You're smarter than your old man."

Scotty fully expected his young partner to charge after St. Pierre in a fit of blind rage after the vicious comment, but with tear-filled eyes, Jack darted towards the telephone on the counter instead. He rushed the operator to connect him to the Darios' and stood impatiently tapping his foot against the counter while wiping his eyes. Seconds later he startled his partners standing near him by shouting into the telephone, "Maria! Oh, Bella. Is everybody okay?" He listened for a while, then said loudly, "Your father is alive? Is he alright? How did he—" Then Jack stood wide-eyed, hearing about the drama that had just taken place at his in-laws' home. Scotty and Joey looked back and forth to each other, and then back to Jack, anxious to hear the details.

A couple of minutes later, Jack ended his call abruptly with, "It's incredible, Maria. Really. Thank God for your father." He paused, then added, "You get back to your mother and Mo. I'll be there as soon as I can." He hung up the telephone and looked over at his partners in a state of disbelief.

"What?' Scotty demanded. "Everybody's okay?"

"Yes. Thanks again to Mr. Dario and his friends," he answered, staring ahead in bewilderment. Scotty and Joey looked at each other, confused, as Jack began relaying the unbelievable story he had just been told. Details were scant, and he was clearly in a rush, but after telling what he knew, Jack finished up with, "And his friends forced those two goons into their own car. They had it in the alley. Then Mr. Dario promised Maria that they would never have to worry about them ever again."

All three stood there quietly, contemplating the reality of what that actually meant and the possible impact it might have on them. Jack ended the brief silence moments later. "I've got to get to my family," he announced as he headed to his office to gather his things.

Scotty and Joey jumped as there came another sudden knock on the door. Jack poked his head back out from the hallway. They looked at each other anxiously.

"Jackie, the inspector is back," Scotty announced with a sigh of relief as he took a few steps towards the door.

Jack cracked a smile of satisfaction and nodded to let Mousseau back in as he moved quickly back towards his office. A short time later, he appeared in the lobby with his hat, the keys to his automobile, and the one last book he had in his possession—the one that Mahoney had put together covertly in case his life was in danger. Ironically, the Quebec boys were now going to rely on the very same book for the very same purpose. Handing it to Inspector Mousseau, Jack said, "Remember our deal, Inspector. Everything and everybody is in here."

29

THE SAINT HAD NO INTENTION OF KEEPING HIS PROMISE. Now that he had the books back in his possession and a major crisis had been averted, it was time to mete out justice. Before that could happen, however, he had two major problems to deal with. The first one dealt with the Quebec operation. With Mahoney already at the bottom of the Detroit River and the ledger book for that branch of the business now missing, continuing to run the operation and taking over the paint shop as the distribution centre was going to be a serious challenge. St. Pierre knew it was going to be impossible to find someone to replace Mahoney and the unique skill-set he possessed. He felt no regret about having his second in command killed for losing the books and betraying him, but St. Pierre did wish he had planned better for someone to step in and replace Mahoney so he wouldn't be in the predicament he now found himself in.

The other problem that caused him concern was the fate of the muscle he had sent to Ducharme's in-laws' earlier that morning. It was unlike the Wolf to have problems handling any situation, and he always checked in with updates. But judging by what he had heard over the telephone at the shop and the fact that St. Pierre had not heard from them in several hours, he realized something had gone wrong. After losing the Russian only days ago, he couldn't afford to lose the tough Polack as well. He needed someone he could trust to rub out the Quebec boys.

By late afternoon, St. Pierre still had not heard from the Wolf or Babe, and so he had to assume the worst. After considerable thought, St. Pierre reluctantly decided that his only move was to go up the food chain for the kind of help he was now in desperate need of. Although he had several dozen people working for him in various roles in the area, the kind of management and muscle he now required to carry on his operations and clean up the mess was only going to be available from across the river. He picked up the telephone and asked the operator to connect him, long distance, with his contact from the Purple Gang in Detroit.

The short, cryptic call went better than the Saint could have ever hoped. In fact, he felt it went a little too well. Maybe it was paranoia due to the threat he had been under recently, but something about the call didn't feel right. Because of the inconvenience, disruptions, and risk his local situation was going to cause the powerful organization, St. Pierre was expecting anger, accusations, and threats. Instead, his contact promised a meeting later that night to discuss possible solutions. And they would even come to him.

Continuing Mahoney's sound advice to keep up his front as William St. Pierre, respectable community pillar—especially at a time of such upheaval—the Saint knew he had to get to the parish council meeting at the church hall in a few hours. He had already missed Sunday mass the day before because of the crisis that Mahoney had created, and his continued absence tonight would be cause for fellow parishioners to make annoying calls of concern, or worse, visit his home bearing all kinds of ridiculous get-well offerings.

The parish meeting began at 7:30 in a small anteroom inside the church hall. The room was uncomfortably warm and muggy, with cigarette smoke clinging stubbornly to the humid air, the result of a long, hot summer day with little breeze. St. Pierre encountered pleasant greetings and inquiries about his health from fellow council members as he walked in fashionably late. With the forced smile that had served him so well over the years, he took the last available chair. Preoccupied by the recent events, his mind began wandering as soon as Fr. Flannigan began with a prayer for guidance from the Holy Spirit and love for one's fellow man—a precursor to their discussions about the committee's charitable donations.

St. Pierre was feeling little love for his fellow man at that moment. Several employees had betrayed him in the last couple of days, including his right-hand man, forcing him to expose his identity. Valuable time and energy was wasted protecting his organization, he had to beg for help from the thankless Jews across the river, and now he was stuck in a church meeting for a couple of hours when he should be out trying to tie up any remaining loose ends.

Even though he did his best to appear somewhat interested, St. Pierre sat near comatose, mentally, as the meeting dragged on as usual. Discussions and disagreements about where to allocate a mere couple of hundred of dollars raised from church charity events continued with no end in sight. While a group of women, including the insufferable O'Hallaren woman, wanted to see it go towards the poor families in the community, others argued that it would be better spent helping fund Sunday school and summer parish camp expenses. While the debate wore on, the Saint secretly fantasized about throwing a handful of hundred-dollar bills in the middle of the table and shouting, "Here! Do all of it so we can end this painful fucking meeting and go home!" The pleasant thought elicited a wicked grin that he concealed by putting his hands over his face in a show of fatigue.

As the council began tackling their last agenda topic for the week—forming a committee to plan the parish picnic in mid-July—they were interrupted by the sounds of hard-soled shoes clacking louder and louder on the terrazzo floors out in the hallway. The parishioners looked at each other, puzzled. When the sounds came to a stop, shuffling behind the meeting room door, similar footsteps were heard behind the back door to the room as well. As the rest of the council looked at each other and wondered aloud what was going on, St. Pierre's instincts told him he was under threat. He stood and scanned the perimeter of the room for possible escape options.

He was too late. Both sets of doors flew open, and pairs of liquor agents and police officers barged in dramatically from each entrance. The officers had their guns drawn, causing a collective gasp from the bewildered committee. As St. Pierre stood helpless only feet from his chair, Inspector Mousseau appeared from behind the group at the main door, sporting a smile of genuine satisfaction.

"What's the meaning of this?" Fr. Flannigan protested as he stood timidly. "This is a place of God!"

Mousseau's eyes locked onto St. Pierre's as he answered, "My sincere apologies, father. But one of your sheep has strayed very far from the rest of the flock." The inspector walked confidently up to St. Pierre, his footsteps echoing loudly in the stunned silence of the room, and announced, "William St. Pierre, you're under arrest for illegal sale and distribution of alcohol, owning and operating a bawdy house, owning and operating a private gaming house, and extortion, as well as accessory to murder."

The parish priest and his fellow councillors in the room would have been inclined to believe an error of staggering proportion was taking place against an innocent, God-fearing man were it not for St. Pierre's instinctive reaction to the arrest. Instead of shock and protestations of innocence while he was being handcuffed, he was enraged. He hissed at Mousseau with a wicked smile that sent chills through the committee members, "You got nothing, Inspector. Nothing. My lawyer will have me out of these goddamned cuffs within the hour." While he was being forcibly escorted to the door, St. Pierre looked around at the wide eyes of his fellow parishioners, realizing his façade was crumbling but unable to control it. As he was being dragged roughly past Mousseau, he looked sideways towards him and in a menacing tone threatened, "You better watch your back when I get out of these, Inspector."

His warning caused the inspector to grab his arm, swing him around, and bring his face within inches of St. Pierre's before he responded with, "You're not going anywhere . . . Saint. We've got all the goods on you now."

St. Pierre was being dragged out of the church hall into the parking lot just as the sun was setting over the river and a shiny grey Model-A Roadster was driving by slowly, taking in the action. The two men inside the automobile, who had just arrived from Detroit through the tunnel, realized that the order they'd been given was now going to be much more difficult to carry out.

....

Jack did not have to wait for the telephone call that Mousseau had promised him to find out about St. Pierre's arrest. Along with Scotty and Joey, he continued hiding out in the paint shop for what seemed like the longest day of his life. He was sure that the Saint would not honour the deal he made with them and felt their lives were still in danger.

Even though Mousseau arranged a couple of trusted police officers to provide security, a combination of boredom, impatience, and tension gripped all three throughout the long day. Every hopeful ring of the telephone had resulted in disappointment as customers called for shop business. Several more knocks on the front door throughout the afternoon made them jump before an officer sent customers on their way. The lunch and dinner brought in by the police during their shift changes were eaten in the office quietly—all three reluctant to believe that the nightmare was indeed over.

A call from Jack's sister later that night, however, changed everything. "Jackie, it's all over. They got him," Annie said in an excited but hushed tone.

Initially, Jack was too confused to be relieved. "What do you mean, Annie? How do you know? Why are you whispering?"

"Grandmother's here with us right now...in the parlour," she explained. "She just came back from a church meeting, and she's in a state. They arrested Mr. St. Pierre there in front of her and the others. She says an army of officers stormed in. She's almost in a state of shock. She said at first they all thought it was a big mistake, but then with the handcuffs on him, Mr. St. Pierre turned into the devil himself—a man none of them could recognize."

Scotty and Joey watched, only steps away in the office, as Jack's face slowly turned from surprise and confusion to sheer relief. The built-up tension in his large shoulders relaxed as his head dropped before he said, "It's good that she saw that. It's good they all saw it." He took a deep breath. "Thank God. I think this thing is finally over, sister." He lowered the handset briefly, looked up smiling at his partners, and repeated more convincingly, "I really think this thing is over."

Less than an hour later, after several reassuring calls were made to update loved ones, Inspector Mousseau made it official with the call he had promised. Jack held the telephone out away from his ear so Scotty and Joey could listen in. Mousseau assured them that he had the full cooperation of a team of "good cops," and that with the evidence that Mahoney's book provided, St. Pierre was headed to jail and those on his payroll were being rounded up.

But the inspector did have words of caution for them. "We are having trouble locating St. Pierre's top brass," he explained. "Mahoney must have left town in a hurry. We know where he lives, and now he's gone. Nothing was taken with him. He even left a large amount of money." Jack and Scotty both looked with a smirk at Joey, who was now feeling even more regret over not helping himself to at least some of the cash when he had the chance.

Jack filled the inspector in about St. Pierre's confession that Mahoney had been killed, but admitted they had no way to prove it.

"And the big thugs he always has around are a concern to us, but we can't find them, either." Mousseau continued. "I'm sure you've dealt with them. A Russian named Wojcik and a ruthless killer by the name of Kaminski . . . someone they call the Wolf. There was a new kid, too, they called Babe."

There was an extended period of silence over the line as Jack looked at his partners and wrestled with the decision about whether the authorities should be informed about the fate of St. Pierre's henchmen. Scotty did not hesitate, moving his head from side to side in warning, and Jack agreed that nothing good could come from being truthful about the street justice meted out by Mr. Dario and his friends. "Well, Inspector," Jack said, "my guess is that they skipped town, seeing as how their boss is caught and the organization is crumbling."

Jack thanked Mousseau for keeping up his end of their agreement and finished the call before all three made a much-anticipated exit from the shop. Although Joey was just anxious to get home to rest and heal up, the emotions ran much deeper for the Quebec boys. Stepping out into the dark, warm night, Jack and Scotty were overwhelmed with a profound feeling of relief and liberation.

Standing beside their automobiles, which were still rendered useless in the shop parking lot, they shook hands with weary smiles, then embraced before they both started their short walk home.

....

Fearing St. Pierre's long tentacles in the Ford City and the Walkerville area, police brought him to headquarters several miles to the west, in downtown Windsor. Sitting handcuffed to a steel pipe on the table in a corner holding room, he looked dishevelled in his scuffed shoes, wrinkled suit, and dented hat. Seeing himself in the reflection of the window, looking out at the dark city, even St. Pierre had to admit that he appeared a far cry from the power, influence, and intimidation he had wielded just hours before. The officers who brought him there didn't even allow him the phone call he requested. In a humiliating show of disrespect, they laughed when St. Pierre demanded his call; they told him that it was late and he would have to wait until the morning. Now, handcuffed in a bright, hot, sticky room, sitting uncomfortably on a wooden chair with an officer stationed just outside his door, he faced the prospect of a very long, sleepless night.

Just after midnight, St. Pierre was shaken out of his repeated head nods by the sound of heavy footsteps coming down the hallway. After a brief, muffled conversation, the loud click of the lock jolted him up, and an officer opened the heavy steel door.

Standing in the threshold was a large, dark-haired gentleman, smoking a cigarette and wearing a tailored suit that even St. Pierre was impressed by.

The man tilted his head slightly, looked expressionlessly at the Saint, then glanced back at the officer and nodded. He put the cigarette between his lips, pulled a thick wad of cash from his pants pocket, handed the entire amount over to the officer, and mumbled in a deep voice, "Go get a coffee, kid."

A broad smile developed on St. Pierre's face as the door closed with a loud clank. "You guys are good," he said. "I didn't even have to make a call."

The gentleman stood across the room, quiet.

"Who you with? Martini? Shapiro?" St. Pierre was agitated with the man's silence. "Or did the Purples send their own man?"

The gentleman smiled, taking another drag.

"It doesn't matter. It's good. Very good. Now you can get me the hell outta here? You must have people on the take in this dump. Can I get out tonight?"

With the cigarette burning between his fingers, the man eyed St. Pierre before turning and taking a few steps to fumble with the dangling strings that hung by the sides of the windows. One by one, the blinds closed, and the darkness that enveloped the city slowly disappeared. He turned around mechanically, walked around the side of the table, and positioned himself between the Saint's back and the cement wall.

Shuffling in his seat from side to side, straining to look behind him with the steel chain of his handcuffs clanking loudly, St. Pierre grew more irritated. "What are you doing? C'mon…go do what you have to do to get me the hell outta here, for Christ's sake!"

With the Saint now barking at him in a growing rage, the gentleman slowly reached into his inside breast pocket. "What have you got there?" St. Pierre yelled. "What are you—" His voice was cut off with a choking gurgle when his visitor quickly wrapped a short piece of piano wire around his neck from behind and pulled forcefully with a technique honed by practice. St. Pierre's feet kicked violently under the table, and his handcuffs rattled loudly against the steel pipe as he instinctively tried to bring his hands up to his throat. The cigarette hanging in the visitor's mouth was wafting smoke up into his squinting eyes and dropping ashes onto St. Pierre's balding head. A short time later, the resistance ended suddenly as the once-powerful crime boss's body slumped lifelessly in the chair, his bloody eyes bulging and his neck bleeding profusely from a straight, clean line.

The visitor calmly used St. Pierre's suit-coat collar to wipe the wire methodically from one end to the other before returning it to his pocket. Noticing a few grey ashes still sitting on top of his victim's slumped head, he gently brushed them off. He went over and pulled the blinds back open, straightened his jacket and tie using the reflection in the window, and casually made his way to the door. He opened it, scanned the empty hallway, and headed for the nearest exit.

It was a joyous and tearful reunion when Jack finally walked into the Darios' home. Little Mo was asleep on the sofa as Maria ran into Jack's arms in the foyer, her parents right behind her, smiling through their own tears. As his wife cried and refused to unlock the embrace, Jack looked over her head at a heavily bandaged and emotional Mr. Dario. He reached out behind her to take his father-in-law's hand, and with more profound sincerity then he ever felt in his life, said *"Grazie, Poppa. Grazie."*

When Maria finally backed away from her husband, she was still crying. "Is everything okay now, Jackie?" she asked, looking up to him for reassurance.

"Yes, Bella. Everything is going to be fine now. Let's go home."

The following evening, only five days after the ledger books were stolen and the Quebec boys' daring plan was launched, all those involved were sitting around the parlour of Jack's mother's home. Scotty and Joey had brought chairs in from the kitchen, Mr. Dario and Maria sat side by side in armchairs, and Mrs. Ducharme and Annie held hands on the sofa. Little Mo was safe at home in the care of his doting Nonna.

It had been a long couple of days of interviews with the authorities for Jack, Scotty, and Joey, and they were happy to be back together, relaxing and having a few drinks. The gathering was more than social, however. The partners felt that it was finally time that the family knew everything.

Once everyone was seated, Jack and Scotty spent over an hour recounting the entire saga of the Ducharme involvement in whisky distribution, its connection to William St. Pierre's local crime group, the Quebec operation, Maurice's murder, Johnny's mysterious disappearance, and their harrowing experiences of the previous few days. Joey added details from his perspective occasionally, and once again Maria acted as translator for her father. Their audience, even those who were involved in the drama, sat enraptured by a story that rivalled the popular gangster news reports of the day. Questions were asked, details were shared, and emotions ran high. A number of times, but especially when her husband's murder was described, Sara Ducharme gasped, broke down in tears, or simply reacted with, "Oh my Lord."

"Now, there's something we all have to be very clear about," Jack said as they were wrapping things up. "Nobody besides all of you knows the full involvement of Mr. Dario, and nobody ever needs to." He looked over at the older gentleman with profound respect and gratitude. As Maria continued to translate, he added, "As far as me, Scotty, and Joey are concerned, we would not be out of this mess or even alive today if it wasn't for him and his friends. But the police and the courts might see things differently. They may want to investigate further or maybe even look into his past. You know the way they sometimes treat immigrants...especially Italians. He doesn't deserve that. So just like the three of us did when we were interviewed, we don't speak of his role in any of this, ever. He was never involved." Everyone nodded in agreement.

After Maria told her father what Jack had said, Mr. Dario's eyes filled with tears again as he looked around the room. He stood, held up his drink, put his other hand on his heart, and in a deep, choked up voice said, *"La famiglia è tutto. Saluti."* Everyone looked to Maria, who also had tears in her eyes, as she translated, "Family is everything." They raised their glasses in agreement.

The room was heavy with emotion when Jack suddenly realized he had forgotten something very important. He stood and laughed lightly as he took his handkerchief out to dry his eyes. As he left the room, he requested, "Everybody, finish your drink. I've got a special treat for you." Smiles began lightening the mood of the room as tears were wiped, glasses were emptied, and everybody was curious as they listened to Jack's big footsteps slapping loudly down the narrow wooden basement stairs.

When he reappeared moments later, he was carrying a brown paper bag with both hands, very carefully, as if it was a priceless relic. With his smile fading, he moved to the middle of the room, slowly reached into the bag, and brought out what looked like a full glass bottle of milk. Scotty recognized it immediately and grinned. The others soon understood as well after Jack brought it over to his sister and placed her hands around it. As she stared off, Jack told her, "It's one of dad's Skim bottles, Annie." She caressed it as her mother reached over to do her own inspection.

Moments later, Jack removed the sealed cap and began going around the room, sharing the renowned Canadian Club whisky, bottled years ago for one of Moose's first Skim customers. Once he gave himself the final pour, Jack looked around the room and held up his glass. Everyone joined him. "To Maurice Ducharme," he announced, eyes welling up once more. "This is where it all began, and this is where it ends."

EPILOGUE

I T TOOK SEVERAL MONTHS FOR POLICE AND LIQ-UOR CONTROL INVESTIGATORS to gather evidence and testimony required for local prosecutors to bring dozens of people involved in St. Pierre's organization to trial. Some cooled their heels in jail cells, praying for an eleventh-hour miracle. Those who cooperated with authorities, turning on their former colleagues by becoming Crown witnesses, enjoyed their freedom but then spent the rest of their lives looking over their shoulders.

A network of powerful men connected to St. Pierre, including bankers, local politicians, police brass, and business owners, nervously waited to learn if they too would be implicated and charged. Others didn't wait. A police captain in Ford City and a warehouse manager at Hiram Walker's Distillery committed suicide – one put a gun to his head while the other jumped from the new Ambassador Bridge – rather than suffer public humiliation or the threat of spending years behind bars.

The mystery surrounding William St. Pierre's murder was never resolved. The police weren't motivated to look too closely into the matter, especially as events had occurred right under their very noses. The public, for their part, seemed content with the crime boss's fate.

By the summer of 1931, local and regional daily news coverage regarding ongoing investigations into the shattered criminal enterprise provided a much-needed diversion from the devastating impact of the economic collapse caused by the Great Depression. Arrests, court cases, verdicts, and sentencing of those who had profited from Prohibition provided fodder for the dailies and radio news broadcasts. Some romanticized these criminal activities into gritty dramas, promoting the Saint to a local version of Chicago's Al Capone. Rumours about who'd been involved in St. Pierre's organization and the possible fate of his missing associates remained a hot topic of conversation for many years.

The United States' repeal of Prohibition in 1933 led to an abrupt end of cross-border illegal liquor. This illicit business completely dried up for local, small-time bootleggers and rumrunners; larger enterprises, however, diversified their criminal activities. Detroit's notorious Purple Gang struggled to make this transition once their relationship with Capone ended, along with the respect and power that partnership granted them. Later that year, the bodies of two Purple Gang leaders were discovered in a car on an isolated country road near Detroit. Each man had been shot numerous times in the face at close range. The murder of their successor in 1937 signalled the beginning of the end of the Purple Gang's dominance of organized crime in Detroit.

Inspector Mousseau did not enjoy his career's crowning achievement for very long. Before all guilty parties were formally prosecuted and sentenced, the 64-year-old became gravely ill. He died in the spring of 1931, but not before honouring his end of the agreement: Jack, Scotty, and Joey were granted full immunity from prosecution. As part of this deal, the trio made numerous court appearances, providing important testimony. They agreed to forfeit bank accounts, including any and all profits from their illegal enterprises. For Joey, this second requirement was easy—he was broke. Jack and Scotty, however, had been planning for years for just such an eventuality. A small amount of cash was turned over to the authorities and their bank accounts were seized. But both men had quietly tucked away large amounts of money into other accounts that were untraceable, thanks to Jack's expertise in finance. Combined with Moose's profits from years before, the duo had amassed a small fortune. At a time when most people were struggling to keep jobs and put food on the table, the partners and their families quietly enjoyed the benefits of their secret wealth.

Joey received a very generous cut of the proceeds, with an understanding that it was to be used to further his education and eventually start a business of his own. Jack and Scotty also ensured

Johnny's family—hard hit by the double whammy of their son's sudden death and the unrelenting economic crisis—were not forgotten. The partners provided his family with two things they desperately needed: first, closure, by explaining their son's fate and the punishment of those responsible; and second, a sizable unofficial death benefit from McLuren's Paints.

Scotty used his proceeds to upgrade and keep his paint shop afloat for years even as business all but dried up. When Canada promised to join Britain and march to war once more in 1939, government military contracts provided local manufacturing with a much-needed boost to climb out of economic despair. McLuren's Paints prospered as a result, using untold amounts of military green and grey paint which adorned all manner of war vehicle and armament that rolled off the assembly lines of re-tooled factories in the region.

Jack's business relationship with Scotty ended following their take-down of St. Pierre. Jack decided to employ his business background for something completely different. The tough times and his access to large amounts of money prompted him to form a real estate company to take advantage of deflated local property values. In a delicious twist of fate, Ducharme Holdings even acquired some properties that had once belonged to the disgraced, deceased William St. Pierre.

By the end of the 1930s, Jack was living a charmed life. He and Maria were happy and living comfortably with their three children - the pride and joy of the

Ducharmes and the Darios. His company had a entire team under his direction, including several managers to handle day-to-day operations.

When war broke out in Europe in the fall of 1939, Jack experienced the same sense of national pride and duty that his father and grandfather experienced so many years before. A successful, well-respected 32 year-old local businessman, he was easy pickings for the Canadian Army officer pool. Major Jack Ducharme served with distinction for nearly five years before returning home to a hero's welcome in 1945. His participation in Canada's successful 1943 campaign to drive the Nazis out of Sicily—the Darios' native land—was a source of tremendous pride for his in-laws.

Jack's return to civilian life following World War Two was much smoother than the years following his father's return from the Great War. He was welcomed back with open arms by his loving family, friends, and neighbours. His real estate company had continued to prosper while he was away; with the postwar economic boom, business flourished beyond expectation. He sold his company and retired in 1958 at the age of 51.

Jack and Maria aged gracefully in their beautiful, modest home on the water, a few miles east of Ford City in an area called Riverside. They revelled in their children's lives and lovingly welcomed numerous grandchildren. Sitting together on their back porch swing, gazing across the river at the ever-expanding Detroit skyline, they often talked about the gratitude they felt for their fathers. Facing a bleak future in Italy, Enrico Dario took a leap of faith and made the arduous trek to Canada. When he was needed most, Dario's selfless acts of heroism helped save lives. And after sacrificing years of his life in a bloody, horrific war, Maurice Ducharme also took a leap of faith into a dangerous and illegal business to provide better lives and opportunities for his family.

Those leaps of faith and sacrifices made would allow the Ducharmes to skim the cream from life for generations to come.

ABOUT THE AUTHOR

Steve Byrne is a retired high school English and History teacher. He resides with his wife Susan in Belle River, Ontario; the couple have three children, Erin, Danny and Sara.

Until the of age 12, Steve lived with his parents and five brothers in a small house near the historic community of Walkerville, prompting an early interest in local history.

In his first novel, **SKIM**, he takes the reader on a journey back to the former Border Cities' communities of Ford City and Walkerville, Ontario during the Roaring 1920's, weaving a mesmerizing tale about the dark side of Prohibition.

Although Steve has always enjoyed reading and writing, his first love in high school and university was athletics. He enjoyed many sports, but had a passion for basketball, eventually playing at at every level, including internationally for the 1983 Canadian Junior National Team.

These days, when he and his wife aren't travelling, Steve enjoys exercise, volunteer work, reading & writing, as well as good food and wine.

Manufactured by Amazon.ca
Bolton, ON

30420691R00243